STRONG TO THE BONE

Other Books by Jon Land

*Published by Forge Books

STRONG
TO THE BONE

A CAITLIN STRONG NOVEL

Jon Land

A TOM DOHERTY ASSOCIATES BOOK
NEW YORK

STRONG TO THE BONE

Copyright © 2017 by Jon Land

A Forge Book
Published by Tom Doherty Associates
175 Fifth Avenue
New York, NY 10010

www.tor-forge.com

Forge® is a registered trademark of Macmillan Publishing Group, LLC.

The Library of Congress Cataloging-in-Publication Data is available upon request.

ISBN 978-0-7653-8464-5 (hardcover)
ISBN 978-0-7653-8466-9 (ebook)

Our books may be purchased in bulk for promotional, educational, or business use. Please contact your local bookseller or the Macmillan Corporate and Premium Sales Department at 1-800-221-7945, extension 5442, or by email at MacmillanSpecialMarkets@macmillan.com.

First Edition: December 2017

Printed in the United States of America

0 9 8 7 6 5 4 3 2 1

For Natalia Aponte, Bob Diforio, and the great Toni Mendez

Agents and friends, who've got my back

ACKNOWLEDGMENTS

Before we start, it's time to give some much deserved shout-outs to those who make it possible for me to do what I do, as well as do it better.

Stop me if you've heard this before, but let's start at the top with my publisher, Tom Doherty, and Forge's associate publisher, Linda Quinton, dear friends who publish books "the way they should be published," to quote my late agent, the legendary Toni Mendez. The great Bob Gleason, Karen Lovell, Elayne Becker, Phyllis Azar, Patty Garcia, and especially Natalia Aponte are there for me at every turn. Natalia's a brilliant editor and friend who outdid herself in these pages, as you'll learn more about in the Author's Note. Editing may be a lost art, but not here thanks to both Natalia and Bob Gleason, and I think you'll enjoy all of my books, including this one, much more as a result.

My friend Mike Blakely, a terrific writer and musician, taught me Texas firsthand and helped me think like a native of that great state. And Larry Thompson, a terrific writer in his own right, has joined the team as well to make sure I do justice to his home state along now with his son-in-law and soon-to-be Texas Ranger himself. I can't thank Pat Epstein enough for the great tour of downtown Austin, or Jay Thies for showing me around Kingwood, home of the great Lone Star Community College. And a special acknowledgment to Bill Miller who helped me smooth out the geography of the Lone Star State, along with all things historical. This is the first time you've seen Bill's name on this page but, trust me, it won't be the last. So, too, I think you'll be seeing Terry Ayers on this page again, and a big thank-you to her for making my scientific jargon sound at least somewhat credible.

Check back at www.jonlandbooks.com for updates or to drop me a line, and please follow me on Twitter @jondland. I'd be remiss if I didn't thank all of you who've already written, tweeted, or emailed me your thoughts on any or all of the first eight books in the Caitlin Strong series. You are truly the wind beneath this particular author's wings.

I promise to stop talking, as soon as you turn the page and join Caitlin for another wild ride.

P.S. For those interested in more information about the history of the Texas Rangers, I recommend *The Texas Rangers* and *Time of the Rangers,* a pair of superb books by Mike Cox, also published by Forge.

You never know how strong you are,
until being strong is your only choice.

—BOB MARLEY

STRONG TO THE BONE

PROLOGUE

But leave us the Rangers to guard us still
Nor think that they cost too dear;
For their faithful watch over vale and hill
Gives our loved ones naught to fear.

—From *Cowboy Songs and Other Frontier Ballads*, collected by
John A. Lomax, The Macmillan Company, 1922

HEARNE, TEXAS; 1944

"Thanks for coming, sir."

"I ain't no *sir*, son," Earl Strong told Captain Bo Lowry, just inside the mud-drenched fence line of the prisoner-of-war camp that had been erected amid the scrub brush and flatlands that dominated Hearne, Texas. "Call me 'Ranger,' 'cause a Texas Ranger is what I am."

Lowry looked up, squinting into the sun to better look Earl in the eye. "My daddy was in Sweetwater back in the oil boom days of the thirties. He's told me stories about you, how you tamed all the lawlessness out of that town all by yourself."

"Well, sir, I did have me a time."

"I'm not a *sir*, either, Ranger," Lowry said, looking down now. "Leastways, not anymore, since I got sent home with a bum leg."

"Where you serve your country don't matter, long as you're serving it. That makes you deserving of the respect, even if it wasn't for that whole mag of bullets you took trying to break out of the beachhead in Anzio."

"Well," Lowry said, shyly, "it wasn't a whole mag."

Earl laid a calloused hand on Lowry's shoulder. "Close enough is what I heard, Captain, all the time while you were saving a whole bunch of your men."

"Tall tale, Ranger, that's all."

"I'm just relating the short of it. My captain filled me in before he sent me up here."

"What else did he tell you?"

"That one of the Nazi prisoners you're holding here escaped."

Lowry nodded, as if that's exactly what he'd expected Earl to say. "Well, there is that, plus a whole lot more, too."

"He kill any of your men in the process?"

"Not my men," Captain Lowry said, his voice strangely noncommittal, "no."

Earl Strong had made the hundred-and-fifty-mile drive from San Antonio up here to Camp Hearne straight from his meeting with Company Captain Tanner Lejeune. The town of Hearne wasn't technically part of his patrol, but technicalities still meant little to the Texas Rangers, and ever since his experiences in Sweetwater in 1931, Earl had found himself dispatched all over the state when the need arose. The same had been true for his father, William Ray, and grandfather Steeldust Jack, legends many times over who'd done their Ranger duty from one side of the state to the other. Steeldust Jack had died just before Earl was born at the turn of the century. But his father had regaled Earl with stories of the man's heroism, first as part of the Texas Brigade during the Civil War at the Battle of Second Manassas and Gettysburg and then as a Texas Ranger battling the likes of John D. Rockefeller.

The long ride gave him the opportunity to reflect on what he knew of Camp Hearne beyond what Captain Lejeune had told him. Like the fact that following the surrender of General Erwin Rommel's Afrika Korps in May of 1943, the United States found itself in possession of more than 150,000 enemy soldiers, nearly half of whom ended up being settled in seventy prisoner-of-war camps right here in Texas, twice as many as any other state.

He'd been told that the reason why Texas became such a popular location for German POWs was the Geneva Convention required them to be moved to a climate similar to the one in which they were captured. Rommel's troops, stationed in North Africa, would've been ill-prepared to survive harsh winters, making Texas the ideal home for them. And the flat terrain made it easier to spot any attempted escapes. Larger camps tended to be near more sizable towns, while smaller ones dotted the rural landscapes like oil wells.

Hearne, Texas was home to one of the larger camps, housing 4,800 prisoners. Shortly after Pearl Harbor, the citizens of Hearne lobbied their congressman to secure it, out of both patriotic loyalty and a sense of duty. The Army Corps of Engineers scoped out the town and liked what they saw. The land was acquired and by the summer of 1943, Camp Hearne was open for business, the prisoners arriving via an endless succession of Pullman trains Earl had greeted himself on more than one occasion.

There was a double fence around the entire camp, the exterior one topped with barbed wire, that included the headquarters building, hospital, and three separate compounds housing prisoners. Each compound was separated from the adjacent one by separate fencing, bracketed by watchtowers manned by machine gun–wielding guards. The buildings themselves had the typical look of standard military barracks, long and narrow, their sloped roofs covered by tarpaper or corrugated sheet iron. To handle the excess amount of prisoners continuing to pour off the trains, smaller shanty-like huts had been erected, featuring canvas roofs held up by matching posts that made them look like glorified tents.

As Earl Strong fell into step alongside Captain Lowry toward a cluster of those rapidly erected huts, he saw guards patrolling the camp both on foot and in weather-beaten jeeps. Earl had heard that soldiers were assigned this duty due either to wounds suffered that kept them from returning to combat, like Bo Lowry, or because they'd been deemed unfit for combat in the first place.

"Is it true what I heard about the non-Nazi and Nazi prisoners coming to blows from time to time?" Earl asked the captain.

"Plenty worse than that. And since the initial outbreak of hostilities, the pro-Nazi forces have pretty much consolidated their hold on power. Reason we've had so little trouble since is that their officers really do rule with an iron fist. They do the camp organizing, settle disputes, partition the work details, and enforce order. But none of them has much to say about Gunther Haut."

"Who?"

"The Nazi who escaped early this morning, not three weeks after he got here. This was where he lived the whole time," Lowry said, stopping just before the closed flap of one of the tented shacks.

"And that would be the prisoner I'm here about."

Lowry parted the white canvas flap and bid Earl Strong to enter. "Actually, you're here about the three men he killed before he jumped ship."

"We ain't touched a thing," Lowry continued, trailing Earl Strong into the shack that still smelled of fresh pine timber, now battling the stench of death, "except to cover the bodies after they were found during a routine check before breakfast. We got MPs on staff, but they don't have much experience with this sort of stuff."

"Then it's a good thing I do," Earl Strong told him.

He figured the temperature inside the uninsulated structure was already approaching a hundred, likely to climb another twenty degrees under the early summer, high Texas sun. Four cots occupied the bulk of the floor space, each with a footlocker squeezed beneath it. A small potbellied stove took up the bulk of the remaining floor space, cold to the touch since it would be several months before it was fired up. Just walking about made for a tight squeeze, but Earl didn't have to walk anywhere to size up what had happened.

The sheets covering the bodies of the three dead Germans were mottled with dark, drying blood up where he judged the heads must be. He figured Gunther Haut had cut the throats of his three bunkmates as they slept before making his way off into the night, not morning, barely twelve hours ago now, Earl confirmed, after pulling back all three sheets to inspect the bodies.

"We figure he stole a knife from the mess hall," Lowry explained, following the Ranger's line of thought.

"Are any of your prisoners assigned to construction details?" Earl asked, aware of the cheap labor they provided to local farmers as well as state road crews.

"They're paid wages on the order of eighty cents per day." Lowry nodded. "Gets deposited into a fund that supports operational expenses."

Earl pointed toward the wound on the nearest dead man's throat from which pools of blood had spouted and dried. "Because these cuts are jagged. Could've been a screwdriver or chisel, if sharpened properly. I've come across similar killings inside prisons."

He eyed the one unoccupied cot, its sheet rolled over a blanket that was tucked tightly into the mattress, revealing a discoloration in the steel frame.

"See that? Looks to me like Haut stole a tool from a work crew, or maybe another prisoner, and filed it sharp as he could right there. Hard to say exactly what it was, and I guess it don't matter much now."

"Haut was assigned to crews building the new inmate structures over in the south yard."

"That explains it then. But it don't explain why he killed his bunkmates, Captain. What can you tell me about the man?"

"I've got his file in my office. He was a Waffen-SS officer attached to Rommel's brigade cadre, the Reich's eyes and ears."

"You said he'd been here three weeks."

"Give or take. Not a lot of time to make the kind of enemies that require killing."

"We can assume he had his reasons, Captain, and that those reasons got something to do with his escape." Earl ran his eyes over the three bodies again, then moved to cover up the one he'd examined closer. "There was no struggle involved here, not even the pretext of self-defense. He murdered his three fellow Germans in their sleep, when he could've just made his way off into the night with none of them being any the wiser."

Lowry followed the sweep of the Ranger's gaze, trying to reconcile his words with the assumptions he'd wrongly formulated. That the murders could be explained away by a man simply wanting to cover his tracks, make sure no one tried to stop him, or alerted the camp guards as to his absence.

"Had Haut been acquainted with these men previous to coming here?" Earl asked him.

"It's possible, but there's no evidence of it. Like I said, we've got more than our share of pro-Nazi versus anti-Nazi conflict among the prisoners, but near as we can tell all four of these men were Nazis to the core and committed to the cause. We separated the two groups out and do our best to keep them segregated now. But the Nazis still run things, make no mistake about it. I told you that, too."

"I thought you run things, Captain."

"I keep order, Ranger, I don't keep charge."

"All the same," Earl told Lowry, "there haven't been a whole lot of escapes from camps like this. I heard it told that, more times than not, escapees end up flagging down a guard or peace officer sent on their trail to bring them back. One fellow was picked up while walking down the side of a main road loudly singing German marching songs. Another escapee was treed by a Brahman bull, quite relieved to return to his life as a prisoner of war upon his rescue. Three more prisoners were caught heading down the Brazos River on some kind of raft, hoping to float back to Germany."

Earl was pretty sure Captain Lowry knew those tales as well as he did, and he might have detailed a few more, had not a slight bulge on the side of one of the covered bodies claimed his attention.

"Now, what we got here . . ."

He eased back the sheet to reveal the victim was holding a heavy rubber mallet, quite capable of bashing in a man's skull, in his death grip.

"Have a look, Captain."

Lowry did just that. "What you make of this, Ranger?"

"Man don't take a mallet to bed, lest he fears he might not see the morning. Yes, sir, he was scared of something for sure."

"Haut?"

"That would be my guess."

Before Lowry could respond, a man wearing a private's uniform barged into the tented shack and approached him, still fighting to get his breath back. He spoke nervously in a hushed tone, and Lowry swung back to Earl Strong before the private had finished.

"You'll have to excuse me, Ranger."

The private followed Lowry out of the tent, and Earl watched them stride quickly across the mud drying in the streaming sunlight toward a half-dozen men dressed in dark suits, sodden by the humidity. They all wore fancy hats, and Earl followed Captain Lowry's boots kicking up flecks of what looked like dried clay in their wake, as the shortest of the suited figures stepped out to meet him. The man held his small hands on his hips, maintaining a rigid stature Earl most closely associated with European royalty.

Lowry was clearly deferring to the man as they exchanged words, pointing a few times toward the tented shack in which Earl still stood. He wasn't much for lipreading, but was pretty sure the short man mouthed *Texas Ranger,* followed by a clearly derisive, even dismissive, shake of his head.

That was all it took for Earl to move from the tented shack into the blistering sunlight, the clay-like ground feeling like beach sand beneath his boots.

"That's right," he said, when he reached the group. "I'm a Texas Ranger, for sure."

Earl addressed that remark to the short man, the subordinates clinging to him, as if attached by rope.

"Well, then, Ranger," greeted the man, who looked somehow familiar, "let me respectfully inform you that your services are no longer needed here."

Captain Lowry cleared his throat, hoping to dispel the tension that had settled over the scene. "Ranger Strong, this is—"

"J. Edgar Hoover," the short man said, extending his hand this time, "director of the Federal Bureau of Investigation. Pleased to meet you."

KINGWOOD, TEXAS

The head emergency room nurse at Kingwood Medical Center handed Dr. Lester Franks a steel clipboard, catching him an instant before he drew back the sheet to check the next patient on the list.

"I think you'll want to bump this one to the head of the class," she said, a look of concern drawn over her features.

He lifted his eyes from the initial exam report after a single glance. "Rape?"

"By all indications. Victim hasn't said much but that's what the physical evidence suggests."

Franks gazed down again. "She was drugged?"

"We got that much out of her. I've already drawn blood and sent it out to be tested."

"Don't hold your breath," Franks cautioned. "If it's GHB, or another from the date rape family, it probably won't show up."

He followed Nurse Rogers to the cubicle where the victim had been placed, but stopped short of drawing back the curtain. "I need you with me on this one."

Nurse Rogers nodded, something in the gesture telling Franks she was coming in regardless.

"I don't see a name here," he said, after consulting the admitting exam report once again.

"She hasn't given us one yet. Like I told you, she hasn't said much of anything."

Franks eased back the curtain slowly, so as not to further stress the victim's already frayed nerves. "I'm Dr. Franks, ma'am. I believe you've already met Nurse Rogers."

The young woman was sitting up on the edge of the gurney, her jeans dirty and shirt torn. Her long, wavy black hair was mussed and grime rode both sides of her face in streaks left by the tears riding her cheeks beneath a glassy gaze. She was tall, even without the well-worn boots she was wearing, and had a complexion that looked vaguely Latino.

Franks stopped a yard from the young woman's bedside, keeping his distance. "I'd like to examine you, ma'am, then order up some tests and X-rays, but I'd like a better idea of what happened first. If you were attacked, we're required to notify the police, but we can hold off on that for a while anyway."

"My father," the young woman muttered.

"What was that?"

"Call my father."

"Glad to, ma'am. But let's start with a name, your name."

"Caitlin," the young woman said. "Caitlin Strong."

PART ONE

It is a cardinal principle in all political associations that protection is commensurate with allegiance, and the poorest citizen, whose sequestered cabin is reared on our remotest frontier, holds as sacred a claim upon the government for safety and security as does the man who lives in ease and wealth in the heart of our most populous city.

—President of Texas Mirabeau Lamar; December 1838,
as reported in *The Texas Rangers: Wearing the Cinco Peso, 1821–1900*
Mike Cox, Forge Books, 2008

I

AUSTIN, TEXAS

"What the hell?"

Caitlin Strong and Cort Wesley Masters had just emerged from Esther's Follies on East Sixth Street, when they saw the stream of people hurrying down the road, gazes universally cocked back behind them. Sirens blared off in the distance and a steady chorus of honking horns seemed to be coming from an adjoining block just past the street affectionately known as "Dirty Sixth," Austin's version of Bourbon Street in New Orleans.

"Couldn't tell you," Cort Wesley said, even as he sized up the scene. "But I got a feeling we're gonna know before much longer."

Caitlin was in town to speak at a national law enforcement conference focusing on homegrown terrorism, and both her sessions at the Austin Convention Center had been jam-packed. She felt kind of guilty her presentations had lacked the audiovisual touches many of the others had featured. But the audiences hadn't seemed to mind, filling a sectioned-off ballroom to the gills to hear of her direct experiences, in contrast to theoretical dissertations by experts. Audiences were comprised of cops a lot like her, looking to bring something back home they could actually use. She'd focused to a great extent on her most recent battle with ISIS right here in Texas, and an al-Qaeda cell a few years before that, stressing how much things had changed in the interim and how much more they were likely to.

Cort Wesley had driven up from San Antonio to meet her for a rare night out that had begun with dinner at Ancho's inside the Omni Hotel and then a stop at Antone's nightclub to see the Rats, a band headed by a Texas Ranger tech expert known as Young Roger. From there, they'd walked to Esther's Follies to take in the famed Texas-centric improv show there, a first for both of them that was every bit as funny and entertaining as advertised, even with a gun-toting woman both Caitlin and Cort Wesley realized was based on her.

Fortunately, no one else in the audience made that connection and they managed to slip out ahead of the rest of the crowd. Once outside, though, they were greeted by a flood of pedestrians pouring up the street from an area of congestion a few blocks down, just past Eighth Street.

"What you figure, Ranger?"

"That maybe we better go have ourselves a look."

2

AUSTIN, TEXAS

Caitlin practically collided with a young man holding a wad of napkins against his bleeding nose at the intersection with East Seventh Street.

"What's going on?" she asked him, pulling back her blazer to show her Texas Ranger badge.

The young man looked from it back to her, swallowing some blood and hacking it up onto the street. "University of Texas graduation party took over all of Stubb's Barbecue," he said, pointing in the restaurant's direction. "Guess you could say it got out of hand. Bunch of fraternities going at it." He looked at the badge pinned to her chest again. "Are you really a Texas Ranger?"

"You need to get to an emergency room," Caitlin told him, and pressed on with Cort Wesley by her side.

"Kid was no older than Dylan," he noted, mentioning his oldest son who was still on a yearlong leave from Brown University.

"How many fraternities does the University of Texas at Austin have anyway, Cort Wesley?"

"A whole bunch."

"Yeah." She nodded, continuing on toward the swell of bodies and flashing lights. "It sure looks that way."

Stubb's was well known for its barbecue offerings and, just as much, its status as a concert venue. The interior was modest in size, as Caitlin recalled, two floors with the bottom level normally reserved for private parties and the upstairs generally packed with patrons both old and new. The rear of the main building, and several adjoining ones, featured a flattened dirt lot fronted by several performance stages where upward of two thousand people could enjoy live music in the company of three sprawling outdoor bars.

That meant this graduation party gone bad may have featured at least a comparable number of students and probably even more, many of whom remained in the street, milling about as altercations continued to flare, while first responders struggled futilely to disperse the crowd. Young men and women still swigging bottles of beer, while pushing and shoving each other. The sound of glass breaking rose over the loudening din of the approaching sirens, the whole scene glowing amid the colors splashed from the revolving lights of the Austin police cars already on the scene.

A fire engine leading a rescue wagon screeched to a halt just ahead of Cort Wesley and Caitlin, at the intersection with Seventh Street, beyond which had become impassable.

"Dylan could even be here, for all I know," Cort Wesley said, picking up his earlier train of thought.

"He doesn't go to UT."

"But there's girls and trouble, two things he excels at the most."

This as fights continued breaking out one after another, splinters of violence on the verge of erupting into an all-out brawl going on under the spill of the LED streetlights rising over Stubb's.

Caitlin pictured swirling lines of already drunk patrons being refused admittance due to capacity issues. Standing in line full of alcohol on a steamy night, expectations of a celebratory evening dashed, was a recipe for just what she was viewing now. In her mind, she saw fights breaking out between rival UT fraternities mostly in the outdoor performance area, before spilling out into the street, fueled by simmering tempers now on high heat.

"You see any good we can be here?" Cort Wesley asked her.

Caitlin was about to say no, when she spotted an anxious Austin patrol cop doing his best to break up fights that had spread as far as Seventh Street. She and Cort Wesley sifted through the crowd and made their way toward him, Caitlin advancing alone when they drew close.

"Anything I can do to help?" she said, reading the Austin policeman's name tag, "Officer Hilton?"

Hilton leaned up against an ornate light pole that looked like gnarled wrought iron for support. He was breathing hard, his face scraped and bruised. He noted the Texas Ranger badge and seemed to match her face to whatever media reports he'd remembered her from.

"Not unless you got enough Moses in you to part the Red Sea out there, Ranger."

"What brought you boys out here? Detail work?" Caitlin asked, trying to account for his presence on scene so quickly, ahead of the sirens screaming through the night.

Hilton shook his head. "An anonymous nine-one-one call about a sexual assault taking place inside the club, the downstairs lounge."

"And you didn't go inside?"

Hilton turned his gaze on the street, his breathing picking up again. "Through *that?* My partner tried and ended up getting his skull cracked open by a bottle. I damn near got killed fighting to reach him. Managed to get him in the back of our squad car and called for a rescue," he said, casting his gaze toward the fire engine and ambulance that were going nowhere. "Think maybe I better carry him to the hospital myself."

"What about the girl?"

"What girl?"

"Sexual assault victim inside the club."

Hilton frowned. "Most of them turn out to be false alarms anyway."

"Do they now?"

Caitlin's tone left him sneering at her. "Look, Ranger, you want to shoot up the street to get inside that shithole, be my guest. I'm not leaving my partner."

"Thanks for giving me permission," she said, and steered back for Cort Wesley.

"That looked like it went well," he noted, pushing a frat boy who'd ventured too close out of the way, after stripping the empty beer bottle he was holding by the neck from his grasp.

"Sexual assault victim might still be inside, Cort Wesley."

"Shit."

"Yeah."

"Got any ideas, Ranger?"

Caitlin eyed the fire engine stranded where East Seventh Street met Red River Avenue. "Just one."

3

AUSTIN, TEXAS

Four firemen were gathered behind the truck in a tight cluster, speaking with the two paramedics from the rescue wagon.

"I'm a Texas Ranger," Caitlin announced, approaching them with jacket peeled back to reveal her badge, "and I'm commandeering your truck."

"You're *what?*" one of the fireman managed. "No, absolutely not!"

The siren began blaring and lights started flashing, courtesy of Cort Wesley who'd climbed up behind the wheel.

"Sorry," Caitlin said, raising her voice above the din, "can't hear you!"

The crowd that filled the street in front of Stubb's Barbecue saw and heard the fire truck coming and began pelting it with bottles, as it edged forward through the congested street that smelled of sweat and beer. What looked like steam hung in the stagnant air overhead, either an illusion or the actual product of so many superheated bodies congealed in such tight quarters. The sound of glass breaking crackled through Caitlin's ears, as bottle after bottle smashed against the truck's frame.

The crowd clustered tighter around the fire engine, cutting off Cort Wesley's way backward or on toward Stubb's. The students, their fervor and aggression bred by alcohol, never noticed Caitlin's presence atop the truck until she finally figured out the workings of the truck's deck gun and squeezed the nozzle.

The force of the water bursting out of the barrel nearly knocked her backward off the truck. But she managed to right and then reposition herself, as she doused the tight cluster of students between the truck and the restaurant entrance with the gun's powerful stream.

A wave of people tried to fight the flow and ended up getting blown off their feet, thrown into other students who then scrambled to avoid the fire engine's surge forward ahead of its deafening horn. Caitlin continued to clear a path for Cort Wesley, sweeping the deck gun in light motions from side to side, the five-hundred-gallon tank still plenty full when the club entrance drew within clear view.

She felt the fire engine's front wheels mount the sidewalk and twist heavily to the right. The front fender grazed the building and took out a plate glass window the rioting had somehow spared. Caitlin saw a gap in the crowd open all the way to the entrance and leaped down from the truck to take advantage of it, before it closed up again.

She purposely didn't draw her gun and entered Stubb's to the sight of bloodied bouncers and staff herding the last of the patrons out of the restaurant. Outside, the steady blare of sirens told her the Austin police had arrived in force. Little they could do to disperse a crowd this large and unruly in rapid fashion, though, much less reach the entrance to lend their efforts to Caitlin's in locating the sexual assault victim.

She threaded her way through the ground floor of Stubb's to the stairs leading down to the private lounge area. The air felt like it was being blasted out of a steam oven, roiled with coagulated body heat untouched by the restaurant's air-conditioning that left Caitlin with the sense she was descending to hell.

Reaching the windowless sublevel floor, she swept her eyes about and thought she heard a whimpering come from a nest of couches, where a male figure hovered over the frame of a woman, lying half on and half off a sectional couch.

"Sir, put your hands in the air and turn around slowly!" Caitlin ordered, drawing her SIG-Sauer nine-millimeter pistol. "Don't make me tell you twice!"

He started to turn, without raising his hands, and Caitlin fired when she glimpsed something shiny in his grasp. Impact to the shoulder twisted the man around and spilled him over the sectional couch, Caitlin holding her SIG at the ready as she approached his victim.

She heard the whimpering again, making her think more of the sound a dog makes, and followed it toward a tight cluster of connected couch sections, their cushions all stained wet and smelling thickly of beer. Drawing closer while still keeping a sharp eye on the man she'd shot, Caitlin spotted a big smart phone lying just out of his grasp, recognizing it as the object she'd wrongly taken for a gun. Then Caitlin spied a young woman of college age pinned between a pair of couch sections, covering her exposed breasts with her arms, her torn blouse hanging off her and jeans unbuttoned and unzipped just short of her hips.

Drawing closer, Caitlin saw the young woman's assailant, the man she'd just shot, in all likelihood must've yanked them down so violently that he'd split the zipper and torn off the snap or button.

"Ma'am?" she called softly.

The young woman tightened herself into a ball and retreated deeper into the darkness between the couch sections, not seeming to hear her.

"Ma'am," Caitlin said louder, hovering over the coed while continuing to check on the man she'd shot, his eyes drifting in and out of consciousness, his shirt wet with blood in the shoulder area from the gunshot wound.

Caitlin only wished it was her own attacker lying there, from all those years before when she'd been a coed herself at the Lone Star College campus in the Houston suburb of Kingwood. Some memories suppressed easily, others were like a toothache that came and went. That one was more like a cavity that had been filled, forgotten until the filling broke off and raw nerve pain flared.

Caitlin pushed the couch sections aside and knelt by the young woman, pistol tucked low by her hip so as not to frighten her further.

"I'm a Texas Ranger, ma'am," she said, in as soothing a voice as she could manage. "I need to get you out of here, and I need you to help me. I need to know if you can walk."

The young woman finally looked at her, nodded. Her left cheek was swollen badly and one of her arms hung limply from its socket. Caitlin looked back at the downed form of the man she'd already shot once, half hoping he gave her a reason to shoot him again.

"What's your name? Mine's Caitlin."

"Kelly Ann," the young woman said, her voice dry and cracking.

Caitlin helped her to her feet. "Well, Kelly Ann, I know things feel real bad right now, but trust me when I tell you this is as bad as they're going to get."

Kelly Ann's features perked up slightly, her eyes flashing back to life. She tried to take a deep breath, but stopped halfway though.

Caitlin held her around the shoulders in one arm, SIG clutched in her free hand while her eyes stayed peeled on the downed man's stirring form. "I'm going to stay with you the whole way until we get you some help," she promised.

The building suddenly felt like a Fun House Hall of Mirrors. Everything distorted, perspective and sense of place lost. Even the stairs climbing back to the ground floor felt different, only the musty smell of sweat mixed with stale perfume and body spray telling her they were the same.

Caitlin wanted to tell Kelly Ann it would be all right, that it would get better, that it would all go away in time. But that would be a lie, so she said nothing at all. Almost to the door, she gazed toward a loose assemblage of frat boys wearing hoodies displaying their letters as they chugged from liquor bottles stripped from the shelves behind the main bar on the first floor. How different were they from the one who'd hurt her, hurt Kelly Ann?

Caitlin wanted to shoot the bottles out of their hands, but kept leading Kelly Ann on instead, out into the night and the vapor spray from the deck gun now being wielded by Cort Wesley to keep their route clear.

"'Bout time!" he shouted down, scampering across the truck's top to retake his place behind the wheel.

Caitlin was already inside the cab, Kelly Ann clinging tightly to her.

"Where to, Ranger?"

"Seton Medical Center, Cort Wesley."

Before he got going, Caitlin noticed Officer Hilton and several other Austin cops pushing their way through the crowd toward the entrance to Stubb's.

"Don't worry, Officer, I got the victim out safe and sound," she yelled down to him, only half-sarcastically. "But I left a man with a bullet in his shoulder down there for you to take care of."

"Come again?"

"I'd hurry, if I were you. He's losing blood."

4

SAN ANTONIO, TEXAS

"Name me something that never changes in Texas besides you," Captain D. W. Tepper said to Caitlin from across his desk the next morning, the office door closed for one of the few times she could remember.

"Summer humidity, I suppose."

"Yup, you can feel it building in the air right now. You notice anything different about my desk?"

"You mean, besides the fact your phone is off the hook?"

"Any notion as to why? Let me spare you the trouble of answering. Because one of the Rangers in the company I'm supposed to be commanding stole a fire truck last night."

"Commandeered, D.W., and I didn't have much of a choice."

"'Course you didn't; you never do. And I suppose you had no choice other than to turn a water cannon on some unruly teenagers."

"They were drunken college students," Caitlin corrected, "and it was close to being a full-scale riot."

"This the part where you tell me they had it coming, like you said about the last, oh, hundred or so people you shot?"

"There was a rape victim inside that building, Captain."

"And you took it upon yourself to shoot a man for stealing her cell phone."

"He did a whole lot more than that before I showed up."

"You sure about that, Ranger? Man's name is Willie Arble. Pickpocket and petty thief with a pecker the size of a pinky toe. Okay, strike that last remark but his sheet's clean as far as rape or sexual assault goes."

"First time for everything, Captain."

"Not in this case. There's DNA all over the victim, but none of it matches Arble's. So you put a bullet through a man's shoulder for pocketing an iPhone." Tepper tapped a Marlboro Red from an open pack and stuck it in his mouth, feeling about his desktop for a lighter, when he suddenly spit the cigarette out. "Goddamn candy butt from the dime store," he said. "Now how you suppose it worked its way into a perfectly good pack?"

"I wouldn't know."

"You have any idea how much these things cost now? Hell, I got a goddamn retirement fund invested in this habit."

"And thanks to it, you may not make retirement."

"Where's my lighter, by the way, the big one I daisy-chained to my desk so it wouldn't go missing like the others?"

"I guess it went missing like the others. If I come across it, I'll let you know."

Tepper retrieved the candy cigarette off his blotter and bit off the part that held the fake filter. "Just like I remember as a boy ..."

"When did you start smoking the real ones?"

"When you joined the Rangers. Wait, no—that was drinking." Tepper's features softened. "I shouldn't be making light of your actions last night, given the chord that young lady being trapped inside must've struck. But even that didn't give you call to unleash the winds of Hurricane Caitlin. And we'd be having a different conversation right now, if Willie Arble was in the morgue instead of a hospital bed."

"If I'd wanted him dead, D.W., he would be."

"And that's supposed to make me feel better?"

"That girl was the same age I was. All I did, after the fact, was take her to the hospital and stay with her until a couple detectives from the Austin police sex crimes squad showed up."

"And what you did before the fact is blowing a shit storm right into my face. When was the last time you shot an unarmed man?"

"I don't know if I ever have."

"That's right. Puts the force of those winds in a whole different category, even for Hurricane Caitlin." Tepper stopped long enough to wrinkle his nose, as if he'd swallowed something bitter. "Remember the pit bull dog I shot that had such a hold on a boy's arm they had to surgically remove its head at the hospital? Who's that remind you of exactly?"

"I got the girl out of there, Captain. I got her help. That's where this ends for me."

"Let's hope so, given shooting unarmed men tends to play poorly, even in Texas. Should I be worried, Ranger?"

"Only about the next time I confront a potential rapist."

Tepper tried another Marlboro only to find all the remaining cigarettes had been replaced with the candy variety. "How about you go fetch me another pack?"

The phone rang, and he answered it, eyeing Caitlin the whole time he listened to the voice on the other end, before angling the receiver toward her across the desk.

"Something you need to hear straight from the source, Ranger."

She came out of her chair to take the phone. "What's going on, Captain?"

Tepper's expression had grown so taut and grave, the deep furrows dug out of his weather-beaten face suddenly looked shallow. "Looks like your part in this isn't finished yet, after all, Ranger."

5

"Your son's a good worker, amigo," Miguel Asuna told Cort Wesley. "I got him stripping a car in less than thirty minutes."

Cort Wesley moved away from the wall of Asuna's office papered with old calendars, his spine stiffening. He'd positioned himself there to make sure his oldest son, Dylan, couldn't see him from his workstation out in the shop. He was halfway to Asuna's desk when the big man flashed him a grin.

"Nah, just kidding. Not about him being a good worker, though. Kid's ever looking for something full-time, I got a place for him."

Miguel's brother, Pablo Asuna, had been Cort Wesley's best friend, the only one still waiting when he got out of the Walls prison in Huntsville after four years, thanks to an overturned conviction. Back when Cort Wesley was working for the Branca crime family, Miguel Asuna's body shop had doubled as a chop shop where stolen cars were brought to be disassembled for parts. He'd once heard Asuna boast he could strip a Mercedes in thirty minutes flat.

Miguel Asuna was twice the size of his dead little brother and, by all accounts, was still living and working on the fringe of the law. As a result, his body shop was filled to the brim, every stall and station taken, with not a single license plate in evidence from this angle. The shop smelled heavily of oil, tire rubber, and sandblasted steel. But the floor looked polished clean, shiny with a coat of finish over the concrete that showed not a single grease stain or even a tire mark. For obvious reasons, Asuna kept the bay doors closed and, with the air-conditioning not switched on, the whole shop had a sauna-like feel fed by heat lamps switched on to dry paint faster.

Months before, Cort Wesley had let Dylan extend his sabbatical from Brown University for the entire school year that had just ended. But only on the condition that he get a job. When the boy's own efforts failed to land him one, his father had called Miguel Asuna, who was more than happy to oblige.

It was hard to even recognize Dylan, Cort Wesley figured, looking at him through the glass of Asuna's office, wearing work coveralls splattered with grease and streaks of grime drawn down his cheeks. He'd clubbed his long black hair up in what they called a "man bun," which made Cort Wesley want to cut it off with a pair of scissors.

"Anyway," Asuna was saying, "that's not why I asked you to come in."

"So I figured."

"Your kid got some kind of hero complex or something?"

"What makes you ask?" Cort Wesley said, already fearing the answer.

"How much you know about the latest issues we got here on the east side of the city, amigo?"

Cort Wesley again made sure he was out of view from Dylan's workstation. "Nothing."

"Not the best of times for us Latinos, with half the country figuring we're all ignorant wetbacks sucking on this country's tits."

"Colorful metaphor."

Asuna's expression hardened, his own coveralls looking like a canvas blanket wrapped around his bulbous frame. "Let's talk about your boy. How he seems to take personal affront to the latest frequenters of East San Antonio."

"And who would that be exactly?"

"American Nazi Party, Aryan Nation—they go by a whole shitload of different names. What stays the same is that they're white assholes looking to let outsiders like us know who's boss." Asuna stopped and shimmied his chair forward. "So last week, I think it was, your boy's outside on a break when he spots a truckload of these white assholes hassling some high school Latinas walking home. Way Dylan describes it, they might as well have been talking out of their assholes, given the shit that was coming out of their mouths."

"What did he do?" Cort Wesley asked.

"He'd just bought a can of Dr Pepper, about to pop it open when he decided to lob it like a hand grenade instead. Shattered the truck's rear window. Girls were able to run away like they were Olympic sprinters."

"But Dylan didn't."

"No, amigo, he did not. Stood his ground right there on the sidewalk, while the truck screeched to a halt and the white assholes piled out."

"Oh boy..."

"Couple of my other guys saw what was happening and got close up to Dylan. Enough to have these white boys covered in tattoos everywhere you could see skin rethink their intentions and leave the premises. Thing you need to be aware of is that they've been cruising by every day since. Sometimes they park across the street and blare heavy rock-and-roll music through their open windows to advertise their presence." Asuna took a deep breath and let it out slowly. "They got their crosshairs trained on your boy, amigo. And, sooner or later, they're gonna do more than park their truck across the street."

Cort Wesley realized he was shaking his head. "All because he stood up for some girls."

"And the illegals I got working for me, too. Let me tell you something else," Asuna said, coming out of his chair, the wood creaking under the strain. "A couple of those punks had their hands on one of those girls. Looked like they intended to drag her into their truck to do God knows what. Your son doesn't throw that pop bottle, maybe we'd know *what* that would've been exactly."

"Thanks, Miguel."

Asuna nodded, his head seeming to merge straight into his shoulders. "You want to get your boy a job with the Parks Department for the rest of the summer, I'll understand. But something else you should know. Another of my guys gave him a pistol, just in case. Problem there is that too often 'just in case' turns into 'rest in peace,' you know what I mean."

"I do."

"I got my guys watching your kid's back, without him knowing," Asuna said somberly. "But these Nazi types got psycho running through their blood. Real punks out to prove they're genuine tough guys by scoring a kill. Some of those tattoos I mentioned? Word is the ones colored red act like a tally, some fucked-up competition. Point being my guys are car boosters and strippers, no match for whatever they're packing."

Cort Wesley nodded. "I know somebody who is."

6

"You probably want to be sitting down for this," Bexar County Medical Examiner Frank Whatley told Caitlin when she didn't take the chair he'd offered her.

"I'm a little confused here, Doc."

"Look, Caitlin—"

"You never call me that. You always call me 'Ranger.'"

"Sit down, *Ranger*. Please."

Caitlin finally did; stiffly, leaving her hat in her lap and feeling it bob up and down in rhythm with her jittery legs.

"Austin medical examiner called me this morning."

"About the girl I brought to the hospital last night?"

Whatley nodded. "The very same. She suffered a broken cheekbone from what appears to be a fist, when she must have resisted. Plenty of bruising consistent with sexual assault, and a dislocated shoulder." Something changed in his expression. "I wish I wasn't having this conversation with you."

"I already know the man I shot didn't do it."

"That's not why I wanted to see you, Caitlin," Whatley said, not sounding like his normal self at all.

"You don't have to parse your words, Doc," Caitlin told him. "It was eighteen years ago now."

"But some things stay with you longer than others."

Frank Dean Whatley had been Bexar County's medical examiner since the time Caitlin was in diapers. He'd grown a belly in recent years that hung out over his thin belt, seeming to force his spine to angle inward at the torso. Whatley's teenage son had been killed by Latino gangbangers when Caitlin was a mere kid herself. Ever since then, he'd harbored a virulent hatred for that particular race, from the bag boys at the local H-E-B supermarket to the politicians who professed to be peacemakers. With his wife first lost in life and then death to alcoholism, he'd probably stayed in the job too long. But he had nothing to go home to, no real life outside the office, and remained exceptionally good at his job.

The Bexar County Medical Examiner's Office and Morgue was located just off Loop 410 not far from the Babcock Road exit on Merton Mintor. It was a three-story beige building that also housed the county health department and city offices for Medicaid. Caitlin had been coming here since she was a teenager, and what struck her was how it always smelled exactly the same, of cleaning solvent with a faint scent of menthol clinging to the walls like paint to disguise the odor of decaying flesh. The lighting was dull in the hallways and overly bright in offices like Whatley's. She'd had occasion to come here plenty often over the years, but normally to discuss cases that fell under Bexar County's jurisdiction, as opposed to Austin's.

"I changed my major to criminal justice after I was assaulted," Caitlin told him, not bothering to elaborate further. "I wasn't sure about becoming a Texas Ranger, until it happened."

"And me always thinking you were born into it."

"After my grandfather died, my heart just wasn't there anymore."

"There was your father."

"I think he wanted me to choose another line of work. I don't think he was happy when I informed him of my decision to change course."

Whatley scratched at his scalp, although Caitlin suspected there was no itch there. "Lone Star College in Kingwood is as good as it gets when it comes to community college."

"You're changing the subject."

"I'm only trying to."

"Don't bother on my account. What did Austin tell you exactly about the victim I pulled out of Stubb's last night? Do they have a line on her real attacker? Is that what this is about?"

"I suppose it is, Ranger."

"What did I tell you about parsing your words, Doc?"

Whatley looked down at his lap, then toward the window, as if suddenly reluctant to meet Caitlin's gaze. "I reviewed the preliminary report from the Austin ME. They do good work up there."

Caitlin waited for him to continue.

"Man who assaulted Kelly Ann Beasley wore a condom, but that college girl scratched enough skin off him to allow for a DNA profile on her attacker."

"Anybody I know?" Caitlin asked, and watched Whatley's expression turn dour.

"Appears so, unfortunately. It's the same man who raped you."

7

HOUSTON, TEXAS; EIGHTEEN YEARS BEFORE

Caitlin's mind flashed back eighteen years to the emergency room she'd driven herself to and the doctor who'd examined her and wrote the initial report.

"My father."

"What was that?"

"Call my father."

"Glad to, ma'am. But let's start with a name, your name."

That doctor had performed all the necessary tests, including those required to assemble a so-called rape kit. So-called because Caitlin detested the name. Made such a perverse act of violence and debauchery sound like something that came out of a box.

Jim Strong had made it to the hospital ahead of the police and took charge of the questioning along with them, the Houston sex crimes detectives more than happy to have the help of a Texas Ranger. Jim made it plain he was there as a father, not a Texas Ranger, and didn't want to provoke any squabbles pertaining to jurisdiction.

After the questioning had passed in a fog, he'd driven Caitlin home—to San Antonio instead of her apartment near the Lone Star College campus.

"You know his name?" Jim Strong asked, his words sounding like they were strained through gravel held in his mouth like chewing tobacco.

"No."

Caitlin watched her father stiffen behind the wheel. "How's that, little girl?"

"Don't call me that."

"I always call you that."

"I just don't feel like a little girl right now. I don't feel much like anything at all."

"Get back to this kid. What was it, some kind of party?"

"He drugged me," Caitlin told her father. "It didn't show up in the blood work at the hospital, but I'm sure of it all the same. The world kept fading in and out. I was in one place, then I was in another. Then I woke up."

"In your apartment. Good thing you managed to get yourself to the hospital like you did, little..."

Jim Strong stopped himself just in time, not wanting to upset his daughter any further. He'd raised her on his own from the time Caitlin was four after witnessing her mother being murdered by Mexican drug dealers. There'd been rape involved there, too, but Caitlin had already hidden herself in a closet by that point.

"So you don't know his name," Jim picked up. "How about what he looks like? Was he a student?"

"His first name was Frank. I never got his last name. He was about your height. Blond hair, blue eyes, nice smile. He got me a drink from the bar in a red Solo cup. I should've known he'd dosed it. There was this look in his eyes..."

"I'll need the address where this party took place."

"You told the Houston cops it was their case."

"I did, didn't I? Their case for sure, but my daughter," Caitlin's father added, looking across the truck's cab at her. "Where'd it happen?" he asked, squeezing the steering wheel tighter.

Beads of sweat dappled his brow, and his cheeks were flushed red with a suppressed, simmering rage he fought hard to keep from spilling over.

Caitlin's throat felt like she'd swallowed a wad of cotton, no words making it through.

"You want to talk about this later?" her father asked.

She finally pushed her voice past the cotton. "No—now, while it's fresh in my mind." The clog started to come back and she forced it down, listening to her own voice as if it was someone else talking. "The party was at a condo, a town house, a few blocks from my apartment. A girl lives there I got to know in Forensics class. We had lunch a couple times at Bill's Café. I don't even know all the names of her roommates. I remember waking up in one of their bedrooms upstairs. I remember his smell all over me and realized it wasn't just his smell. Then I blacked out again and next time I woke up I was on my own couch. Took some time to come all the way to, and then I drove myself straight to the hospital."

"Okay, so you don't know Frank's full name. What about whether he was a student or not?"

"I don't remember seeing him around campus."

Caitlin thought her father was writing all this down in his mind.

"But you'd know him, if you saw him again."

"For sure. And there's something else I just remembered: look for a man with scratches down his face, or neck maybe."

"Why?"

"Because when I finally came to, I saw there was blood under my fingernails. The doctor at the emergency room took samples," Caitlin had continued. "But he thought they might not yield much, when it comes to DNA."

"Why's that?"

"I don't know, something about degradation." Caitlin could tell that upset her father, adding to his fury and frustration. "It was so hard for me to keep from jumping in the shower, I wanted to wash all of him off me so much," she continued. "I was actually turning on the shower when I changed my mind. Never even took off my clothes before driving to the hospital."

"But you brought a change with you, because you knew they'd need the ones you were wearing for evidence," Jim Strong noted. "Smart."

"I was thinking, just not very clearly."

"Understandable, under the circumstances."

Jim Strong let out a deep, growling breath, while Caitlin held hers briefly.

"What are you gonna do, Daddy?"

"Say my prayers that your granddad's not still alive, or I'd have to cordon off the whole city of Houston."

Caitlin swallowed hard. "You know that talk we had about me not being sure about a career in law enforcement, becoming a Ranger, after all?"

"I do."

"I think I've changed my mind."

8

SAN ANTONIO, TEXAS

"You can tell all that from a preliminary report?" Caitlin asked Doc Whatley, finally finding her voice again.

"Austin ME's office are the ones who came up with the match from the database."

Caitlin felt the familiar clog return to her throat, pushing her words through it now, as she had done eighteen years ago. "Off the blood that was under my fingernails?"

Whatley nodded. "Whoever hurt that girl last night was a surefire match for whoever it was that hurt you."

Caitlin shifted one way in her chair, then back to the other. "Austin police say anything about how the girl is doing?"

"I didn't ask. Sex crimes cops said they'll be in touch with you to discuss anything you may recall from the crime scene. They believe the assault occurred on the same couch where you found her. They collected the cushions as evidence last night and also found a button that may have come from the assailant's shirt."

"Victim say anything about him to the Austin PD?"

"Caitlin . . ."

"I'm just asking."

Whatley gave her a long look before responding. "She said she didn't remember very much, couldn't even be sure which of the guys she'd been dancing with it was, if any. Her blood test came back negative, but it's pretty clear her assailant slipped her some GHB, or something like it."

"Figures," Caitlin said, feeling herself grow stiff and anxious again. "What about the man I shot who was swiping the victim's wallet and cell phone?"

"I didn't ask about him," Whatley told her, his expression tightening in concern. "You don't have any ideas about pushing yourself into this case, do you, Ranger?" Whatley asked her, the concern ringing in his voice.

His phone rang before he could finish his thought. He lifted the receiver, listened more than spoke, and jotted down a few notes before his eyes retrained themselves on Caitlin.

"Yes, Captain," he said into the phone. "She's here right now.... Sure, I'll tell her. Maybe we can carpool."

Whatley hung up the phone, tore the top sheet off his notepad, and lumbered out of his chair.

"Whatever you were thinking of doing, Ranger, it'll have to wait."

"Where we going, Doc?"

"What may or may not be a crime scene."

Caitlin rose, too. "Usually, Rangers don't get the call until that's been confirmed."

"Except in this case," Whatley told her, "the local PD isn't sure."

9

San Antonio, Texas

"God's supposed to be merciful, but I wouldn't want to bet the farm on that," Guillermo Paz said to the man holding the hard cardboard plate out before him in the soup kitchen's line. "See, He's got a temper and a mean streak, and a capacity for vengeance like you wouldn't believe. You see where I'm going with this?"

At nearly seven feet tall, Paz found himself looking down at the man named Benny whose eyes kept shifting this way and that, unable to focus on anything for very long at all. His hair was long and tangled into oily knots that smelled like rancid, standing water. The man had been banned for a week after starting a fight with those seated around a table in the Catholic Worker House courtyard, because he claimed it was his. Paz had evicted him as peaceably as possible, learning in the days since that Benny was a homeless veteran with a long record of petty theft and assault.

This was Benny's first day back, pushing his plate skittishly closer to the ladle with which Paz had scooped up some mashed potatoes.

"I'm telling you this," Paz continued, as the line backed up behind Benny, "because I've gotten into my own share of scrapes I've come to regret later, so many I can't even count. Call me lost, if you want, call me the cold-blooded killer I've been for as long as I can remember. I'm still a killer, but not the cold-blooded kind anymore, since I found God or, at least, have kept looking."

Guillermo Paz was no better at dispensing advice here at the Catholic Worker House on Nolan Street than he was at doling out food. He gave out overly large portions, and spent so much time talking with the unfortunate souls who stopped in for lunch pretty much every day that the line, inevitably, snarled.

But he was just trying to do the right thing here, feed their minds and souls, as well as their bodies. The food for the former being copies of passages from his favorite philosophers he made at Staples to hand to those who came through the line, because he believed they were in need of them. But, to a man and woman, visitors to the single-story, former residential home wanted to enjoy their food, use one of the computers free of charge, shower, do their laundry, or just go someplace where they could be part of a community. They sat at round wooden tables covered in white cloth, squeezed into a pair of adjoining rooms Paz took for the former residence's living and dining rooms.

Paz tried to get Benny to meet his stare, but failed. "See, the priest I'd been visiting for years at the San Fernando Cathedral lives in a nursing home now, after suffering a stroke. I was the one who found him outside the confessional, blood dribbling out one of his ears and staining his white hair red on that side. I wanted to pray for him while I waited for the paramedics to arrive, but I was too pissed at God for letting this happen."

Paz looked down again, saw Benny had moved on without his mashed potatoes, leaving him speaking to another man with one of his eyes narrowed into a slit. "That's why I'm here," he continued, anyway. "Because getting angry at God was to disrespect all I'd learned from my priest. I prescribed some penance for myself, figured that would make my priest happy. Give us something to talk about—well, me anyway, since he can't talk anymore—next time I visit. I miss talking to him, so I'm talking to you instead. Just about the same thing, because my priest always let me ramble on. I think he wanted me to think things out for myself, instead of relying on him to do it for me. I've tried auditing college philosophy classes to expand my horizons, visited a psychic to expand my universe, taught English to new immigrants to expand my nature. But you know what?"

Another figure stood sheepishly in Paz's massive shadow now.

"Tennessee Williams wrote that 'Hell is yourself and the only redemption is when a person puts himself aside to feel deeply for another person.' In other words, I started figuring I could help folks like you as much with words, as with meals. So I began making my copies over at Staples, figured I'd try my hand at being a spiritual guide and food server at the same time, since I never had any experience with either before. I'm probably too old for the seminary, and they probably have a strict no-gun policy there anyway. But this is the next best thing, even though not many of you take the handouts I leave on the tables. Nobody even noticed I made sure they were printed in both English and Spanish. I like to think I'm all-inclusive, since in my past life the ethnicity of my victims never made any difference at all."

Paz figured God's tolerance for his murderous actions could only get him so far, the fact being that while he'd long ago lost track of the number of people he'd killed, the Almighty certainly hadn't. But it was one he'd failed to kill that had changed his life forever, back when he was still with the Directorate of Intelligence and Prevention Service, better known as the Venezuelan secret police. He'd been retained to kill a Texas Ranger, a woman of all things, a fact that bothered Paz not in the least, until their eyes met in the midst of a gunfight, and he saw what had been missing in his own. He'd never returned to Venezuela after that, calling Texas and America home now, thanks to an arrangement with Homeland Security that kept Paz inoculated from prosecution. All he needed to do was the bidding of a shadowy subdivision, under the leadership of an equally shadowy man, chartered to keep America safe from within through any and all means necessary, means that often amounted to Guillermo Paz and the killers in his employ who'd formerly filled his ranks in Venezuela. Most didn't speak English, and the ones that did didn't speak much, anyway. They waited for his call, and when it came, they answered.

Paz was grateful for their presence, as much as anything because it aided his efforts in keeping his Texas Ranger safe. The woman was a walking magnet for trouble. Paz was convinced that the multitude of threats continually plaguing the country owed their presence in Texas directly to her. In the cosmically charged universe, he believed nothing ever happened by chance alone, and Texas had somehow become the epicenter of efforts by an unholy assortment of villains to do America harm. As if the state lay at some metaphysical low point to which everything bad ultimately settled, to be dealt with by the likes of him and his Texas Ranger. Paz even figured the gunfight that had brought them together eight years before had been the work of the universe.

"Where was I?" Paz asked the shape before him, looking up from his freshly packed ladle of mashed potatoes.

"I need your help, Colonel," Cort Wesley Masters told him.

10

San Antonio, Texas

Cort Wesley sat across from Paz at a table in the courtyard shaded by the thin shadows cast by some saplings. "I don't think the supervisor likes you, Colonel."

Paz shifted uneasily on a chair too small to accommodate his vast bulk. "If I wasn't a volunteer, she'd fire me. Thinks I talk too much."

"You do."

"Words are less painful than bullets, and I've been too free with dispensing both for too long. So this help you need, does it have something to do with our Ranger, outlaw?"

"No. My son Dylan."

"He's in trouble," Paz said.

"Nothing new. Boy seems to attract it."

"Now who does that remind you of?" Paz asked lightly, not really seeking an answer.

"If it's not over a girl," said Cort Wesley, "it's for standing up for someone else or some cause."

"I'm guessing the latter in this case," Paz said.

Cort Wesley watched Paz's eyes gleam in the narrow bend of light, weighing every word as if he were fixing his aim on a target. "He's taking some time off from college—a semester, something like that. I got him a job working at Miguel Asuna's body shop. Apparently there's a gang menacing the local Latino population. In a word, Dylan told them to go fuck themselves."

"That's more than a word, outlaw."

"It's also a problem. Miguel thinks the gang may have Dylan marked. He keeps pushing things, they're sure to push back."

Paz nodded. "You tell the Ranger about this?"

"I'm telling you."

"She and I have different approaches to such things."

"That's why I'm telling you, Colonel. And I'm wondering if you or your men could keep eyes on him for a time, until I sort through this and learn a bit more about this gang."

"Is that all?"

"I trust your discretion."

"You didn't always, outlaw," Paz said, holding his stare now. "Miguel Asuna's brother, Pablo, was the one whose face I held against a fan belt to get him to tell me where I could find you. He never did, as I recall."

Cort Wesley felt himself stiffening. "People change."

"I've been doing my best."

Cort Wesley looked around him, another set of homeless men taking an unshaded table that had just been cleared by a volunteer staff member. "Explains why you're here."

"I miss my priest."

"How's Father Boylston doing?"

Paz looked surprised. "You know his name?"

"You told me, Colonel. I remembered."

"He's still breathing. That's about all I can say. I think he'd be pleased that I'm working here." Paz rocked forward, his arms so big they almost rubbed up against Cort Wesley's when he laid them on the table. "I'm happy to help, outlaw."

"I'd do it myself, but it would piss Dylan off something crazy, if he found out. You know Asuna's body shop?"

"I'll find it. Handle the bulk of the watching myself, and have my men fill in as needed."

"First time I've heard you mention that you needed anyone, Colonel."

Paz leaned back again. "Only from noon to two. That's when I work here."

II

ELK GROVE, TEXAS

Armand Fisker laid the revolver down atop the old-fashioned blotter and moved behind the teacher's dusty desk, crossing his arms.

"One way we could do this," he said, addressing the three big men squeezed into a trio of tiny desks across the front of the classroom, their faces shiny in the glow of the bright overhead lighting, "is to let the three of you assholes go for the pistol and see who gets there first. The other is to grow up, grow some balls, and keep making ourselves a shitload of money."

Fisker ran his gaze from one man to another, the three of them leaders, respectively, of the Bandidos, Cossacks, and Hells Angels biker gangs in Texas. To a man, they were reluctant to look back, their stares ranging from indignant to petulant. But none of them made a move for the gun, which left Fisker shaking his head.

"You boys talk a hell of a good game when you're spraying a Waffle House with machine-gun fire," he continued. "Let loose, have at it, and let the bodies fall where they may. Know what? Let's try this a different way."

And, with that, Fisker retrieved the revolver, popped open the cylinder, and yanked out three of the cartridges. Then he spun the cylinder, so the gang leaders could see the three cartridges still tucked into their slots, before snapping it back into place.

"Let's play a little Texas roulette," he said, grinning at the term he'd just coined.

Thunder was rumbling over the mesas looking down over Elk Grove, a storm coming that darkened the day to near night, enough for the windows to throw Fisker's reflection back at him. His hair was jet-black and combed straight back to wipe out any semblance of curls or waves, and better highlight the icy blue eyes that were sharp enough, somebody once mused to him, to cut a man's throat. His arms bore the tightly banded, sinewy muscles bred by plenty of hard labor, his shoulders naturally broad and chest inflated by the weights he continued to push up, uncompromised by age. The window glass's distortion made his neck look thin and birdlike, an illusion cast in contradiction to his block-shaped head that featured a ridged jawline and protruding forehead. His jowls looked puffy, and when Fisker smiled, the reflection of his teeth was so gleaming white, he thought maybe it had been a flash of lightning in advance of the storm.

Fisker rotated the .357 Magnum's barrel from one man to the next, holding it briefly on each. "Any of you don't want to play Texas roulette, I understand. Feel free to get up and walk out of here. Just don't think you can ever come back. Once you're history, you're a name in a book and nothing more. Take all that money I've made you and go sun your fat ass in some tropical paradise." Fisker held the gun steady. "So who's staying and who's going?"

None of the big men tucked snugly into the desks before him moved a muscle. Fisker aimed the .357 straight at Hacksaw, head of the Bandidos.

"That gunfight at the Waffle House in Waco and all the bullshit since stops now," Fisker continued, holding the pistol steady with finger poised on the trigger. "I called you boys here to my own backyard, my home, the ghost town I rebuilt from the ground up to get that straight. Your pissant squabbles have hurt business and that needs to stop today. We play our cards right, the sky's the limit."

Hacksaw didn't look like he was even breathing, eyes tight on the revolver, as if he'd spotted something inside the bore. Fisker pulled the trigger.

Click.

Hacksaw started breathing again.

"We play our cards wrong, we're as fucked as a two-dollar whore," Fisker resumed and, without missing a beat, spun the cylinder and resteadied the Magnum on Arlo Teague, head of the Hells Angels Texas chapter. "My daddy didn't lay all the groundwork for what we're building to see it lost in a shit storm of pansy-ass bullshit over who gets what city or what Podunk town."

Fisker curled his finger over the trigger and pulled it again.

Click.

Frank Fulton, head of the Cossacks, was grinning when Fisker aimed the Magnum straight for him, after spinning the cylinder a third time.

"Offer's still open, Frank, if you want to take your leave."

Fulton's response was to sandwich his hands around the pistol and press the bore dead center against his forehead. "Let's do this."

"You wanna talk territory, Frank," Fisker said, starting the trigger inward, "let's talk about the whole goddamn U. S. of A."

Click.

Fisker laid the Magnum back atop the desk where any of the gang leaders could grab it. "Guess I underestimated you boys," he said, coming around the desk toward the blackboard. "Now that we've got that behind us, school is in session."

The ghost town of Elk Grove, in its heyday, had been home to twelve hundred who liked living in a dirt-rich town carved out of the South Texas prairie two hundred miles south of San Antonio in McMullen County. Its population had varied considerably through the years, in accordance with the fluctuating nature of the state's oil booms. By the time the sixties arrived, the oil had all dried up, followed by the water when a dam broke to the west and the town's faucets started yielding nothing but air. The residents left, pretty much en masse, their small homes that dotted the town's outskirts falling into deep disrepair, along with the town's single L-shaped main drag of buildings.

Fisker had first spotted the town from a helicopter and knew he'd found exactly what he'd been looking for. A location literally off the world's map, where he could settle his people unbothered from the rest of the civilization. McMullen County was so sparsely populated that nobody much cared, especially when Fisker made hefty campaign contributions to the presiding sheriff, judge, and officials at the county seat. He made sure all taxes were paid on time and fashioned an insular world where not a single call had ever been placed for assistance of any kind to the outside world.

Fisker's first order of business had been to rebuild the homes and central buildings to their pristine, original condition. He used his own people, or their own people, to work construction, certain elements kept secret to the point where some of the work was done only at night. So, too, he made sure no Confederate flags or any other symbols were displayed anywhere in the open or publicly. Nothing to rouse the suspicions or raise the concerns of anyone who might be passing by, stumble in, or be paying a routine service visit to restock the propane tanks that fed the town all of its power. Elk Grove was as self-contained as it got, a slice of down-home Americana that, except for its soul and secrets stored within its dark underbelly, looked carved out of a Norman Rockwell painting.

"Lesson number one," Fisker continued to the three men, whose knees were all rubbing up against the underside of their kid-sized desks, when he reached the blackboard. "We gotta go along to get along, and get along to get ourselves where we're supposed to be. As in this..."

With that, Fisker yanked on a partially exposed pull-down map of the continental United States, held in a spindle. The map was so old and faded, he wasn't even sure Alaska and Hawaii were included. He pulled too hard, eased up when he heard a slight tearing sound, then jabbed a finger into the center of the map.

"This is where we're supposed to be," he told the leaders of the three motorcycle gangs. "This is our territory. We got product spilling in from Mexico, as well as points south and north of the border in Canada. We got a distribution network that puts Walmart and Amazon to shame, and a firm presence in all fifty states you can see right here. Well," Fisker added, correcting himself, "forty-eight, anyway."

Hacksaw, leader of the Bandidos, raised his hand.

"Speak your mind," Fisker told him.

"Product's the problem. We could move ten, even twenty times the pills we're moving now through our territories, and our suppliers are getting less and less reliable."

"Goddamn Fed crackdown's hitting us hard," said the leader of the Cossacks, nodding in agreement.

"Maybe we waste a few of the motherfuckers, they'll turn to thinking different on the matter," suggested Arlo Teague of the Hells Angels.

"That's one way of doing business," Fisker told him, "if you want that business to dry up to nothing, and a crackdown like nobody's business to put us behind bars."

"Behind bars is where your daddy started all this," Hacksaw noted. "At least, that's what you've always said."

"True enough. You can build an empire behind bars but it's not as easy to run one from there," Fisker told the three of them. "We keep our noses as clean as we can, and we keep stuffing our pockets full."

Hacksaw shifted in his desk and the whole thing lifted into the air from the effort. "You want an empire, we're gonna need more pills; more Oxies, Vikes, Percs, and crystal meth. A lot more."

Fisker pulled down on the map just hard enough to make it snap back into place with the *thwack* of a gunshot. "That's the other reason I called you boys here today. Because this supply problem is about to become a thing of the past."

He looped around the teacher's desk again and retrieved the .357 Magnum. The three gang leaders paid him no heed at all, barely acknowledging his action, until he pressed the pistol's bore against his own temple.

"Fair's fair, right? If I was a better leader, if I'd schooled you on the way things needed to be when I should have, all this bullshit would've stayed in the can. But I didn't and that blame's mine to shoulder."

Click.

"Now," Fisker said, sliding the big gun back into his holster, "where were we?"

12

It wasn't like any crime scene Caitlin had ever seen before; it wasn't like any crime scene at all.

The man, potential victim, sat slumped in a reclining chair in his apartment's living room, facing a widescreen television much too big for the room. The picture flared, but the volume had been muted, likely the single alteration that first responders had made to the room, so they could go about their duties without sound blaring in stereo. The victim had rubber tubing tied around his bicep to inflate veins now holding still blood. An empty vial of what must've been heroin rested on a table squeezed up against the chair arm, and Caitlin spotted the telltale spoon and lighter nearby as well.

"Well, check out what we got here," a voice called out, and Caitlin looked up to see a big figure lumber out of what must've been the bedroom. "A genuine Texas Ranger at our little ole crime scene."

It took her another second to recognize Detective Frank Pepper from their one previous, and unpleasant, encounter. She'd heard he'd been fired from the Houston police department shortly after that, but had no idea he'd gotten a job down here. The San Antonio police detective's badge dangling from his neck told her otherwise; Caitlin was barely able to hold her tongue.

"Nice to see you again, Doctor," she said, calling him by his nickname.

Pepper's expression bent into a snarl, recalling the uncomfortable history they had between them. "That's what my friends call me."

"Your friends down here know what else they called you up in Houston? 'Peepers,' wasn't it, on account of how you were prone to strip-search female suspects rousted on a traffic violation?"

"I lost my seniority, the years I had in, and most of my pension," he groused. "Isn't that enough for you?"

"You did that all on your own, Detective."

"Bullshit. I dared to cross the mighty Texas Rangers, and this is the price

I paid for it. Low man on the totem pole getting put on diddly shit cases that don't even reach the bottom of the barrel." Pepper swung his eyes that were too small for his head around the room, as if seeing it for the first time. "But since you're here, I guess maybe you're swimming in it, too. And I don't recall requesting any Ranger involvement."

"That's not your call," Caitlin said, turning toward Doc Whatley, who was already in the preliminary stages of examining the body. "Right, Doc?"

"Right," Whatley echoed, not paying attention to her.

Pepper scratched at his scalp, drawing a sound like sandpaper against wood. "We don't need the Bexar County ME to diagnose a drug overdose."

"Paramedics thought otherwise," Caitlin noted.

"For good reason," Whatley said, retrieving a syringe that had slipped under the recliner. "This is still full. Victim must've dropped it before shooting up. So it wasn't an overdose that killed him."

The paramedics hovering nearby nodded, as if they'd already figured that much out.

Pepper moved closer, wanting to see the syringe for himself. "So he'd shot up already. OD'd before he could shoot more poison into his vein."

"Check out his arm," Caitlin said, gesturing toward the still puffed-up parts beneath the rubber tubing looped round his bicep. "There are scars from plenty of past needle marks, but nothing fresh. Not only did the victim not overdose, he was clean until…" She looked back toward Whatley. "Can you hazard a guess as to the time of death?"

"Last night."

"Makes sense," Pepper said. "A neighbor found him this morning, when she stopped by to return some plates."

"What's the man's name?" Caitlin asked him.

"Tyrell Liston." Pepper paged through his memo pad. "Claimed he was related to Sonny, the fighter that then–Cassius Clay beat to claim the heavyweight title."

"That the man's primary claim to fame?"

"That and the fact that he spent a year in Huntsville on a drug beef going back a decade."

"My guess is that's where he got clean, or at least started to," Caitlin suggested. "Search the apartment and you'll probably find a bunch of stuff labeled 'NA' for Narcotics Anonymous."

"So you think somebody killed him and made it look like an overdose?"

"Doc?" Caitlin said to Whatley.

"No signs of foul play at all here yet, but . . ."

"But what?"

Whatley went back to his examination of the body. "I'm not ready to say yet. But the paramedics made the right call in alerting the medical examiner's office. There's something here that they . . ."

"They *what?*" Caitlin echoed, prodding Whatley to continue.

"Tyrell Liston's been dead for a while, Ranger."

"I thought you put the time of death as last night."

"Dying, then. He'd been dying for a while. Weeks maybe, days at least. Based on the way the blood's settled, I'd say he barely moved from this chair for the whole day before he died, at the very least."

Before Whatley could continue, one of the patrolmen Frank Pepper had assigned to canvass the apartment building returned, half out of breath.

"We found another body, Detective," he said, leaning against the wall to steady himself.

It was a woman, found dead in her bed two floors up from Tyrell Liston's apartment. The patrol cop explained that he'd caught the smell while knocking on her door, and fetched the building superintendent. Then rushed back down here, once he was sure.

At Caitlin's urging, only Whatley entered the apartment and returned after the ten minutes it took for him to perform a rudimentary examination of the woman's body.

Caitlin closed the door behind him. "Well?"

He held up the iPhone he used as a camera and extended it toward her so she could see the screen. "Look familiar?"

It was a picture of the female victim's eyes, the whites so yellowed they looked like somebody had taken a paintbrush to them.

"Same as Tyrell Liston," Caitlin realized.

"It's too early to make any definitive pronouncements, Ranger, but this is consistent with catastrophic liver failure in both cases," Whatley affirmed. "And that's not all of it, either."

"All of *what?*" Detective Frank Pepper asked him. "Hey, I'm talking to you."

Whatley looked back toward Caitlin, clearly not wanting to say anything more, where he might be overheard.

"Doesn't matter, anyway, Detective," Caitlin said, easing her phone from her pocket. "Things here just changed in a big way in a big hurry."

She hit a number on her speed dial.

"Who are you calling?" Pepper demanded.

"Homeland Security," Caitlin told him. "And I want you to begin an evacuation of the entire building."

13

WASHINGTON, D.C.

The chairman of the House Oversight and Reform Committee leaned so far forward, her microphone barely picked up her next words.

"Let me get this straight, Mr. Skoll," Congresswoman Sheila Decker said to David Skoll. "You purchased Redfern Pharmaceuticals in order to buy control of drugs currently on the market, but operating at a loss."

Skoll mimicked her motion, only strains of his voice reaching the microphone. "That's correct, ma'am."

"And would you like to explain to this committee why a purportedly successful hedge fund manager like yourself would knowingly make a deal that would lose money?"

"Because the drugs in question were remarkably undervalued."

"By which you mean *underpriced*. That's correct, isn't it, Mr. Skoll?"

"If you say so, Madam Chairman." Skoll smirked.

His lawyers had advised Skoll to be temperate and humble in his re-marks, and avoid being the wiseass the public had already branded him.

Skoll ignored them.

They recommended he dress like a thirty-eight-year-old successful busi-nessman, and not wear his trademark jeans, T-shirt, and sneakers. Dress for the occasion, they told him.

Skoll had dressed for the occasion in jeans, sneakers, and a T-shirt.

They'd warned him to make sure he shaved and got a haircut.

Skoll's face currently featured three days of beard stubble and his hair, worn exactly the way he had since high school, still hung down to his shoulders.

"And what do you say, Mr. Skoll? What do you say about raising the price of a dozen drugs by up to ten thousand percent virtually overnight?" Decker put on her glasses in order to read from the list before her. "Drugs to fight HIV, hepatitis C, malaria, MERS..." She took off her glasses again. "Older drugs, long in circulation, you purchased in order to turn them into so-called specialty drugs. What do you have to say to that, sir?"

"That I wasn't expecting to cause such a fervor," Skoll said into the micro-phone. "That I wished I owned a drug that could cure the kind of stupidity that keeps people from seeing that, with the increased profits, I'll be able to pump more money into research and development. That undervaluing drugs in the marketplace has the very real effect of depressing the kind of innovative research that can save lives in the future."

"And what about the people who are no longer able to afford the drugs you now own, which they need to stay alive?"

Skoll popped a stick of gum into his mouth and worked it audibly about his mouth, another thing his lawyers had warned him not to do. "Madam Chairman, I lost my father to ALS. There's no drug that can cure ALS. Re-cently, my mother was diagnosed with early onset Alzheimer's disease. There's no drug that can cure that, either. And there never will be—for ALS, Alzheimer's, or any other modern-day scourges—because it costs a billion dollars to develop them. And the only way to raise that billion dollars is to raise the price of drugs already on the market. You want to blame someone for my actions, blame the Food and Drug Administration for creating such an onerous approval process."

"Tell that to the loved ones and families of victims who'll soon be dying because your prices aren't so bearable to them and their budgets," Congresswoman Decker told him. "And you can do just that, because they're next on our list to testify. So stick around, Mr. Skoll."

"I don't have to, Madam Chairman. I've already been subjected to parades of protesters outside my home and office with their signs and their placards, showcasing their ignorance at the behest of politicians like you, who are persecuting me because I've long refused to donate to your political campaigns."

Skoll waited for the murmurs rising through the chamber to quiet before continuing.

"That's right. I have in my possession campaign fund-raising solicitation letters from half the members of your committee, sent over the course of the past election cycle. If you'd like me to produce them..."

"That won't be necessary, sir."

"Even yours, Madam Chairman?"

A few chuckles rose through the crowd this time, Skoll ready to resume the moment they subsided.

"Unfortunately, Madam Chairman, my company doesn't make a drug to treat hypocrisy."

"I'm guessing nobody would be able to afford it anyway, Mr. Skoll," Decker snapped back at him. "And, on that subject, perhaps we should discuss the fates of the two other pharmaceutical concerns you previously obtained. They're both in bankruptcy now, is that correct?"

"Through no fault of mine, Madam Chairman. Those companies were severely overleveraged and my attempts to right their ships by raising specialty drug prices came too late."

"The numbers suggest otherwise. The numbers suggest that you were the one who leveraged both companies in order to pay off investors of several other failed investments you had made on their behalf. You used price gouging to overstate their actual worth and then borrowed against that increased line without putting a single dollar back into the companies."

"Those allegations are both unfounded and unproven."

"Not for long, Mr. Skoll," Decker reminded, "if the U.S. attorneys in four different states have their way—and that's not to mention an investigation already under way by the Securities and Exchange Commission. Looks like you're going to be spending a lot of time in hearings like this one, sir."

Skoll took the wad of gum from his mouth and let the camera see him stick it under the table at which he was seated. "Speaking of which," he said, rising, "my time is valuable and I've wasted enough of it here already. I need to get back to work."

Decker rapped her gavel several times to still the crowd's audible reaction to Skoll's indignation. "What is Lot U-two-five-seven-F?"

Skoll froze in place behind his chair.

"Do you need me to repeat the question, sir?" Decker asked him. "I believe this coding in question indicates a drug for which a clinical trial is being conducted at Redfern. Is that correct?"

"That's confidential."

"So do you deny knowledge of, or any association with, a clinical trial for a drug known as Lot U-two-five-seven-F?"

"I do deny it, because it's none of your damn business."

Decker smiled smugly. "I'd remind you, Mr. Skoll, that I'm here to do the people's business."

"If that's what you'd like to call it."

"One more time, Mr. Skoll: what is Lot U-two-five-seven-F?"

"I have no idea."

"And you say that under penalty of perjury?"

"I say that because it's the truth, Madam Chairman. And standing here being berated by you doesn't make it any less so."

"Then perhaps you should take your seat again," Decker suggested, to a smattering of chuckles in the gallery.

Skoll remained in place. "Not if it means continuing with this farce."

"This committee hasn't excused you yet, sir. We're called the Committee on Oversight for a reason, Mr. Skoll, and that would seem to be something you're badly in need of. And I'll ask you one last time, what is Lot U-two-five-seven-F?"

"And I'll tell you one last time that it's none of your business," Skoll insisted, hoping Decker and the other committee members couldn't see the cold sweat beginning to soak through his shirt. "I was called here today to testify about drug pricing, which I have done in good faith. I wasn't prepared for questions about any clinical trials my company may or may not be engaged in."

"This committee has taken the liberty of expanding the scope of its investigation. We would, of course, be happy to revisit this matter at another time," Decker said, eyes boring down on Skoll from the dais.

"There's no matter to revisit, because there's no such thing as Lot U-two-five-seven-F at my company."

"Then I suppose you have nothing to worry about on that end, do you?"

Skoll wished he'd had something witty to say, some harsh retort held on his tongue like a sharp knife ready to poke flesh. But all he could think of was how Congresswoman Sheila Decker could possibly have learned of the existence of Lot U257F, and how many others might be aware of its existence as well. Because if they knew everything…

"Mr. Skoll, I would ask that you take your seat, so this hearing may continue."

"No," Skoll heard himself say to Decker. "No." Repeating it louder. "I will not take a seat and you can continue this hearing without me."

The gallery broke into a chaos of voices as David Skoll made his way toward the exit to the accompaniment of camera clicks and whirs.

"I'd strongly advise you to reconsider this decision," Decker's voice blared, her gavel rapping constantly against the hard wood to still the disturbance in the hearing room.

Unable to help himself, Skoll stopped just short of the door and, before a bevy of cameras and a packed gallery following his every move, he gave Congresswoman Decker the finger.

14

Smirking now, Skoll pressed forward out the door. He felt his phone vibrate with an incoming text he didn't read until he made it through the milling crowd and into the back of his limousine.

Skoll's hand trembled. He had to remind himself to breathe as he reread the message. Then he pressed out the number of the person who'd texted him and listened to it ringing. The clamminess he'd felt in the committee chamber had stayed with him, so he reached up to lower the air-conditioning in the limo's rear.

"Is it contained?" Skoll asked as soon as he heard the click of the line being answered, not waiting for some perfunctory greeting.

"Unfortunately, yes," the voice said back to him.

"Why's that unfortunate?"

"The two latest victims both lived in the same apartment building."

"Oh, shit . . ."

"That was my thought. Texas Rangers evacuated the complex. Homeland Security's involved."

"Texas Rangers, Homeland Security," Skoll said, shaking his head. "How about the Sixth Fleet, maybe the Eighty-second Airborne—are they on their way, too?" He felt his phone vibrate and checked the screen for the caller ID, immediately recognizing the Texas exchange. "I've got to take this other call. I'll ring you back."

Skoll took a deep breath and swapped out the new call for the old one.

"I watched the hearing on television," greeted the voice on the other end of the line. "You looked like shit."

"I'm flying back this afternoon. Can we talk then?"

"Sure, we can, Davey, and we can talk now, too. See, your note's come due."

"Whoa, whoa, whoa, we've got a deal!"

"That's right, we do. Next time I'd recommend a more careful review of the terms."

"Look, I've done everything you asked."

"And now I'm gonna ask for more, Davey, on account of demand exceeding supply. Means I need that supply upped. You know, capitalism at its best."

"I'm under federal scrutiny. They could have a warrant to listen in on all my calls. Let's meet up when I'm back."

"Give me a time."

"Tonight," Skoll told him. "My place."

"Works for me, Davey," said Armand Fisker.

PART TWO

"Here lies he who spent his manhood
defending the homes of Texas."

—epitaph on the gravestone of Texas Ranger
William "Bigfoot" Wallace, 1817–1899

15

Guillermo Paz stood at the edge of the shadows darkening a tight alleyway next to a boarded-up building across the street from Miguel Asuna's body shop on the east side of the city. He'd originally planned to begin watching over Dylan Torres, the oldest son of Cort Wesley Masters, tomorrow. But something had made him come here late in the afternoon, just as the light of the day began to bleed away.

Paz had been dispensing toilet articles in sample sizes that had been donated to the Catholic Worker House, when the thought struck him like a slap to his spine. He got those feelings often, having inherited a kind of second, even third, sight from his mother, who everyone in the Caracas slum he'd grown up in thought was a *bruja*, or witch. They stayed away from her as a result, even the most hardened criminal element afraid to cross Paz's mother, lest they risk a spell being cast against them, or worse.

Paz had to admit he'd been scared of his mother for a time, too, right after the first instance he'd witnessed her abilities truly on display.

He'd been ten years old when he'd found his first priest bleeding to death from a knife wound suffered for trying to help the local impoverished lot the gangs sought to control. He held the man's head in his lap, his own tears falling onto his robes, as the man took his last breath. He closed the glazed eyes and crossed himself the way the priest had taught him, silently swearing to avenge him. Then Paz went about collecting the bread and vegetables the man had died for that had spilled out of the grocery bags when he fell.

He'd found his mother crying when he returned to the tiny, clapboard house with a tin roof they shared with his four siblings, having been struck by one of her visions she called *desfallecimientos,* which was Spanish for spells.

"I didn't steal it," Paz said, laying out his small share of the food the priest would've allotted him. "I didn't take anything that wasn't mine."

"But you're going to take plenty in the years to come," his mother told him. "You're going to take more lives than I can see. Your fate was sealed today and now I see why, just as I see the blood staining your clothes."

Paz looked down at his shirt and pants. They were still moist with blood from where the priest's wounds had leaked onto him.

"I didn't hurt anyone, *madre,*" Paz insisted.

"But you will, you will hurt many, more than you or I can count."

"I'll find another priest," he said, refusing to let himself cry. "I'll pray."

"It won't matter," said his mother. "The smell of blood will be forever strong on you, Guillermo."

And, true to his mother's words, it had been, until the day he first crossed paths with his Texas Ranger. He'd spilled plenty of blood since, but the smell of it no longer clung to him the same way.

Paz had begun his vigil today, because a vision of Dylan Torres had struck him while he was passing out those toiletries. The young man's image had popped into his head and hadn't moved. That wasn't a good sign, among those with which Paz had familiarized himself, building his own lexicon for the sensory perceptions that set the world around him crackling with static electricity that prickled the surface of his skin.

True to what he'd sensed, a black, extended-cab pickup truck began edging its way into his field of vision. It had windows tinted so dark, they reflected the last of the day's sunlight like mirrors. The steel bed was black, too, the tires extra wide, and the loud engine made the truck sound like a race car revving. Both rear quarter panels were decorated with Confederate flags, whether painted on or decals, Paz wasn't sure. He thought he was looking at a cliché come to life, this batch of human excrement right out of central casting.

Paz backed farther into the shadows of the alley to avoid being seen, finding himself next to a Dumpster overflowing with chunks of what had been the boarded-up building's brick façade. He wondered what new sign would hang over the door once the renovations were finished; he had trouble picturing something like a Starbucks moving in here. More likely a bodega or food joint that accepted EBT cards and featured a sectioned-off check-cashing station way in the back.

Paz watched the truck slow, brake lights flashing on and then off again when it passed Miguel Asuna's shop. It continued on, the driver accelerating with a screech of his tires when a pair of Latino boys rushed across the street, jamming on the brakes just when it seemed he was intent on running them over.

Paz thought he heard laughter coming from inside the cab.

Just then, some of Miguel Asuna's workers emerged from his body shop. They carried themselves uneasily, their shoulders stiff, maybe from glancing back over their shoulders too much. Illegals for sure, afraid to report harassment at the hands of the likes of the men inside the black truck.

Paz watched the big truck reverse with a squeal of its oversized tires, then grind to a stop when it drew even with the four Latinos who'd emerged from the auto body repair shop. It crawled down the street in rhythm with the pace of the workers who did their best to ignore it, even though Paz heard ugly taunts being tossed out of the truck's passenger side.

Paz was thinking seriously about intervening, when Dylan Torres emerged through the same door, still wearing his coveralls and pulling his arms through a jean jacket. He stopped to light a cigarette, another thing his father Cort Wesley Masters would likely put the boy over his knee for doing, and then tossed it aside when he spotted the black truck's brake lights and his fellow workers moving in a tight cluster even with it.

Uh-oh, Paz thought, even before he saw the pistol flash in Dylan Torres' hand.

16

San Antonio, Texas

Dylan jogged up even with the driver's-side door and rapped on the blacked-out window with the butt of the Glock 17 nine-millimeter pistol one of Miguel Asuna's illegals had given him.

Dylan had just started banging again when the truck jerked to a halt and the window slid down. The pungent scent of weed washed over him, the driver sneering from behind a set of hooded eyes slowed by the joint he and his posse had been sharing. The stench of rank perspiration trailed the smoke out of the cab, strong enough to turn Dylan's stomach.

"What the fuck you want, spic?" asked the driver, whose hair was almost as long as Dylan's.

"I'm only half spic."

"Guess that means we need to hate you only half as much," the driver said, drawing a laugh from the truck's three other occupants.

Dylan held the pistol low by his side, a round already jacked into the chamber, making sure the driver could see it. "Why are you bothering them?"

"Who," the driver wanted to know, "your spic brothers?"

"*Half* brothers, remember? I'm only half spic."

"So is it the spic half sticking up for them?"

"It's the white half holding the gun."

"So how exactly are they gonna deport only half of you?" The driver jammed the truck into park. "I say we carve you in half, one little ball on either side. Hey, how do they say 'little balls' in Spanish?"

Dylan looked down the street, the workers he ate lunch with every day just about to turn the corner, meaning they were almost safe. "Why don't you step out of the truck, so I can whisper it in your ear?"

The rear window on the driver's side slid downward and an acne-scarred, greasy-haired kid about Dylan's age propped a sawed-off shotgun on the sill. Kid had a round fat face and jowls so big they hung off his face. So ugly Dylan had to look away.

"Why don't you drop the gun?" the driver said, tapping his own revolver on the gleaming finish of the truck's door. "Nice piece. Better yet, hand it over and we'll call things even."

"Why don't you come out here and take it?" Dylan said, still holding the Glock low.

His words sounded brave, but he was cursing himself for not noticing the driver work the .357 into position. His father would kill him for that, if the driver didn't.

The driver grinned, his tiny eyes looking even smaller. "No, you're gonna hand me the gun, real slow and careful, and in return we're gonna let you keep those little balls of yours."

"*Cajones pequeño.*"

"Huh?"

"Little balls in Spanish. You wanna step out of that truck and suck them?"

Dylan was ready to fire as he said that, barrel tilting upward from his hip. The driver had started to right his pistol, the kid in the backseat raising his sawed-off out the open window.

Then something hit the truck's hood with enough force to leave a huge dent. In the next instant, the windshield exploded, and Dylan saw what looked like a brick wedged into the shattered glass.

"What the fuck?" the driver squealed. "What the—"

Two more bricks left huge dents in the roof before he could finish, clangs sounding from impact in the cargo bed, before one sailed through the open rear window, grazing the face of the greasy kid in the backseat. He grunted, almost lost hold of his sawed-off, and lurched forward to get it back in his grasp.

Boom!

The blast must've deafened those inside the truck, the shotgun shell tearing a horizontal divot down a long portion of the quarter panel.

"Shit!" the driver bellowed. "Shit, shit, shit!"

The sky was raining bricks now, the truck under some indescribable siege that left the driver jerking it into gear and screeching off from the onslaught, bleeding smoke from its tires.

Dylan cupped his balls through his coveralls in his free hand, hoping the driver was watching him in the truck's side-view mirror.

"Eat this, asshole!" he yelled out, kicking aside one of the stray bricks that had seemed to fall from the sky.

17

SAN ANTONIO, TEXAS

"Ranger," D. W. Tepper had said, as soon as he arrived at the now evacuated apartment complex, "if they outlawed shit in the whole state of Texas, you'd still find a way to step in it."

"Nice to see you, too, Captain."

Tepper took a box of Marlboro Reds from the pocket of a suede jacket swimming with fringe. Caitlin recalled it had been a gift from the grandson of Buffalo Bill Cody. "Say, does this apartment complex allow smoking?"

"I wouldn't know," Caitlin told him. "I was too busy evacuating the residents."

"Our friend Jones arrive yet?"

"He wouldn't say where he was when I reached him. Only that he was turning around and heading our way."

"Yeah, half of Homeland Security would be out of a job, if it wasn't for you." Tepper popped a single cigarette from the box and stuck it in his mouth. "Well?"

"Well what?"

"I was waiting for one of your lectures about my lungs filing a grievance and ruining my golden years you already turned to lead."

"I'm done trying to talk you out of killing yourself, D.W."

"Really?"

"Really."

"Well, this is cause for celebration."

He took out his lighter, snapped the top open, and flicked at it with no success.

"What the hell?" Tepper started, giving it a closer look, squinting. "Somebody yanked out the goddamn wick. You wouldn't know anything about that, would you, Ranger?"

Dusk fell without any of the first responders emerging from the complex.

"What did the Rangers do for excitement back in the day before we had terrorists?" Caitlin asked D. W. Tepper.

"You mean besides hunting dinosaurs? Well, we did have the likes of Bonnie and Clyde and John Wesley Hardin to deal with. And your grandpa, he even went up against the Nazis."

"Earl Strong spent time in Europe?" Caitlin asked, trying to reconcile the apparent discrepancy with what she knew of her grandfather's history.

"Nope, he went up against them right here in Texas...."

18

HEARNE, TEXAS; 1944

"Nice to meet you, sir," Earl Strong said to J. Edgar Hoover. "It's not every day the director of the Federal Bureau of Investigation comes to Texas."

"Well," Hoover said dismissively, looking up at Earl, whose boots made him more than a half-foot taller, "this particular case warranted an exception."

"It sure does, given the unprecedented nature of a Nazi war criminal loose on our soil. But I find myself curious about one thing, Mr. Hoover."

"What's that, Ranger?"

"Well, I drove out here in my truck directly after receiving the call. Assuming you got the call in the relative vicinity I did, I'm wondering how it was you got out here all the way from Washington so fast, 'less you got a plane faster than the kind in the comic books my boy reads," Earl said, referring to his ten-year-old son, Jim.

Hoover wet his lips with his tongue, even more reluctant to meet Earl's gaze. "Was there something else, Ranger?" he asked.

Earl wondered if he was supposed to pay more deference to the man, maybe kneel on bended knee to kiss his ring. He liked most of what he'd heard and knew about the FBI, respecting their prowess at outthinking and outgunning the kind of criminal vermin the Texas Rangers had been battling for an additional century or so. When it came to the kind of up close and personal confrontations on which lawmen staked their reputations, though, he hadn't heard much indicating FBI types were up to the task. Neither great shots nor particularly good at putting down the wild-eyed bandits and gunmen who'd battled the Rangers since the time of Stephen Austin.

"Well, sir," Earl replied, "it just seems obvious you were already on your way here, before you could possibly have gotten word of these killings. And, since a case like this is hardly becoming a man of your stature, I've got to figure that you had an interest in the suspect, Gunther Haut, even before these murders went down."

"What's your point, Ranger?" J. Edgar Hoover asked him.

"I'm just wondering about the basis for your interest in this particular prisoner, that's all."

Hoover forced a smile that rode his face like he had gas he couldn't pass. "If I didn't know better, I'd say you were interrogating me."

"I'm sorry, sir. I meant no disrespect. It's just that if there's something you know about Gunther Haut, something that brought you all the way out here, it could be a great help to my investigation into the murders of his three bunkmates."

"Are Texas Rangers always this prone to jumping to erroneous conclusions?"

"I'm not sure I'm following you, sir."

"You're assuming I came to Texas because of Gunther Haut, instead of considering the possibility I came to Texas for an entirely different reason that just happened to overlap with the murders and escape here at Camp Hearne."

"Just happened," Earl repeated.

"It's called a coincidence, Ranger."

"I know what it's called, sir, and that leads me to another problem I'm having with your presence here, and thus your involvement. Haut was here for three uneventful weeks, with no disturbances or any forewarning of what happened last night. So I'm wondering if maybe he got word somehow that you were headed this way, and that's why he's in the wind now with blood on his hands. And that makes me wonder what it is that made Gunther Haut, one of over seventy thousand German prisoners of war held currently in Texas, so important to bring you halfway across the country."

Hoover started to step closer to Earl, then changed his mind. One of his fancy shoes was untied, and both were plastered with grit and the orange clay dirt unique to this part of Texas that clung to his soles like gum.

"I think I can make this simpler for both of us, Ranger," the head of the FBI offered. "What we have here is a jurisdictional issue, federal versus state. While the Federal Bureau of Investigation has every intention of working cooperatively in this process with Texas, this is a federal matter given that the land on which it occurred is a duly registered facility of the United States government. I'm sure we can agree on that much."

"Actually, sir, that's not entirely true," Earl said, as respectfully as he could manage. "The federal government has made it clear that it's not liable for any damage incurred as a result of these prisons being placed on Texas soil. And it's my understanding that the federal government has only leased the land these camps reside on. That means any crime committed inside one has to be treated like any crime committed in Texas and, at this point, that don't really matter a bit anyway."

Hoover was kicking at the soft, claylike dirt now with the toes of his shoes. "Am I missing something here, Ranger?"

"No, sir. What's missing is Gunther Haut, currently a fugitive on Texas land the federal government has no claim to or jurisdiction over. So until I'm told otherwise by the parties I answer to, I'm going to stay on the job, if you don't mind."

"Well, the fact is I do mind," Hoover told him, his neck getting red from both the agitation and the day's building heat. "And I intend to inform your superiors in Austin as such. I'm sure you'll be hearing from them promptly." Hoover nodded at the surety of his own words, seeming to look at Earl differently. "You never served in the war, did you?"

"No, sir, I didn't. Too much damage done by past gunfights. Army docs said they would've thought I was sixty years old, if they didn't have my chart right in front of them. I couldn't serve my country, no, so I decided to stay home and keep serving my state. One of those gunfights, by the way, took place in Sweetwater during the big oil boom. I had a run-in with Al Capone's boys from the Outfit, who'd been attracted by the lawlessness of those boom towns they must've seen as good for business."

"I seem to recall something about the incident you're referring to. Such incursions by organized crime into law-abiding places in the country was one of the considerations behind the formation of the FBI in 1935."

"Well, sir, what you don't recall is the help I requested, but never received, from the Bureau of Investigation you headed up at the time and had been for a decade, after your appointment at the ripe old age of twenty-nine."

Hoover fidgeted, started kicking at the drying mud again, but then stopped. "We consider Nazis at large in this country to be a major security problem the FBI is completely dedicated to dealing with. We don't have time to consider distractions, like something that happened ten years ago, or a local investigation that may hamper our federal one here today. In a word, Ranger, this isn't your problem."

"That's more than a word, Mr. Hoover, and so long as Camp Hearne is located on Texas soil, my job is to bring the man who murdered his bunkmates while they slept to justice. Now, you can conduct your own investigation, the army can conduct theirs—hell, I don't care if the Girl Scouts of America thinks they've got a dog in this fight. The more the merrier. But right now, I think I'm gonna get myself back to the actual crime scene," Earl said, Hoover finally meeting his stare, his eyes wide with contempt. "One of us here has a job to do."

Captain Bo Lowry stood anxiously at the open flap of the framed, tented shed from which Gunther Haut had disappeared after murdering the three fellow German prisoners sharing the space. For Earl Strong, meanwhile, the aroma of blood hung heavy in the stale air. He noticed the same claylike dirt on his boots that had coated the shoes of FBI Director J. Edgar Hoover. He'd left a trail of it across the shed's plank flooring and cursed himself for disturbing the scene, even in such an innocuous way.

But that was just the start of it. While he'd been speaking with Hoover, the bodies had been removed and the cots stripped clean to the mattresses that remained sodden with blood from where the victims had bled out.

"Something seems to be missing, Captain," Earl said, turning with hands firmly planted on his hips.

Lowry stiffened even more. "On orders of Mr. Hoover, sir."

"Is that a fact? Did Mr. Hoover give instructions as to where the bodies should be taken?"

"I'm not at liberty to say, sir," Lowry said, like a man with a gun to his head.

Before Earl Strong could voice further objection, a soldier trotted up to Lowry and spoke softly to him. Lowry asked a single question and got his answer, never once taking his eyes off Earl.

"Your commanding officer phoned the camp, Ranger," Lowry said, a measure of relief creeping into his voice. "Looks like you're needed elsewhere."

"And where would that be exactly?"

"The Driskill Hotel in Austin, sir. There's been another murder."

19

"And who was it?" Caitlin asked Tepper, after he'd stopped, enthralled by the tale of her grandfather's run-in with J. Edgar Hoover. "What did my grandfather find when he got to the Driskill Hotel?"

The captain's gaze drifted over her shoulder, Caitlin turning to find the familiar figure of Jones striding through the area authorities had cordoned off from the public.

"Guess we're gonna have to pick this up later, Ranger," Tepper said to her.

"Well, well, well," Jones smirked, when he reached Caitlin and Tepper, "if it isn't the lady who's keeping my entire department funded."

"I thought your department had a blank check, Jones," Caitlin said, by way of greeting.

"In the past five years, we've expended more resources in Texas than any ten other states combined. Care to guess who's responsible for that?"

Captain Tepper took a step back from them. "Think I'll leave you two to catch up. Locals over there are looking pretty antsy."

Caitlin followed his gaze. "I notice they're smoking, D.W. Means you might find a lighter."

"That thought had crossed my mind, too," Tepper said, already turning away. "Just make sure you don't shoot anybody while I'm gone."

Caitlin and Jones moved out of the direct spill of the big work lights that had been set up outside a tent erected to serve as a command post, away from the constant parade of uniformed and civilian figures coming and going.

"I'm glad you're so appreciative of my efforts," Caitlin said to Jones.

"What did your captain mean by that 'don't shoot anybody' remark?"

"I shot an unarmed man last night."

"And you're here instead of behind a desk?"

"The man was picking the pockets of a sexual assault victim. I thought the cell phone he'd just pinched was a gun."

Jones was left shaking his head. "Loose cannon doesn't even begin to describe you, Ranger. No wonder I hear there's a big Hollywood studio looking to do a movie based on your life. I hear they're going call it 'Strong to the Bone,' because that describes you perfectly. If they happen to contact you, just remember to leave Homeland out of the script."

"I guess that means they won't have to pick an actor to play you. I was thinking Tom Cruise."

"He's too small."

"I'm sure he gets that a lot."

Jones circled his gaze about, as if to remind himself where he was. "Did you and your boyfriend really hijack a fire truck and hose down a bunch of college kids outside Stubb's Barbecue in Austin last night, *before* you shot that unarmed man?"

"If that's what you want to call it."

"What do you call it, Ranger?"

"Stopping a riot," Caitlin said.

"I hear a few of the kids you wet down are filing lawsuits against the city of Austin. Good luck using that as your defense."

Caitlin couldn't say exactly what Jones did with Homeland Security, especially these days, and doubted that anybody else could, either. He operated in the muck among the dregs of society plotting to harm the country from the inside. Caitlin doubted he'd ever written a report, or detailed the specifics of his operations in any way. He lived in the dark, calling on the likes of Guillermo Paz and the colonel's henchmen to deal with matters always out of view of the light. When those matters brought him to Texas, which seemed to be every other day, he'd seek out Caitlin the way he might a former classmate.

She'd first met him when his name was still "Smith," and he was attached to the American embassy in Bahrain, enough of a relationship formed for the two of them to have remained in contact and to have actually worked together on several more occasions. Sometimes Jones surprised her, but mostly he could be relied on to live down to Caitlin's expectations.

The fall of night kept Jones's face cloaked in the shadows with which he was most comfortable. Caitlin tried to remember the color of his eyes but couldn't, as if he'd been trained to never look at anyone long enough for anything to register. He was wearing a sport jacket over a button-down shirt and pressed trousers, making him seem like a high school teacher. He'd even let his hair grow out a bit, no longer fancying the tightly cropped, military-style haircut that had been one of his signatures for as long as she'd known him.

"The two hundred people you evacuated from the complex were all taken to San Antonio's Southwest General Hospital to make use of the new quarantine procedures we put in place," Jones told her. "So far, about half of them have undergone preliminary examinations that have revealed nothing out of the ordinary, no indication whatsoever that they've been afflicted by whatever killed the two victims inside."

"Good news."

"Really? Do you have any idea what you pushing the panic button on this one is going to cost?"

"Why, are you paying? Give it a rest, Jones, I was just following procedure and you know it."

"And all that washes just fine, until nothing turns up and Homeland's budget dips another five million into the red. When I get called on the carpet for that, I'll tell the new administration that you were just playing things safe, the same way you were when you shot a man armed with a cell phone."

For some reason, Jones's remark stung Caitlin. No matter how hard she tried to push the shooting from her mind, along with the associated memories of her own past it conjured, it came roaring back. She wondered who she'd really wanted to shoot last night; the man she'd suspected of being Kelly Ann Beasley's rapist or her own from eighteen years ago.

"And you're anticipating the new administration having a problem with that?" Caitlin managed finally.

"They have a problem with everything."

"Including that private jet you've been flying around on lately?"

"Comes with the job these days. Time is money and, in Code Red cases, the country needs first responders on the scene before social media can control the narrative."

"Sounds like you've mastered a whole new vocabulary, Jones."

"That also comes with the territory. Oh, and did I mention that the preliminary water and air samples taken on-site have come back negative?" Jones peered over Caitlin's shoulder. "Friend of yours, Ranger?"

Caitlin turned to follow his gaze and recognized Doc Whatley's squat shape through his yellow biohazard suit, as he lumbered her way. She watched him struggle to remove the soft helmet with affixed respirator, finally managing to let it flop downward behind him like the hood of a sweatshirt. His face was red from a combination of exertion and the hood's confines.

Whatley stopped just before Caitlin and bent over slightly with hands on his knees to catch his breath. "First time I've ever put one of these on and also the last."

"Let's hope so, Doc."

Whatley noted Jones's presence and cast him a sidelong, disapproving glare. "Is there anything we can keep local these days?"

"Not something like this," Caitlin told him. "Jones just told me the residents we quarantined are checking out fine, and the samples taken inside the complex so far reveal nothing awry."

"I wouldn't know, Ranger, because I've been busy with the two bodies we found," Whatley said, eyeing Jones again, as if to determine how much to share in front of him. "They got something in common, all right; just not what we were expecting."

20

San Antonio, Texas

Cort Wesley came straight to the Catholic Worker House as soon as he received Guillermo Paz's phone call. He found the former head of the Venezuelan secret police wrapping up a service held in a cramped, makeshift chapel that all of the homeless men staying the night were required to attend.

He was standing just outside the door when a man with gray hair and glasses, wearing an ID badge dangling from a lanyard, approached him.

"You need to go inside. It's a rule."

"It's okay," Cort Wesley told him, caught off guard. "I'm not staying."

"We don't allow visitors after dark," the man told him.

"I'm not visiting . . . Well, I am, just not one of your guests. I'm here to see the colonel."

"Colonel?"

Cort Wesley cursed himself for not being more careful, having no idea what Guillermo Paz had told those who ran the facility about himself. Certainly not the fact Paz had gained the rank of colonel in the Venezuelan army, before moving on to run the country's secret police. Cort Wesley was spared the need to respond further when a pair of doors opened and the homeless men who'd be staying the night flooded out, each holding a brand new toothbrush.

"I hand them out after every sermon," Paz explained, suddenly behind him, having appeared out of nowhere. "A local drugstore's been kind enough to donate them. Come on, outlaw, you can help me set up before the next group comes in. First service is in English, the second in Spanish."

"Sorry I missed the sermon, Colonel."

Cort Wesley followed Paz inside the chapel, a temporary altar consisting of an ornamental cross sitting atop a plain wood table situated in the front. Paz handed him a Walgreen's bag full of toothbrushes and the two of them began laying them across every seat, row by row.

"How much do you want to know, outlaw?"

"Whatever you have to tell me."

Paz stopped dispensing toothbrushes long enough to give Cort Wesley a long look. "You're not going to like it."

"I told you," Paz said, when he'd finished telling Cort Wesley what had transpired late that afternoon.

"You really rained bricks down on the truck?"

The big man shrugged. "It was either that or kill its occupants. I didn't see a third option at the time."

Cort Wesley had laid the Walgreen's bag on the nearest chair, his free hands clenching into fists. "That kid in the backseat had a shotgun aimed at Dylan?"

"Close enough. The driver with the Magnum, too."

"And he still didn't back down?"

"It looked like he wanted to make sure he gave his coworkers the time to get clear."

"Kid's never going to learn, goddamnit, not until he gets himself killed."

"What would you have done, outlaw?"

"Same thing probably, now that you mention it. But that's different."

"Not from your son's perspective."

They went back to dispensing the toothbrushes, laying them upon each of the seats that would be filled in a matter of minutes.

"The philosopher Arthur Schopenhauer wrote that, 'Politeness is to human nature what warmth is to wax,'" Paz resumed.

"I'm going to pretend I know what you're talking about."

"You look at your son and you see yourself, and it makes you realize no man is invincible. Not you, not me, not the Ranger, not Dylan. His actions force you to let loose the same nature you reject in him. You judge him, but don't want him to judge you—that's why you asked me to watch over the boy, instead of doing it yourself."

"I would have rained something other than bricks down, Colonel," Cort Wesley conceded.

"Of course, you would. In his writings, Plato imagined a cave where people have been imprisoned from birth, chained so that their legs and necks are fixed, forcing them to gaze at the wall in front of them and not look around at the cave, each other, or themselves. Thus that wall is all they know of the world, all they have to judge it by. But behind the prisoners burns a fire, and all they can see of it are the shadows cast on the wall by the fire. So all they know of the world are those shadows and to them the shadows are all that inhabit the world, because in their imprisonment they can only see what their perspective allows them. And that same perspective leaves them believing all the sounds they hear stem from the shadows."

"Is this the part when you tell me what you're really talking about, Colonel?" Cort Wesley asked him.

Paz extracted a scrap of paper from his pocket. "Here's the black truck's license plate number, so you can find out for yourself."

21

ALAMO HEIGHTS, TEXAS

Armand Fisker walked around the sprawling wood-paneled library in David Skoll's gated mansion. The heads of big game animals hung from the walls, their glass eyes staring down blankly, as if to accuse anyone who met their stare of killing them.

Fisker turned to look at Skoll instead. "This place looks like one of those hunting lodges where you can bag a lion or tiger, if you're rich enough."

"I've been on a couple of safaris like that, one in Africa. For the right amount, they bag it for you," the smaller man said with a smile.

"Is that supposed to impress me?" Fisker said, not bothering to hide his disgust at the notion.

"Hey, I bought this place fully furnished. The animal heads came as part of the package."

Fisker had forgotten that. He knew the previous owner had fled the country, leaving a mountain of debt and an army of ruined lives behind. The state had seized and sold off his assets, this estate being prime among them. Nearly fifteen thousand feet of living space spread over four levels along the posh Alameda Circle in the tony subdivision of Olmos Park. The ornate staircase spiraling upward reminded him of some European palace, the entire mansion built around a sprawling, banquet hall–sized room that could accommodate upward of a hundred guests at a time. Seven bedrooms and seven baths, he remembered Skoll telling him. A whole bunch of fireplaces to warm those cool Texas nights, a pool, statue-laden landscaping, and a guest cottage more than twice the size of the home in which Fisker had been raised.

"How's your asshole feel?" he asked Skoll.

"Sore."

The man had the boniest shoulders Fisker had ever seen and had squeezed his thin frame into a pair of even thinner jeans that looked more like a second denim skin. The jeans looked stiff and starched, and Fisker had the notion that Skoll was more likely to discard a worn pair than wash them.

"But I imagine you've got a drug for the pain, don't you, Davey?"

"I was going to ask you for one."

"That supposed to be funny? You shouldn't joke with a man you're in to for over a hundred million dollars."

Skoll's plump, unmarred face crinkled in a mixture of surprise and condescension. "Check your balance sheet, Armand. The number of prescription pain pills I've peeled off the line for you."

"I took that as a gesture of goodwill on your part, Davey."

"Goodwill? Under the watchful eye of FDA inspectors? Do you know what the penalty is for moving this level of prescription pain meds?"

"Do you know the penalty for not honoring your debt to me?"

"We had a deal, Armand," Skoll said, directly beneath a buffalo head that looked to be snorting.

Fisker took a step closer to him, just enough to make Skoll flinch. "Let's rewind a bit to you bleeding cash from this Ponzi scheme you've been running out of the hedge fund that bought you this place. You were about to jet off to Bolivia, when you had the good fortune to learn of my interest in your services."

"Ecuador," Skoll corrected, "where there's no extradition treaty with the United States. And my cash flow issues remain only a temporary setback, caused by the boycott of some of Redfern Pharmaceuticals' most profitable drugs."

"You mean the ones you raised the prices on a million percent or something?"

"What the market will bear."

"And how's the market been bearing? Not very good, since the only thing keeping you afloat right now is my cash and good graces. I save your ass and you balk at this one small favor?"

Skoll pawed at the Persian carpet that cost more than Fisker's first house with a pair of custom-made cowboy boots that added two inches to his meager height. "How much of an increase are we talking about?"

"Double."

"Double? Remember those FDA inspectors I've got crawling up my ass? You think it's easy hiding case lots of narcotics that vanish into the wind?"

"You want me to take my business back to Canada?"

"You struck a deal with me when they couldn't keep up with demand, so go ahead. Maybe you should think about putting your people back in meth labs where they can blow themselves to shit."

"How much you lose on that Alzheimer's drug that went bust?"

"What's the difference?"

"I'm curious, that's all."

"A hundred million, give or take."

"Nice round number. Pretty much what you're in to me for, right? You know how many pills that is exactly? The answer is not enough, not even close. That's why you're going to double production in that manufacturing plant you got running up in Waco. Put on an extra shift if you have to. I need to move the pills into the streets in a month's time."

"That's impossible."

"I don't think you understand our problem here. If I can't deliver the goods, consumers will find somebody who can. That'll leave me with a turf war on my hands you can bet will grow into a shooting war, which is bad for business. My business, as well as yours. Guess you might say we're joined at the hip now."

Skoll stepped out from the shadows cast by the buffalo head. The recessed lighting above struck him in a way that made his face looked shiny, a man approaching forty trapped in a sixteen-year-old's body with hair that looked like a boy's hanging down over his face. Fisker watched Skoll toss it aside with a flick of his head and then mop the rest into place with a hand.

"You buy those jeans in the boy's department, Davey?"

"They're custom-made," Skoll said, with a smirk.

"Custom-made to look like you've outgrown them? Now, that's truly something. Way they're hugging your crotch, it looks like you're dating them."

"I'll up the production," Skoll relented, "but it's going to take more than a month."

"Is it now? Well, then, maybe I should take this fancy house as collateral. See what it'll fetch on the open market. Hell, I'll even throw in the animal heads for free."

"The fuck you will, Armand. The fuck you—"

Fisker's fist smashed into Skoll's face. His head whipsawed to the right, the spittle flying from his mouth trailed by teeth when Fisker hit him again. The second blow was so hard, it actually lifted Skoll's boots off the ground and dumped him atop the carpet, the blood pouring from his mouth and soaking it in a widening pool.

Fisker wondered if the stain would ever come out as he bent over Skoll, hands placed casually on his knees, the one he'd hit him with twice already beginning to swell and throb. "Now you know what it feels like to be helpless, like animals from those dime-store safaris. Like shooting birds in the backyard, Davey. You know what isn't? Hunting men. There's places you can do that. I know because I've done it, and I hold you in the same esteem as those hapless fucks I've bagged. I can't remember a single one of their faces, but I remember yours, with and without the teeth you just spit out. What's gonna happen from here, is that you're going to have production doubled within the month. I don't care if you have to disguise my Oxy as aspirin tablets or allergy pills."

Skoll tried to say something, but only a frothy gurgle emerged.

"You wanna try that again, Davey?"

Gibberish this time.

"See, you might be able to hide from the United States government in Ecuador, Bolivia, or wherever it is you intend to flee. But you can't hide from me, because I'm not in this alone. Look at France, Germany, Russia, Italy, even jolly old England. We are goddamn everywhere and where we ain't yet, we will be soon. See, Davey, our time has come."

Skoll tried speaking again, almost managing a few words.

"One more time, son."

"What if..." Skoll managed, before his words dissolved anew.

"What if what?"

"What if I... had something else?"

"Something else?"

Skoll nodded desperately, so fast it looked like his head might shake itself off. "Something else you could use, something a lot more valuable than Oxy," he managed, and spit out a huge phlegm-soaked wad of blood.

Fisker put a hand behind Skoll's head and eased him to a sitting position, then gave him a handkerchief he kept stuffed in his pocket to press against his mouth. "I'm all ears, Davey. But let's see if we can find those teeth you spit out first."

22

SHAVANO PARK, TEXAS

Caitlin had just sat back down on the front porch swing of the modest two-story home, when Cort Wesley's truck pulled in to the driveway. With his younger son Luke at a posh boarding school in Houston and older son Dylan away at college most of the time, they'd found themselves with the house to themselves on the nights she stayed over. Then Dylan had elected to take some time off from college at Brown University—still undecided when, or even if, he was planning to go back.

"Looks like you had the same kind of day I did," Caitlin said, rising as he headed up the walk toward the stairs.

"Remind me never to have another kid, Ranger," he said, letting out some breath.

"Dylan?"

Cort Wesley nodded. "You wouldn't believe me if I told you. I'm going upstairs to check his closet for a black rubber suit because I believe he thinks he's Batman. Protector of lost souls."

"I don't think that was Batman, Cort Wesley."

They embraced when he reached the porch and settled onto the porch swing together, which rocked back and forth under their weight. Caitlin leaned over and picked up a bottle of Freetail Brewing Company's Original Amber Ale, Cort Wesley's favorite craft beer made right in San Antonio, and handed it to him.

"What's Dylan gotten himself into this time?"

Cort Wesley realized the cap wasn't a twist-off and used his thumb to flick it up into the air, just like his father had taught him when he was eleven. "Protecting his Latino coworkers at Miguel Asuna's auto body repair shop."

"From what?"

"A new racist element to hit San Antonio," he told her, taking a sip of his beer.

Caitlin snatched her bottle of genuine, old-fashioned root beer from the porch's plank floor.

"Since when do you drink root beer, Ranger?"

Caitlin took a gulp and ran it around in her mouth, before swallowing. "There was a time when I used to mix root beer with bourbon. Funny thing is it tastes the same either way."

Cort Wesley looked at her over his beer bottle. "You were a drinker?"

Caitlin drank some more root beer, the words she'd been rehearsing suddenly eluding her. "There's something I need to tell you, Cort Wesley."

"Likewise, Ranger."

"You go first."

"Let's flip for it," he suggested instead.

"Got a coin?"

He scooped the cap he'd popped off his beer bottle from the plank floor. "How about a bottle cap? Up side or down, you call it."

"Down."

Cort Wesley flipped the bottle cap in the air. It clacked back down to the porch, bounced a few times, then settled with the company's logo shining straight up in the porch lighting.

"You get to go first, Ranger," he told her. "Why do I think this has something to do with what went down in Austin last night?"

"Maybe because it does." Caitlin rolled her root beer bottle between her hands, so Cort Wesley could see the rest of the contents sloshing around. "I didn't come to drinking these with bourbon out of nowhere."

"That's the way it usually is, isn't it?"

"But I had a special kind of motivation, back when I was in college...."

23

KINGWOOD, TEXAS; 1999

"How come you're not drinking?" the young man, holding a red Solo cup, said to Caitlin, amid the swarms of people brushing past them in the jam-packed town house.

"Maybe because I don't drink," she responded, instantly regretting the fact that she'd come to the party in the first place.

"The bar's downstairs."

"I'll see you when you come back up."

"Come on, keep me company. What's your name anyway?"

"Caitlin."

"I'm Frank."

"You look old to be a Lone Star College student, Frank."

"I did four years in the army before I enrolled. ROTC's paying my way." He scowled at a floppy-haired kid who bumped into him and didn't bother to apologize. "That's why I look so much older than these kids. Being out in the world does that to you. You look older, too."

"I'm not," Caitlin said, not elaborating further on the fact that she'd just turned twenty, about the average age of the people in attendance.

"I didn't say you were, only that you looked it. That's a compliment, in case you didn't realize."

Frank flashed a friendly, comfortable smile that put Caitlin more at ease. She hadn't been making friends any better in college than she had in high school. So when a couple of fellow second-year students told her about the party at another friend's house and insisted that she come, Caitlin promised she'd be there. Of course, initially anyway, she had no intention of going. But then those girls would go the same way the friends she'd never made in high school had, and Caitlin thought this was a fine opportunity to begin working on her social skills.

Caitlin felt Frank take her hand and didn't pull away, because the gesture felt more natural and friendly than flirtatious. He had sandy brown hair, deep brown eyes, and a lean, hard body made for the tight, faded jeans he had fitted over his worn boots. She had to admit she'd noticed him earlier in the night, a few times in fact, kind of fantasizing about the notion of him coming up to her.

And now he had. Now, here she was with a young man a few years her senior who hadn't spent the last hour bro-hugging other guys after racing through beer chugs with them. There was also the fact that the two "friends" she'd met up with here had already disappeared into the room that had been emptied of furniture and turned into a steamy dance floor, smelling of stale sweat.

"That offer still open?" Caitlin asked Frank, trying to sound casual.

"What offer was that?"

"Go down to the bar with you."

He smiled playfully. "But you don't drink," he said, mocking her earlier words.

"Come on," she said, mocking his in return, "I'll keep you company."

It was a triplex apartment located in a tightly congested assemblage of matching structures in a Millwood subdivision not far from Caitlin's apartment in the Lodge at Kingwood complex. Lots of space for the three roommates living here, including the ground-level rec room, where a pool table had been covered with a cheap tarpaulin and dueling scents of spilled beer, strong perfume, and cheap cologne hung in the dead air. It wasn't as hot or crowded as the dance floor down here, but it was close. A stranger to such crowds, Caitlin found herself instantly regretting accompanying Frank, then realized she'd inadvertently grabbed his hand again to avoid losing him in the clutter of bodies.

"You got a hell of a strong grip for a girl," he noted, raising his voice to carry it over the music blaring from a pair of wall-mounted speakers.

"Jealous?"

"Curious."

"Get your drink."

Frank came back to the corner Caitlin had settled in with a red Solo cup for her, too.

"I hate drinking alone," he said.

"I hate drinking period," she said, holding it in her grasp. "Maybe you forgot that already."

"Nope, but you looked thirsty and the punch is as close to a soft drink as they've got. Not much stronger than old-fashioned Hawaiian Punch. And I only brought you half a cup. See, I'm not a bad guy," Frank said, flashing that smile again.

"Not half a bad guy," Caitlin said, finding a comfort with him that had eluded her so often in the past.

And breaking with that past, not resigning herself to spending the rest of her college years wallowing in the same misery that had defined high school, meant making at least a few compromises. So she took a sip from the red cup, and damn if the contents didn't taste exactly like Hawaiian Punch, true to Frank's words. She couldn't even detect any alcohol.

So she took another sip.

Then a third.

The heavens didn't open, she didn't feel sick to her stomach, dizzy, or light-headed. And Frank was still there, the dim lighting making his strong features appear softer and more attractive, his sandy brown hair hugging his face and scalp just right.

"My father's a Texas Ranger," Caitlin said suddenly, loud enough to carry her voice over the din of music and dueling conversations.

"I'll drink to that," Frank said, raising his Solo cup in the semblance of a toast.

"I'm studying law enforcement here. But I'm not sure I want to be a Ranger yet."

"I was thinking about police work," Frank told her. "Nice fit after the service. We got a police tradition in the family, military, too."

"That's nice."

"Want me to fill your cup halfway again?"

Caitlin looked down, surprised to see that she'd drained the whole thing. "I think I'm good."

Frank flashed a smile that made Caitlin's insides melt. "You're a whole lot better than good, girl. You're as good as it gets."

Just then, Caitlin caught the reflection in a mirrored Budweiser sign of an attractive coed with waves of black hair that tumbled back past her shoulders. She had ridged cheekbones and a gleaming smile that showcased the confidence Caitlin only wished she possessed. But the next instant revealed the reflection to be *hers*, Caitlin left seeing herself in an entirely different regard, for the moment anyway.

"Hey," she said to Frank, "you wanna dance?"

24

SHAVANO PARK, TEXAS

Caitlin realized she'd laid the root beer down somewhere in the midst of telling the story and picked it up again. The bottle was empty, but she had no memory of draining it, just like she'd had no memory of what happened after she'd drained her half-filled Solo cup that night at the party eighteen years before.

"I don't remember going upstairs," Caitlin continued. "Last thing I remember before I woke up was dancing, I think with Frank, but I'm not sure."

She could see the banded tension in Cort Wesley's neck, the tight sinews seeming to flex.

"You were in the same house when you woke up?" he asked her.

Caitlin felt herself nod. "In a bedroom that smelled like lavender. That's what I remember more than anything—the lavender smell. My jeans didn't feel right and I realized my panties were gone. I found them on the side of the bed. I'd gotten the jeans back on, and my shirt over my bra that was only half-fastened. I must've forgotten the panties."

"So," Cort Wesley started, seeming to think one syllable at a time, "you think Frank spiked your punch with GHB, something like that."

"I can't say for sure it was Frank, but somebody did."

"Your father never found who it was?"

Caitlin shook her head. "And he never found Frank, either. He interviewed all the people I remembered seeing at the party, including the students living in that apartment where it took place. Nobody knew anything about a guest matching his description or personal history."

"What about Lone Star College?"

"There wasn't much they could do officially, given that the incident occurred off school property."

"I was talking about enrollment or registration records for any student matching Frank's description," Cort Wesley corrected.

Caitlin shook her head slowly. Telling the story had made it feel heavy and stuffy. She hadn't recounted all of it in years and the feeling she was left with reminded her why.

"I looked at the college ID photos of every male student enrolled at the time, and didn't recognize a single one of them."

"No Frank?"

"No Frank. And I can't even tell you for sure he was the one who assaulted me."

"Seems obvious," Cort Wesley said, fidgeting and lifting up his beer bottle in the hope of finding more inside.

"What's wrong?" Caitlin asked him.

Cort Wesley laid the empty bottle back down. "What's wrong? How about the fact that you're just telling me about this now?"

"I don't like talking about it."

"But this is me you're talking to."

Caitlin took a deep breath. "After I stopped mixing bourbon with my root beer, I gave up trying to figure out who'd assaulted me. The hospital confirmed what I knew already, and my dad drove in to pick me up. Took me straight home, even though I know he wanted to start questioning anyone and everyone. We never talked much about whatever progress he ended up making, but I could tell it wasn't to his liking."

"What else do you remember, Ranger?"

"Trying to forget the whole damn thing. And being scared all the time, looking back at every young guy who gave me a second glance to see if I remembered them, to see if they were the one. I think I committed myself to becoming a Texas Ranger driving back home that day with my dad."

Cort Wesley didn't look convinced. "Maybe you should sit down with a sketch artist and see what he comes up with for this Frank."

Caitlin blew into the rim of her root beer bottle to produce a whistling sound. "I haven't told the story to anyone in a long time, Cort Wesley."

His facial muscles had tensed and his jaw looked locked in place. "But you just did, and I don't think you woke up this morning with the express goal of spilling your guts, which tells me there's something else in play here."

"Austin PD did a rape kit on the girl I pulled out of Stubb's last night." Caitlin swallowed hard, felt her breath lodge in her throat. "Her assailant's DNA was a match with mine."

Caitlin had rehearsed those words so much while waiting for Cort Wesley to get home, she thought saying them out loud would have no effect on her. But she felt the tears start to spill before she could get ahead of them with a swipe of her sleeve. Cort Wesley wrapped an arm around her shoulder and drew her in close, waiting for her to resume on her own.

For a time, Caitlin didn't think she would, but pushing more words out might stem the flow of her tears, and she picked up again, after clearing her throat. "According to Doc Whatley, there's a definite match but no ID on who the DNA belongs to yet."

"You never thought to tell me this before?" Cort Wesley said, his words trapped somewhere between a question and a statement.

"I wouldn't have today, if that DNA match hadn't surfaced. Tough enough being a female Texas Ranger without being a female Texas Ranger who was sexually assaulted. And when it happened, I don't know, I guess I blamed myself a bit."

"Too much."

"Nobody made me go to that party, Cort Wesley."

"That's like saying it's your fault your car got stolen because you parked it on the street."

Caitlin could feel the heat radiating off him, his muscles tightening beneath his shirt and his free hand squeezing the beer bottle so tight, she was afraid it was going to crack.

"It makes sense now," he said suddenly.

"What?"

"Why you shot that man in Stubb's last night."

"I never wanted to kill anybody more than I wanted to kill him."

"If that were the case, he'd be dead right now."

"That's what I told Captain Tepper. I guess reason prevailed. I didn't see him swiping that girl's cell phone and wallet, I saw him raping her and I felt like it was me. Trying to set things right, I guess."

"By ruining your career?"

"In that moment, nothing else mattered. There was that night eighteen years ago, another victim, and someone I could finally punish." She took a deep breath and looked up at him. "Your turn, Cort Wesley."

"Huh?"

"You said you had something to tell me, too."

"Oh, yeah. Never mind."

She eased herself from his grasp. "Don't do that."

"Do what?"

"Think you have to treat me with kid gloves, all of a sudden."

Cort Wesley forced a smile. "I thought I always treated you with kid gloves." He pulled the scrap of paper, on which Guillermo Paz had scrawled the black truck's license plate number, from his pocket. "I need to know where I can find the owner of this truck, Ranger."

PART THREE

I now propose to render reasons why the Texas Rangers are superior and the only class of troops fitted for such service. They are excellent horsemen, accustomed to hardship, and the horses of Texas having been raised on grass, can perform service without requiring grain... except to recruit their strength for a few days, when returned from a hard scout; the Texians are acquainted with Indian habits and also their mode of Warfare. They are woodsmen and marksmen. They know where to find the haunts of the savage and how to trail and make successful pursuit after them.

—Governor Sam Houston in an April 1860 letter
as reported in *The Texas Rangers: Wearing the Cinco Peso, 1821–1900*
Mike Cox, Forge Books, 2008

25

PFLUGERVILLE, TEXAS

Kelly Ann Beasley lived with her parents just outside of Austin in the beautifully manicured Pflugerville subdivision on Brown Dipper Drive, notable for the fact that virtually every tree in the community was still a sapling. Some had yet to shed the ties that bound them to waist-high stakes driven into the ground to hold them steady so they'd grow straight and tall.

Caitlin found that an apt metaphor for life, though human beings were seldom granted the same luxury past childhood that for Kelly Ann had ended the night before last. Her house was sided in faux brick that looked natural set against the auburn shutters and taupe garage door. She noticed the welcome mat was upside down.

An Austin detective had called ahead on her behalf, so she'd be expected. Kelly Ann's mother answered the door before Caitlin could even ring the bell, staring at her badge as much as her face after closing the heavy door behind her.

"I googled you after that detective said you were coming," Carolyn Beasley said, once greetings were exchanged. "I thought your name rang a bell. Now I see why."

"I've been in a few scrapes, ma'am, that's all."

"My daughter's in the television room," Beasley continued. "She's pretty much moved in there. If you'd like I could..."

"That's okay, ma'am, just point me in the right direction."

Kelly Ann Beasley was curled up, pillow in her lap, watching cartoons that dated back to when Caitlin was a little girl. And that's what she looked like sitting there on the couch: a little girl smiling and chuckling the day away, so the world beyond this room couldn't touch her.

Except for a broken right cheekbone that had swelled to twice the size of the left one, and an arm held in a sling to support her dislocated shoulder.

"Remember me, Kelly Ann?"

Kelly Ann looked at her, focusing on the Texas Ranger badge just like her mother had, then quickly back at the wall-mounted television. "A little. It's all still a blur. But I've been meaning to call to thank you for what you did."

"It was my job."

Kelly Ann turned her way again, holding her gaze on Caitlin this time. "No, you were off duty. Somebody told me that. I don't remember who."

Caitlin sat down in the chair nearest to Kelly Ann. She felt suddenly hot and light-headed, as if she was having a flashback to that night at the party in Kingwood when the contents of half a Solo cup had turned her life upside down, and there'd been no one to rescue her.

"I'd like to ask you some questions, Kelly Ann, if that's okay."

Kelly Ann lifted the pillow from her lap and hugged it against her chest with her one good arm. "I already told the detectives everything I could remember."

"Would you mind if we went over it again?"

"The police told me I wouldn't have to answer any more questions," Kelly Ann said, suddenly reluctant to look at her.

"I'd like to ask you a few myself, if that's okay," Caitlin said softly.

"Could you come back later? Tomorrow?"

"It's important, Kelly Ann, and it's important we do it now. I wouldn't be here if it wasn't."

She studied the television, as if Caitlin wasn't in the room at all. "I don't want to talk about it anymore."

"I know how you feel."

Kelly Ann slowly turned her gaze toward her. "How?"

Caitlin swallowed hard, just as she had last night before telling Cort Wesley her story, the familiar lump forming in her throat. "Because it happened to me, too. A long time ago, when I was just about your age. Your mother recognized me when I got here, on account of all the men I've shot in the line of duty. People ask me all the time how it is I keep at it without all that gunplay taking its toll. I mostly just shrug off their questions, but the truth is I think every time I fire my gun, I'm really shooting at the man who hurt me. I can't put a face on him, but I can put a face on all these others."

Kelly Ann tightened her stare, seeming to see Caitlin an entirely different way. Suspicious at first, then almost like she was looking in a mirror. The glow off the television screen that took up most of the wall formed the room's only light, keeping her features lost to the shadows where she seemed comfortable. Her hair was tied up in a bun and she was wearing a loose-fitting tracksuit with her name and a number embroidered across the left collar.

"Thirteen." Caitlin nodded.

"No one else ever picks it, but it's my favorite number." Kelly Ann seemed to perk up, at least slightly. "I play volleyball. We won our division this year."

"Did you go to the party with your teammates?"

Kelly Ann nodded. "But we got separated. Hard to keep track of everyone in all those people."

"I've read the statement you signed," Caitlin told her. "So I'm up on all the facts. But when this happened to me, I left some things out, either because I was embarrassed or didn't remember—I don't really know which to this day."

Kelly Ann swallowed hard, looking like a little girl in the meager light coming off the television. "How old were you?"

"Twenty."

"I just turned twenty-one. Did they ever catch the guy who . . . hurt you?"

"Not yet," Caitlin said, just firmly enough as she held Kelly Ann's stare. "It's been over a day since you spoke to the Austin detectives. I'm wondering if you may have remembered anything else."

The young woman shook her head. "Sorry, no."

"Don't be sorry. This wasn't your fault, none of it. Not now and not then."

"Did you know the man who hurt you?"

"Not until that night. A guy handed me a glass of punch that had been spiked with a so-called date-rape drug. I say 'so-called' because I hate that term. It's a rape drug. No reason to give dating a bad name."

Kelly Ann swallowed hard again. "Is whatever I say to you confidential?"

"Insofar as I won't share it with anyone outside the immediate circle of the investigation, you bet."

"Does that include my parents?"

Caitlin nodded, and leaned forward in her chair to put less space between her and Kelly Ann. "You're a legal adult, so it sure does."

"You promise?"

"I promise. Scout's honor," Caitlin said, making what she thought was the proper hand gesture.

"I was never a scout."

"Neither was I, but I think it still works. And if you want to tell me something about the man who assaulted you, I'll even keep that between us, if it's truly what you want."

Now it was Kelly Ann who leaned forward, lowering her voice when she spoke. "It wasn't a man."

26

ELK GROVE, TEXAS

Armand Fisker sat at his big desk on the second floor of what had once been the town hall, overlooking the central square that dovetailed around a corner toward a secondary row of now similarly closed-up stores. From this angle, it was easy to picture Elk Grove before circumstances had rendered it a ghost town. Fisker imagined oil workers, soaked in crude, slogging along the muddy streets in knee-high rubber boots. Women in long dresses, with their parasols open, walking the plank sidewalks. Clusters of children running this way and that, turning on a dime as if they were a flock of birds. A town content in its existence, with no foreknowledge of its impending decline and doom.

He sat at his desk, waiting for his computer to fire up, with his right hand encased in a bowl of ice to soothe his knuckles, still swollen from the beating he'd given the pissant Davey Skoll the night before. In almost any other scenario, Skoll would be no different than the mud Fisker scraped out of the grooves of his boots, to be disregarded and discarded. Skoll was a shining example of everything that was wrong with American society and civilization. The country, and the world, would be much better places with his kind bled into extinction, going the way of the dinosaurs or, at the very least, reduced to living amid the shadows of society, off the map and off the grid. But he fulfilled a purpose for Fisker, a damn important one, too, that might be about to expand.

What if I had something else? Something else you could use, something a lot more valuable than Oxy.

Fisker could hardly believe the next words out of Skoll's broken mouth; the ones that had followed those. And if he was speaking the truth...

Fisker chose not to complete the thought. He'd called this meeting to share the news with his international counterparts, who could use their imaginations just as well as he could.

Fisker didn't like computers and never had. Didn't like trusting secrets to all that metal and wire, that faint hum of something whirring invisibly inside, heating up when left on for too long a stretch. He didn't trust anything he couldn't see out in the open. For all he knew, miniature robots were crawling around inside the housing, stealing whatever they could get their tiny hands on.

But the Dark Web was different. The Dark Web, as his tech people explained it to Fisker, was a secret labyrinth of warrens and alleyways where he could do his business without fear of the authorities catching on. His daddy had started the ball rolling, from prison of all places, where he'd founded the Aryan Brotherhood, a loose assemblage of mostly biker-types that built chapters in virtually every prison across the country. Paying more, and far bigger dividends when those chapters expanded to outside prison walls, encompassing virtually every major biker gang, and thus every major population center, in the U.S.

Armand Fisker had expanded on his father Cliven's vision, not just beyond concrete walls topped with barbed wire, but also across the ocean to Europe, where carefully chosen counterparts operated as much under the radar as he did. Violence, Fisker had learned the hard way from his father, was bad for business. Uniting rival biker gangs, Fisker worked toward cornering the nation's and eventually the world's drug distribution business. In his operation, violence was to be abhorred and avoided at most costs, though not quite all.

And business was booming, due mostly to a swell in the ranks of like-minded people not just in America, but also in England, France, Germany, Italy, Austria, and various smaller nation-states in an ever-expanding landscape across the world. Men who were true leaders and shared his values now roamed within the highest corridors of power across the globe.

The computer flashed to life, colors filling the screen, and the doorway to the Dark Web opened with a click of his mouse on an icon one of his tech guys had preset for him. The other four participants in the call were labeled ENGLAND, FRANCE, GERMANY, and ITALY, no other sign of identity other than the bar grids that bounced and wavered when they spoke. Always in English, the one rule Fisker maintained over the group he had founded. His business brethren might be foreigners, but Fisker found comfort and familiarity in the fact that they spoke the same language.

"The meeting will come to order," Fisker said, his voice aimed toward the computer's speaker as he took his hand from the ice and dried it with a towel. "We left off the last meeting with an update on the unfortunate fates suffered by numerous elements of our competition in the trade. So fuck 'em, and let's move on. We've all done a little gunrunning and arms dealing in our time. Penny-ante shit mostly to pay a few bills. So what if I told you boys there was a way for us to expand our horizons even further, climb the food chain to the top, and I do mean the very top?"

"And how would we do this exactly?" asked Germany.

"The same way we've gotten this far," Fisker said, recalling what a blood-ied Davey Skoll had insisted he could provide. "By getting rid of anybody in our way. And what I got to share with you is the means to do just that."

Fisker gazed out the window while awaiting the response, spotting a dark pickup truck he didn't recognize edging its way down the street beyond.

27

SOUTH TEXAS

Caitlin was already gone when Cort Wesley awoke with his head pounding and his mouth dry as a dust. Had he drank that many beers or was he just getting too old to drink any at all?

Sitting up sent pangs through his head, his eyes tired and the color washed out of the world before him. But he still managed to spot the handwritten note Caitlin had scrawled for him in her scratchy penmanship on her side of the bed.

Here's the address that truck you asked me about is registered to, it began, finishing after the address with, *Be careful!*

He was on the road heading south for a town called Elk Grove twenty minutes later, swigging the first water bottle tucked into his cooler to chase away his hangover. He tried programming the address into his truck's navigation system, a little ball spinning around until it was replaced by a message Cort Wesley had never seen before:

LOCATION NOT FOUND

He wanted to punch the damn screen, but opted to reenter the information instead. When this produced the same result, he tried his phone, coming up with the history of the town of Elk Grove and not much more. Because, it turned out, the town didn't exist anymore. It had been abandoned years before when the oil boom had gone bust and a new superhighway had rendered the nearby access roads obsolete.

So how could the truck Guillermo Paz had rained bricks upon be registered there?

"Now, there's a mystery, bubba, if ever there be one," said Leroy Epps, suddenly filling the passenger seat beside him.

The spectral shape's lips were pale pink and crinkled with dryness, the morning sunlight casting his brown skin in a yellowish tint. The diabetes that had planted him in the ground had turned Leroy's eyes bloodshot and numbed his limbs years before the sores and infections set in. As a boxer, he'd fought for the middleweight crown on three different occasions, knocked out once and had the belt stolen from him on paid-off judges' scorecards two other times. He'd been busted for killing a white man in self-defense, and had died three years into Cort Wesley's four-year incarceration, but ever since always seemed to show up when Cort Wesley needed him the most. Whether a ghostly specter or a figment of his imagination, Cort Wesley had given up trying to figure out. He just accepted the fact of Leroy's presence and grateful that his old friend kept coming around to help him out of one scrape after another.

Prison officials had let Cort Wesley attend Leroy's funeral in a potter's field for inmates who didn't have any relatives left to claim the body. He'd been the only one standing at the graveside, besides the prison chaplain, when Mexican laborers had lowered the plank coffin into the ground. Cort Wesley tried to remember what he'd been thinking that day, but it was hard since he'd done his best to erase those years not just from his memory, but from his very being. One thing he did remember was that the service was the first time he'd smelled the talcum powder Leroy Epps had used to hide the stench from the festering sores spawned by the diabetes that had ultimately killed him. And, in retrospect, for days after the funeral Cort Wesley had been struck by the nagging feeling that Leroy wasn't gone at all. The scent of his talcum powder still hung heavy in the air inside his cell, and Cort Wesley woke up at least once every night, certain he saw Leroy standing there watching over him, grinning and sometimes even winking when the illusion held long enough.

"Wasn't no illusion, bubba," Leroy said today, as if reading his thoughts. *"I was there then, just as I be now. Say, you got any root beers in that cooler in the backseat there?"*

"Help yourself," Cort Wesley told him.

Leroy turned his gaze toward the windshield, peering out far beyond anything Cort Wesley could see. *"Would seem you're headed up my way."*

"How's that, champ?"

"Place we're going is a ghost town, ain't it?"

"Was that a joke?"

"You see me laughing? But, yeah, I guess it was. Kind of."

"It's not a ghost town anymore, not if that truck's registered to somebody living there."

"Ranger tell you that?"

"She ran the license plate."

"After you ran your mouth so much, you never caught up to what you were saying."

Cort Wesley fished out a Hires Original Root Beer he'd packed in the cooler just in case Leroy paid him a visit during the ride, and placed it in the passenger-side cup holder. "Say what you mean, champ."

"Question being, exactly what you meant by what you told her and what you didn't."

"You always talk in riddles now?"

"No sirree, bubba. Must be the morning. Was never a morning person on Earth, and I ain't no more of one since I came to be where I am now. How you figure on that, when I'm in a place where time's not supposed to make a dime's bit of difference? What I'm talking about is you not telling the Ranger lady the truth, the whole truth, and nothing but the truth."

Cort Wesley reached over and twisted the cap off the Hires he'd placed in the cup holder for a ghost.

I must truly be nuts....

"I told her I'd asked Paz to keep an eye on Dylan. I told her what happened after Dylan mixed it up with a truckload of punks with Confederate flags painted on both rear quarter panels, how Paz had used bricks to diffuse the situation."

"Diffuse the situation," Leroy said, casting a bloodshot eye toward the Hires Cort Wesley had just opened to let the aroma filter out. *"What's that mean exactly? I'll tell you what it don't mean, bubba. It don't mean you being so scared of your own boy, you gotta ask others to do your business for you."*

"I think I'll turn up the radio," Cort Wesley said, but stopped short of working the controls mounted on the steering wheel.

"Let me find us a station worth listening to. Ride south to the music of the blues. Say, you know that story about Robert Johnson going down to the crossroads to trade his soul to the devil in exchange for the blues?"

"Sure."

"What if I told you it was true?" Clouds covered the sun, making Leroy's eyes suddenly look shiny in the truck's cab. *"I know this on account of Robert Johnson telling me so himself."*

"I'm not scared of Dylan, champ."

"Nope, just scared of not having his approval, afraid he'll drift away on account of your tendency to judge him."

"Kid dropped out of an Ivy League school. What was I supposed to do?"

"Just what you done. And he didn't drop out, he's—"

"—taking some time off," Cort Wesley completed for him.

"Problem being that what you asked the big man to do is something you woulda done yourself up until maybe the day before yesterday. There's 'nother word for that 'sides fear."

"And what's that?"

"Love, bubba. What else?"

Cort Wesley jostled his hands on the steering wheel, accidentally switching the radio to a station playing a John Coltrane song.

"Now that's what I'm talking about," Leroy Epps said, leaning back in the passenger seat with hands cupped behind his head.

"Why don't you make yourself useful and tell me about this ghost town we're headed for, champ?"

Leroy didn't move an inch, the sunlight streaming through the windshield again seeming to pass right through him. *"Nothing good there I can see, but plenty bad in ways like we've never seen before. If I was sending you a sign about what you're riding into, it would be to stop your watch or maybe make that clock on your dashboard with the numbers freeze up solid. Time doesn't move where you're headed. Or maybe it winds backwards."*

Cort Wesley swept his gaze over the parched and barren world around him, the four-lane that looked like it headed nowhere. "I must've missed the turnoff somewhere. I don't even know where I am right now, and the GPS isn't worth shit out here."

"What's GPS?" Leroy asked him.

"Helps steer you in the right direction."

"Yup, you can use that, all right."

Cort Wesley tried working the navigation system again without success, gazing across the seat to find Leroy Epps, and the open bottle of Hires he'd tucked into the beverage holder, both gone.

28

ELK GROVE, TEXAS

Cort Wesley went back to following the old directions he'd been able to pull together from a stop at a gas station and farm stand, and finally found himself in what must be Elk Grove. There were no welcome signs to greet him, no banner strung over the town's main square to proclaim the coming of Founder's Day or something like that. There was just dust rising over the flattened, hard-packed, unpaved streets and furtive eyes held on him from behind cracks in window blinds.

He cruised slowly down the street, then doubled back when he reached a residential cluster of tiny homes renovated out of the clapboard shacks used by oilmen, who did nothing but sleep in them during the boom days.

Approaching the center of town again, he saw the landscape had sprung to life in the form of three men standing before him wielding shotguns.

Cort Wesley slowed to a halt, put the truck into park, and slid down the window. Then he watched two of the men fall in deferentially behind the third as they approached. The leader was tall and wiry, with an anvil-shaped head and a torso that looked too big for the rest of his body. A nest of stringy black hair emerged from beneath his cowboy hat, stained by sweat along the brim.

"You must be lost, stranger," the man said, reaching the window.

"Aren't we all?" Cort Wesley said lightly, drawing no reaction from the man. "But this is Elk Grove, isn't it? Because if it's Elk Grove, then I'm not lost at all."

The wiry man in the cowboy hat took a step back from the truck's open window, the two men flanking him tensing.

"I'm looking for Ryan Fisker," Cort Wesley said.

The wiry man stiffened, his frame seeming to fill out as if someone had pumped it full of air. "And why would you be looking for Ryan Fisker?"

"He got into a scrape with my son that almost went to guns yesterday. I thought I'd come here and make things right. Get it all behind us."

The wiry man with the big chest and shoulders bred of pumping heavy iron said nothing.

"I got this address from the DMV. Since his truck may have suffered some damage in the fracas, I thought I could square that, too."

"Why don't you just be on your way?" the wiry man said, taking another step back to put him in better position to use his shotgun.

"As soon as I have a talk with Ryan Fisker."

The wiry man took off his hat to reveal jet-black hair brushed straight back, save for the stringy patches that had clumped together under his cowboy hat. "I'm his father. You can have your talk with me."

Cort Wesley felt a chill of realization pass through him. "You're Armand Fisker. My dad did time with your dad, Cliven, in Huntsville. Sometime in the early eighties, I think it was."

Fisker's expression flattened, his cheeks puckering, as if channeling the breeze that had suddenly come up.

"Your dad founded the Aryan Brotherhood there," Cort Wesley recalled. "Made his bones killing black inmates and built something that sprouted chapters across the country like wildfire. That's an auspicious act to follow. Think you're up to the task, Armand?"

Fisker's face canted like a curious dog's. "Do I know you?"

"Our paths crossed a few times when I was working for the Branca crime family out of New Orleans. My job was to keep the Latino gangs from moving in on the drug trade. I believe you cut a deal to supply the Brancas with crystal meth they moved through the most impoverished neighborhoods in cities across the Deep South. I believe your daddy started the whole operation from prison and built it up from scratch, until somebody shanked him in the shower."

"You want to drive out now or never, cowboy? Your choice."

Cort Wesley rested his forearm casually on the open window, making sure Fisker could see his other hand still poised on the steering wheel. "Your son's been driving around East San Antonio, rousting illegals who mean him no harm, Armand. That big truck of his, painted with Confederate flags, has become a regular sight. My boy was just standing up for a few of the illegals he works with. So if you have a sit-down with your son to show him the error of his ways, then the past stays the only thing we've got between us. Just tell Ryan to take his hate posse somewhere else, so you and I can go about our business like none of this ever happened."

Fisker hacked up a thick glob of spit. "Mister, why don't you get out of that truck, so we can finish our business right now?"

Cort Wesley watched the two men who'd accompanied Fisker to the street take up positions in front of the truck, shotguns aimed from low on the hip and ready to fire.

"I get out of this truck, Armand, and one of us is going down so hard, he isn't likely to get up again. If that's what you want, I'm coming out. I'll kill you first, then the two guns I spotted in those windows on either side of the street, and then the two men blocking the road. If you want to see that go down, just say the word and I'll pop the latch. If it isn't, tell your men to stand aside and I'll be on my way."

Cort Wesley watched Fisker weighing the situation, the steely bent of his eyes indicating there was only one way this could go, before his mind got the better of him and he motioned to the two gunmen poised before the truck. One moved to the left, the other right, clearing the street.

Cort Wesley had readied himself to drive on, when Fisker clamped a hand on the hot metal where his forearm had just rested.

"You and I might've once had business together, cowboy, but we got no business together anymore. So once you're on your way, lose this place in your GPS."

Cort Wesley gunned the engine. "That ought to be easy, since my GPS couldn't find it."

He drove off, eyes rotating between his mirrors and the road ahead, one hand on the wheel while the other clutched the Smith & Wesson nine-millimeter pistol he'd tucked between his legs.

"Well, that went well," said Leroy Epps, suddenly beside him again with half-finished Hires in hand.

"Got a feeling we haven't seen the last of Armand Fisker, champ."

Leroy winked a gleaming eye at him. *"Nice to see I'm not the only one who can steal glimpses of the future, bubba."*

29

SAN ANTONIO, TEXAS

"I've never seen anything like it before," Doc Whatley told Caitlin after closing his office door behind him.

"Last time we had a closed-door meeting, I think you told me somebody was planning to poison chewing gum with the bubonic plague."

Whatley was clearly not in the mood to smile. "I completed the autopsies on those two bodies we recovered yesterday, Ranger."

"Got a cause of death for me?"

"Take your pick."

"Is this multiple choice, all of a sudden, instead of fill in the blank, Doc?"

"That's as good a way of putting it as any, given that all the organs in both subjects failed, each and every one."

"Cause of death," Whatley continued, "could be listed as kidney failure, liver failure, acute pancreatitis since the pancreas in both of them has shriveled to what look like supermarket bags. Or how about respiratory failure since their lungs were filled with necrotic tissue it normally takes a lifetime of smoking to generate? And neither of them were smokers. I know that much from their medical records, the same records that confirmed something I noted at the scene."

"What's that, Doc?"

"They were both recipients of organ donations."

"Liver and kidney, respectively, both within the past two years."

"You drawing a link between that and what killed them?"

Whatley scratched at the scalp revealed beneath his thinning hair. "What killed them was catastrophic, and virtually simultaneous, organ failure. If there's a link there, I can't see it."

"Pretty big coincidence otherwise, Doc."

"You're the Texas Ranger. I'll leave that for you to decide."

"Then you know what I'm going to say next."

"And I'm already running a check to see if there are any indications that the pattern goes beyond these two. That's going to take some time."

"So we're ruling out anything pertaining directly to the apartment complex itself."

"Three hundred people live there," Whatley reminded her. "And only two of them died of catastrophic organ failure, both of whom received donated organs. That's where you'll find your connection, Ranger."

"What about other residents who may have received donated organs?"

Whatley nodded, picking up on her thinking. "On the chance they might be next, because something environmental in the complex might be to blame, having somehow weakened their already compromised immune systems."

"In which case we'd need to warn them and fast."

"Already working on it."

"And the hospitals where the transplant surgeries took place..."

"Checking into that, too," Whatley said, nodding again.

"And what if what killed them actually has its roots in the donated organs they received? Imagine if the liver and kidney in question came from—"

"—the same donor," Whatley finished for her. "One thing I can say for sure is that isn't the case: the two victims had different blood types."

"Looks like you're ahead of me, Doc."

"First time for everything, I suppose."

Caitlin started to stand up.

"By the way," Whatley continued, "your captain called me yesterday in search of a history lesson."

"How's that, Doc?"

Whatley scratched at his scalp again. "Well, apparently you got him thinking about your granddad chasing an escaped Nazi prisoner of war across the state back in 1944. He asked me to fill in some details for him."

Caitlin sat back down. "Why don't you fill them in for me first?"

30

Austin, Texas; 1944

"Thanks for coming, Ranger," the manager of the Driskill Hotel said when Earl Strong climbed out of his pickup truck, parked directly before the entrance. "Locals want no part of this one and I'm having trouble keeping a lid on things to avoid spooking the guests."

Earl looked up at the marquee of the famed hotel. "As I hear told, this building's already got its share of blood staining the walls."

"Nothing like this," the manager told him. "You'll see what I mean as soon as we get upstairs."

The manager's name was Arliss Weatherby and he'd been in the process of anxiously checking his watch when Earl Strong pulled up after the two-hour drive from Hearne, traveling southwest on Route 79. Earl had heard talk that construction would soon be under way on much bigger highways that might stretch as far as four lanes in both directions. He always accepted the information with a shrug, wondering if there was alcohol on the speaker's breath, given it was hard to picture that much concrete carving up a state as massive as Texas. In Earl's mind the state was still best traversed by horse, but he hadn't worked a case on horseback since way back in 1931 when he'd battled all manner of miscreant, along with Al Capone's Outfit, in Sweetwater. That said, his powder-blue Chevy pickup was the second love of his life after his son, Jim.

Equipped with the latest General Motors V-8 engine, it had automatic overdrive transmission, power steering, power disc brakes, chrome accessories, Flowmasters, Dolphin gauges, tilt steering, a woodgrain Grant wheel, louvered hood, relocated gas tank, lowered suspension, and staggered twenty-inch aluminum KMC Nova wheels. Earl could recite those features as smoothly as the salesman who'd sold him the truck, giving him the military discount, even though Earl had spent the war fighting crime in Texas, instead of the Nazis. The salesman had convinced his boss that being a Texas Ranger more than qualified Earl there.

In the course of the drive from Hearne, he'd started wondering if the killing he'd been sent to Austin to investigate was as much a ploy to get him out of FBI Director J. Edgar Hoover's hair as anything. Hoover had a well-earned reputation for not fancying opposition of any kind, and it was clear back on the clay-rich soil of that prison camp that they'd gotten off on the wrong foot.

Then again, Hoover's history with the Rangers had been tainted for a while already, dating back to Ranger Frank Hamer's doggedly successful quest to bring Bonnie and Clyde to justice in 1934, after FBI efforts to do the same had failed at every turn. It had been Governor Miriam "Ma" Ferguson herself, no friend of the Rangers at all, who called Hamer out of retirement to take up the chase, which he promptly did in the company of a band of equally able, retired Ranger lawmen he'd put together himself. In Texas, the bureau would always be playing second fiddle and Earl figured that ate at Hoover's insides something awful.

One look at hotel manager Arliss Weatherby was enough to convince Earl that his being summoned here was no ruse. The man was tied tight as baling wire, his nerves a jumble and his embroidered white handkerchief already sodden with sweat and grime from a constant blotting of his face, so red in the heat of the Texas day that it looked almost purple. Then again, the Driskill was the most well-known hotel in the capital city, and maybe even the entire state, having played host to all manner of events and parties featuring dignitaries and politicians, so Weatherby was certainly facing some pressure here.

"Housekeeping staff found the body," the hotel manager related, patting at his shiny face with his handkerchief again. "I gave the maid and her supervisor the rest of the week off."

"Mighty kind of you," Earl noted, wondering what his life would be like if he'd been given a week off for every body he came across, especially if that included the ones he dropped himself. "But I'm more interested in the guest's identity."

Weatherby consulted a leather-trimmed notepad, squinting for want of reading glasses. "Abner Dunbar. His registration lists his profession only as 'oilman' and his employer as Standard Oil."

"John D. Rockefeller's old company."

"Is that important?"

"Not particularly," Earl Strong replied. "Beyond the fact that my grandfather Steeldust Jack Strong had a run-in with him back in the late nineteenth century. Now, how about you show me to the room in question?"

Earl rode the hydraulic elevator upward, trying to remember if there'd ever been another time when he'd been called to investigate two different murder scenes in a single day. Weatherby had posted private uniformed hotel security guards on either side of a door in the middle of the hall. A short, dapper-looking man in a tweed suit and bowler hat stood across from them, balancing his weight on a single leg, the second one folded up behind him, dress shoe heel pressed against the wall.

"This is Mr. Brimble," Weatherby said, by way of introduction. "The hotel detective."

"Works for you?"

"The owner."

Earl flashed Brimble a look, realizing he had a thin mustache, too. "Then he can report to the owner, after I report to you."

"I worked for Scotland Yard," Brimble said in a thick London accent. "My grandfather investigated Jack the Ripper."

"Did he catch him?"

Blood was the first thing Earl noticed once in the room, first by the powerful coppery stench, and then the spray across the bedcovers and walls. Against his better judgment, he let Brimble accompany him inside, curious to see how the famous Scotland Yard operated.

"Somebody slit his throat," Brimble said, looking down over the body, which was stripped down to his underwear.

"You got any observations that are less obvious?"

"Only Americans kill men in their sleep."

"Is that a fact? Then I guess it's a good thing this man wasn't sleeping, or even lying down. The way the blood sprayed indicates he was sitting up, likely right here on the edge of the bed. You see that depression in his forehead?"

Brimble crouched and laid his hands on his knees. "Yes, I do."

"Revolver barrel did that. The killer was holding it against his forehead when he cut poor Mr. Dunbar's throat."

"To avoid making a racket, I assume."

"Your assumption would be correct, Scotland Yard."

Earl moistened a towel in the luxurious bathroom that came complete with one of those toilet-like things for women they called a bidet, and swabbed it across the area of the wound on Abner Dunbar's throat.

"Should you be doing that, Ranger?"

"I trust myself to do it more than I trust anyone else. And..."

Earl stopped, the wound looking all too familiar. "Well, I'll be damned…"

"What is it?" Brimble asked, drawing closer.

"A coincidence, we can hope, but this isn't the day for them."

"I'm not following you, Ranger."

"I came here straight from the German POW camp in Hearne where one of the prisoners escaped, after cutting the throat of his three bunkmates. Near as I can tell, those wounds were identical to this one. Same general circumference, made by the same or similar straight-edged tool sharpened to an edge, as opposed to something more serrated."

"Same killer?"

"That would be my initial evaluation," Earl said, moving his eyes away from the body and the blood, and sweeping them about the room furnished with handmade wood furniture and real oil paintings hanging from the walls.

Then his gaze edged downward. "Don't move," Earl said to Brimble.

"Why?"

"There's clay dust on your shoes."

Brimble looked down, shook his head. "And I just had them shined in the lobby."

"When?"

"Oh, a few hours ago maybe."

"Step back."

Brimble did.

"Holy shit," said Earl.

Earl used an old toothbrush he always carried to push as much of the clay dust as he could into one of several plastic bags he always kept tucked in his pocket. The thick nap of the carpeting must have pulled it from the soles of the killer's shoes. He still had a sizeable portion left to go when he heard a commotion in the hall just ahead of the room door opening all the way.

"You again," said J. Edgar Hoover, entering in the company of the same suited figures Earl recalled from Hearne. "Doesn't Texas have any other Rangers?"

Earl rose from his crouch. "One or two, Mr. Hoover. They happened not to be in the area at the time."

"My lucky day," the first and only director of the FBI said, shaking his head.

"Not his, unfortunately," Earl said, bending his gaze down toward Abner Dunbar.

"We'll take things from here," Hoover told him.

"Didn't you say almost the same thing to me at the POW camp?"

Hoover didn't bother nodding. "It was true then, and it's just as true now."

"Fact that the director of the FBI is a long way from home at a second murder scene tells me you suspect a connection with that triple homicide committed by Gunther Haut in Hearne. Does that sound about right, Director?"

J. Edgar Hoover gave the body a closer look. "You're not an educated man, are you, Ranger?" he asked, the condescension in his voice as palpable as the smell of blood in the air.

Earl watched Hoover's lackeys ease forward to stand between him and their boss. "I never went to college, if that's what you mean."

"I also mean schooled in the basic tenets of criminology and modern forensics."

Earl didn't feel much like getting into a pissing contest right then. "Rangers tend to work scenes where the nearest medical examiner might as well be on Mars and the local elected law never faced a criminal in his life. Under those circumstances, folks tend not to ask for diplomas."

"But these are different circumstances, aren't they?"

"I'm still waiting to hear why that is exactly, Mr. Hoover."

"You're way out of your league, Ranger."

Earl sidestepped to hide the presence of the clay dust sprinkled over the carpeting, and tucked the plastic bag into which he'd sifted samples into his pocket. "Being this is Texas, sir, I was about to say the same thing to you."

31

"That clay dust," Caitlin said. "My granddad must've recognized it from the prison camp in Hearne."

"Can you believe Earl Strong talked to J. Edgar Hoover that way?" Whatley asked her, instead of responding to her comment.

"My granddad was never one to mince words with anyone. And it sounds like he suspected something fishy about the director of the FBI's presence in Texas right from the get-go. With good reason, too," Caitlin added, "starting with the fact that Abner Dunbar being in Texas at the same time Gunther Haut escaped couldn't have been a coincidence. Dunbar must've been waiting for Haut to show up at the Driskill Hotel. This was something big for sure."

Whatley drummed his fingers on his desktop, choosing his next words carefully. "Should I ask how it went in Austin?"

"Like stepping out of a time machine," Caitlin told him. "I promised myself I'd never feel that helpless again and, there I was, reliving the whole experience through the eyes of a fellow victim."

Whatley again looked hesitant to continue. "Was she helpful at all?"

"She believes her attacker was a woman."

"Say that again?"

"That was my reaction, too, Doc."

"Doesn't exactly jibe with your own recollection."

"Except I really don't have any. I'm thinking about getting a sketch artist to put something together on the guy who gave me the spiked drink. See if we can age it eighteen years and see if it jogs Kelly Ann Beasley's memory."

"Except she doesn't believe her attacker was a man in the first place."

"I don't need to tell you that those date-rape drugs tend to play hell with whatever memory you've got left when you wake up." Caitlin hesitated, trying to figure out how to best phrase her next question. "Any chance Austin's lab findings were wrong on this, Doc?"

Whatley shook his head, looking as sad as the rare times he opened up about losing his family. "I double-checked them myself, Ranger."

Caitlin shook her head. "All those years apart, two different cities, same MO...If there's any sense to be found there, maybe someone else needs to find it."

"When it...happened, we all tried not to think what Jim Strong would do to your attacker if he ever found him."

"Spare the ghost of my granddad the trouble."

"You believe in them?"

"What?"

"Ghosts, Ranger."

Caitlin thought of Cort Wesley's "friendship" with Leroy Epps and those times she was certain she spotted her father and grandfather together grinning at her from shaded tree groves, still wearing their Ranger badges with holsters strapped around their waists. "I don't know if that's what I'd call them, but I definitely wouldn't rule it out."

Whatley's eyes moistened behind his glasses and he took them off to rub at the sockets as if to block his tears. "I see my boy and my wife from time to time. They both still look to be in pain, like they're frozen in the final moments of their lives: my son getting knifed by those gangbangers and my wife in a hospital bed after alcohol had rotted out her insides. I thought the pain was supposed to end when they died. I hope that doesn't mean they're in hell, Ranger."

Caitlin felt her phone buzzing inside the pocket of her jeans, but didn't answer it. "It's us who visit hell from time to time, Doc. What you think you're seeing is something you just dragged back with you. Your son's someplace where there are no gangbangers to hurt him, and wherever that is, your wife is there, too."

Whatley sniffled. "I'm not normally a sentimental man."

"How long have you known me?"

"All your life."

"You don't have to put a label on what you're feeling with someone you've known that long, Doc."

Her phone buzzed again and, this time, Caitlin excused herself to check it, finding CORT WESLEY lit up in the caller ID.

"How'd it go in Elk Grove, Cort Wesley?" she asked without saying hello.

"Just fine if you like towns that don't exist anymore and people who aren't supposed to be living there," he told her. "I'm going to need something else from you, Ranger."

32

WACO, TEXAS

"How come they call you Dobby again?" David Skoll asked the tech automation whiz, who'd helped design this fully automated pharmaceutical manufacturing plant that had gone online just a few months before.

"Not Dobby. Dobby was a character from *Harry Potter.* It's *Dobie.* And they call me that, because my last name is Gillis."

"So?"

"My mother's favorite TV program growing up was a show called *Dobie Gillis.* It was actually called *The Many Loves of Dobie Gillis,* but nobody ever referred to it that way."

"Never heard of it."

"Ask your father."

"I can't; he's dead."

"Er, sorry."

"Don't be, Dobie. That's where all my money came from. The best thing the son of a bitch ever did for me was drop dead and leave me a boatload of cash. That's what I have to take from our relationship, and I'm fine with it. I'll take money over memories any day of the week."

Skoll returned his attention to the technological marvel of a world revealed beyond the observation glass below, nary a human in sight in a massive area the size of five football fields laid next to each other.

"I heard recently that before too long the most employees a place like this will have is two: a man and a dog," Skoll resumed. "The man is there to feed the dog and the dog is there to make sure—"

"—the man doesn't screw up."

"You heard it, too."

Gillis nodded from behind his horn-rimmed glasses. He was in his midthirties, but his paunchy frame and thinning hair made him look older, despite wearing yesterday's jeans and a T-shirt that read I BRAKE FOR ASSHOLES.

Automated assembly lines were hardly anything new; auto factories had been using robots to perform menial line tasks for decades. The difference here at Redfern Pharmaceuticals, the company Skoll's hedge fund had acquired at a virtual fire sale after manipulating the stock price, was Gillis had taken that principle a whole bunch of steps further.

Instead of being moored or anchored to a fixed slot, a number of the "Bots," as Gillis called them, moved independently about the line, performing quality-control checks. Kind of like giant, man-sized, sophisticated versions of the robotic vacuum cleaners capable of memorizing room layouts and intuitively deciphering how to avoid getting trapped in a corner or against a piece of furniture.

Gillis's Bots, on the other hand, looked more culled from something out of the first generation of *Terminator* machines as portrayed in the film series. Skoll had enjoyed his share of dalliances out in Hollywood and had put some hedge fund capital into a couple of studio film slates—not because he ever expected them to turn a profit, since he knew Hollywood didn't work that way. Being a player, though, gave him the in he needed to meet actresses, which, given his looks and money, almost inevitably led to the next step.

Of course, those looks had suffered a beating, literally, at the hands of Armand Fisker the night before. Skoll noticed Gillis eyeing the makeup job he'd done on the black-and-blue spots, and was late to their meeting here at the Redfern Pharmaceuticals manufacturing plant in Waco because of a necessitated stopover at his dentist's office to get his temporary teeth installed, so he'd at least look good as new.

Right now, he couldn't take his eyes off the giant humanoid-like machines rolling along atop wheels built into their undersides.

"I can see why you gave them those armlike extremities," Skoll said to Gillis, "but why build them with neck and head-like extensions?"

"Because people accept robots better when they look more like us," Gillis explained. "Call it a sense of familiarity. Maybe it's even more than that, since almost every robot made to resemble humanoid dimensions has its 'brain' function in its head." Gillis flashed Skoll a look like something had just magically occurred to him. "Maybe you should think about building a different kind of assembly line."

"I'm considering that, as we speak," Skoll said, visions of dollar signs dancing in his head at the mere thought of landing military contracts someday.

That would enable him to tell the likes of Armand Fisker to go fuck themselves, he thought, watching four of the wheeled, eight-foot-tall contraptions rolling about the various stations of the line below that molded, stamped, cut, apportioned, packaged, boxed, and labeled the dozen drugs manufactured at this facility. Exposed cables ran from their narrow torsos up to their steel shoulders, looking like muscular, rubbery sinews. Their legs were combined into a single base and their arms were capable of full articulation to the point Gillis claimed they could retrieve a single pill that had spilled off the line with their pincers without crushing it. The robots whisked about, stopping at every juncture where a red light garnered their attention to signal something awry. Skoll watched as they freed clogs of cardboard or stuck foil wrapping, moving on to reboot dispensing systems that had shut themselves down to avoid overheating. The robots couldn't join a union, didn't complain about working conditions, never bartered over overtime, needed no medical benefits, and couldn't testify against him in court. So Skoll firmly believed Redfern Pharmaceuticals had uncovered the perfect formula for a thriving business:

Remove people from the equation.

Gillis had programmed these robots with a rudimentary artificial intelligence that allowed them to both learn from their labors and deduce simple repair tasks not necessarily included in their programming. And the results spoke for themselves. Since Redfern's Waco facility had replaced three hundred workers with a pile of diodes, microchips, rubber, and steel, productivity had increased threefold. On their best days, human workers couldn't even begin to replicate the pace and efficiency of machines. And machines didn't carry germs, infections, or environmental toxins capable of contaminating the pharmaceuticals they were charged with producing, adding an extra benefit to the equation.

"I'd like to hear more about the military versions of our friends down there," Skoll said to Gillis, eyes riveted to the scene in the sprawling plant beneath him.

PART FOUR

Boys, you have followed me as far as I can ask you to do unless you are willing to go with me. It is like going into the jaws of death with only twenty-six men in a foreign country where we have no right according to law but as I have [gone] this far I am going to finish with it. Some of us may get back or part of us or maybe all of you or maybe none of us will get back.... I don't want you unless you are willing to go as a volunteer.... Understand there is no surrender in this. We ask no quarter nor give any. If any of you don't want to go, step aside.

—Texas Ranger Captain Leander McNelly; November 1875,
as reported in *The Texas Rangers: Wearing the Cinco Peso, 1821–1900*
Mike Cox, Forge Books, 2008

33

Armand Fisker pulled back the cover on his son's truck halfway, enough to reveal dings and dents that looked like the kid had gotten caught in a hailstorm of mythic proportions.

"When did you plan on telling me about this?" he asked Ryan, who hovered behind him.

"There's nothing to tell, Dad."

They'd taken the biggest house in the former ghost town for themselves, and then worked on building this garage. Those weeks gave Fisker hope, both for his son and their relationship. In the course of the build, it got so he could actually envision Ryan following in his footsteps, picking up the mantle when he stepped down. It was different between him and his dad, because Cliven Fisker had gone to jail for murder at the age of thirty, when Armand was nine, and died there just after his son's thirty-fifth birthday. Plenty of what he'd done before, and everything he'd done in Huntsville, had laid the groundwork for what Armand Fisker was building now. Taking the foundation his father had laid for a base and building a massive, ever-expanding structure atop it. Thinking about it that way made it seem oddly similar to building the garage with his own son, a metaphor of sorts.

Except that's where things stopped. Ryan was every bit the hothead his grandfather had been, owning every bit of the temper and rashness of Cliven Fisker, while combining it with none of the cunning or intelligence. That damn cowboy's story about what Ryan was up to in East San Antonio was more or less typical. The boy lacked the subtleties necessary for dealing with people and inspiring them to follow him. And, instead of learning the business here by his father's side, he was content to terrorize and bully others to wash himself in his own sense of power and superiority. If Ryan wasn't his son, Fisker would've already deemed him an utter piece of shit incapable of living up to whatever potential his last name afforded.

"Why don't we start with who did this to your truck?" Fisker asked, not about to let it go.

"I thought maybe somebody was stripping a roof and got a bit careless."

"Bullshit!" Fisker wailed, slapping his son across the face.

"Ouch! What the fuck you—"

Fisker slapped him again. "Don't you ever swear at me, boy! I'm not one of those lackey losers who follow you around 'cause you happen to share my last name."

Ryan's eyes had already teared up from the slaps, but the remark seemed to stun him even more, leaving his mouth hanging open with air leaking out the way it did from a tire with a nail stuck in it.

"That hurt, son? Good, 'cause I meant it to. I'm gonna ask you again, who did this to your truck?"

"I didn't see him," the boy said, sniffing now, but stopping short of wiping his eyes for the satisfaction it would give his father.

"It wasn't the white kid you were rousting?"

"No, I had eyes on him the whole time. I think the bricks came from an alley across the street."

"His father came to see me."

"Whose father?"

"The white kid's. Fancies himself a badass. Used to work for a second-rate crime family out of New Orleans who couldn't shine your grandfather's shoes."

Ryan Fisker took in a deep breath and held it briefly. "I'm gonna get him."

"Say that again."

"I'm gonna—"

Fisker's third slap, the hardest yet, cut off his son's words and left a scarlet palm imprint across his cheek. "You're gonna cut this shit out, that's what you're gonna do. It ends now, all of it. You wanna go roust illegals and mix it up with some white kid who figures he's a superhero, do it on a bicycle, because you've lost your driving privileges."

"You can't—"

This time, Ryan stopped his own words when Fisker got his hand into slapping position again. "What is it you were saying?"

"Nothing."

Fisker walked the long length of the big truck, pulling back the cover as he went, revealing more of the pockmarks, dings, and shattered glass. "That's right—nothing. Which pretty much describes all you've made of yourself. Until now, I guess I've been looking the other way, since you kept your behavior at a distance. But what you did yesterday brought a stranger out here, to our home and place of business. That makes him a threat and he came to Elk Grove following the trail you left. County sheriff's on his way out here right now to help me figure out how to clean up *your* mess. And until it's cleaned up, you and your loser running buddies are gonna stick around smoking weed and playing video games, things normal losers do, which for you is an improvement. Hey, if you've got any questions, feel free to stop me."

Ryan sniffled again, looked down, and kicked at the garage floor. Fisker figured maybe what he should do was take a knife to his boy, instead of an open hand. Scar up that pretty face and hair he'd inherited from his mother Fisker had long told him had run off years before, along with a pissant attitude and spineless nature. He'd been fooling himself for too long about the prospects for his one child's future. Left to continue on this track, Ryan would end up in prison getting fucked instead of being the one doing the fucking. The polar opposite of his dad and grandfather. Time for some tough love, in other words, starting today. Help the kid turn over a new leaf.

"Know what I should do?" Fisker challenged, from the front of the dented truck to his son at the rear. "Make you pay out of your own pocket to get this fixed at that body shop where those illegals you rousted work. Has a nice ring to it."

"I think he was part Mexican," his son said out of nowhere.

"Who?"

"The kid, the one who drew a nine-millimeter on me. Or doesn't that count for anything?"

"The count was four guns against one and I'm sure you boys were packing the heavy artillery."

Fisker watched his son swallow hard, the palm impression showing no sign of fading from his cheek. "Do I really have to get the truck fixed at that place?"

"No, but only because that would mean venturing out of town. We got a couple boys on the payroll who know their way around body work," Fisker said, running his hand along the truck's finish, and feeling it dip into the spots where the bricks had left their mark. "I think I'll have them take a look at the damage."

"Thanks, Dad," Ryan said, still kicking up dust from the floor.

"Oh, don't thank me, son. You're gonna be doing the heavy work, including giving the truck a paint job that'll look showroom fresh. These boys are gonna be there just to teach you the tricks of the trade. That way, you'll be ready if I decide to have you swap places with that kid in East San Antonio. Part Mexican or not, he sounds like the kind of boy I'd rather have by my side than you. Of course, I've got a feeling his father isn't going away anytime soon, thanks to this stunt y'all pulled off. Maybe I'm gonna have to kill him on account of you, in which case maybe I'll have you pull the trigger to see if you can kill a man without wetting your undies."

Fisker heard someone clearing their voice and turned toward the driveway where the McMullen County sheriff was standing, his frame equally divided between sun and shade.

"We need to talk, Armand," he said, his expression grim and four. "We need to talk now."

34

Donnell T. Gaunt was serving his twelfth consecutive two-year term as sheriff, his complacency over reelection reflected in the belly that hung over his belt. His round face, beet-red from the heat of the day that had lingered into early evening, featured bulging jowls and eyes that looked like tiny marbles recessed amid the flaps of skin beneath coarse, thinning hair.

"I ran that name for you," he said to Armand Fisker.

"And since you drove all the way out here for a heart-to-heart tells me what you found can't be good."

"That would be an understatement, Arm. You want the bad news or the bad news?"

There wasn't much shade where they stood in the front yard, and the sheriff's face seemed to grow redder with each breath and word. Fisker enjoyed watching Donnell Gaunt roast in the dwindling sunlight, reminding him of the pleasure he'd taken in setting fire to ants as a boy.

"Why don't you decide, Sheriff?" he said to Gaunt.

"The stuff you told me about Cort Wesley Masters was easy to confirm. His criminal record working for the Branca crime family, the four years he did in Huntsville on a murder beef gone bad, his release after he was exonerated by a DNA test. The rest, well, let's just say it raises more questions than answers."

"And, as in the rest, you mean . . ."

"The years before and after what I just told you. Masters served in the Army Special Forces during the Gulf War in the early nineties, a genuine Green Beret. I'm going to assume you didn't know that."

"You'd be assuming correctly," Fisker acknowledged, trying very hard not to appear rattled by what he was learning about the father of the boy his son had nearly gone to guns with, before bricks had rained out of the sky.

Sheriff Gaunt was nodding, his head looking like a basketball set on a spindle, bobbing up and down. "Which means you couldn't have known that when I pinged him in the system, the request came back flagged."

"How's that?"

"A polite way Washington says to bug off, meaning there's stuff in Masters' file I lack the security clearance to access."

"Was that the bad news or the bad news?"

"Take your pick, because there's more. Not long after he got out of prison, Masters' girlfriend was gunned down. His two sons would've been killed, too, if a Texas Ranger hadn't saved their lives. They've been an item practically ever since."

"Masters is a fag?"

"The Texas Ranger is a woman."

"Caitlin Strong?"

"I see you've heard of her."

"All of Texas has heard of her, for Christ's sake. And you're telling me they're a goddamn couple?"

The sheriff nodded. "I guess it's a good thing you were polite and reasonable when Masters paid a visit. It would be a real bad idea to involve the Texas Rangers in our affairs."

"Am I breaking any laws I'm not aware of?"

"You're pure as the driven snow, as far as I'm concerned. Elk Grove not being on the state tax rolls will certainly roil some folks in Austin, though, if the Texas Rangers make it their business to raise a stink."

Fisker weighed Gaunt's words carefully, gaze cheating back to the garage where he'd left the son who'd made all this trouble for him. "What would you suggest, Sheriff?"

"What did Cort Wesley Masters want?"

"I don't really know, because we didn't get that far into the conversation."

"He didn't mention the Texas Rangers?" Sheriff Gaunt asked, the degree of foreboding in his voice palpable.

"We back to that again?"

"A pissed-off father can't do much damage to what we've built here, Arm. The Texas Rangers, well, that's something else again."

Fisker took a sudden step forward that pushed Gaunt all the way into the sun, where the steaming rays resumed the roasting of his face. For some reason, he took even more pleasure in the man's discomfort.

"I believe you've developed an inflated opinion of your worth here."

The sheriff looked ready to stuff his hat back on his head, only to realize he must have left it in his cruiser. "I have no idea what you're talking about."

"You keep saying 'we,' Donnell. There is no *we*. *We* didn't build anything here—I did. You're just along for the ride and the walk to the bank to deposit the money contributed to make sure you hold office comfortably."

"Hey, you called me on this. You want my help or not?"

"You mean the help I'm paying for?"

"Then here's some more of your money's worth, Arm: there's a whole bunch of weird shit that came up when I cross-referenced Caitlin Strong with Masters."

"How's that?"

"Can't say exactly. All I can tell you is that they're both involved with somebody in Washington who wants to make sure that association stays secret. What matters to us—excuse me, partner, to *you*—is that these are people you absolutely don't want prying into your affairs. So I'm gonna give y'all my advice, even if you didn't ask for it or pay for it. Make him go away, Arm. Whatever it takes, even if that includes your boy's left nut."

Fisker thought about how little value that would have, but kept it to himself. "Masters didn't exactly leave a number where I can reach him."

"Let me see if I can track it down for you." Gaunt squinted into the sun. "Beats risking the Texas Rangers showing up, maybe with warrants in hand."

Fisker took a single step closer to him, the bulbous man seeming to shrink in his shadow. "I don't like your tone, Donnell."

"Well, that's too fucking bad. I'm the only cover you've got when it comes to shit like this, and you damn well better appreciate that fact."

"The monthly stipend I'm paying you isn't enough for your efforts all of a sudden?"

"Not if it means going up against the Texas Rangers. You don't want to make me choose sides."

"I don't?"

Gaunt held his eyes, which looked swollen over with excess flesh, on

Fisker, not squinting anymore. Then he stepped back, turned around, and surveyed the town, virtually all of it visible from this vantage point.

"You think you're the first man in my county I've done business with over my years in office?" he said without looking back toward him. "You think I've been reelected a dozen times taking chances and making enemies I can ill afford? Like I said, we got a good thing going. But it's fragile and prone to breakage."

"What would you suggest we do to shore it up, Sheriff?"

Gaunt looked back his way, his face glowing with sweat. "Glad you asked, Arm, glad you asked."

35

San Antonio, Texas

"When I asked for a sketch artist," Caitlin said, closing the door to the Ranger Company F headquarters conference room behind her, "I wasn't expecting to see you."

The honorary Texas Ranger known as Young Roger popped his laptop open. "That makes two of us, since I didn't think the description would be coming from you directly."

"Day for surprises, then," Caitlin said, taking the chair directly across the table from Young Roger as he fired up his computer.

"What'd you think of the show at Antone's, Ranger?"

"Your band keeps getting better, the Rangers just might lose you to the road."

"No worries there." He grinned. "I enjoy my day job too much."

Young Roger was in his midthirties now, but still didn't look much older than Dylan. Though a Ranger himself, the title was mostly honorary, provided in recognition of the technological expertise he brought to the table that had helped the Rangers solve a number of Internet-based crimes ranging from identity theft, to credit card fraud, to the busting of a major pedophile and kiddie porn ring. He worked out of all six Ranger Company offices on a rotating basis. Young Roger wore his hair too long and was never happier than when playing guitar for his band the Rats whose independent record label had just released their second CD, the contents of which had made up their set at Antone's. Their alternative brand of music wasn't the kind she preferred, but it had grown on her, and hearing it live had given her a fresh perspective on the band's respective talent.

"I'm dating Patty," he said, looking at his screen.

"Who's Patty?"

"Our blue-haired guitarist."

"I think it was purple a couple nights back. If you're going to keep dating her, that's something you should maybe notice."

Young Roger looked up, the program he needed to access to compile Caitlin's sketch open before him. "You ever color your hair, Ranger?"

"Not like that. But I did go through a blond phase as a little girl for a while that led me to take some lacquer to my bangs."

"You're kidding."

"I wish I was. The can I found in the garage looked blond, but it was actually yellow to match the shutters on our house. Needless to say, things didn't go well."

"Well," said Young Roger lightly, "you always said you were socially impaired as a kid."

"I was paint impaired until my hair grew out. I had to beat up a whole bunch of boys who razzed me."

"No girls?"

"Sure, but it seemed wrong to hit them. And you don't have to do this."

"Do what?"

"Try making it easier. I'm doing this because I want to, because it might help another victim."

Young Roger laid his fingers on the laptop's keys. "Then let's get started."

Creating a usable sketch of the man who may have sexually assaulted her eighteen years before meant revisiting that night and all that came with it.

The doubts, the questions, and the guilt. What could she have done differently? Why did she take that Solo cup from the young man named Frank? How could she have made it so easy for him to overpower her?

Revisiting all that made Caitlin feel weak and vulnerable, bringing back not only the memories, but also the feelings of inadequacy and angst that had dominated her life for months afterward. The Texas Ranger Caitlin had become had been forged from that experience, and she had forgotten how badly she wanted to leave all of it behind her for good.

I'm doing this because I want to, because it might help another victim.

True enough, Caitlin thought of her words just spoken to Young Roger. The real truth, though, was the person she really wanted to help was herself. Deal with this last bit of her past that remained unresolved that had led her to nearly kill a man two nights before.

"You want me to come around to that side of the table?" Caitlin asked Young Roger.

"No, I'd rather you form the face, to the best of your recollection, in your mind. I don't want my work to distract you from that."

"Whatever you say. It's been some years since I laid actual eyes on the man in question, so hopefully my recollection proves to be good enough. Houston police did a sketch eighteen years ago, but it didn't lead them to a suspect. According to Doc Whatley, the same DNA was found on that more recent victim I told you about." Caitlin watched Young Roger's eyes flash, as if he'd gleaned the gist of what she was saying. "Where should we start?"

"As basic as it gets. Eye color?"

Caitlin closed her eyes and pictured the young, good-looking man named Frank. Though eighteen years had passed, his face came back in a heartbeat, frozen like a snapshot.

"Blue," Caitlin said, "but dark, not icy or pale."

"Got it," Young Roger said from behind his computer, keys clacking away.

"Why are we starting with the eyes?"

"Windows to the soul, as they say. Getting the eyes right gives me something to build the face around, and everything else will fall into place."

"Navy blue. Seems strange to describe his eyes that way, but that's what I remember."

"How'd they ride his face?"

"As in …"

"Flat, protruding, sunken, or set back. Pick one."

"Flat."

Young Roger went back to working the keys. "That's the most popular answer."

"Do I get a Kewpie doll?"

"No, another question: hair color?"

"Dirty blond."

"Describe it."

Caitlin closed her eyes again. "Shaggy, hanging low over the ears and shoulders." She opened them. "Like a musician."

"You mean a rock star."

"Not a star, more like the drummer in your band."

"Steve." Young Roger nodded, clacking away. "So far, he's the spitting image of the man you're describing."

"I didn't notice."

"Steve's a drummer. He's used to that."

Thirty minutes later, Young Roger turned the laptop her way so Caitlin could get a notion of what he'd done so far, before the real detail work was added.

"Close," Caitlin said, "real close."

Twenty minutes after that, his rendition of the young man she knew only as Frank looked more like a photograph, to the point that Caitlin shuddered, dredging up her last memory of him just short of the dance floor before her world had faded to black.

"Houston police never found him?" Young Roger asked her.

Caitlin couldn't take her eyes off the screen. "They tracked down as many guests from the party as they could find."

Young Roger looked down, then up again. "And you're saying, after all these years, he did it again?"

"During a college graduation party at Stubb's Barbecue."

Caitlin watched him swallow hard. "We'll need to age the picture then. How many years was it again?"

"Eighteen."

Young Roger started clacking away at the keys again. "Let me do a basic aging, so you'll have a better idea of what he looks like today. Give you something to work with while I come up with some more options."

A knock fell on the door, and Caitlin turned as Captain Tepper poked his head in. "A minute, Ranger?"

"Jones wants to see you," he said, once they were in the hallway.

"He couldn't call me himself?"

"Maybe he figured you wouldn't like what he had to say. Maybe he asked me to deliver a message. Maybe I told him to eat dirt and tell you himself."

"That doesn't sound good."

"You're the one who keeps dragging this asshole to Texas, Caitlin."

"You want to give me a hint, Captain?"

"I don't believe Jones, or all of Homeland for that matter, is prepared to be blown over by Hurricane Caitlin."

"That bad?"

"Doesn't make any sense from where I'm sitting."

"You're standing, D.W."

"But I was sitting when I took the son of a bitch's call. He said to tell you he's on his way."

"Call him back. Tell him to meet me at our usual place in Marble Falls."

"Why Marble Falls, Hurricane?"

Caitlin pictured Young Roger in the conference room, clacking away at coming up with a rendition of the man she knew only as "Frank," aged eighteen years beyond the night of her assault. "So I can stop there on my way to Austin."

36

"Is one of those for me, Jones?" Caitlin said, noting the two heaping pieces of chocolate cream pie set before him in a corner booth at the Bluebonnet Café.

Jones checked his watch dramatically. "It's still Pie Happy Hour, Ranger. Order a slice, plus one, for yourself. You can mix and match, if you like."

"Kind of describes your work at Homeland, mixing and matching. But I'd go easy with the calories, if I were you. That six-pack of yours is already down to one."

Jones forked a chunk of pie into his mouth, leaving whipped cream across his upper lip. "I don't drink, so this is how I relieve stress. Just so you know, my diet was going great until you called yesterday."

"Nothing of note at that apartment building, as it turned out. So why you still around?"

"Because maybe I was wrong and you found a whole new pile of shit to step in."

"You want to say that in a language I can understand?"

"Tox screens on those two bodies we pulled out of the complex came back with the same anomaly."

She settled into the booth across from him. "Doc Whatley didn't say anything about that."

"Maybe because he didn't know. Maybe because the analytics I have access to are a thousand times beyond that museum you call the Bexar County Medical Examiner's Office. Jesus Christ, all that money I've funneled here from Homeland, you'd think you could spring for a used electron microscope or something."

"Right, I'm sure all the accident victims we scrape off the freeways would appreciate that."

Jones took another bite, more whipped cream left drizzled across his upper lip. Caitlin was going to tell him to wipe it off, then decided not to.

"What do you mean by an anomaly?" she asked him.

"A drug we can't identify."

"Whatley told me both victims had received organ transplants, a liver and a kidney respectively."

Jones finally dabbed his mouth with a napkin. "Maybe I should reevaluate my assessment of his office."

"So the two bodies, otherwise not connected, were both taking something you can't identify. We need to share pie for you to tell me that?"

Jones dabbed at his mouth again, as if forgetting he'd already wiped it clean. "I need you to back off your latest crusade."

"What crusade would that be?"

Jones worked his fork, but didn't lift another piece of pie toward his mouth. "You rescued a potential rape victim from Stubb's Barbecue in Austin, then interviewed her outside the presence of the Austin PD. Now I understand you want to show her a sketch of a man who's a potential suspect. Have I got that right?"

"Not really. First off, there was nothing 'potential' about Kelly Ann Beasley being a victim. Secondly, the official police term is 'sexual assault,' not rape. And I had permission from the lead Austin sex crimes detective on the case to interview her. As for the sketch, it's somebody I've got something of a history with I thought might be connected."

"And what made you think that?"

"Guess you don't know as much about me as you think, Jones."

He pushed a double forkful of pie into his mouth and spoke while chewing. "You mean the fact that you were raped—excuse me, *sexually assaulted*—yourself, when you were about the same age as Kelly Ann?"

"Where'd you go to charm school?" Caitlin asked him. "I think I might enroll."

"Good. You could use it, the way you plow through the state of Texas with no regard for the collateral effects of your actions or any respect whatsoever for jurisdictional boundaries."

"You're sounding very official today, Jones."

He laid his fork down and glared at her across the booth. "I need you to back off this, Ranger."

"Back off what?"

"The investigation you've got no part in, anyway. It's a local matter, not a Texas Ranger matter."

Caitlin glared back just as hard. "Texas Rangers don't need an invitation to join an investigation, Jones. And this happens to be a personal matter, in case I didn't make that clear."

"You made it crystal clear, Ranger, just like I'm making my order to you."

"Order," Caitlin repeated.

"Call it whatever you want."

"Does bullshit count?" Caitlin asked him.

She eased from her pocket one of the copies Young Roger had made for her of his sketch of the man she remembered only as Frank, aged eighteen years. Unfolded it and slid it across the table toward Jones.

"This man mean anything to you?"

Jones gave the picture a first look, but not a second. "Should it?"

"He may have been the man who raped me eighteen years ago." Saying those words made Caitlin feel as if needles were jostling around her stomach.

"You mean, *sexually assaulted* you."

"It was called rape back then."

"So is that who you were picturing when you shot that lowlife in Stubb's?"

Caitlin pulled the computer-generated sketch back across the table. "Actually, Jones, I was picturing you."

"I think I'm doing you a favor by telling you to back off the case. Leave things be."

Caitlin tapped the sketch with her finger. "As soon as I show this to Kelly Ann Beasley to see if it jogs her memory." She started to pull her finger away, then changed her mind. "Who is this guy and why are you protecting him?"

Jones traded his cleaned plate for the fresh piece of chocolate cream. "Who said I was protecting him?"

Caitlin looked down at the face that had once been handsome and was now worn with time. His sandy brown hair was darker, stringier, and thinning, and his eyes had been dulled by the years. "Is he Homeland? Does he work for you?"

Again, Jones didn't bother looking at the aged sketch. "How many ways do you want me to say this?"

"As many as it takes to make me forget about my duty."

"Duty to who, Ranger?" Jones scoffed, expression coming up just short of a scowl. "Sounds like your duty's to yourself, by tracking down the piece of shit who hurt you and got away with it. Like I said, I'm doing you a favor here."

"How's that?"

"You got bigger fish to fry than ghosts from the past."

"Get back to that anomaly you found in both victims from the apartment complex," Caitlin said, eager to change the subject. "The drug the tox screen revealed."

"We haven't identified it yet. And don't try to sidetrack me. I want your word you're going to let this sexual assault thing go."

"Mine or Kelly Ann Beasley's?"

"Is there a difference?"

Caitlin rose and slid out of the booth, snatching up the sketch on the way. "That's what I intend to find out."

37

SAN ANTONIO, TEXAS

One good thing about his son Luke being away at boarding school and Dylan being pretty much on his own was that Cort Wesley got to spend more time in the gym. He'd had to steal time to work out much over the past seven or so years, so that came as a welcome relief. Truth be told, he wouldn't trade the experience of being a father for anything in the world, but it was nice to have some time for himself again.

He'd chosen to join the District gym on Broadway because it was new and featured a pair of climbing walls in addition to the regular complement of fitness equipment and free weights. Today he started out with cardio because he needed to sweat out his experience with Armand Fisker from the morning, as if the residue had seeped in through his pores and needed to be excised from his system. He remembered how his father would spend hours in the steam room at the Y to flush the alcohol from his system following a bender, when Cort Wesley was a boy. Take Cort Wesley with him and leave him in the corner with a comic book until he felt like returning, his son an afterthought as always.

The irascible Boone Masters, who'd died pretty much friendless and alone in a hospital bed—at least, that's what Cort Wesley had thought for the better part of his life. Then he learned the true source of his father's passing, that he'd gone out a hero, but never wanted his son to know that particular truth about him. As if it might tarnish the reputation for wantonness Boone Masters had worked so hard and long to cultivate.

Benching on the District's Smith machine to spare his shoulders, though, stoked fresh thoughts in Cort Wesley's mind. Boone Masters hadn't wanted him to know the truth, because he didn't want his death to be hard on his son. Better he go out being hated than being missed or mourned. He preferred the reputation of a hard ass and a drunk to the man who was actually much purer at the core, but kept his morality tucked into some secret pocket somewhere.

Thinking of his own sons made Cort Wesley push the weights harder, as if exercise were some magic elixir that could hold him in place while his boys and the world spun faster around him. He welcomed those thoughts as distractions from the moral stink of Armand Fisker that rode him like skunk oil. What he needed was a shower, not a workout, but all the soap in the world couldn't cleanse him of the ugliness he'd encountered in the former ghost town of Elk Grove.

Cort Wesley had just formed that thought when his phone rang. He snatched it from the pocket of his workout shorts.

"I'm outside Miguel Asuna's body shop, outlaw," Guillermo Paz said. "You need to get over here."

38

"She doesn't want to see you again, Ranger," Kelly Ann Beasley's mother said to Caitlin through the crack in the front door.

Caitlin had taken off her Stetson and was holding it low by her hip. "I just need to show her a sketch of the man I think may have hurt her."

"As I understand it, this isn't your case."

"I'm assisting the Austin detective heading things up."

"It was Detective Diaz who advised me not to let you see my daughter again."

Caitlin couldn't make any sense of that and didn't bother trying. "I just want to help, ma'am. Why don't we do this? Why don't I leave the sketch with you and you show it to Kelly Ann whenever she's up to it? If she recognizes the man, you can have her call me or Detective Diaz. Does that sound okay?"

The woman nodded stiffly and Caitlin handed over one of the sketches she'd brought along. She flirted with the notion of telling Kelly Ann's mother the whole truth behind her involvement, but stopped short of doing so since it was clear the woman wasn't budging.

First Jones trying to warn me off, and now this. What's going on?

The woman's eyes met Caitlin's, something inside her trying to get out.

"Do you have something you'd like to tell me, ma'am?"

Kelly Ann's mother shook her head. "I'm sorry you wasted a trip."

"Please tell your daughter I was here and I hope she's feeling better."

"I'll do that, Ranger."

She flashed another copy of Young Roger's aged sketch of the man she knew only as Frank to the hostess, servers, and bartenders at Stubb's Barbecue. Several said he looked familiar, but couldn't say from where. Others gave the sketch a second look, even a third, before telling her they could be of no help identifying him, either.

That left Caitlin back at square one, the person who might be the most help to her unwilling to talk, and the ones willing to talk being unable to help. She spoke to Stubb's manager last, who barely even regarded the sketch before telling her he'd never seen the man before.

"Maybe you should take a longer look."

"I don't have to," the man said. "I told you I'd never seen the man before."

"Neither has anyone else who works here. But they all gave the sketch a closer look. Is there something I should be reading into that?"

"Yeah," the manager told her. "The dinner rush is starting and we've got a new owner who won't like it if I don't tend to my job."

The manager walked off before Caitlin could press him further, trying to pinpoint the look in his eyes after he'd glanced at the sketch, when a call came in from Captain Tepper.

"You in Austin, Ranger?" came his greeting.

"You must be psychic, D.W."

"Either psychic or caught in another storm whipped up by Hurricane Caitlin, take your pick. Jones was here."

"I'm sorry to hear that."

"Just like I was sorry to hear what he had to say. I'd tell you you're off the Beasley case, but you were never on it and you wouldn't listen to me, anyway."

"Right on both counts, Captain."

"Look, I can handle the Category Ten–force winds you bring about. But right now those same winds are aimed at some folks who can't. Jones gave it all to me, but not until he called Washington to get my security clearance upped."

"That doesn't sound good."

"Because it's not. So drive yourself on back here and I'll lay it all out for you. And don't even think about making another run at Kelly Ann Beasley before you hit the road. She is strictly off-limits and that's for her own good."

Caitlin realized she'd walked back outside while she'd been talking, her boots crunching some stray shards of broken glass left over from the other night. "You want to tell me what's going on here exactly?"

"Sure, Ranger. You may be able to walk on water, but quicksand's a whole other thing. So get down here, before it swallows you up altogether."

39

EAST SAN ANTONIO, TEXAS

It was pretty much over by the time Cort Wesley arrived, Miguel Asuna's illegals handcuffed and taken away in a county jail short bus, Asuna left answering questions for a trio of men with ICE stenciled over their windbreakers. He spotted Dylan leaning against the 1996 Chevy truck he'd restored to pristine condition, looking forlorn and alternately brushing and blowing the stray hair the breeze kept dropping over his face. It was the work he'd done on the truck that had given Cort Wesley the brilliant idea to get him a job here, a simple enough thing that had turned out to be not so simple at all.

Guillermo Paz emerged enough from an alley across the street to grab Cort Wesley's attention, and he started toward him instead of moving straight to Dylan.

"There was nothing I could do, outlaw," the big man said apologetically.

"This was my doing, Colonel. I paid a visit this morning to the father of the kid whose truck you dinged up. I'm guessing this is payback." Cort Wesley could see from across the street that Asuna's conversation with the ICE officials wasn't going well and flirted briefly with the notion of calling Jones, before remembering he wasn't one to stick his neck out, especially when another government agency was involved. "So, there you go, father and son, each of us with the uncanny ability to make any situation worse."

"This isn't about either one of you," Paz told him.

"What's it about then?"

"According to Albert Einstein, 'The world is a dangerous place to live, not because of the people who are evil, but because of the people who don't do anything about it.' See my point?"

"Not particularly, Colonel, no."

"Both you and Dylan tried to do something about it."

"And that seems to have made the world more dangerous for both of us," Cort Wesley said, casting his gaze across the street again, "along with Miguel Asuna and his illegals."

His eyes swung back toward Dylan, still leaning against his truck, suspended between thoughts and actions, no doubt blaming himself for this, just as his father was.

Well, Cort Wesley thought, *at least we've got that much in common.*

"I'm going to go talk to my son," he told Paz. "Thanks for calling, Colonel."

"Outlaw?"

Suspended between sun and shade, Cort Wesley stopped and turned back around.

"One of my priest's favorite quotes, from Proverbs twenty-four, twenty: 'For the evil man has no future; the lamp of the wicked will be put out.'"

"Stay tuned," Cort Wesley told him. "I may need your help in putting out Armand Fisker's light once and for all."

40

East San Antonio

"This wasn't your fault, son," Cort Wesley said before Dylan had even acknowledged his presence. "It was mine."

The boy brushed the black hair from his face and looked at him, confusion framing his features. "What am I missing here?"

"Caitlin ran that truck's plates for me. Turned out the asshole hassling those illegals is the grandson of a genuine piece of shit my father went up against in prison. A man named Cliven Fisker who founded the Aryan Brotherhood while behind bars."

"Those guys I messed with are Nazis?"

"I don't think they call themselves that, but close enough. Cliven Fisker's son's name is Armand. I paid him a visit this morning, looking for his son who goes by the name of Ryan, according to his truck registration."

Dylan shook his head, his expression mixed between dismay and disgust. "So first you send the big guy to babysit me and then you go see this Armand Fisker to, what, tell him to take away his kid's milk and cookies?"

"I didn't realize who he was until I got there."

"Oh, that makes me feel a lot better."

They turned their gazes to the county jail bus pulling away, bracketed both in front and behind by unmarked, government-issue sedans that must've belonged to Immigration and Customs Enforcement, the guys in the windbreakers.

"I'll make this right, Dylan. I've got favors I can call in."

Dylan held his gaze on the convoy as it drove down the street. "I should have backed off. It wasn't even my fight."

"'The world is a dangerous place to live, not because of the people who are evil, but because of the people who don't do anything about it.'"

"Who said that?"

"The big guy," Cort Wesley said. "And Albert Einstein before him. Nothing wrong with trying to do something about it."

"Apparently, there was, Dad." Dylan looked away, then turned his eyes back just as fast. "Why'd you ask Colonel Paz to watch me? Why didn't you do it yourself or just talk to me?"

"Would you have listened?"

"No."

"There you go then. I didn't want to deal with the fallout, if you caught me watching your back."

Dylan canted his head toward the alley where Paz was standing. "So you sent *him?*"

"It worked." Cort Wesley shrugged.

"Did it?"

"You're alive."

Dylan blew the hair from his face with a burst of breath. "What are we gonna do about this, Dad?"

"*We?*"

"You heard me."

"Let me handle it."

"I'm not very good at that."

"First time for everything."

Dylan gave him a long look. "Tell me more about the Fiskers, father and son."

"They've resettled a ghost town down in McMullen County."

"The two of them?"

"Along with a couple hundred of their closest friends, from what I could see. Fisker has turned the nation's biker gangs into upstanding businessmen; they've cornered the market on the distribution of black market narcotics, Oxycodone and Vicodin, most notably, along with their old staple of crystal meth."

"So what's his son doing rousting illegals?"

"Being an asshole, same as his father, though on a much smaller scale."

"You think they have talks like this?" Dylan wondered, only half-whimsically.

"Well, I can imagine the one they had when Armand Fisker saw the damage done to his boy's truck."

41

ELK GROVE, TEXAS

Armand Fisker figured he'd check in on the progress on the repairs Ryan was making to his truck before heading out to Waco to pay a visit to Davey Skoll.

Since he'd left Ryan in the garage, he'd had supplies and the proper tools brought over and sent one of his guys with body shop experience to get him going. He pulled in to the driveway to find the garage door closed. Fisker parked, turned off the engine, and hit the automatic garage door opener before climbing out of his truck.

It slid upward to reveal a wash of smoke, releasing the pungent scent of weed. Ryan and a couple of his loser running buddies bounced up off the garage floor, two of them fanning the smoke away, while his son stamped out a joint. Beyond them, the truck looked exactly the same as it had that morning, supplies and auto body repair shop tools piled alongside it.

"Get lost," Fisker said to Ryan's two friends, who scampered away so fast, one of them tipped over a gas can. "Were you confused about what I told you?" he asked his son.

The boy stood stiffly before him, his narrow shoulders inherited from his mother. "I was just taking a break, Dad."

Fisker nodded, feeling his heart hammering against his chest. "Those illegals you were trying to chase back home have been arrested. Since you don't have to bother with them anymore, you'll have plenty of time to work on your truck."

"You had them arrested?"

"I had some calls made," Fisker said, righting the plastic gas can before it leaked over the floor. "Those two losers I just sent home, they were with you when the truck was damaged?"

"Uh-huh." His son nodded.

"I don't want you hanging around with them anymore."

"They're *my* friends."

"Glad to hear it."

Fisker watched his son's spine stiffen. "I'm twenty years old. You can't tell me who I can and can't hang out with."

Fisker carried the gas can toward the shelving where it belonged, loosening the cap as he walked. "You're right, son, you are twenty."

Drawing even with Ryan, he drew the gas can backward and flung its contents all over him. The boy recoiled, banging into the rear bumper of the big truck that looked to be the only part that had escaped damage from the onslaught of bricks.

"But I can tell you anything I want to tell you. You got that?"

His son spit gasoline out of his mouth, started hocking up more immediately.

Fisker took a silver cigarette lighter from his pocket and flicked it to life, the flame shooting out. "I don't smoke, but I carry this because it's all I've got left of my father. He didn't leave me anything and I got this out of his drawer, since you're not allowed lighters like this in Huntsville where he got shanked to death in the shower. I also ended up with the organization he built and expanded it worldwide. I used to hate him, because he never believed I could do something like that, and every time I grow our business bigger I think of him." He edged closer to Ryan, moving the lighter out so the flame was between them. "You want to tell me why I shouldn't burn you alive right now and save us both the trouble?"

"Dad . . ."

"That your answer?"

Ryan recoiled against the truck's cargo bed door, looking even slighter than usual. Fisker liked watching the glow of the lighter flame shining in both the boy's eyes.

"There's two things in the world, son, two things and only two: assets and liabilities. You're either one or the other, and there's nothing in between. Something you need to know: your mother didn't run off, like I told you. That was a lie. She was a liability. Got busted for drugs and sold me out to avoid prison time. I guess she didn't know I had friends in that jail who let me know what she was up to."

Fisker let his words settle in before continuing, liking the pain that had sprouted on his son's face. Wouldn't surprise him if the kid started bawling his eyes out, crying for his missing mommy.

"Every time I look at you, I think of her. The two of you are alike in every damn way, including being a pain in my ass."

"What'd you do to her?" Ryan asked between raspy whimpers, the gasoline dripping off his hair and clothes.

"Had her deposited in a junkyard compactor, after I strangled her. Because she'd become a liability." Fisker flashed the lighter in front of his son's eyes. "Just like you. So look into my eyes and tell me I won't do it, son, look into my eyes."

"Dad," the boy whined.

"Look into my eyes!"

Ryan did, using all his will.

"You think you're strong, you think you're tough, because you can scare a bunch of wetbacks who are scared already. But you can't scare a punk kid your own age who stood up for them. Maybe I can make a trade with Cort Wesley Masters, you for his boy straight up." His gaze lifted over Ryan to the dinged-up truck. "Hell, I'll even throw the truck in, as is. Sound fair?"

"I'm sorry, Dad, all right? I'm sorry," Ryan managed, his voice cracking and spittle trailing the words from his mouth. "What do you want me to do?"

Fisker moved the lighter's flame so close to him, he thought his son's clothes might catch. "What I tell you. I want you to do what I tell you. But you didn't do that this morning, so I've got no reason to believe you'll do it now."

"I'll fix the truck!"

"Yes, you will."

"I promise!"

"I hope you're not talking to me, son, because I don't give a shit." He flicked the top of his father's lighter back into place, extinguishing the flame. "You're a liability now, and until you show me something that proves different, I'd avoid open flames at all costs. Because you're gonna wear those clothes for a while, until I tell you to take them off, undies included. Something to remind you of the difference between assets and liabilities."

"You'll see," Ryan said, holding his face so rigid, his chin stuck out like a blade.

"What am I going to see exactly, son? Enlighten me, please."

His son's jawline straightened to a rigid block, making him look more like Cliven Fisker than his dead mother. "You'll see," the boy repeated.

PART FIVE

The Rangers have given the people of Texas protection from redskin, Mexican raider, frontier robber and desperado, mob violence and the more modern forms of defiance of law and order. They have not done so without leaving many of their comrades on the field of battle. Their record has brought glory not only to the Rangers themselves but to all of Texas. The Ranger has become symbolic of the heroism with which Texas has been carved from the wilderness. For these things, the Ranger deserves the high place of honor given him.

—*The Dallas Morning News*, August 24, 1936

42

Captain Tepper was smoking a cigarette, boots almost as old as he was propped up on the desk before him, when Caitlin walked into the room.

"You know, I tried to retire last year, Ranger."

"Really?"

Tepper nodded and eased his boots back to the floor. "Uh-huh, for the third time, actually. And Ranger headquarters in Austin gave me the same answer each time: no. Know why? Because they knew no one they put in my place could handle you. Hell, not that I've been doing a very good job at all in that regard. Did you really violate a direct order from our friend Jones?"

"He's not our friend and since when did you start taking his side?"

"Since it became a matter in Homeland's purview, not ours."

"You're talking about Kelly Ann Beasley."

Tepper rocked forward in his chair. "Who you went to see, even after Jones warned you not to."

"He didn't give me a reason."

"He didn't think he needed to, beyond whatever it was he said he told you." Tepper shook his head and stamped out the remainder of his cigarette in a heavyweight ashtray he kept chained to his desk with a computer cable so

Caitlin wouldn't steal it. "Man actually thought you were going to take his words at face value and go merrily on your way." He gazed at his pack of Marlboro Reds, as if he were already longing for another. "Hey, notice anything, Ranger?"

"Besides the fact that your office smells like a barroom before smoking was outlawed in them, you mean?"

"I was talking about the fact that I put the cigarette out when it was halfway done. See, you've had more of an effect on me than you thought. I only smoke half of each one I light up now. Give me some credit."

"You think that's going to put years back on your life, D.W.?"

"Take less of them off, anyway. Look, Caitlin, I'm deeply appreciative of you doing your best to keep me alive, but both of us know your interests are self-serving, since you don't want to have to break in a new commander by ignoring his orders, too."

Caitlin sat down in the chair in front of Tepper's desk and put her boots up on the edge. "Doc Whatley picked up the story of my granddad investigating that POW camp murder."

"Is that a fact? Where'd he leave off?'

"At the Driskill Hotel, where the body of a man believed to be working for Standard Oil was found."

"Named Abner Dunbar, as I recall." Tepper nodded. "Here's what happened next...."

43

AUSTIN, TEXAS; 1944

Earl Strong left the crime scene in the able hands of J. Edgar Hoover and the FBI, and rode the hydraulic elevator down to the lobby, marveling at the way the cab operated. A black man wearing a uniform like a train porter's sat on a stool working the controls. Going up and down all day, every day, the floors the cab opened onto always the same. Earl found himself wondering if he'd be better off in a line of work more like that, and tipped the man a dollar after he'd slid open both the grate and door itself.

"Thank you, sir."

"Keep up the good work."

From the elevator, Earl went straight to the Driskill Hotel's front desk, making sure his Texas Ranger badge was in full view of the clerk.

"You got the registration card for Abner Dunbar?" he asked.

"Sure do, Ranger. That FBI man asked me to pull it and I'm holding it right here for him, if you want to take a look." The clerk lowered his voice. "Did you know it was J. Edgar Hoover himself?"

"Is that a fact?"

The clerk fished the registration card from a drawer and slid it across the desk. It listed a Dallas address in Dunbar's scratchy scrawl, above where he put Standard Oil as his employer. Earl Strong slid a ten-dollar bill across the shiny countertop in its place.

"The Driskill's such a busy place, it's not hard for a little registration like this to go missing," he said, watching the clerk's eyes widen at the sight of the bill.

"Happens all the time," the man said, covering it with his hand and making the ten dollars disappear with a magician's skill.

"Something else you need to know," Earl told him, feeling the need to explain a clear indiscretion for a lawman. "Those folks from Washington upstairs are no friends of Texas. They're here purely to suit their own interests and would shit on the Lone Star flag itself if it furthered their cause. They've got no claim to that registration card or anything else."

"What registration card would that be?" the clerk asked him, grinning.

DALLAS, TEXAS

The address Abner Dunbar had listed on the registration card took Earl Strong to a modest bungalow on the outskirts of Dallas at the virtual meeting point between country and city. It was the kind of tract home rented by the case lot by oil companies to house their workers who came and went based on the whims of the pumpjacks that dotted the horizon, churning day and night.

That made Earl wonder if Dunbar's employment with Standard Oil might actually be real and not a ruse, as he checked the windows and doors in the hope of finding one open. When he didn't, being no good at all when it came to picking locks, Earl scooped up a rock from the garden and hammered out a windowpane on the back door. Then he carefully reached through the jagged breach and unfastened a chain lock before popping open the door lock and entering the kitchen.

The thing about kitchens was that, in Earl's experience, they always smelled of something. The residue of cooking odors clinging to the paint, wallpaper, and appliances maybe. It was always there, as much welcoming as sad, given how often Earl paid visits to homes of those already deceased.

Like Abner Dunbar.

He checked the refrigerator and found it virtually empty, save for a couple bottles of pop and some sticks of butter. Closing it, Earl started from the kitchen into the living room area, passing by a pair of doors leading into identical bedrooms when a man's shadow shifted against the far wall. That was enough, instinctively, to tell Earl where the man behind the shadow was standing, and he spun around the half wall without breaking stride.

He saw the revolver before he saw the man holding it, jerking his whole arm upright, just as the man pulled the trigger. The deafening roar blew air through Earl's ears and rained ceiling plaster downward. Earl punched the gunman in the face with his free hand, then hit him a second time for good measure. He noted a mustache below a pair of ice-blue eyes already glazed over, as the man slumped down the wall he'd crashed into, his shiny, pressed suit squeaking the whole way.

Earl stuck the revolver, the kind the British army used, in his belt and handed the kerchief he always carried in the event of a dust storm down to the man, whose nose was currently gushing blood. "You FBI? Did J. Edgar Hoover send you?"

The man looked up at him, his eyes coming back to life. Earl anticipated any number of things happening next, though not what actually did.

While holding the kerchief firmly against his nose to stanch the flow of blood, the man extended a hand upward to shake Earl's. "Captain Henry Druce, British Special Air Service," the man said in the thickest British accent Earl had ever heard. "Nice to meet you, Ranger."

Earl sat in a stiff-backed fabric chair, facing the couch on which Henry Druce sat, currently easing his ID wallet back into his pocket. The vinyl material was stiff beneath him and Earl thought he spotted the tag from a local furniture store still protruding near one of the couch's arms.

"So I guess this means the FBI didn't send you," Earl told him.

"You mentioned Mr. Hoover in particular," Druce said. "Might you have crossed paths with him already here in your state?"

"At the scene of a triple murder in Hearne on the grounds of one of the German prisoner-of-war camps we got here in Texas. But I'm guessing you already knew that."

"And what would be the basis of such an assurance?"

"Can't say. It's what my gut told me. What my gut isn't telling me," Earl continued, "is whether your presence is connected to Abner Dunbar's murder."

Druce's face flashed genuine surprise. "Dunbar was murdered?"

"Unless he cut his own throat and then managed to hide the knife, he sure was. In Austin at the Driskill Hotel, where the pipsqueak J. Edgar showed his face again."

Druce nodded, processing the new information Earl had just provided. "And this hotel, would it be in reasonably close proximity to the camp in question?"

"Austin's the only city in spitting distance and the Driskill is the first choice of many who visit the city." Earl leaned forward. "That was your turn, now it's mine. What's a captain in the British SAS doing in Texas on the trail of a murdered man on Standard Oil's payroll?"

"The same thing as you, I fully expect, Ranger: chasing criminals, though quite a bit different ones in my case."

"How'd you get in?" Earl Strong asked him.

"I picked the front door lock."

"Never my strong suit."

"So I gathered when I heard the glass break."

"You saw me coming?"

Druce nodded. He was a dapper-looking man with a neat mat of helmeted hair—the same color as his mustache—plastered to his scalp. His skin was pale and Earl recognized his eyes, now that they weren't glazed in pain and shock, as a gunman's or, in this case, a soldier's.

Captain Henry Druce kept the kerchief pressed against his nose, as he resumed. "I heard your truck first. It alerted me somebody was probably coming."

"So here we both are, in what looks to be the temporary home of a dead man. I'm here because the cut across his throat matched the cuts that killed the three bunkmates of an escaped German prisoner named Gunther Haut. That name mean anything to you?"

"Not in itself, Ranger. It's Abner Dunbar I tracked here to Texas."

"All the way from England?"

"Me, yes. But Mr. Dunbar hails from Chicago. He is, in fact, employed by Standard Oil in their international department, specializing until a few years back in a specific country."

"Don't tell me," Earl said, leaning back again. "Germany."

"You weren't actually in the war. Would I be correct in that assumption, Ranger?"

Earl nodded, slightly embarrassed by the question he got a lot, as if he'd let down the country while remaining in Texas. "I got so much shrapnel in me already, Captain, I figured others could share in the wealth. And I believe you're suggesting Abner Dunbar is a German spy, bought and paid for by the Third Reich. Have I got that right?"

"In a manner of speaking, yes"

"What manner would that be exactly?"

"A spy, to me, implies someone who infiltrates an army or government in order to steal secrets. That doesn't describe how the late Mr. Dunbar earned the money deposited into a Swiss bank account at all."

"What does, Captain?"

Druce pulled the now sodden kerchief from his face and touched his fingers to his nose to make sure it had stopped bleeding. "We need to back up a bit first."

"How far?"

"I was speaking figuratively."

"I'm about as good at speaking that way as I am with picking locks, so I'd rather you just lay it out for me."

Druce continued checking to see if his nose was still bleeding, and returned Earl's kerchief to his nostrils when he saw it was. "The war in Europe is effectively over, and Germany lost. I say it that way, because it's inevitable, and the smartest and most cunning Nazis are planning for that inevitability by circling the wagons, to use American vernacular, and racing to preserve their most vital human assets."

Earl smiled and shook his head. "Now that's a mouthful."

"It also explains my job, which is to prevent that from happening."

"Keep the Nazis from preserving those vital human assets."

"That's right." Druce nodded. "I'm the commanding officer of something called Operation Loyton. Its purpose is to track down Nazis, many of whom are already in the wind."

"But not all."

"No, not all."

"And I'm also guessing that some of these vital human assets ended up in American prisoner-of-war camps. Say, Gunther Haut, for example."

Druce nodded again. "You're a smart man, Ranger."

"Smart's got nothing to do with it, Captain. The director of the FBI shows up from Washington and now here you are all the way from England. Even a dumbass ought to be able to figure out neither one of you would've come all this way for our great weather."

"It is a touch hot, I must say."

"Summer's coming. You ain't seen nothing yet."

Something changed in Druce's expression, Earl figuring he was seeing the man's core for the first time. "Oh, I've seen plenty, Ranger, and I wish I could forget plenty of it."

"Doesn't work that way, though, does it?"

"No magic bullet I've been able to find yet."

Earl stood up to stretch a bit and remembered Druce's revolver was still wedged through his belt. He eased it free and handed it back to him.

"Yeah, well, Captain, in my estimation a bullet's only good for one thing anyway. And we were talking about how it is that Operation Layton brought you to Texas."

"A small number of these high-value assets, as we're calling them, are currently interred in several prison camps across your state. We believe it was Abner Dunbar's job to make contact with them and, whenever possible, facilitate their release."

"You mean escape."

Earl watched Druce hedge for the first time. "It's political."

"What is?"

"War, to begin with. Ever read von Clausewitz, Ranger?"

"Can't say that I have."

"Von Clausewitz once wrote that, 'War is regarded as nothing but the continuation of state policy by other means.'"

Earl didn't bother to pretend he understood a word of that. "I'd like to get back to what brought you to the United States, if we could."

"I just explained that."

"Sure, about how this now-deceased Dunbar fellow was responsible for taking care of these high-value Nazi assets, some of whom are currently interred on Texas soil. But only one of them, Gunther Haut, murdered three fellow inmates and then proceeded to kill the man you're suggesting to me was supposed to be helping him. You want to tell me how that jibes with your thinking, Captain?"

Druce shifted uncomfortably on the couch. "I can't. I didn't even know Dunbar was murdered, until you told me. And I'm taking you at your word that Gunther Haut was responsible."

"Don't take my word, take the evidence. Identical means of killing and a trail of clay dirt that stretches between Hearne and Austin."

"Clay dirt?"

"Common in the drier, more desolate areas of the state. Hearne isn't all that, but it's enough, and I found traces of the same clay dirt in Dunbar's hotel room in Austin that I spotted at the prison camp. Which begs the question, Captain, why Haut would kill a man in business to help him."

"I have no idea."

Earl Strong leaned back and crossed his legs. "I believe you do, sir."

"Do you take me for a liar, Ranger?"

"I didn't say that. There's a big difference between a lie and an omission. So I guess I'm calling you an 'omitter.'"

"I don't believe there's such a word."

"Being *omitted* from the dictionary doesn't make it so."

"In any case, I've told you everything I'm able to."

"But not *everything.* I'm going to venture a guess here, so feel free to stop me if I stray too far off base. I think Gunther Haut is what brought you to the United States as part of this Operation Loyton of yours. I think somebody, the late Abner Dunbar probably, got word to him you were headed this way on his trail. That may well have been what spurred his escape."

Druce hadn't stopped him, but neither did he confirm Earl Strong's suspicions. Just sat there on the couch, looking like he was ready for tea to be served, or whatever it was Brits like him drank.

"And where do the murders of his three bunkmates fit into your scenario, Ranger?"

"I think Haut was afraid they'd figured something out about him. He wanted to make sure neither you, nor somebody like me or J. Edgar Hoover himself, had anyone to tell us what that was."

"Then why kill Dunbar?"

Earl crossed his arms and leaned back in his chair, nearly tipping it over. "I'm going to let you take a shot at that one, Captain."

"I truly have no bloody idea."

"Yes, you do. You've got a whole lot of ideas you don't want to share with me, for whatever reason. I figure you know something about Gunther Haut that explains pretty much everything that's happened in the past twenty-four hours."

"Suspicion isn't the same thing as knowledge, Ranger."

"No, but you've got to start somewhere, and it's suspicion that brought you across the Atlantic, because there's something more important here to your operation than back home to catch all those important Nazis who otherwise might slip through the cracks, once the war ends."

Druce rose stiffly. "Gunther Haut cannot be allowed to slip through the cracks. You need to trust me on that."

"You're not giving me a whole lot of reason to, Captain."

"I will as soon as I'm sure, Ranger. You have my word."

Earl rose, too, and extended his hand, the two men shaking. "Then it looks like we've got ourselves an understanding, and maybe even something of a partnership. I can help you with the lay of the land and keep your presence here secret from J. Edgar Hoover by running a little interference."

"I'd appreciate that," Druce said.

"But I'd be cautious, if I were you. See, I've got to figure Hoover knows the same thing you do, or he wouldn't have come down here on Haut's trail, either. And he was already en route to Texas before he could possibly have learned of the murders, which tells me that it's not a killer Hoover's after, it's something else."

"Any satisfactory conclusion as to what, Ranger?"

"No, sir, not yet," Earl said, shaking the life back into the hand with which he'd shaken Druce's. "Guess I'll just wait until you're ready to tell me. In the meantime, what do you say we search this place to see if we can figure out what this Abner Dunbar was really up to?"

44

SAN ANTONIO, TEXAS

Captain Tepper had fired up a fresh Marlboro Red by the time he finished, Caitlin watching it burn down toward the halfway point.

"My granddad never told me that story," she said, "not even a part of it."

"I'm sure he had his reasons."

"You don't know them, even now?"

"He never said, and I gave up asking, Ranger. He and Captain Henry Druce must've come up with something, anyway. I checked Druce out in the years that followed. He took this Operation Loyton to France next, where he and his SAS team were supposed to meet up with leaders of the French Resistance to help find the Nazis he was looking for. But they had the misfortune to parachute into the Vosges Mountains at a time when the German army was reinforcing the area. Most of Druce's team got captured, and he ended up the hunted instead of the hunter. He died in 2007 at the ripe old age of eighty-six, after winning the Distinguished Service Order for his heroic actions operating behind enemy lines."

"Which, apparently, included Texas."

"Your granddad never had occasion to tell me what happened next. But I'm going to hunt down the rest of that story, if it kills me, Ranger."

Caitlin watched him stamp out his cigarette just past the halfway point in his ashtray that looked the size of a small tire. "It'll have to get in line, D.W."

"Speaking of which," Tepper said with a frown, but left it here.

"Speaking of *what*?"

"Should I be worried about you?"

Caitlin eased her boots off the front edge of his desk. "No more than usual."

"But there's nothing usual about this particular case, is there?"

"You already pulled me off it, Captain."

"Even though you were never on it to begin with, so excuse me if I take no solace in whatever you assure me on the matter. I'd tell you this is one you really need to keep your distance on, if I thought you'd listen. So instead I'm going to suggest you have a talk with somebody far better schooled in such things than a moth-eaten log like me."

Caitlin stiffened. "And who might that be?"

"A kind of specialist."

"As in a psychiatrist, a shrink?"

Tepper's expression remained uncharacteristically flat and noncommittal. "We've got one on staff now. What's the harm?"

"This an order, D.W.?"

"Just a suggestion at this point."

"At this point," Caitlin repeated, as if that might make more sense of Tepper's meaning.

"I never worry when you go off half-cocked, Ranger, because I know sooner or later you're going to hit what you're aiming at and whatever it is deserved to be shot. But this is different. It's not about insubordination, or living in another century by your own rules, or embracing the notion of the old-style lawman. It's about a terrible thing that happened to you and never got resolved. The sore's been festering ever since and now the bandage has been stripped off. That already got one man shot and I don't want you launching any more harpoons at this white whale of yours that has resurfaced after eighteen years."

"But that's not why Jones warned me off Kelly Ann Beasley, is it?"

Tepper shook his head. "That had nothing to do with you or the girl, or the assault she suffered at the hands of the same attacker who assaulted you. It's all about her father."

"Her father?"

"Beasley isn't Kelly Ann's real last name. I don't know what her real last name is, because her father's a whistle-blower placed in Homeland's version of witness protection, after he detailed a certain Fortune 500 company's ties to unsavory Third World governments."

"Holy shit," Caitlin could manage.

"The man's got assassins looking for him across the entire planet, and you ran roughshod into his life, threatening to tear the cover off everything."

"This doesn't change the fact that Kelly Ann *whatever's* rapist is still out there," Caitlin reminded.

"And, even if you catch him, the girl's circumstances make it impossible for her to get involved. Chances are Jones will have the whole family out of Texas once he finds a new place to stash them. Hard to prosecute a case without a victim, Ranger."

"There's another victim, Captain," Caitlin told him, "in case you've forgotten."

45

"We really have to wear this shit?" Armand Fisker wondered, squeezing his hands into latex gloves while the surgical mask dangled from his throat.

David Skoll looked up from the bench where he'd just pulled similarly disposable plastic booties over his shoes. "We can't risk contamination of any kind to the production line."

Night's fall beyond had done nothing about the sordid humidity roasting the air. Fisker had learned the meaning of truly oppressive heat during his own brief stretch in Huntsville before a witness mysteriously recanted his testimony. As luck would have it, his seven-year-old son disappeared after being dropped off at a school bus stop. That night, the man found a jewelry box with a boy's severed finger inside. Turned out that the finger was clipped off another boy waiting to be embalmed at a local funeral home, but it did the trick by making the appropriate point.

Fisker nodded grudgingly toward Skoll, and sat down to fit his booties on, too. "Nice of you to finally show me the place, given that I got as much stake in it right now as you do. Hey, I see you already got your teeth fixed. I'd like you to send me the bill. Least I can do for going off on you the way I did. I've been dealing with a heavy load of shit, and something happened yesterday that just put me over the edge. I took my shit out on you, and I owe you an apology for that. It won't happen again."

"I appreciate that," Skoll said.

Fisker waved a finger at him, half flippantly and the other half in reproach. "As long as you don't cross me."

He left things there, enjoying the fact that Skoll had no idea how to take his comment.

"Is this where you make the wonder drug?"

"I'd hardly call it a wonder drug."

"It is to me, and right now that's all that matters."

"Yes, it was made here until production was suspended."

"Clinical trial, that's what you called it."

Skoll nodded. "Lot U-two-five-seven-F," he said. "We would've marketed it under the name Axiol."

"What's that mean?"

"I made it up."

"And if this Axiol, Lot whatever, had worked, how much would you have made?"

"Personally?"

"Say it any way you want."

"A billion dollars over ten years."

"In your pocket?"

"In my pocket. At minimum."

Fisker pulled on the elastic of his surgical mask, ready to fit into place. "And how hard would it be to start production up again?"

They walked amid the fully automated machines, spread over nearly four acres of space. Their steady hum pushed a hollow feeling through Fisker's ears. Made it feel like there was something crawling around in his head that was exacerbated by the *thwack* of pills being pressed into patches of foil and the *smack* of the identifier codes being stamped onto hundreds of pills at a time by what looked like alien typewriter keys. There was also the thud of shipping cartons being placed on pallets by automated forklifts, to be righted when necessary by robots towering over both of them that paid neither he, nor Skoll, any heed at all.

"Looks like we got more in common than I thought, Davey," Fisker said through his surgical mask.

"Really?"

"I use the same kind of pallets for my pills and weed. I'll show you the whole operation when you come to visit Elk Grove. Every bag I ship through my biker gangs is logged and bar-coded. Anything comes back for reasons like incarceration or damage, I charge a restocking fee, just like Walmart."

Fisker watched Skoll pretend to be interested, not giving a shit.

"Before the good Lord dropped you into my life, Davey, I was getting most of my pills from north of the border, via the Hells Angels. Given that they practically run the nation of Canada, there wasn't much room for negotiating the bikers' own particular exchange rate. So I bought a meatpacking company, just so I could hollow out sides of beef and pack them with vacuum-sealed packets of cash. Refrigerated trucks cross the border without anybody looking twice, and come back the same way with pills tucked into the beef, instead of money. Great system, but the deal we got working beats it to hell."

Fisker and Skoll kept to the aisles, lined and retrofitted to the specifications of the rolling man-sized machines that needed to negotiate them. Fisker watched another of the humanlike things fixing a machine that was supposed to stack boxes. A malfunction had snagged the line that promptly started up again under his eye, the robot that towered over him rolling past him, on to its next task.

"And to think, Davey, we got this failed clinical trial of yours to blame for an association between us that's about to expand big-time. How many people dead so far thanks to this Axiol?"

"Just under two hundred."

That drew a grin from Fisker. "Man oh man, that makes you a mass murderer, a gen-u-ine serial killer. How is it you're not behind bars already?"

"It was a double-blind study conducted over the entire country, the test subjects assigned numbers to replace their names. I'm the only one who knows their names. And since they're scattered over a number of states, it's not as bad as it seems."

"Oh, it's bad all right," Fisker told him, "it's super bad—for these subjects anyway. But for me it's Christmas come early. It's fucking Santa Claus leaving a present under my tree that's sure to keep on giving for a long run of time. And you can manufacture Axiol as a pill, powder, liquid, even an aerosol, right?"

"The aerosol is a heavier lift," Skoll told him, sounding stiff and unsure, staying just out of arm's reach on the chance that Fisker decided to punch him again. "But we can produce the drug in any form you want."

"God works in mysterious ways, don't he, Davey?"

"You're not asking God to give you the power to kill millions of people, Arm, you're asking me."

Fisker kind of liked the fact that Skoll was having one of his morally superior moments, a breath's-length belief that he was the one holding the power. Fisker let him enjoy it just long enough to remind the kid what his life had been like before Fisker had become his de facto business partner. Let him get a sense of the way the world used to work for him, so it would hurt even more when the realization that those days were long gone struck him anew. Fisker liked seeing weakness on people's faces even more than pain, and weakness looked especially good on those used to wielding strength like a jackhammer.

"Who says I'm gonna kill anybody, Davey?" Fisker resumed, after he'd let Skoll's comment linger just long enough. "You just said how God works in mysterious ways. Well, I do, too. And what you accidentally came up with in those research labs of yours can help me along a bit. Man who carries around an unloaded pistol is an idiot. I'd like to know I've got some fresh ammo I can load, if I ever need it."

"In case you've forgotten," Skoll said, "I just got professionally reamed by a congressional subcommittee that's laser focused on my business dealings. They even asked about the same clinical trial you're interested in."

"For different reasons, obviously."

"I can skirt my way out of all these insider trading and market manipulation charges, Arm. But I won't be able to skate on a slew of deaths that will inevitably be connected to my wonder drug that's not so much of a wonder."

"It is to me, Davey, it is to me."

Skoll said something in response, but Fisker didn't hear him, too busy sidestepping to clear a path for one of the automated forklifts. It was lugging boxes, stopped by its sensors when they recorded his presence.

"We pull this off," Fisker continued, "and your debt is paid in full. Hell, I'm even gonna cut you in for a percentage of the profits once we're square. No need to thank me, Davey. What are friends for?"

46

Elk Gove, Texas

Armand Fisker had lost track of time. It was almost nine o'clock when he finally climbed behind the wheel of his truck for the drive back to Elk Grove. The latest spate of good fortune was just what he needed to relieve the pressure he'd been feeling. His father might have been one of the most feared men on the planet at times, but he'd never taken a fist, strap, or belt to his son, not even once.

Here he was, though, knocking out a business partner's teeth and pouring gasoline on his own son in less than a single day's time. He needed to get a handle on his emotions, start holding them in check. His son Ryan and Davey Skoll were different sides of the same coin, entitled and privileged sorts holding onto their respective daddy's coattails, heritage to blame for any success they had achieved and likely ever would. Fisker didn't feel bad for giving Skoll a beating that had separated him from a couple teeth, but he hadn't felt right about what he'd done to his boy, even while he was doing it. The whole thing felt sour, his actions as much to deflect from his own sense of failure at raising his son right. Kid should be by his side, helping to run things by now. Instead he was smoking weed and rousting illegals.

It was a day, though, for apologies. First, Fisker had come as close as he could to telling Davey Skoll he was sorry for knocking out a couple of his teeth. Now he needed to do similarly with Ryan. Fisker decided on a grand gesture, in search of redemption as well as a relationship. So, reaching the outskirts of Elk Grove, he settled on telling Ryan he was going to have the repairs on his truck taken care of, sparing the boy of the need to slave away at the impossible task for someone unfamiliar with body work.

The garage door was closed, and Fisker hit the button to open it as soon as he pulled into the driveway. Already mapping out what he was going to say to his son, he saw the garage was empty, both Ryan and his dented-up truck gone.

47

Guillermo Paz sat at his priest's bedside at the Menger Springs Senior Living Community. The side rail had been lowered so he could feed the man his dinner consisting of watered-down oatmeal the texture of drilling mud to make it easier for him to swallow. Paz was the only one who could get him to eat anything at all, convincing himself that Father Boylston could still grasp the meaning of his words, even if he could no longer respond to them. Strange that he hadn't even known the priest's name until Father Boylston had been brought here after suffering his stroke.

"I want to believe in miracles, Padre," Paz said as the old man worked his mouth feebly and then managed a swallow. "I want to believe I'll walk in here one day to find you back to your old self again, at least enough to keep me on the straight and narrow like you used to. But we have to face the fact that maybe the doctors are right and the damage was too severe to hope for any improvement at all."

Paz dabbed the spoon into the bowl of soupy oatmeal and eased it forward. His priest opened his mouth a crack and sucked up the meager contents with a slurping sound.

"I know you can't talk to me anymore, Padre, but you can still listen and that's almost as important. Because if you get tired of living like this, and want to meet God on a personal level, find a way to give me the word and I'll help you out. I've sent more people with the Ferryman up the River Styx than I can count, but never somebody who asked me to punch their ticket for them. But if that's what you want, just say the word, so to speak, and you'll be walking and talking wherever it is you're headed."

The old priest finished working that spoonful down his throat and opened his mouth for the next. His once bright eyes were dull and lifeless, his thinning white hair flattened to his scalp in some places and sticking up askew in others. The room was laced with deodorizing spray to hide the stale scents of bodily waste and dried, scaly skin wracked by bedsores. Paz detested injustice of all kinds, but this seemed like the ultimate one. For a man who'd given his life to others to have his own snatched from him this way.

"Blink twice and I'll know you understand what I'm saying and that you're ready to go check into a different zip code. When I killed the man who killed my priest back home in the slums, I did it up close and personal. I even used the same knife he did, and I wanted it to hurt. But death doesn't have to hurt, and sometimes life is a lot more painful. The philosopher Rousseau wrote that 'Man is born free, and he is everywhere in chains.' So blink twice if you want my help getting those chains off you, just like you helped me shed mine."

Paz watched his priest swallow the latest spoonful without blinking twice. He realized Father Boylston's lips were trembling in anticipation of more oatmeal, and he quick readied the next spoonful. Scooping too much up for the old man to manage and needing to shake some of it back into the bowl, Paz watched the old man swallow and then waited again for the two blinks, relieved when they didn't come.

"If you change your mind, Padre, the offer still stands. I'm glad you're not ready yet, because I need someone to talk to like this, even if you can't talk back. You know how I always get those feelings before the bad times come? Well, I've got another one. Different from all the others, but just as bad. That's why I needed to see you, because I was there when a body shop got raided today and all these illegals got hauled away. Government officials hoisted open this big bay door, and all I saw beyond it was darkness. Then the darkness burst outward and, for a moment, swallowed everything before me. But it's not just the darkness that got out, Padre, it was something hiding inside it. Whatever the nature of that evil is, it's loose now, and I know I'll be seeing it again, probably soon. Only this time I'll be ready."

48

"You're still shaking, Cort Wesley."

"That's what breathing the same air as Armand Fisker will do to you, Ranger."

"Dylan coming home?"

"I think he's staying at a friend's house."

"And you let him?"

Cort Wesley took another sip of the Freetail Brewing Company's Original Amber Ale that had become his favorite and wrinkled his nose at the taste, leading Caitlin to tip her bottle of Hires toward him.

"Maybe you should follow Leroy Epps's lead, like me."

He laid the bottle down on the porch floor and leaned back in the swing, rocking it slightly. "It's lukewarm. How long have I been drinking it?"

"A half hour, maybe."

"That explains it."

"But not why you're letting a lowlife like Armand Fisker get into your head."

Cort Wesley looked at her in the spill of the porch light that splayed the shadows of the nearby juniper bushes across Caitlin's face. "You run him through your system?"

She nodded. "Just the boilerplate stuff at this point. I'm thinking I need to get more detailed, maybe go have a talk with him myself."

"The man might be a lowlife, Ranger, but he's got his own town and who knows how many bikers and other assorted dregs of humanity doing his bidding. Did I tell you my dad crossed paths with his in Huntsville?"

"Cliven Fisker, founder of the Aryan Brotherhood," Caitlin recalled.

Cort Wesley tried his beer again "Foundation of everything Armand Fisker has built today. But what does a man need his own town for?"

"The McMullen County sheriff, Darnell Gaunt, fancies himself a true nineteenth-century lawman, right down to letting the local outlaws buy his loyalty. Rangers have crossed paths with him on numerous occasions. We've hauled him into federal court a bunch of times for various violations of the criminal code, mostly involving the treatment of illegals in his county. I think he's still appealing four cases."

"Takes a lot of money to do that, Ranger."

"And now we know where it's coming from." Caitlin held the old-fashioned root beer bottle in her lap. "You want me to take a run at Fisker?"

"As in an official visit?"

"Define official, Cort Wesley."

"The kind where you shoot him if he doesn't cooperate."

She took another sip, revealing her bottle had gone lukewarm, too. "Wishful thinking. What about letting the whole thing go?"

"You're forgetting about Dylan's part in this. He hasn't been right since we took on ISIS in Houston, like he's standing on some kind of edge. We handle this wrong, maybe he goes over. He's blaming himself for those illegals getting hauled in. We don't do something, I'm worried he will."

"In other words, you're worried his fuse is burning again."

"It's like he's on some kind of cycle. Maybe it's the moon."

"The moon didn't create the assholes he's come up against," Caitlin said, and blew into the top of the Hires bottle, making a whistling sound.

"Leroy Epps does the same thing," Cort Wesley noted.

"Maybe he taught me."

"Nothing surprises me anymore, Ranger."

She slid closer to him. "How about I call Jones about these illegals, see if there's anything he can do to intervene?"

"Maybe Paz could deputize them."

"They know how to shoot an assault rifle?"

"They know how to chop a car. How about some clerical work?" Cort Wesley asked lightly, guzzling a hefty gulp of beer as if the taste had returned.

"Only clerical work the colonel requires is somebody to fill out all the death certificates he generates."

Cort Wesley looked away, then back at her, Caitlin noticing the muscles in his neck were flexing. "I can't believe I'm thinking this. . . ."

"Thinking what?"

"Asking Paz to deal with Fisker."

"I can't believe it, either."

"I'm worried about Dylan, Ranger. He's not going to let this go. He ends up forcing the issue with Armand Fisker's son, cleaning his clock or worse, what do you think Fisker does?"

Caitlin felt herself stiffen. "This goes to guns, whatever Fisker's building in Elk Grove will have to contend with the whole of the Texas Rangers, Cort Wesley."

His face was caught in the jittery spray of headlights, and Caitlin followed their origin to the driveway, where Dylan's 1996 Chevy pickup rumbled to a halt, bleeding oil and gushing tar black smoke from its tailpipe. The engine sputtered before shutting off altogether, Dylan closing the driver's door gently behind him and heading stiffly up the walk with his hair bouncing in a halo around him.

"Why are the two of you looking at me like that?" he asked, stopping between them and the front door.

"Glad you came home," Cort Wesley said to him, his words sounding like he was reading someone else's line.

Dylan stopped just short of reaching for the latch. "Maybe I just need to pick up a few things, so you can stop babysitting me."

"What's that supposed to mean?" Cort Wesley shot back, Caitlin laying a hand on his knee to keep him calm.

"A truck followed me a good part of the way home. Doesn't the big guy have anything better to do with his time?"

Caitlin felt Cort Wesley's leg harden under her grasp, and then lifted her hand off when he started to rise. "I think we better sort this out, son, because that truck wasn't—"

A barrage of gunfire swallowed the rest of his words, the line of windows over their heads blown out as all three of them hit the porch floor.

49

Pistol already in hand, Caitlin scanned the front yard, locking on dark shapes silhouetted against the night. She put the count at four, though it could've been five, Cort Wesley already answering their fire, which peppered the railings, blew out more windows, chipped divots from the shingle-like siding, and took out the dangling light fixture, sending it crashing downward.

"Stay down!" he cried out, when Dylan started to push up with his hands.

"I'm getting the shotgun!" the boy rasped back to him, dragging himself closer to the front door.

"I said, stay down!" Cort Wesley tried again.

Caitlin fought to collect her thoughts, measuring the enemy force by the concentration of their fire and muzzle flashes flaring in the night beyond. Dylan was crawling forward, and she stretched out a hand to restrain him, but he shook it off and kept pulling himself along.

"Goddamnit!" Cort Wesley wailed between his own shots, his anger aimed at his son.

"Four or five?" Caitlin called to him, just loud enough for Cort Wesley to hear over the fire she'd added to his.

"Five, by my count. They're firing full auto. Lousy shots."

"Lucky for us."

"Stay where you are, son!" Cort Wesley blared, stealing a glance back at Dylan, who'd just reached up for the front door latch when a blistering volley blew divots out of the wood. "What did I say?"

"Cort Wesley," Caitlin started.

"Cover me, Ranger."

And she watched Cort Wesley launch himself up and over the railing in a single fluid motion that drew a fresh concentration of fire from beyond.

Caitlin emptied the rest of her SIG-Sauer's magazine and snapped a fresh one home. Ratcheting a round into the chamber and opening fire again from her prone position, she smelled the combination of chipped lumber and gun smoke. An earlier round taking out the porch light had proven a godsend in that it enabled her to better spot the motions of the dark shapes before her converging on the house. Cort Wesley had been right; there were five. She fired to hold them at bay and give them something to think about more than anything. And the hesitation in their fire, accompanied by the wild sprays that followed, told her gunfights had likely not been in their vocabulary until tonight.

She encountered that a lot with an assortment of bullies, mob lackeys, and gangbangers who know only how to wield overwhelming force against those who couldn't, or didn't, fight back. The failure of their initial ambush would normally have made these kinds of gunmen flee. The fact that they were still firing away was a testament to their determination, but also to their stupidity.

Caitlin started in on aiming for her targets. She glimpsed one pitch sideways and then go down, uttering a cry that sounded more like a boy's than a man's.

Ryan Fisker...

A picture of a truck with him behind the wheel, packed with his fellow tough guys barely college age from Elk Grove, filled her mind, right down to the dents left by the bricks tossed by Guillermo Paz.

Crack!

She thought it was another gunshot at first, then felt the surge of chilled air surging out from the house through the door Dylan had crashed through to grab the twelve-gauge shotgun from its spot. Kept within easy reach ever since a different set of gunmen had killed Cort Wesley's ex-girlfriend, his mother, Maura Torres, and would have killed Dylan and his younger brother, Luke, too, if she hadn't been there.

Caitlin rolled under the porch swing, bettering her position, when the first of the flaming Molotov cocktails crashed through the house's windows.

Cort Wesley caught the first gunman, poised beyond the cover of an old elm tree straddling his and his neighbor's yard, in his sights. The back of his mind recorded the distant blare of sirens in the same moment a sliver of moonlight peeking out from the clouds revealed this shooter to be no older than Dylan. A lumbering blob of a shape barely contained by the substantial width of the elm tree's base.

Cort Wesley wanted to shoot him but couldn't. He looped around the yard instead, the front porch aglow with flame bursts that had erupted from inside his house.

Just kill him!

He heard the words in his head, not from Leroy Epps, but the same disembodied voice he'd first heard in Iraq during the Gulf War. He hadn't even known Leroy then and could only imagine what the ghost of his old friend would have to say about Cort Wesley gunning down a kid whose M16 trembled atop the tree branch upon which he'd rested it.

Cort Wesley came up from behind the kid and hammered him hard in the soft, vulnerable part of his head certain to knock him out. He felt bone recede on impact, the nine-millimeter's butt seeming to dig through his skull like a shovel. The kid, who smelled like fast-food onions and grease, didn't go down, but pitched forward, his face smacking a tree branch that kept his unconscious frame propped up on his feet.

One down, he thought. *Old Leroy would be proud.*

But then Cort Wesley heard heavy, untrained feet pounding across the grass, automatic fire spraying the air above him when he hit the ground, steadying his pistol.

Caitlin was down to six shots, maybe five. Her nostrils clogged with the clashing scents of gasoline, burned fabric, and nitrogen-rich fire-extinguisher foam. She pictured Dylan inside the house, abandoning the shotgun in favor of putting out the flames set by the Molotov cocktails crashing through the windows. The boy faced again with an unimaginable assault where he should've been safe. The last time, only Caitlin's intervention had saved him. Tonight, there was a shotgun, soon to replace the fire extinguisher she could hear spraying throughout the first floor.

She wondered which of the shapes scurrying beyond belonged to Ryan

Fisker. She knew she'd wounded one of those who'd accompanied him so far, but couldn't spot his shape or any other right now amid the hazy glow of the LED streetlights over the yard. That all changed when she saw a shape rushing Cort Wesley's way, trying to balance an assault rifle, and letting loose with a wild torrent of fire that was as likely to find Cort Wesley as not.

Caitlin sighted in, about to pull the SIG's trigger when it looked like somebody yanked the world out from beneath her target.

Cort Wesley had fired twice while still rolling, the kid going down as if a hole had opened under his feet. He thought he detected a blood burst from the kid's skull, the air turning misty red in his mind's eye.

He twisted around, still churning over the ground, close to a gore-strewn patch where whatever had blown out of the dead kid's skull had landed. Two more of them were converging on the porch, seizing an opening, unleashing twin fusillades of fire that spilled planters, took out the wind chimes hanging alongside the door, and exposed pocks of wood beneath shattered siding. He tried to discern Caitlin's shape as he sighted in on them, yanking back on his trigger to take one in the leg and maybe back with at least one of the three shots. Sighting in on the second, when fresh fire sliced up the ground around him, coughing grassy divots into the air and filling his nose with the scent of the fertilizer he'd laid the week before.

50

Shavano Park, Texas

Dylan's nostrils were on fire, scorched by a combination of smoke, heat, and the blowback from the corrosive chemicals raining out of the fire extinguisher nozzle. He sprayed without restraint, where there were flames flaring and where there weren't, the hot night air hitting the conditioned cool of the house like a ram.

He didn't realize he'd discarded the drained extinguisher until he heard it clang to the floor and then launch into a noisy roll. He looked down to find the twelve-gauge Remington he'd picked out with his dad the day after Cort Wesley Masters had moved into the house in his grasp, with similarly no memory of having hoisted it from its perch by the door.

It felt heavy, as heavy as it had all those years ago when he'd held it in the store for the first time. Like he was thirteen again, half expecting a reflection of that boy's face to look back at him when he crossed before a still whole window that blew out under a fresh burst of gunfire, just after he'd crossed it.

Dylan started to drop to the floor, but caught himself halfway and kept moving toward the front door, still open part of the way. He'd held guns before where the possibility of squeezing the trigger was very real, most recently just the other day in East San Antonio, but never with the foreknowledge that he was going to fire. Pulling the shotgun's trigger was as certain in his mind as using the fire extinguisher's nozzle to douse the flames kicked up by the exploding Molotov cocktails.

He knew it was him the gunmen had come for, the same kids, no doubt, who'd been chased off by the hail of bricks sent raining down upon them by Guillermo Paz the other day. He'd wondered up until that moment if he were truly capable of firing the pistol he'd been holding low by his hip. But Dylan held no such doubt tonight about firing the big shotgun his hands squeezed tight.

The thought he was about to kill somebody filled his mind and choked off his breath, as a surge of heat blew into him and he shouldered the front door all the way open.

Caitlin had heard the first boy cry out, then spotted him rolling back and forth on the grass, screaming as he tried to reach around for a spot in his buttocks. It was like listening to a baby's cries, the same sound she recalled coming from the kid one of her initial shots had winged, and she had to remind herself such innocence stopped there. This boy and the others had followed Dylan home with assault rifles at the ready, military grade tuned to full auto. That was the ticket they held and now it was getting cashed.

Or so she tried to remind herself, so as not to consider they were still kids.

A second shape, taller and more athletic, stumbled up the stairs, likely as unnerved by the downed boy's horrible wails as she was. Caitlin had two bullets left in her SIG, but wasn't going to shoot him. Planning to use the fact that the kid seemed oblivious to her presence to jump him. But then Dylan appeared in the doorway behind the twelve-gauge's gaping barrel, the kid's M16 leveled straight for him. Dylan was about to die in the very same spot where his mother had fallen dead the day she'd saved his and his brother's lives.

Not on her watch.

Caitlin felt the breath catch in her throat as she fired. Her first bullet took the kid in the side of his neck, one hand jumping to the wound while the other clung to the trigger. All this recorded in the pause between heartbeats, as she fired again and blew a wash of blood, bone, and brains through one side of his skull and out the other.

The force of the bullet threw him back and to the side, crashing through the porch railing and dropping into the garden Cort Wesley had begun lovingly tending below, crushing his latest plantings that had just sprouted their first petals.

"Dylan!" she yelled out.

But he was already past her, streaking down the stairs into the blackness of the yard and the sight of Cort Wesley pinned down under an onslaught of fire.

Cort Wesley made it to the cover of the tree, his ears ringing from the constant percussion of the bullets clacking around him. He dropped behind the thickest part of the base, adjacent to where the lumbering tub of a kid was still propped up unconscious, bark spitting around him from the constant spray of automatic fire.

Cort Wesley lurched out to sight down on the shooter, just as a spray of bark lifted under a fresh fusillade of fire, either a bullet graze or wood shard stinging Cort Wesley's wrist and sending his pistol flying.

Damn!

He hadn't faced down all manner of lowlife and miscreant these past few years to get gunned down by a punk only tough enough to roust illegals who couldn't fight back. And if he went down, that would bring the off-spring of Armand Fisker, a waste of sperm if ever there was one, that much closer to Dylan. He thought of his own father, Boone Masters, dying alone and unloved in a hospital bed, a man he'd never truly known until years later after far too much time had passed for it to truly matter. He wasn't about to let Dylan and Luke grow up that way. Having missed the early parts of their lives, he had no intention of missing the rest of them.

There had to be *something,* because there was *always* something.

He just had to find it.

The kid in the tree still had his M16 shouldered, held to him by its strap, and Cort Wesley twisted toward him. He heard the clack of an ejected mag hitting the ground. The snap of a fresh one being slammed home greeted him just as he lunged to his feet, twisting toward the assault rifle firmly in his sights slung from the fat kid's shoulder.

Cort Wesley got it up and leveled between the tub of lard and the tree itself, hit the trigger before the oncoming kid hit his.

Click.

The gun was empty.

Caitlin rushed down the stairs in Dylan's path, stopping just long enough to scoop up the wounded kid's M16. Lifting it from the ground when he grabbed her leg, more reflexively than defensively, his terrified eyes begging for help, for something.

Caitlin tried to kick herself free, but his grip wouldn't give, locked onto her like a flex cuff in desperation and terror. She finally knocked it off with the butt of the M16, swinging toward Dylan when she heard the shotgun's roar.

Dylan recognized the kid as the driver of the big black pickup he'd confronted outside the body shop where his father had gotten him a job. The kid wasn't looking at him, never even noticed him, too busy righting his mean-looking assault rifle at something else:

His father.

Dylan remembered the most frightened he'd ever been in his life, waking up screaming from a nightmare at the age of six. His mother rushed in and all Dylan could do was blabber on about a dark figure with a sword knocking on his window, wanting to get inside so he could take him away the way he'd taken a classmate who'd been killed in a traffic accident.

"The Green Ripper, Mommy!" he wailed. "The Green Ripper wants me, too!"

Dylan had slept with the lights on for weeks, barricading the window the "Green Ripper" had been tapping on. No one understood the source of his fear, because it wasn't the Green Ripper he thought was coming for him; it was the *Grim Reaper.*

Death itself.

And now death had returned, minus the scythe and black shroud, death in the form of the kid standing before him about to kill his father.

Dylan had heard about moments where time froze up solid, but never believed it was actually possible until that moment. Time just stopped. The world wasn't moving, the kid wasn't moving, his M16 wasn't moving.

Only Dylan was moving, the Remington twelve-gauge in concert with him. He never remembered pulling the trigger, never recorded the muzzle flash exploding from the bore. All he remembered was the kid blown backward off his feet, arms splayed to the side like they were wings flapping, before he hit the ground soundlessly to Dylan's ears that had been deafened by the blast.

Had he fired once or twice? Had he fired at all? Was this just another bad dream?

Then someone was taking the shotgun from his grasp and he saw lips mouthing, *Dylan, Dylan, Dylan,* but he still couldn't hear and recognized nothing around him, as he sank to his knees in his father's grasp.

PART SIX

Captain R. A. "Bob" Crowder transferred to the Ranger force from the DPS Bureau of Intelligence in 1939. In 1955 the inmates at Rusk State Hospital for the Criminally Insane rioted and took hostages, giving Crowder a chance to live up to the "One riot, one Ranger" legend. Alone, Crowder walked into the maximum security unit to meet with the leader of the riot. The two men exchanged words, and within an hour, the riot was over and the hostages were freed. Before Crowder agreed to enter the building, however, the Ranger talked to the lead inmate on the phone and informed him that, although he was coming in alone, he would have a Colt .45 on each hip. "I want to tell you one thing," said Crowder. "I'm not comin' in unarmed because you've already got three people over there as hostages and I don't want to be the fourth one—and I'm not going to be. I just want to tell you this. If somethin' goes amiss, I know who's going to fall first."

—"Lone on the Range: Texas Lawmen" by Jesse Sublett,
Texas Monthly, December 31, 1969

51

SHAVANO PARK, TEXAS

"Well, Ranger," Captain Tepper said, a Marlboro at the ready in his right hand, "this is one royal mess."

Caitlin looked at him from the top of the porch steps where she'd sat down, hoping to quell the queasiness in her stomach. The feeling was a mix of nausea and the worst indigestion she'd ever had, sometimes rotating between the two and sometimes roiled by both at the same time.

"I killed a kid tonight, D.W.," she said, looking down again. "I never even saw his face. I killed a kid I wouldn't even recognize if his ghost walked right up to me."

"Would looking him in the eye have changed anything?"

"I'll never know, since I didn't get the chance."

Tepper sat down next to her on the top step and took off his hat. "Nobody's tougher on you for that loose trigger finger than me, Ranger. But if there's another way this could've gone down tonight, I can't see it. Sometimes you force the issue—that's true enough. But tonight the issue forced you."

"I still killed one kid and put two bullets in another."

Tepper had never appeared more grim and dour, the look of a man holding an entire lemon in his mouth having claimed his expression. He gazed out toward the last two dead bodies being loaded into the coroner's wagon under Doc Whatley's supervision. Shavano Park police department detectives had listened to Caitlin's story and were still listening to Cort Wesley's, while the techs continued taking measurements and an overall inventory of the crime scene.

"What do you suppose the combined ages of the three victims were?" Caitlin asked him.

Tepper started to lift the cigarette toward his mouth before changing his mind again. "I'd rather count up the expended shells from all the rounds they shot off. You mentioned they were firing on full auto. You want to tell me how kids no older than my grandchildren can get their hands on that kind of firepower?"

"Real hard to believe, being that this is Texas and all."

"They're illegal in this state, too, Ranger."

"Then I imagine that's a question for the father of the boy Dylan shot to save Cort Wesley: Armand Fisker."

"Not a conversation I'm looking forward to having," Tepper groused.

He finally lit up the Marlboro and took a long, deep drag. Beyond them, the endless array of flashing lights sprayed a kaleidoscope of color about the street. Cort Wesley was still being interrogated separately by Shavano Park detectives and sheriff's department deputies inside the house, explaining why Caitlin had staked a claim to the porch in case things got out of hand there. Something that could easily happen when five gunmen show up to kill your son.

Just as fast as he'd started the cigarette, Tepper dropped it onto the step even with his boot and stamped it out. "From where I sit, the three of you are gonna come out of this just fine."

"At least I won't have to see the face of the kid I killed every time I close my eyes for a while."

"Do yourself a favor, then: don't read the papers or watch the news tomorrow." Tepper looked down at the ruined cigarette, as if to wish he hadn't stamped it out. "You talk to Dylan yet?"

"There wasn't a lot of opportunity, given that neighbors had already called the Shavano Park PD and they showed up not more than a minute later."

"He didn't see the body?"

"Captain?"

Tepper's expression looked genuinely pained from trying to mince words. "What that shotgun did to Armand Fisker's boy."

Caitlin shook her head.

"You're going on administrative leave, effective immediately," Tepper said abruptly.

"Say that again."

"With pay," he added.

"And that's supposed to make me feel better?"

Tepper rose to his feet and laid a boot on the second step, his knee on that side creaking as he leaned in toward her, pain from more than his arthritis spreading across his features. "This is different than the other shootings, Ranger. You know that as well as I."

"Even though I'm going to come out of it just fine?"

"This one's sure to get political, drag every enemy you've made over the years out from the woodwork. And that's a long line, if I need to remind you. Especially since Willie Arble, the man you shot in Stubb's the other night, has filed suit against the Department of Public Safety."

"You can't be serious."

"The suit alleges excessive force and there's a school of thought already brewing that he's got a good case."

"I thought he was a rapist, D.W."

"Tell it to the judge, as they say," Tepper said, before his voice took on a cautionary tone. "On second thought, better not, because that would make your history part of the story here, who you were really shooting at when you plugged Arble."

Caitlin let his remark stand.

Tepper took off his Stetson and held it against his side, releasing the sweet smell of the Brylcreem he still slathered into his thinning hair every single day, making it look pasted to his scalp except for the patches that took less kindly to his hat. "History's not your friend in this case, Ranger," he resumed.

"I'm going to find the man who raped Kelly Ann Beasley, Captain."

"You mean, the man who raped you."

Caitlin pushed herself to her feet. "Guess the ending to that movie somebody wants to make about me isn't written yet, is it?"

Tepper turned his gaze over the flood of activity that continued under the spray of police floodlights and the spots blazing into the eyes of the bevy of news reporters going live from the scene with the best rendition of events they could assimilate. "Since it's your story, Ranger, you can bet it'll be bloody."

He'd barely finished his sentence when a distant roar reached a crescendo, and turned deafening. Caitlin swung with him to the head of the street where an endless parade of motorcycles sped forward, enclosing an armada of SUVs and pickup trucks.

Tepper peeled back his jacket to expose his .45. "Like I was saying."

52

Shavano Park, Texas

The roar of motorcycle engines drew Cort Wesley from inside the house, along with the Shavano Park detectives who'd been interrogating him, reaching for their guns as well.

Cort Wesley stopped just behind Caitlin and Captain Tepper. "Armand Fisker and friends, no doubt," he said, smelling of the ash and char leftover from the fires started by the Molotov cocktails inside the house.

"You visited his home, Cort Wesley. I guess he's returning the favor."

Shavano Park police officers had confiscated their firearms, along with the Remington twelve-gauge, as evidence. Caitlin had backups inside her SUV parked in the driveway, but didn't figure the local cops would take kindly to the notion of her getting into a second gunfight in the same night. But she and Cort Wesley moved toward the street anyway, watching the convoy stop on a dime, the bikers making no effort to disguise either the long guns they were wielding or pistols holstered to their belts.

A passenger door on the lead truck opened, and Armand Fisker dropped out, instantly in motion and shadowed by a good portion of the army that had accompanied him here.

"Where's my son?" he cried out, steam blown from his mouth with the words that split the stone-cold silence of the night. "Where the fuck's my son? You hear me over there? I want my son's body!"

Captain Tepper cast Caitlin and Cort Wesley a gaze lodged somewhere between a scowl and a frown. "Two of you better hang back to keep this from going to guns."

Caitlin ran her eyes across the lawn, taking note of cops both exposed and having taken cover behind anything they could find, all with pistols drawn and ready. Twenty guns at most, maybe, against as many as sixty. And pistols versus assault rifles to boot, for the most part. But there were three other Rangers on scene now, in addition to her and the captain, which provided some cause for hope if things turned bad.

She watched Tepper move through the assembled officers from various law enforcement bodies and stop fifteen feet from Armand Fisker in the spill of the headlights streaming from both trucks and motorcycles.

"Mr. Fisker, I'm Captain D. W. Tepper of the Texas Rangers and I'm mighty sorry for your loss."

"Where's my son?" Fisker raged, storming forward into the same spill of light that had captured Tepper. "You give me my goddamn son!"

"I'm sorry, sir, I can't do that. His body's already been hauled away."

"Where?"

"That's a police matter, sir. If you and me can talk, I might be able to—"

"I'm not talking to you, I'm not talking to anybody! If I got something to say, I'll let my bullets speak for me, until I get my son back."

Tepper stood there rigidly. "That's not going to happen right now, much as both of us might want it to. You want, I can take you to him, sir, but it's got to be just the two of us."

"Sure, so you can gun me down the way he was gunned down."

"Sir, he was firing a fully automatic M16. We've found two expended magazines we believe came from it, meaning he fired sixty shots before he went down. You want to explain how that makes him a victim here?"

"Who shot him?"

"That's under investigation."

"You're a Texas Ranger, true old-school. So why don't you just hand over the shooter to me and we'll call it even?"

Caitlin watched Tepper take off his hat and flap it against his side. The Brylcreem he'd slathered on made his hair appear shiny in the spill of the streetlights, but her angle made him look like a single David facing an army of Goliaths. She thought back to the times of her father and grandfather, wondering how many times they'd found themselves standing up against the kind of crowd Tepper was confronting now.

"Nothing can make this even, sir, after the loss you've suffered," he said, his voice echoing slightly in the still night air. "But that doesn't mean making it worse is the way to go, either."

Fisker gazed past Tepper toward the yard and the police, Rangers, and sheriff's deputies, all with guns drawn, dotting the lawn. "Why, I'd bet he's around here right now, maybe inside that house. So what's it gonna be, Captain? You gonna give the shooter to me or am I gonna take him?"

Tepper made sure Fisker could see his hand close to the old-fashioned .45 he still carried. "Stand down, sir."

"How many of us you think you can get with that dinosaur of a gun?"

"One is all I'm thinking about right now."

Fisker nodded, as if processing the information. "I'll bet it was the pansy ass, Mexican-loving punk that did the deed. Kid who drew down on my boy and vandalized his truck the other day. You telling me my boy didn't have the right to get a little payback?"

"Not packing fully automatic weapons he didn't, Mr. Fisker. You want to explain to me how your son and his friends acquired the military-grade M16s they brought along for the ride? Seems like a lot of firepower to get a little payback. More like they were going to war."

And they lost, Caitlin thought to herself, feeling naked without a weapon and finally starting to backpedal, with Cort Wesley, toward her truck and the weapons tucked inside a locked spare tire compartment. Her father always said it was better to have a spare gun instead.

"Here's what we're going to do," Tepper was saying to Armand Fisker.

"You're gonna get back in your vehicle and drive off with your friends, and I'm going to watch you do it."

"Is that a fact?"

"One way or another."

Fisker looked down at the street, then up again. "I already lost a son tonight. I don't have much else to lose."

Caitlin could see where this was going, the inevitability of it. The sense of it felt like a thick fog settling over the scene. Starburst firecrackers about to shoot out of Fourth of July cannons. She had an AR-15, a shotgun, and two extra pistols in her SUV. Enough to make the odds better, but still not very good.

That's when she heard a roar almost as loud as the one the biker convoy had announced itself with, ahead of an ash-gray pickup truck with massive oversized tires blazing onto the scene from the other end of the street behind a blinding floodlight array. Tearing across lawns and plowing over trash cans and mailboxes, en route to spinning to a screeching halt between Tepper and Armand Fisker on the street.

Caitlin watched a dark torrent of gunmen in flak jackets and tactical gear pour out of the truck's bed in a stream equal to the flood from a clown car. They positioned themselves fearlessly before Fisker's army in a semicircle, with M4 assault rifles steadied before them. This as the driver's door opened and the massive shape of Guillermo Paz emerged, wielding twin M4s that looked like toys in his grasp.

The bikers froze at the sight of the sudden and formidable threat before them, their surly confidence draining with the breath misting before their mouths. Caitlin expected Paz to do any number of things in the next moment, from chasing Fisker and his men off with a spray of fire over their heads to providing a philosophical backdrop on the error of their ways.

"¡Vete!" he ordered flatly instead, his voice knifing through the night air. "Leave!"

A moment of hesitation followed, no sound but the trees shifting in the breeze and the blare of a television through an open window nearby. Then a motorcycle engine flared to life, followed by a second, and a third. Ultimately, it grew into a roar Armand Fisker had to shout over for Captain Tepper to hear him.

"This isn't over, Captain! Not by a long shot!"

Tepper stood silent and stiff, as Fisker headed back to his truck amid the flood of motorcycles swinging around and tearing off around him.

53

Shavano Park, Texas

"How'd you know, Colonel?" Caitlin asked, drawing even with Paz's huge shape.

He kept his focus trained dead ahead, turning toward her only when the engine sounds faded out in the distance. "Jones thought you could use my help."

"Jones?"

"And it looks like he was right," Paz said, fixing his gaze forward again, as if Armand Fisker's biker army was still there. "He told me the boy killed one of the attackers."

"It was Armand Fisker's son," Caitlin nodded. "Dylan saved Cort Wesley's life."

Paz turned all the way to look at her directly, his eyes sad and his expression long. "Sophocles' message in *Oedipus the King* is that all heroism is ultimately tragic. He questions to what degree we can actually succeed at doing the right thing without paying a price for it. Even if we do everything right, in Sophocles' mind, act on the best information available and with the best of intentions, we are still bound to be haunted by what we do in pursuit of good. Because sometimes in doing good, it's necessary to unleash the dark side that can never again be chained."

Paz's statement brought Caitlin's thinking back around to the kid she had killed, and then to the lawsuit filed against her, indirectly, by Willie Arble.

Could she have handled things a different way in Stubb's? Did she really have to shoot him?

"I don't know any other way of dealing with animals, like the ones we just saw, when they're off the leash, Colonel," she said, forestalling the need to answer those questions.

Paz nodded once. "George Orwell once wrote that 'People sleep peaceably in their beds at night only because rough men stand ready to do violence on their behalf.' But that speaks nothing about the effects on these so-called rough men. Nietzsche and Schopenhauer both believed that violence, once embraced or resorted to, is not easily shunned."

"Like for you, Colonel?"

"And you, Ranger." Paz turned back to the street, his stare utterly blank, his next words spoken so quietly they were almost lost to the night. "I saw the darkness again today, before I heard from Jones. I knew something was coming."

"Well, it came."

Paz turned his head slowly. "This is just the beginning. The fuse has been lit, the true nature of this darkness to reveal itself only once it burns down."

"That's what I'm afraid of, Colonel."

54

SHAVANO PARK, TEXAS

"One of us needs to talk to Dylan, Cort Wesley," Caitlin said, when the activity finally began to die down, save for a number of media personnel who seemed prepared to camp out to get the full story.

"I was thinking both of us. You know, double-team him," Cort Wesley said, not bothering to hide his discomfort over doing it alone.

"You remember the first man you killed?"

"It was more of a boy, and so was I at the time. He pulled a knife, tried to rob me and the girl I was dating at the time. I stuck it into him, as she reached into her handbag."

"You ever see her again?"

"Turned out she was reaching for a thirty-two caliber she kept in her bag. If I hadn't killed the kid, she would have. But, no, I never saw her again. Her father found out who I was and didn't want his pristine daughter associating with a criminal."

"Your father was the criminal."

"The girl's father failed to see that distinction. How about you, Ranger?"

"A junky who was holding a tour group inside the Alamo at gunpoint."

"You shot your first man *at the Alamo?*"

"I came in to negotiate. He wasn't in a talking mood. I didn't have a choice."

"You didn't have a choice tonight, either, Ranger."

"It show that much?"

"That kind of pain is hard to disguise, but it'll pass."

"I'm not so sure of that," Caitlin told him.

"Someone real smart once told me it's not the person you shoot, it's the gun."

She shrugged. "Easy to make pronouncements like that when I'm not aiming at anybody."

"What are we supposed to tell Dylan? How are we supposed to help him get through this?"

"How'd he look to you, Cort Wesley?"

"Normal," he said, gazing back toward the house where detectives were finishing up their questioning. "That's what scares me. I don't want this to just run off him. I want it to hurt. I don't want him to think that because it's okay for us to gun down people for the good, that it's okay for him, too. And Paz is right: this isn't over, Ranger, not by a long shot. Armand Fisker isn't the type to let bygones be bygones."

Caitlin watched the detectives emerge from the house. "How about we go have that talk with Dylan?"

55

"This was all my fault," Dylan said, seated at the edge of his bed. "And don't try to tell me it wasn't."

Caitlin stood on the left of him, slightly closer than Cort Wesley, who stood on the right. When Dylan kept his gaze fixed downward, she let her stare linger on him. For some reason Caitlin had expected him to look different, as if the ordeal had changed him in some way. Instead, though, he looked younger and more vulnerable, time rewound back to his fifteenth birthday or so. His hair hung over a large measure of his face, smelling of musk and oil, the room itself smelling sour and stale, as if he'd dragged the ugliness of what had happened inside with him.

"You ask those punks to terrorize illegals?" Cort Wesley challenged. "You ask them to talk wise and strut their guns after you inquired about their presence? You ask them to come here tonight and fire over a hundred rounds our way? You didn't ask them to do any of those things, the way Ryan Fisker asked for a bullet tonight."

Dylan snapped his gaze upright. "You think I don't know that? You think I'm sitting up here regretting what I did?" He shook his head. "Not for a minute," the boy insisted adamantly, though the cracking of his voice and tears welling in his eyes said otherwise. "I'd do it again in a heartbeat, and I would've shot him again if he didn't have the good sense to die." Sounding less convincing now, as if he were reading lines that someone else had written for him. "You wanted me to go back to school," Dylan said, clearing his throat to try and stop his voice from cracking.

"I wanted you to do what was best for you, son."

"And if I'd gone back to school, none of this would have ever happened."

"That's not entirely true," Caitlin said, interjecting herself into the conversation. "Fisker and his posse would still have terrorized those illegals; there just would've been no one there to stand up for them."

"But they'd still have jobs, wouldn't they? ICE wouldn't have up and arrested them all. And the three kids who got killed here tonight would still be alive."

"So now you're feeling sorry for them, too?"

"I don't feel sorry, I don't feel bad. I just feel stupid." Dylan's eyes moistened again, and he swiped a sleeve across his brow, sniffing as he turned to Cort Wesley. "I'm going back to Brown next semester, in time for summer football camp."

"That's good, that's real good," Cort Wesley told him.

Dylan looked back at Caitlin, sniffling again and wiping his nose this time. "How much trouble am I in?"

"You'll have to ask Coach Estes about that."

"I'm talking about tonight, I'm talking about...what I did."

Caitlin sat down on the bed next to him, fighting the urge to wrap her arm around Dylan's shoulder and reel him in against her. "We got something called the Castle Law in Texas, and under its tenets, you're free and clear. Beyond that, you were acting in clear defense of another on your own property. Did I mention this was Texas?"

Dylan looked past, more than at her, as if unsure Caitlin was there at all. He looked even younger, dating back to the first time Caitlin had seen him, standing at the front door of this house with his mother's body lying at his feet.

"I never even realized I was doing it," he said, in that boy's voice. "I don't remember pulling the trigger."

Cort Wesley checked his phone. "I'm going to try your brother again at his boarding school in Houston. I want him to hear about this from me before he sees it splashed all over the internet."

56

"He doesn't know what to say to me," Dylan said to Caitlin, after Cort Wesley was gone.

"Neither do I."

Dylan puckered his lips but didn't blow out any breath this time. "You come closer." He turned to look at her. "Should I feel bad? About what I did, I mean."

"You mean, killing somebody who was about to do the same to your father? I remember something my first instructor at the police academy said about turning the other cheek, besides that it was bullshit. He said that it was as much of a sin to let yourself be hit, as it was to strike another. Biblical teachings and misplaced morality for its own sake belong to people who are already lying dead on the ground. If you let somebody kill you because you feel it's wrong to kill him, who's really to blame for you dying?"

Dylan gave her a long look. "Are you asking me?"

"It was more of a rhetorical question. Maybe I was asking myself as much as you."

He ran a couple fingers through his hair. "How long's it gonna hurt the way it does now?"

"That depends on whether you feel you had a choice or not."

"I didn't."

"That's right. Your dad would be dead now otherwise. You want to tell me how you'd feel right now, if you didn't fire?"

"I feel like I got hit by a truck."

"Beats a twelve-gauge shell, Dylan," Caitlin said, realizing she was trying to convince herself of the very same thing.

57

ELK GROVE, TEXAS

Armand Fisker stood on the roof of the town hall building, one of the few structures still whole when he took over Elk Grove. Its original corrugated tin roof that held the day's heat like an oven remained in place. Right now, Fisker felt he was standing in a sauna, as much from the heat flaring inside him as out.

He'd deal with recovering his son's body tomorrow; nothing else he could do now but stew in his own thoughts. The fact that Ryan had disobeyed him, the fact that the boy's behavior had drawn attention to his work and presence here, the fact that the boy had led his posse of morons to exact violent revenge for no more than showing him up, were all rendered insignificant in the face of the boy's death. Everything was rendered meaningless.

His own father, Cliven Fisker, hadn't let prison stop him from building a nationwide organization based behind prison walls like the ones he'd die within. That loose, patchwork amalgamation of the Aryan Brotherhood prison gangs had formed the basis for everything Armand Fisker had built outside of such walls. Now, standing on the town hall roof and looking over a world of his own creation, he could only think of the metaphorical ones that were closing in on him.

Picturing his son lying on the ground and taking his last breath choked Fisker up. He wished he could have cried, but it seemed he'd forgotten how. The boy who'd done the shooting, Cort Wesley Masters' kid, had to die; there was no doubt about that. And he would, along with the war hero and the Texas Ranger, because that was the way things were done, even though Fisker knew that would provide only a small measure of satisfaction.

Fisker wished he could unleash Davey Skoll's accidental creation on them all. Let the sons of bitches go out that way: weak, helpless, and shitting their pants when their intestines failed, along with all their other organs. Even getting all of them, though, wouldn't be enough to still his pain. He needed to make a mark that extended far beyond Texas. He needed to do something that would swallow the likes of Caitlin Strong and Cort Wesley Masters.

They represented order.

Fisker represented chaos, a chaos from which he and others like him could emerge stronger than even their wildest dreams suggested. Not just in America, Fisker insisted to himself, *everywhere.*

That thought sent Fisker back to his office, where he switched on his computer and used the instructions taped inside his top desk drawer to log on to the Dark Web. The message he sent to a dozen associates around the world represented a call to arms of sorts, a means to vastly expand their power, influence, and thus, their revenue.

Money, after all, was power.

From the infamous Walls prison in Huntsville, his father had eventually forged chapters of the Aryan Brotherhood in prisons across the world. Though small in design and intention back then, those chapters had morphed into much larger movements beholden to Armand Fisker today that owed their origins, in large part, to what Cliven Fisker had built. The chapters went by a variety of names now, much of the funding that supported their more politically driven efforts stemming from control of the drug trade in their respective countries. They could call themselves anything they wanted, but the fancy titles were just another way of saying Nazi. In Austria, it was the Freedom Party; in Germany, the National Democratic Party; in France, the National Front.

All of them had eyes on far more power than they currently wielded, and which Armand Fisker now had the capacity to deliver. The means to bring on the chaos they longed for, the chaos that would allow them to take control of their countries. And he wanted to share the means to do that with others who thought as they did, cut from the same cloth as he was. Fisker had never personally formed a political thought in his life, but found the notion of chaos, of civilization spinning off its very axis, just what the world, and he himself, needed right now.

But not this way, not via email no matter how secure the Dark Web might be. No.

His message would provide scrambled instructions to head to Texas immediately for a meeting. A bunch of men joined by the same goals, values, and concerns in the same room for the first time. Christmas was coming early for them, because Armand Fisker would come to that meeting bearing gifts. In his mind, the definition of a criminal was a businessman who thrived on chaos. And, after tonight, more than anything he wanted to rain chaos down on the world.

Starting here.

In Texas.

58

AUSTIN, TEXAS

"You didn't have to come all this way to thank me for sending Paz last night, Ranger," Jones said to Caitlin, looking up from behind his desk.

He hadn't risen when she walked in unannounced, just kept rotating his gaze between a trio of wall-mounted televisions tuned to each of the major news stations. Caitlin noticed the office was bathed in murky lighting, in spite of the blazing morning sunshine, because Jones chose to keep his blinds drawn as a deterrent against snipers.

He gestured toward the televisions. "You made the news again."

"Tell me how excited I look about that."

"Blowback?"

"Let's just say I'm here today in a less than official capacity."

"You need a job, Ranger?"

"More like my head examined, if I ever even consider that, at least on a permanent basis."

"Interesting qualifier."

Caitlin looked around at the surprisingly elegant furnishings and walls filled with Texas-centric prints, paintings, and photographs. "You got an office like this in every state capital, Jones?" she said, changing the subject.

"Just here, where I seem to spend the bulk of my time."

"I need a favor."

"You mean, besides the one I did for you last night?"

"What do you know about Armand Fisker?"

Jones's office was located in the same gleaming office tower as *Texas Monthly* magazine a few floors up at 816 Congress Avenue, directly across from the state capitol building. It was a simple suite of three offices and an adjoining conference room, with a reception area Caitlin doubted was ever staffed, just as she felt pretty sure the other two offices remained unoccupied, despite being furnished. Jones's considerably less than aboveboard dealings kept him from working out of the J.J. Pickle Federal Building, which would've been more appropriate for his job description, if he'd had a real one.

"You didn't come all this way to ask me that."

"Pretend that I did."

Jones leaned forward. "I did my share of reading about him both before and after last night."

"Why before?"

"You think your cowboy boyfriend was the only one the colonel gave the license plate of the truck he bashed up?"

"This in anticipation of the insurance claim against Homeland, Jones?"

"Paz might be your guardian angel, but he answers to me."

Caitlin tried not to laugh, but a chuckle emerged anyway. "Yeah, keep telling yourself that."

"He didn't show up last night because of that psychic connection he's got with you, he came because I sent him."

"After you read up on Armand Fisker. What can you tell me about what Homeland has on him in the system?"

"He's not really on our radar."

"His goddamn father established the Aryan Brotherhood from behind bars, and word is Fisker has built that into a nationwide drug distribution network, from coast to coast. And he's not on your radar?"

"Exactly." Jones nodded. "Drugs are the concern of other government agencies."

"You don't see drugs as a Homeland Security issue?" Caitlin felt her temperature start to rise. "But let's look at this another way. You know the only thing harder than uniting Israelis and Palestinians, Shia and Sunni Muslims, or Democrats and Republicans? Biker gangs, Jones. And, from what I've learned, Fisker has the Cossacks, Bandidos, Hells Angels, and a dozen or so smaller offshoots eating out of his hand. I'd call that an enemy force operating on American soil. Homegrown terrorists even."

"What else would you like to know about Fisker?" Jones asked her, instead of responding.

"Anything about him that stands out, makes you raise an eyebrow. Something like him appropriating an entire abandoned town for his own use and declaring himself the law."

"That town's taxes and fees are all paid up, all their paperwork has been filed with the county seat on time and aboveboard, and he's got the politicians doing his bidding because he's opened a perpetual campaign fund to serve the election needs of anyone he wants to buy."

Caitlin couldn't help but shake her head. "And none of that riles you?"

"You rile me, Ranger, but that doesn't make you a threat to Homeland Security."

"About that job opportunity at Homeland . . ."

Jones rose and moved around to the front of the desk where he sat back down leisurely on its edge. "Uh-huh."

"Given my administrative status with the Rangers, I need a new portfolio to hang my hat on for a time."

Jones pointed at her shirt. "You're still wearing your badge, Ranger."

"It comes with the wardrobe."

"And if somebody you need to question happens to notice it . . ."

"I'll let them draw their own conclusions. But I wouldn't mind introducing myself as a liaison for Homeland Security."

"Is that the career change you're looking for?"

"Has a nice ring to it, don't you think?"

"I think you'd be working under me. How's that sit with you?"

Caitlin smiled. "I don't want to ever find myself under you, Jones, but I need a calling card while my membership in Club Ranger is suspended."

Jones grinned back at her, even broader. "Maybe you should've thought of that when you disregarded a direct instruction I gave you."

"You mean about a sexual assault victim whose family is hiding out in Homeland's version of witness protection? Did it even occur to you to just tell me that, instead of playing your usual game of pin the tail on the asshole?"

"There are policy lines even I won't cross, Ranger. It comes down to weighing the family's overall safety versus the investigation of a crime."

"Kelly Ann Beasley was raped, Jones."

"And she can't identify her attacker."

"Neither could I," Caitlin said, too abruptly to consider her own words.

"This isn't about her, it's about you," Jones said, trying to sound as sensitive as he could. "You'd risk endangering Kelly Ann's safety to catch the man who assaulted you."

"Assaulted both of us," Caitlin corrected.

Jones gave her a longer look. "Kelly Ann didn't remember anything about her real attacker, when you talked to her?"

"She thinks it was a woman."

"Whatever that means."

"I can't make any sense out of it, either."

Jones's teeth began sawing at his upper lip. "I wish I could give you some leeway with this, Ranger, but I can't risk putting that family in any more danger."

"I understand, Jones, just like I would've understood if you'd laid it out like that for me to begin with."

"Best I can do is make you a duly appointed and official contractor for the Department of Homeland Security. How's that?"

"Good for starters."

"Starters?"

Caitlin moved a step closer to him, more of the light from the recessed ceiling fixtures finding her. "You ever hear the stories about prisoners of war from Nazi Germany being housed in Texas?"

"Over a hundred thousand at one point, I think." Jones nodded.

"Did you know J. Edgar Hoover came down here on the trail of one who escaped the camp in Hearne after killing three fellow POWs?"

Jones's brow crinkled. "Hoover himself?"

"That's right."

"Now, that's news to me. Quite a surprise."

"He butted heads with my grandfather, Earl Strong."

"That's not a surprise at all."

Caitlin let the moment settle between them, before resuming. "My grand-dad teamed up with a captain in the British SAS named Druce. Something about hunting down Nazis the Reich was determined to protect, so it could live to fight another day. Gunther Haut, that escaped prisoner I just told you about, was apparently one of them."

Jones clacked his still-spanking-new-looking boots against the desk. "If you know all this, what do you need me for?"

"Because all Captain Tepper knows of the story ends with my granddad and this Druce joining forces to get to the bottom of what was really going on. I was hoping you could run a check to see what Homeland's files have to say about the matter."

"Don't you want me to deputize you first?" Jones asked her.

59

Austin, Texas

It hurt to ask Jones for help, but it wasn't like Caitlin had a lot of choices, either. Outside, the heat offered welcome respite from the sixty-eight chilling degrees at which Jones kept his office thermostat set. The warm air vanquished the clamminess and dank feeling that had glued her shirt to her skin, but not the sense of heaviness and unease that came every time she relived that night from eighteen years ago.

It wasn't another game, as Jones suggested. It was the pure honest truth that she wanted as few people as humanly possible to know what had happened. Because sharing the story made her feel weak and vulnerable all over again, nothing like the Texas Ranger who was strong to the bone, at least in Hollywood's mind. She realized now more than ever that the one remedy for the chalky feeling that had returned to her mouth, along with the bad taste, was to catch the man who'd done this to her.

Otherwise, how many other Willie Arbles would she shoot? How many others had she shot already?

But catching the perpetrator promised to be no easy task by any stretch of the imagination, especially with no help coming from Kelly Ann Beasley. But Caitlin couldn't let go of this second chance to get the man who'd nearly destroyed her life.

As if on cue, her phone buzzed with a text message from Young Roger:

Some different looks for your suspect

She scrolled through fresh versions of the sketch he'd done for her, each providing a different "look" to the suspect's face, based mostly on hairstyle, length, and relative amount of loss. There were eight in all of the man she knew only as Frank, each providing a different sense of his potential appearance today.

Her phone buzzed with another incoming text from Young Roger, just as she finished her perusal of the shots.

And call Doc Whatley

Given her current status, Caitlin guessed Whatley would want no record of any call made, or email sent, to her. Having her call into his office offered Whatley insulation from the picture of insubordinate behavior contacting her might have suggested. The doctor covering his ass, just like everybody else did.

A skill I've never picked up, Caitlin thought to herself, as she touched the name WHATLEY in her contacts.

"I won't tell you who I am," she greeted, after he answered.

"Good," Whatley said back to her, "and I won't ask."

"I understand you've got something to share," Caitlin said, not bothering to add "with me" to insulate Whatley further from any issues that might arise from their still being in contact.

"Not over the phone and not at the office, either."

"What's this pertain to, Doc?"

"Those two bodies we hauled out of that apartment complex where a contagion of some kind was initially suspected. I found something in my analysis I think will be of interest to the Texas Rangers."

"How about Homeland Security?" Caitlin asked him, recalling Jones's mention of an unidentified drug showing up in the tox screens performed on the two victims. "Because I'm currently moonlighting. Unofficially."

"Well, Ranger, Officer, or whatever I'm supposed to call you, it just so happens what I've got to share might be of even more interest to them."

60

AUSTIN, TEXAS

Caitlin stopped off at a Staples store to make prints of Young Roger's sketches, figuring that was a lot more professional than jogging through the shots downloaded onto her phone. She had them printed on photo-grade paper to seem even more official, then headed over to Stubb's Barbecue.

Captain Tepper would be pissed at her for following up on a case without formal credentials, Jones would be pissed at her for continuing to search for Kelly Ann Beasley's rapist, and Doc Whatley was already pissed at her for not coming straight back to San Antonio. Maybe these new sketches would yield nothing more at Stubb's Barbecue than the original version had. What chance did she really have that a bartender, manager, bouncer, or member of the waitstaff would recall a single face among thousands? What chance was there that anything would stick out amid all that crowding, and overshadowed by the virtual riot that had broken out during the night's final hours?

But this wasn't about Jones or Tepper or even about being a Texas Ranger. This was about what had happened to her eighteen years ago. It was as if every criminal, terrorist, and madman she confronted from behind the cinco peso badge was the personification of the man who'd sexually assaulted her. Until she found him, the battles and the wars would just keep coming, because deep inside Caitlin wanted them to continue stoking the fires that had been simmering ever since that night.

She parked her SUV down the street from Stubb's Barbecue and stepped out, sketches in hand and Ranger badge still pinned in place. Let the workers in Stubb's draw their own conclusions; she'd deal with the fallout later.

Caitlin hadn't told Cort Wesley about her intentions and didn't want him tagging along, when Dylan needed him far more than she did right now. Not only might the boy be in very real danger from the long reach of Armand Fisker, he also would have to deal with the upshot of killing somebody with the insulation of shock soon to wear off, if it hadn't already.

No such insulation cushioned her from the reality that she'd killed a kid of Dylan's age the night before. And Caitlin wondered how much of her well-earned reputation for violence was owed to the night of her own rape. Were all the men she had killed no more than projections of the entity who'd hurt her in a way that would never heal entirely? Was her comfort with a gun no more than a defense mechanism rooted in her obsession to keep the world safe from men she was convinced were evil because she'd been unable to keep herself safe when it mattered the most?

Going to that party had been a mistake, not leaving when she lost track of her friends had been a mistake, taking that Solo cup from a stranger had been a mistake. And she'd been paying for those mistakes ever since, following her forebears into the Texas Rangers to hide behind a badge in order to quell the demons unleashed eighteen years before.

Caitlin wondered where those Hollywood producers had come up with "Strong to the Bone" as the title for her life story. She felt anything but that now. Her bones felt as brittle as the rest of her, ready to snap in a stiff wind or go soft and rubbery in a Texas downpour. She didn't want to be here. She wanted to be with Cort Wesley and Dylan, where she could help sort out the feelings that had besieged them, instead of facing her own.

She kind of hoped that Cort Wesley, or even Paz, would be waiting outside the entrance to Stubb's ahead, having figured on her making just this move and riding in to stand by her side. Caitlin liked that notion and the support that came with it. Maybe she was strong to the bone, but right now she needed propping up.

Neither of them were anywhere around, though, and she entered the restaurant alone and headed straight for the hostess whose name tag identified her as "Kim."

"You may remember me from the other day, ma'am," Caitlin greeted, after Kim had finished her phone call.

Kim's eyes went straight to her badge again. "Of course, Ranger. Sorry I couldn't have been more helpful. I hate hearing that something like that happened here. Well, anywhere really," she added.

Caitlin laid the manila folder containing the revised sketches she'd printed at Staples on the counter between them and opened it. "Me, too, Kim. Which is why I had some more work done on the sketch of the suspect to give us a few other options. I was hoping you could give them a look."

"Sure." The young woman nodded and started flipping through them.

Kim wasn't much more than Dylan's age, or the kid she'd killed last night. She wanted to tell her to be careful, to be alert when she walked to her car after her shift was over, to not trust a stranger's disarming smile or the contents of a glass he might hand her.

"Oh," Kim said suddenly, looking up and then back down at the face that looked shiny on the photo-grade paper. "This could be . . . It looks like . . ."

"Take your time, Kim."

She looked around to make sure none of the waitstaff was nearby. This time of the day, between lunch and dinner, was relatively quiet with shift changes and busboys prepping the tables for the coming dinner rush.

"I can't say for sure, but it looks like one of our bartenders." She angled the sketch so they both could regard it. "He's got a shaved head, just like this. Like I said, I'm not sure, but . . ."

"What's his name?"

"Doyle," Kim said. "Frank Doyle."

Frank, Caitlin thought, feeling something icy drag down her spine.

"When is Frank scheduled to work next, Kim?" she managed, teeth chattering a bit.

"He's here now, stocking one of the bars outside."

61

Caitlin went back outside through the entrance and walked to the end of the building, where an opening between it and the next one provided access to the large, flattened dirt patch where live music played on any of three stages. She spotted a sprawling bar straight ahead, already stocked and unmanned. But a tall, strapping figure wearing a denim shirt with sleeves rolled up to the elbows was raking at the dirt before the bar to cover a few stray puddles left over from a sudden downpour the previous night.

The figure's back was to her, giving Caitlin time to superimpose him against the man who'd handed her the Solo cup half-filled with punch eighteen years ago. She didn't recall that Frank being this tall or broad. But a man could change a lot over so many years, and she recalled him wearing sneakers, not boots like the pair he had on now, which could have accounted for a couple extra inches anyway.

Only one way to find out, Caitlin figured.

She approached him slowly, feeling her own boots crunching over gravel and dirt already dried by the sun.

"Mr. Doyle," Caitlin called when she was just close enough, continuing when he started to turn, "I was wondering if I could trouble you for a few minutes. I've got some questions about the other..."

Caitlin glimpsed the rake coming up and around, a mere instant before she recognized Frank's eyes. She realized he'd shaved his eyebrows as well, wondering if his baldness was due to illness instead of choice.

His chest muscles rippled as he swung the rake, Caitlin backtracking a single step and arching her spine, so its tongs whistled past her, spraying a thin fountain of dirt. She could have tried to pull her gun in that moment, but Frank bull-charged her, figuring he could overpower her with his size and brute strength.

In the flash of an instant, time rewound to reveal a slighter figure with long sandy brown hair and a charming smile that shined beneath his twinkling eyes, Caitlin smitten by his looks and his charm. The moment passed as quickly as it came, and she stepped to the side and kicked one of Frank's legs out. He stumbled on for a few steps, ready to fall, but he didn't right away, and when he did it was hard and face-first into the ground.

Caitlin could have drawn her gun then, slapped the cuffs on him, and gone about this by the book. But this might well be the man who'd stolen her sleep and haunted her dreams, a man whose actions had forever changed her life. How long was it before she could let someone touch her again? How long before she could be alone in the same room, or just share the same space, with a man without questioning his motivations and intentions? How long before she stopped believing that people, even strangers who met her gaze, could read her shame and embarrassment, looking into her eyes and seeing the ugliness that had penetrated her soul? How long before she got her life back?

She'd visualized this moment from her first day at the police training academy, the opportunity to face her attacker and look him in the eye, as she dispensed the payback she'd long thirsted for. And right now, more than anything, she wanted to hurt Frank Doyle, eighteen years of pain, heartache, and guilt finally boiling over.

Frank staggered back to his feet, eyes narrowed in surprise at the gun still holstered on her belt.

"Go ahead," she heard herself say, like it was someone else, "finish what you started. Go ahead and try."

He lumbered toward her, limping on the leg she'd swept out, with the look of a man who'd done some bouncing and so-called tough-guy work in his time, but not especially skilled or trained as a boxer or martial artist. He had six inches on her, though, and that reach counted for something.

Caitlin didn't wait to find out what. She lurched toward Frank Doyle, making it look like she was going to let loose with a flurry of blows with her hands, when she snapped her foot out and smashed his other knee from the inside.

Frank started to double over, then surprised her by lunging forward, and grazed her under the chin with an uppercut that would've knocked her silly, if it had hit full force. Still, it rattled her teeth and left both sides of her jaw feeling as if they were working independently of each other. He stormed her, Caitlin anticipating a body blow, but he bull-rushed her again instead, successfully this time.

Caitlin hit the hard, flat ground with an impact that shook her spine and stole her breath. She recovered her senses as Frank worked to straddle her, his face twisted in hate and exhaustion.

Just like he, or someone else, had eighteen years before. Mounted her like a dog in heat and had his way with her, while she lay dazed and unconscious.

Not this time!

Before he planted himself atop her, Caitlin got a knee up. Frank dropped straight onto it, making it less design and more fortune, but either way, she could feel his balls mash inside his jeans. He grunted and fell off to the side, already teetering on his knees, when Caitlin tightened her palm by curling the fingers over, and then slammed the heel of her hand into his nose, cracking the cartilage on impact.

Blood exploded from both his nostrils and Frank keeled over to the side. The gurgling sound that wheezed from his mouth made her think he was done, finished, and Caitlin reclaimed her feet. She'd lost her hat in the fracas and decided to retrieve it from the dirt between his downed form and the patch of ground he'd been raking.

Caitlin picked up her Stetson, flapped it clean, and turned back toward the man she couldn't vanquish all those years ago, but had today. Breathing hard as she fit the hat back upon her head.

Frank came at her again, the speed and power of the move springing out of nowhere. Caitlin went with it, propelled backward and stumbling over the discarded rake. The shadow of the bar overtook her, an instant before Frank's force projected her up and over the polished wood finish. Her splayed boots shattered a host of bottles and glasses, sent an entire shelf tumbling down upon her.

Caitlin looked up from the plank bar flooring, her shoulders propped up against a trash can, just in time to see Frank lunging at her with the jagged edge of a broken bottle. She deflected his first blow, then rerouted his second upward, drawing a nasty gash up his left cheek almost to the eye to match the blood still oozing from his nose.

When Frank jerked backward, recoiling instinctively, Caitlin grabbed hold of the metal trash can behind her in both hands and slammed it into his face. He pitched over to the side hard, Caitlin stumbling to her feet over him, as she discarded the trash can, now dented to the specifications of his face that was taking on a purplish glint from the swelling. Then she hopped back over the bar, retrieved her Stetson yet again, and laid her hands on her knees to get herself settled.

Caitlin heard a *plop* and watched Frank hit the hard ground after rolling off the bar's top. He made it back to his feet, first wobbling about and then listing from side to side, a small-bladed knife flashing in his right hand.

Caitlin moved her hand toward her SIG-Sauer in response.

"Gaw head, shoot me!" he raged, starting toward her unsteadily with both knees swelling up and seeming to bend inward.

Caitlin had as much of her breath back now as she needed. "That would be too easy," she said and moved her hand away from the SIG.

Frank spit out the blood that had collected in his mouth from his busted nose. The eye that had taken the brunt of the damage from the trash can was half-closed and his forehead looked vaguely simian shaped from the swelling.

"I don't even remember you," he sputtered, through the froth, drool, and blood oozing from his nose and mouth. "How's that make you feel?"

Caitlin backed off from him and sidestepped under the roasting sun. "But I'll bet you remember Kelly Ann Beasley from the other night, don't you?"

She continued to circle before Frank, getting him positioned just the way she wanted to. Let him poke and thrust at her a few times with the knife, blows she effortlessly avoided.

Why have I not shot him?

Because that would be too easy, just like she'd told him. Use her gun, shoot him here and now, and he'd be the winner, just like he'd been for eighteen years. Just like he was last night when she'd killed a kid and two nights before that when she'd shot Willie Arble.

Frank had recovered his footing, his knife starting to come dangerously close to Caitlin, when the sun hit his eyes. She watched him turn his head away and tuck his face low against the blinding rays. He probably never actually saw the blows she unleashed that pounded his solar plexus, ribs, and throat. Either way, Frank was standing and then he was lying on a heap on the ground, the old-fashioned switchblade separated from his grasp.

Caitlin kicked it aside, only then realizing the fight had drawn an audience of diners and workers from inside Stubb's, either through the window, out on the back deck extended from the restaurant, or having claimed a position on the hard-packed dirt for themselves.

"You lost, Frank," she said, twisting his hands behind him. "And you're under arrest."

62

ELK GROVE, TEXAS

"You sure this is a good idea, bubba?" the ghost of Leroy Epps asked Cort Wesley from the passenger seat of his truck. *"I mean, as I recall, things didn't go so well the first time we came out here and they can only get worse this time."*

"Sorry I forgot to pack your root beer, champ," Cort Wesley said to him, squeezing the wheel tighter.

Dylan was back home, under the watchful eye of Guillermo Paz. Cort Wesley had told the colonel he was driving up to Houston to pick up Luke. He was sure Paz knew he was lying but didn't care, since it was better than saying he was going to pay a visit to the man who'd raised holy hell in the street last night. Circumstances aside, he figured Armand Fisker had that coming to him, along with a message Cort Wesley wanted to deliver in person.

"Last night was a pickle, wasn't it?" Leroy resumed, peeking into the backseat to make sure there was no cooler packing root beer there. *"That boy of yours sure is a chip off the old block."*

"That a good thing or a bad thing?"

"Depends on your perspective. From where I be, right and wrong look distinct as black and white. Man can't hide his intentions or the contents of his soul from those of us on the other side. There ain't no gray."

"Where you going with this?"

"Your boy shares your soul, bubba. He's a gen-u-ine piece of work, an anachronism costumed as one of them rock and rollers that drives the girls crazy."

"Biggest word I've ever heard you use. Anachronism," Cort Wesley repeated.

"Don't try changing a subject you brought up. Your boy's a walking contradiction."

"And you think that applies to me, too?"

"You look in the mirror lately?"

"As little as possible. Normally, only when I'm shaving."

"Imagine a mirror where you could see the inside of folks, too, bubba. That's the perspective from this side, biggest difference there be between the two realms. I look inside your boy, I see your ilk. I saw it last night when he gunned down that boy whose soul was black as pitch."

"You're just trying to make me feel better, champ," Cort Wesley said, the outskirts of Elk Grove almost upon him.

"Not my call to make you feel better or worse. I tell it as I sees it," Epps said, his sometimes lifeless, bloodstained eyes glowing and bright. *"Not my business neither to tell you what you already know about what's been. I'd rather we conversate on what's to be."*

"Conversate?"

"You got an issue with my vocabulary today?"

"Just tell me what's on your mind."

"'Sides the fact that this drive is a mistake? I know what you're doing and I know why, and it's as bad a notion as notions get."

"Can you be a bit clearer?"

"Not if you ain't gonna open your mind to what I got to say."

"It's open."

"How can you even tell? There's so much clutter in your thoughts. You figure the best way to keep Armand Fucker away from your boy is to draw him onto you. Not sure

if you're doing some deflecting or distracting, if you'd like to clarify, but it won't work either way."

"Why's that?"

"Because Armand Fucker got enough hate and ugliness in his soul to go around, more than enough to allocate on you and your boy. And you got yourself riding straight into a shit storm."

What had been a mere speck on the horizon filled out ahead of him as the shape of two McMullen County sheriff's department cruisers parked nose to nose across the road, blocking both sides.

"See what I mean, bubba."

Cort Wesley shot the ghost of his old friend a look, then turned back to a pair of deputies standing before their cruisers, tightening their grasps on the shotguns they were holding. He looked to his right to see if old Leroy had any more pearls of wisdom to dispense, but the ghost was gone, leaving a slight impression in the passenger seat.

Cort Wesley pulled his truck to a halt on the side of the road, climbed out, and approached the roadblock with his hands in the air. The deputies jacked rounds into the chambers of their twelve-gauges in virtual unison, as the rear door to one of the cruisers opened and a man he recognized from a Google search as Sheriff Donnell Gaunt stepped out.

"Road's out ahead," he told Cort Wesley, the hands planted on his hips nearly disappearing into the rolls of fat layered around his torso.

Cort Wesley left his hands in the air. "I want to talk to Fisker. Tell him, it's—"

"I know who you are, Masters. This road's closed to avoid the kind of trouble you bring with you."

"Tell Fisker I want to see him."

"Nothing you can say about your boy blowing a hole in his that he wants to hear."

Cort Wesley took a few steps closer. "It's not about his son, it's about his father."

63

Armand Fisker arrived at the roadblock ten minutes later, four thugs armed with assault rifles piling out of the sleek, dark SUV ahead of him. He moved straight toward Cort Wesley in their shadow, stopping on the other side of the cruisers blocking the road.

"You got something you want to say to me?"

"Father to father, man to man, I'm sorry."

Fisker stiffened. "And that's supposed to mean something?"

"You need to hear this from me, because I'm the one your boy was sighting on. He'd just popped in a fresh magazine to do the job, when my boy did what he did."

"Scattered my son's guts across the roadbed, you mean."

"You ever see what an M16 on full auto can do to a man?"

"Once or twice."

"I've had considerably more experience."

"On account of you being a war hero, a goddamn Green Beret? Like that's supposed to mean something to me."

"It's not," Cort Wesley told him. "What's supposed to mean something to you is the fact that your son had his finger on the trigger of a fully racked magazine when my son dropped him with a round from a twelve-gauge. There anything you find unfair in that picture?"

"Just the fact that my boy's dead and yours isn't. And the sheriff told me your coming here was about my father, not my son."

"It's about both. See, we had a history between us long before yesterday."

"I don't think I follow you."

"My father was in the Walls prison at the same time Cliven Fisker was running the whole show, members of his Aryan Brotherhood killing what they called 'niggers' or 'darkies' to prove their mettle to him, like initiation rites."

Fisker shook his head and laid his hands on the boiling hood of one of the cruisers, letting the heat singe his palms. "You come here to tell me something I already know?"

Cort Wesley leaned as close to Fisker as the hood would allow. "I came here to tell you he went too far and that's what got him killed, just like your boy last night. I guess it runs in the family."

Fisker jerked his palms from the sizzling paint and backed off, stopping just short of swinging all the way around. "I believe we're done here."

"Not quite, Armand," Cort Wesley told him. "One of those 'darkies' killed on your father's behalf was a friend of my father's, a man who'd kept him safe when he first went in. Two weeks after somebody forced a bottle of bleach down that man's throat, your father got shanked in the shower."

"If you're trying to make amends for your boy, hero, you're going about it the wrong way."

"Just a little clarity on the history we got between us, Armand: it was my dad who shanked yours."

64

ELK GROVE, TEXAS

"I thought it best you hear that straight from me," Leroy Epps said, picking up Cort Wesley's exchange with Armand Fisker when they were back on the road, Cort Wesley still half expecting a fusillade of fire to rain down on his truck. *"Did I hear right? You really say that to him, bubba?"*

"You heard right, champ."

Cort Wesley thought he heard the leather creak, as Leroy settled back in the passenger seat. *"Man, I could really use a Hires now. I'd settle for whatever you can scrounge up at the next gas station. Watching over you's a full-time job and I thought my working days were done a whole long time ago."*

"Isn't that what angels do?"

"Who said I was an angel? You see any black wings sprouting from this here body?"

Leroy stopped there and turned his gaze out the window, as if seeing the landscape for the first time, resuming with his gaze still aimed in that direction. *"You really think you improved your cause back there?"*

"I'm not sure that's what I was trying to do."

The ghost swung back toward him, his motion a blur, his spectral appearance fading for a moment. *"That's the smartest thing you've said all day, including back there. Those are the kind of sumbitches used to hang folks like me for entertainment at a weekend barbecue. You just tried to put out a fire with gasoline and, if things go bad, it's your boy who's gonna get burned. Did you ever think of that?"*

"I was trying to make this personal enough to take Dylan out of the picture, remember?"

"Fisker's got an army, bubba."

"I've gone up against worse."

Leroy's expression turned even dourer. *"I'm not sure about that. I'd like to tell you the man's got a dark soul, but I'm not sure he's got any soul at all."*

"He's got blood pumping through his veins, though, and that's what I intend to spill."

Leroy reared back his head and chortled, his laugh pushing out a curtain of mist through his spectral mouth that seemed to envelop him.

"Something funny, champ?"

"You ever sit back and listen to yourself? Man oh man, you are a walking cliché!"

"This coming from a dead man who steals my root beer."

"You're missing the point, bubba."

"Why don't you enlighten me?"

Leroy's expression flattened, the furrows deepened by his laugh filling in. *"I didn't know your daddy was the one who put Cliven Fisker out of the world's misery. You said it was over Fisker killing that friend of his who kept him safe when he first went in."*

"There's more, champ. Boone Masters was doing a three-year stretch for robbery. This would be back in the early eighties, just before he joined up with Caitlin's father, Jim Strong. Cliven Fisker ordered the murder of a young black inmate who was the son of a man who'd taken the rap for my father years before and died in prison for it. My father figured he owed him that much. Armand Fisker was probably a little older than me at the time."

"I never had no idea."

Cort Wesley turned toward the passenger seat, where Leroy's physical form faded and then sharpened again. "Guess it never came up."

"So now you're keeping secrets from me?"

"Boone Masters isn't my favorite topic of conversation, in case you forgot."

Leroy's form solidified again, to the point where Cort Wesley could smell the talcum powder he'd used on his diabetes-bred sores to quell the rotting stench emanating from them. *"My point, bubba, is that if I had no idea your daddy shanked Cliven Fisker, how much else from those years might we not be aware of?"*

"Pertaining to Cliven Fisker, you mean."

"Man dies in prison, he leaves a whole lot of secrets locked in his cell behind him. Everything Armand's got was born behind those same walls. We want to find out what's going on at the root of all this shit, that's where we'll find it."

"In Huntsville. At the Walls."

"Was there another prison where we shared a cell?"

"Don't crack wise with me, you damn ghost. And Huntsville is the last place in the world where I want to go right now."

Leroy leaned back and folded his arms behind his head. *"We got a long trip ahead of us, bubba. What you say we stop off and pick up some Hires for the ride?"*

65

ALAMO HEIGHTS

"Come on, baby, let's have some fun," David Skoll said to one of the two beautiful women he was lying in bed with, the one who hadn't passed out.

She muttered something unintelligible, smiling softly with her eyes closed, when Skoll spread a line of cocaine over her exposed breast and snorted it, finger pressed against his free nostril.

"This ever goes legal, I'm getting the merchandising patent," he said, as the first of the brain rush struck him.

Both women had passed out now, Skoll wondering if he should bother dispensing with the hundred bucks he usually tipped. Who knows, before too long he might need every penny he could get his hands on. Facing off against the government was bad enough on its own, and now he had Armand Fisker front and center in his life, instead of just a peripheral participant.

Packing for Ecuador had become an even more attractive proposition, turning state's evidence against Fisker a slightly less appealing one. He could have his lawyers test the waters, see if the FBI or Justice Department was interested. Not seeing witness protection as a viable option, though, where exactly did that leave him once the deed was done? Fisker could get to him anywhere. Those damn bikers he commanded would off somebody for a thirty-rack, one can for every bullet in an AR-15 magazine.

He never should have spilled the beans to Fisker about the wonder drug that wasn't so much a wonder. A drug that was supposed to improve, and even save, millions of lives that ended up a potential weapon of mass destruction in the wrong hands.

Like Armand Fisker's.

Maybe Skoll should have his lawyers contact Homeland Security. This seemed more up their alley and maybe they could deport the son of a bitch to Guantanamo. Skoll had some gangster friends he could talk to about a more permanent solution, but they were greaseballs who didn't make much of a match for Fisker's biker army.

The other girl, the brunette, was stirring now, coming awake, her mouth making cracking sounds from the dryness all the cocaine she'd snorted had left behind. Her eyes opened and she stretched a hand up to run through Skoll's long hair that made him look like he was still in high school. That made him think of the invite list to his fortieth birthday party in two years.

"You're pretty," she said.

Skoll held the back of her hand, while she fingered his sweat-dampened locks that smelled like motor oil right now. "So are you, darlin'."

"I want to club this back in a ponytail. Make you even prettier."

"Maybe later," he said, moving her hand from his hair to his groin. "First things first."

The brunette slid down him, feeling like a snake slithering across his chest.

She replaced her hand with her mouth, while Skoll waited for the cocaine to work its magic. How many lines had he done today exactly, a little after-noon delight he figured he had coming to him? Maybe he should just go back to sucking the white powder up his nose, until his brain exploded. Go out with a bang in the same moment the brunette, or the blonde, finished their business. Fuck the world, the government, and Armand Fisker, too. Truth was, Skoll hated Ecuador.

Down below, the brunette's head was gyrating like crazy, but nothing was happening. Absolutely nothing.

What the fuck?

Well, Fisker had taken his balls, so why should he be surprised? Maybe he needed the man's permission to get a hard-on now.

His phone chimed with a special ring reserved for only those he couldn't put off. He groped for it and dragged it to him with AF in the caller ID.

"Hey, Arm," he greeted, as the brunette continued trying to bring him to life. "I was just thinking about you."

PART SEVEN

They were men who could not be stampeded.

—Colonel Homer Garrison, Jr., director of
Texas Department of Public Safety, 1939–1968

66

They sat on opposite sides of the big oblong table in the conference room adjacent to his office, Caitlin staring at Jones as if to make sense of what she was seeing.

"How's your first day as a Homeland Security agent going, Ranger?"

"When was the last time you were in an all-out brawl?" Caitlin asked him.

"I can't remember."

"If you don't count a few hours back, neither can I."

Jones's gaze softened. "I told them to hold Frank Doyle as a person of interest for Homeland. That won't hold up for long."

"I won't need long to question him."

"Come again, Ranger?"

"I think he's the man who raped me, Jones. I think he raped the Beasley girl, too. Check with the hostess. Doyle was on stage security that night, maybe just a few feet from where Kelly Ann was dancing. My guess is we'll learn he was on break or something around the same time she was sexually assaulted downstairs in the restaurant."

She rubbed the shoulder that had started to act up on her, a residue of her fight with Frank Doyle. It hurt her jaw to speak or swallow, and her head throbbed from where she'd slammed into the bar outside Stubb's Barbecue.

She didn't feel dizzy or nauseous, prime indicators of a concussion, but she'd felt light-headed a few times, passing it off as a lingering spike in her blood pressure produced by the altercation.

"Frank Doyle's refusing to provide a voluntary DNA sample," Jones told her.

"Maybe you don't need him to. After that fight, I've got plenty of his DNA all over me."

"That's a thought."

"And you wouldn't need a warrant, or anything like that. What about Kelly Ann Beasley?"

"What about her?"

"I was hoping I could show her Doyle's mug shot, see if it strikes a chord. After all, I'm working for Homeland Security now."

Jones stiffened. "She and her family are off-limits, Ranger. I thought I made that clear."

"So the investigation of her rape disappears into the wind."

"I have to think of the bigger picture here."

Caitlin thought of the rage, anger, and hatred that had simmered inside her unchecked for eighteen years, most of it tucked away beneath the surface, eating at her until it had finally spilled forth this afternoon in the heat and dirt outside Stubb's Barbecue. Each blow she struck to Frank Doyle felt like rewinding time, getting a few of those years back. Who knows, a few more blows and she might have taken the clock back all the way before the night of her assault.

"There is no bigger picture than this, Jones," Caitlin said coldly. "Maybe if somebody had ever forced themselves on you, you'd know what I was talking about."

He leaned forward and crossed his arms on the scratched-up table. "Let's change the subject."

"To what?"

"Armand Fisker."

"I figured he might be on Homeland's radar. You sent Paz because you must've gotten wind that Fisker was en route with his private army in tow. You got someone inside his organization, right? Otherwise, you would've come clean when the subject came up originally."

Jones remained noncommittal. "We're onto Fisker for running drugs and guns from coast-to-coast through biker gangs organized out of the Aryan Brotherhood. He's turned pond scum into millionaires. Franchised out distribution networks by state and region, utilizing a separate force to deal with the competition. You want to know why so many of the Colombians and all the other drug gangs who don't drive Harleys turned tail and went home? Look no further than the private army you saw first-hand last night."

"You want to tell me how a man like that operates under the radar?"

"Because he's not actually under it, Ranger, so much as flying stealth. Like the way he set up shop in Elk Grove, bringing all the right people and turning local law enforcement into enablers. You know what his organization calls itself?"

"No."

"Because it doesn't have a name. Fisker is street-smart in the same way his father was. He's turned corruption and bribery into an art form, and bikers into businessmen who wear three-piece suits and park their hogs in the private garages of high-end office buildings. If estimates of his reach are any indication, he employs more people than IBM ever did."

Caitlin shook her head, something unsettling in Jones's tone. "You sound like you admire him."

"I may have, until last night. Storming a suburb of San Antonio was hardly the best thing for business. Looks like his son's killing finally flushed him out. Has a Shakespearean ring to it, doesn't it?"

"I didn't know you read Shakespeare."

"Figure of speech, but I'm sure there's an allusion in there somewhere."

"*Hamlet* comes to mind, maybe *King Lear* and *Macbeth*, too. You know, the mad king syndrome."

Jones smirked. "Whatever you say."

"You have my official Homeland creds yet, Jones?"

"No, something better: the next part of the story involving your grand-father and J. Edgar Hoover."

67

Earl and Captain Henry Druce searched the home of Abner Dunbar until the late afternoon sun bled away and twilight bloomed in the Texas sky.

"You ready to give me a clearer idea of what it is we're looking for?" Earl finally asked him.

"I believe I already did."

"No, you said it was some kind of list. You didn't say exactly what kind. Dunbar being involved in resettling these Nazi assholes made me figure it must be a list with names like that of Gunther Haut. Now I'm figuring it's something else."

"Such things don't happen in a vacuum, Ranger. You want to stop such an operation like this in its tracks, you need to do so at the source. Those men like Dunbar are ultimately beholden to."

"And that would be…"

"Plenty of powerful Americans who never really did support your country's entry into the war. This same plenty would have much preferred either you stayed out of things altogether or, even, cozied up to Germany."

"These being businessmen?"

"The name Joseph Kennedy mean anything to you?"

"Of course, it does. A man cut from the same cloth as John D. Rockefeller who my own granddad had quite a tussle with back in his time."

"Then it may interest you to know, sir, that Rockefeller's Standard Oil of New Jersey shipped fuel to Germany through neutral Switzerland in 1942, at the same time millions of American and British people had to fend with rationing coupons and lines at the gas stations. And, speaking of gasoline, I'm sure the name Henry Ford means something to you."

"It sure does. I drove a Ford truck for a time, Captain."

Druce stepped farther into the light of Abner Dunbar's living room they'd been searching to no avail. "Then, sir, it may also interest you to know that

Ford trucks, until quite recently, were being built for the German occupation troops in France with direct authorization from Dearborn, Michigan."

"I can go that one better," Earl said. "Did you know Colonel Sosthenes Behn, the head of the international American telephone conglomerate IT&T, flew from New York to Madrid to Bern during the war to help improve Hitler's communications systems and fine-tune the robot bombs that devastated London? Or that IT&T built the Focke-Wulfs that dropped bombs on British and American troops? Or that crucial ball bearings were shipped to Nazi-associated customers in Latin America with the collusion of the vice chairman of the U.S. War Production Board in partnership with Göring's cousin in Philadelphia? All this while American forces were desperately short of those same ball bearings."

Druce's eyes widened in surprise. "I must say, sir, that I was not aware of any of that. It's a pleasure to be in the company of such a learned man."

Earl scratched at his scalp. "Well, Captain, I don't know about any of that. I read lots of newspapers to ease my guilt over the fact I'm here instead of over there. And when I read those kind of stories, it makes me feel like a man doesn't have to go all that way to find his share of vermin."

Druce checked his watch. "Speaking of which, we must consider the possibility that your friend Mr. Hoover will be here before too much longer."

Earl turned his gaze about the room, imagining he was seeing it for the first time. "We've been wasting our time. Man charged with this kind of mission wouldn't leave anything of note anywhere men like us could find it."

"Dunbar wasn't working alone, Ranger. He was part of a network with a reach that extends into the United States and every country in Europe. If we don't find some clue as to the other spies he was working with, I'm afraid the killer you're chasing will slip away forever."

Earl's eyes settled on the mail slot built into the front door, beneath which a stack of envelopes lay, some captured in a rubber band. "I believe I've got another idea."

The next morning Earl and Captain Druce rode the elevator in the Lone Star Gas building up to the twelfth floor and the office of Witchell Long, president and owner of the company that had provided the building its name. Located on St. Paul Street in Dallas, the thirteen-story tower had been completed in 1931 as an Art Deco masterpiece, although Earl had no idea what Art Deco actually was.

The elevator opened into a spacious reception area, already humming with activity centered around the biggest wooden double doors Earl had ever seen. They looked hand carved and custom fitted to allow someone as big as Paul Bunyan to pass under the arch without ducking.

Earl led Druce to a reception desk set directly before those doors, making sure the woman eyeing them suspiciously could see the Texas Ranger badge pinned to his chest.

"Ma'am, I'm here to see Mr. Long."

"Is he expecting you?"

"No, he's not."

"And you don't have an appointment?"

"No, we don't. But it's vital I see him and I don't expect to take too much of his time."

The woman nodded, eyes shifting back and forth between Earl and the badge that glistened in the bright reception area lighting. "If you could give me some notion as to what this is about, I'd be happy to buzz Mr. Long."

"I'm afraid I can't do that, ma'am. This is a personal matter involving Mr. Long's family, and I'm not at liberty to share the details with anyone but him."

"Mr. Long's son has been in and out of trouble with the law," the woman said, more to herself than either of them. "Why don't I go in and see if he's available?"

The woman emerged from Witchell Long's office inside of a minute later, holding one of the big double doors open for Earl and Druce. "He'll see you now, Ranger."

Earl passed the woman, tipping his hat to her with Druce on his tail. He closed the door behind them and engaged the bolt before he turned to find a big man, who looked to be a better fit for the oilfields than the boardroom, rising from behind the biggest desk he'd ever seen. Witchell Long looked to be as close to seven feet as six, carrying more of his three hundred or so pounds around his midsection than he used to, but still looking as if he could wield a sledgehammer just fine. He had tawny skin with tiny cracks that made it look like leather tanned by the sun and a scalp that featured only a dollop of hair on each side. He laid a pair of hands that might have been slabs of meat atop his desk blotter and studied Earl Strong and Henry Druce as they approached.

"You said you had business pertaining to my family, Ranger," he said stiffly, as if that came as no surprise to him. "Something you can share only with me."

In Earl's experience, all rich and powerful families had plenty to hide and the ruse he'd just used to gain access to one of the most successful business-men in all of Texas had never failed him, not even once.

"I do indeed, sir. There's something I need to show you that'll help explain things."

With that, Earl extracted Abner Dunbar's phone bill that he'd found beneath the mail slot the day before and laid it on the desk. "Sir, could you confirm for me that the numbers I've circled are yours, both home and here at the office?"

Long's eyes narrowed warily, and he placed a pair of spectacles over his nose to better see the circled numbers, taking his gaze from Earl in order to regard them. He left his other meat slab of a hand propped on the desk, never noticing the Ranger ease the ballpeen hammer from the pocket of his brown suede coat.

"Could you please explain what this—"

The hammer strike that smashed the knuckle on his pinky finger froze Long's words there, his mouth gaping for a scream that never came. He col-lapsed back into his chair, which rocked violently backward. Earl clamped a hand over his mouth when it snapped back forward, and kept Long's hand, the one with the pinkie already swollen to twice its normal size, trapped in his grasp.

"I'm going to speak plainly, Mr. Long," Earl started, "to waste as little of your valuable time as possible."

The big man was breathing heavily, his flushed face twisted in agony, eyes that suddenly looked too small for his head darting about as if to measure his options.

"This here phone bill," Earl said, flapping the pages before Long, while Captain Druce looked on in silent amazement, "belongs to a man I believe you're acquainted with named Abner Dunbar." Earl laid the phone bill down, where Long could still see it. "He's now deceased, in case nobody else has told you, killed we believe by a Nazi prisoner of war being held in Texas he was charged with helping get to safety. This man here is Captain Henry Druce of the British Special Air Service whose job it is to ferret out Nazis like him. Mr. Druce informs me that there's a whole bunch of big business-men who don't let anything as pointless as patriotism get in the way of making a buck. And since the late Mr. Dunbar made a whole bunch of calls to you, I'm going to assume that you're one of them."

Long finally caught his breath, his red face dappled with beads of sweat now. "I have no idea what you're talking—"

Earl lashed the ballpeen hammer downward again, this time crunching the knuckle on Long's ring finger that blew up as big as a golf ball, again clamping his free hand over the man's mouth to stifle his scream.

"Neither of us has time for bull crap here, sir. You are going to tell us all about your involvement with whatever Abner Dunbar was up to. You're going to serve us some names and spill everything you got inside you on the sub-ject. If you don't, I'm gonna keep breaking your knuckles until I run out, and then I'm gonna push you out that big window there to see what three hun-dred pounds of bullshit looks like splattered across the sidewalk. How's that sound?"

"You're out of your mind!" Long rasped through flecks of blood-streaked drool leaking out his mouth, from biting his tongue. "Who sent you here? Who ordered this investigation? I'll have your badge! I'll put the Texas Rang-ers out of business once and for all. Do you even know who I *am*?"

"I'm starting to get a real good idea, yes, sir," Earl said, his stare boring into Long's face, as if trying to find his tiny eyes narrowed even further into slits.

"Abner Dunbar is, *was,* in my employ, in charge of opening new venues of business across the Southwest. And if you think that in any way—"

This time Earl's hand swallowed the rest of his words, ahead of bringing the hammer down on his middle finger.

"Seven more to go, sir, and since you know so much about the Rangers, I'm going to assume you know I won't stop until all ten look like you squeezed marbles inside your skin. Good news is I'm not really interested in the business dealings that made you party to this—my guess is slithery creatures like yourself are well versed in avoiding illegality in the formal sense. So, being the big dealmaker that you are, here's the deal on the table: you tell me what you know, in general, and about a Nazi prisoner named Gunther Haut, in particular, and our business is done. Alternative is hitting the sidewalk with all your fingers busted. And I don't believe a third option's in the cards, is it, Captain Druce?"

"It most certainly is not, Ranger Strong."

Earl turned back to Witchell Long. "Let's start with Gunther Haut, sir. Dunbar was waiting for him at the Driskill Hotel in Austin, when Haut showed up and killed him."

"That wasn't my doing!" Long insisted, his words strung out to sound more like a harmonic whine.

"Then why don't you tell me what your doing was exactly?"

"I have business associates in Europe," Long started, through rapid heaves of breath, "who are indeed sympathetic to the Nazi cause. They said they were in contact with any number of German scientists who loathed the Nazis as much as we all do, who'd been forced into their service. These scientists were looking for a lifeline, once the war drew to a close."

"In other words, they were looking for a way to avoid being on the wrong end of a rope."

Long managed a labored nod that seemed to shoot fresh stabs of pain through him. "In a manner of speaking, I suppose. These scientists have developed entirely new technologies to extract oil and gas from deeper in the ground. Energy is the future, Ranger, and they could assure that future belongs to America."

"So now you're a patriot."

"You think you have to ride a horse to be a patriot?"

"I ride a Chevy."

"And the Texas Rangers, such noble patriots and heroes, how many Indians did they massacre in cold blood?"

"Not nearly as many as were riding in to kill them first. Just stick to the subject. What did your Nazi friends ask you to do with regards to Gunther Haut? He was too young to be a scientist."

"They didn't go into details. It was a matter of . . . resettlement. My international dealings have afforded me a wealth of contacts in smoothing over certain issues of identity and nationality. Borders mean nothing in business, but sometimes it's necessary to travel with different papers, even passports, so as not to stoke interest in parties who may have their own best ends in mind."

"I have no idea what you just said, sir, except that it sounds like you were supposed to provide Gunther Haut with a new name, birth certificate—the whole ball of wax. And Abner Dunbar was your middleman, the one who got his hands dirty so yours could stay clean. Is that about it?"

This time, Long nodded only once, gnashing his teeth against the pain that had flared anew.

"Speaking of the wrong end of a rope, sir, you wanna explain to me how that doesn't make you a traitor?"

Long was breathing noisily now, trying very hard not to turn his gaze toward the hammer still clutched in Earl Strong's hand.

"I guess you don't," Earl said, when he remained silent. "Let's try this next: what were Dunbar's orders regarding Gunther Haut's safety?"

"He was to set up a safe house for him, where Haut would remain until more permanent arrangements could be made."

"Because all this happened fast, right? Haut had only been at the prison camp in Hearne for three weeks."

"Somebody wanted him out of there very badly, Ranger. We were supposed to have more time. The killings in that camp by his hand came as a surprise."

"And now Mr. Dunbar will be leaving Austin in a pine box. Sounds like somebody in Hearne figured something out about Haut he wasn't supposed to. That would be the first thought most folks would entertain on the subject. But here's what's sticking with me. Dunbar checked into the Driskill, *be-*

fore Haut killed his three bunkmates. You want to try explaining that to me, sir?"

Long remained flat-faced, as if pretending not to hear him.

"Yeah, I figured that would be your answer."

And, with that, Earl covered Long's mouth yet again and slammed the ballpeen hammer down on Long's index finger knuckle, pulling his hand away when the man started gagging for breath.

"Why don't we try that question again?"

"Haut was important to them!" Long managed, through a twisted mask of agony.

"Important to who?"

"My German business associates!"

"You mean *Nazi* business associates, don't you? And why was he so important to them?"

"They didn't say." Then, staring into Earl Strong's eyes, "That's the God's honest truth, Ranger!"

"I believe it is. Now, work with me here, Mr. Long, because I'm of the opinion that the timing of all this was anything but accidental. That tells me you and those business associates of yours had somebody on the inside of that camp. A soldier, officer—somebody. You got a name for me?"

Earl raised the hammer back overhead when Witchell Long failed to respond.

"No, wait! *Wait!* It was the commanding officer!"

"Captain Bo Lowry?" the Ranger posed, with no small degree of surprise.

"I don't know his name. I didn't need to know his name."

"But you're saying he was in on it."

Long's eyes were still teary from the pain. "Gunther Haut wasn't the first prisoner whose escape was facilitated, Ranger."

"But I'd wager he was the first who killed three fellow inmates before strolling out the gate. That tells me they'd figured out what made him so important. Maybe he spilled the beans, maybe he talked in his sleep, maybe he just liked killing folks the way I like taking a ballpeen hammer to the knuckles of traitors."

Long's expression wrinkled with disgust, as if revolted by Earl Strong's words. "Don't blame me for putting the future first, Ranger. The difference between the simple man and the successful one is the vision to see far ahead, not straight ahead." His eyes made no secret of his message, as they widened out of the slits into which they'd narrowed. "Then there are those who can't stop living in the past, with no regard for the future."

At that, Earl slammed the ballpeen hammer down on Long's thumb knuckle.

"I got no more questions for you, sir. That one was just on principle."

68

SAN ANTONIO, TEXAS

"You can't stop there," Caitlin protested.

"I have no choice," Jones told her.

"What's that supposed to mean?"

"The rest of the file was redacted."

"Redacted?"

Jones nodded. "For reasons of national security."

"Come again?"

"State secrets, that sort of thing."

"My grandfather was involved in state secrets?"

"Explains why he never told you this particular story, doesn't it?"

"So you don't know what happened when he returned to the prisoner-of-war camp in Hearne to see what the camp commander was up to? You have no idea what it was Earl Strong had stumbled upon?"

Jones shrugged. "I'm trying to locate the rest of the file now. It's probably tucked away in storage somewhere. Just give me some time, and you'll know if your grandfather took a ballpeen hammer to Captain Lowry's knuckles, too."

Caitlin shook her head. "Who the hell was this Gunther Haut?"

"Beats me. All I can tell you is that no record of him exists after that day."

"No surprise there, Jones."

"But here's one, Ranger: there's also no record of him ever being interred in Hearne. I uncovered the logs featuring the names of nearly all five thousand POWs who passed through those gates, and there's no listing whatsoever for a Gunther Haut."

"Which means somebody scrubbed those records clean. Which means somebody with that capability must've had reason to." Caitlin thought for a moment. "What do you figure J. Edgar Hoover's part in this was?"

"I don't."

"But he must've known, at least suspected, what made Haut so important to the Nazis and their sympathizers over here. Maybe he'd figured out what Witchell Long couldn't tell my grandfather because he didn't know." Caitlin hesitated and gave him a longer look across the conference table. "Doesn't the notion of Nazis running around Texas make your skin crawl, Jones, at least a little?"

Jones flashed a slight smirk. "After all I've been through in this twilight zone of a state of yours, *nothing* could make my skin crawl." The smirk vanished. "You mind if I speak plainly?"

"Since when did you need to ask?"

"I think I get it now," Jones said, looking straight at her. "This obsession of yours with the past, with trying to link every case you're on to something one of your ancestors was involved in."

"I'm not following."

Jones's stare continue to bore through her. "You can't remember all of that night from eighteen years ago, aren't sure who really assaulted you. So maybe you figure if you can get a better handle on the past, sooner or later that part of it will come back to you, too."

"Dime-store psychology coming from you ain't worth a nickel, Jones."

"Changing the subject won't change the fact you know I'm right. And figuring out who Gunther Haut really was won't bring you any closer to what happened after you finished whatever was inside that red Solo cup."

Caitlin pushed herself back to her feet, her chair scraping across the hardwood floor when she shoved it backward. "Then I guess we're done here."

"Hold on there," Jones said when she headed for the door. "Where do you think you're going?"

"To meet up with Doc Whatley."

"I hope you remember you're not an active Texas Ranger right now."

"This is Homeland Security business. Scout's honor. I'll brief you, as soon as I'm done."

Jones's phone rang, a fresh smirk claiming his face when he checked the caller ID. "How about that? It's Masters. You want to talk to him?"

But Caitlin was already out the conference room door.

69

HUNTSVILLE, TEXAS

"Where'd you say you were?" Jones asked Cort Wesley.

"Huntsville. The Walls prison, specifically," Cort Wesley told him.

"Which side of the fence?"

"I need access, to see an inmate named Darl Pickett."

"You want to tell me what this is about, cowboy?"

"Let's see what Pickett has to say first, if he's even still alive, Jones."

Cort Wesley had learned from inquiring at the gate that Warden Della-hunt had finally retired. He'd stayed in touch with Dellahunt sporadically since his release and believed the warden to be the quickest route by which he could gain entry to the Walls to visit Darl Pickett. With Dellahunt no longer in charge, Cort Wesley needed another way to speed through the red tape of an ex-con paying a prison visit.

Pickett had been old when Cort Wesley was an inmate nearly a decade before, and he'd been there at the time Boone Masters was jailed at the Walls as well, and plenty of years before that to boot. Pickett had been rounded up as a peripheral player in an organized crime RICO beef. He'd served as a mob accountant, an absolute whiz with numbers. With a good lawyer, he might have done a couple years behind bars at most. Thanks to a bad one, though, he earned himself a lifetime stretch, due to being tied in conspiratorial fashion to a series of murders that had nearly earned him a seat in the electric chair.

By the time he was up for parole for the third time, the outside world no longer held any claim over or interest for Darl Pickett, and he'd accepted his permanent home as the prison where he served as an inmate trustee and unofficial historian. Pickett would be in his seventies now, maybe even eighties, a man who'd found a form of contentment and simplicity inside an eight-by-eight cell from which he'd been permitted to come and go as he pleased.

"This Darl Pickett hasn't had a visitor in over twenty years," Jones said, when he called Cort Wesley back. "The new warden thought I was crazy when I told him Homeland had some questions for him."

"That's because everyone Darl's known for fifty years is either dead or still jailed."

"Where do you fit into that mix, cowboy?"

"I'll let you know when I figure it out myself, Jones."

Darl Pickett had skin as yellow as the whites of Leroy Epps's eyes, before he'd turned into a ghost. His entire face was sallow, skin sagging in patches on the verge, it seemed, of sliding off altogether. A patchwork quilt of what looked like reptilian ridges and bumps from a lack of sunlight and the lousy air inmates were forced to breathe, as if the state of Texas processed it just for them.

"Boone Masters!" the old man greeted, confusing Cort Wesley for his father.

He took a seat opposite Cort Wesley in the otherwise empty visitors' area of the prison, lined with tables and chairs that were intentionally uncomfortable. The exception had been granted for Darl Pickett because of his age, special status as an inmate, and the fact that Cort Wesley was here on behalf of Homeland.

"I haven't seen you in . . ." The old man's eyes wavered, as if he'd lost control of his thinking. "How long has it been now?"

"Quite a while," Cort Wesley told him.

"Long time."

"Quite."

"I've been in here forty-six years, eight months, and six days as of today. That's seventeen thousand and forty-seven days in total, counting leap years. That's four hundred and nine thousand, one hundred and twenty-eight hours. That's twenty-four million, five hundred and forty-seven thousand, six hundred and eighty minutes."

"Like you said, Darl, a long time," Cort Wesley said, amazed at how the man brightened when reciting numbers from the world in which he was most comfortable.

Pickett scratched at his scalp, bald except for a few stray patches of white hair. "When'd you get out? I forget now."

"A few months back."

"And how's that boy of yours, the one you're always bragging on?"

Cort Wesley felt something sink in his stomach. "He's fine."

"Bet he missed you while you were inside."

"Hard to tell, Darl, him being a teenager and all. You know how teenagers are."

"Sure I do," Picket said, even though it was clear he didn't.

But that gave Cort Wesley an idea. "My son's the reason I'm here, Darl."

Pickett's wan expression looked to be genuinely concerned. "How's that, Boone?"

"Cort Wesley's started running with Cliven Fisker's son. Goes by the name of Armand."

The old man's hands began to shake atop the table, but he didn't seem to notice. "Cliven and Armand are both names with six letters. Fisker has six letters, too. Did you know eight percent of people have the same number of letters in their first name as their last?"

"No, Darl, I didn't."

Pickett looked up, his eyes suddenly bright and sharp. "I'm worried about your boy, Boone."

"So am I. That's why I'm here: to find out everything I can about Cliven Fisker, steer my boy away from his family if there's cause."

"Oh, there's cause all right, plenty of cause. Something like eight to the nth power, even though nobody really knows what the nth power means."

"Why's that, Darl?"

The brightness in Pickett's ancient eyes, one with a cataract that looked like a piece of snot stuck on his pupil, faded, his gaze narrowing. "Why what, Boone?"

"Why's Cliven Fisker trouble?"

The old man looked around, as if trying to remember where he was. "What's your boy's name again?"

"Cort Wesley."

"Who's that?"

"My son."

"Sure." Picket nodded, grinning. "The one you're always bragging on."

"I'm worried about him, Darl."

"Why?"

"That's what I need to ask you. Tell me about Cliven Fisker."

"Who?"

"Cliven Fisker, the inmate who founded the Aryan Brotherhood from inside here."

"Why you asking about him?"

"Because I'm worried about my son."

"What was his name again?"

"Cort Wesley."

Pickett's expression tightened again. He reached across the table and captured Cort Wesley's forearm in a wizened, bony grip that felt more like claws than fingers.

"You tell that boy to steer clear of anyone with the last name Fisker. You tell him to steer clear of anyone with six letters in their last name, just to make sure he listens."

"Is Fisker dangerous, Darl?"

The old man jerked his hand from Cort Wesley's forearm and rocked himself backward in the plastic chair. "Oh, I don't know. Is a rabid dog dangerous? Is a wounded moose dangerous? Is a woman during that time of the month dangerous? Is Cliven Fisker dangerous? The answer is yes, to all of the above. You know he ordered the death of a Negro boy because he looked at him wrong?"

"No, I didn't," Cort Wesley said honestly.

"Uh-huh, it's the truth. Kid just made eye contact with him because he didn't know Negroes aren't allowed to do that. It's as sure a death sentence as killing the president. Did you know I met Lee Harvey Oswald?"

"You did?"

"Saw him anyway. I was in a cell when they brought him into Dallas police headquarters. They walked him right past me. I didn't even know Kennedy had been killed. And I don't know what I was doing in that jail at the time, either. Do you?"

The dull lighting made it hard for Cort Wesley to get a read on Darl Pickett's constantly shifting expression, so he'd know how to react to his lucid moments when they came. Trying to get information out of the man reminded him of mining for gold: you probably won't find much, but the only way to find anything at all is to keep chiseling away at the wall before you.

"Tell me about Cliven Fisker, Darl."

"He's dangerous."

"Besides that."

"It's *why* he's dangerous, *what makes* him dangerous."

"What's that? Tell me."

"You won't believe me, Boone. Nobody ever does."

"Why don't you try me, Darl?"

70

Huntsville, Texas

Pickett's face blanked, his eyes seeming to lock on a wall clock he'd just noticed. "Is it really one o'clock?"

"No, Darl, it's almost five. That clock must've stopped."

"Time stops for no man, Boone. You should pass that along. Time stops for no man." The old man's eyes refused to leave the clock. "Maybe you can wind it up like a watch, make it start working again."

"We can try."

Pickett's uncertain eyes sought Cort Wesley's out. "What day is today?"

"Saturday."

"They all seem the same to me lately, Boone. Only way to tell them apart is by what they're serving in the cafeteria. We have taco Tuesday now."

"That sounds good."

"On Fridays we get fish sticks and on Saturdays we get chicken that looks like fish sticks. Did I have them for lunch today?"

"I guess."

"You weren't there?"

Cort Wesley swallowed hard. "I got out, Darl, remember?"

"When that happen?"

"A while back."

The old man looked down, his lips quivering. "I don't remember. I have trouble remembering things sometimes. Like the name of that boy of yours you're always bragging on."

"Cort Wesley."

"Who's that?"

"My boy."

"I knew that. I never forget a name."

For Cort Wesley, sitting here talking to Darl Picket felt like being stuck in a riptide. Only choice you had was to go with it, since fighting the riptide would only get you drowned, which gave him an idea.

"Did you have lunch with Cliven Fisker today, Darl?"

"Nope, not today. Did once, though. Him and me swigging moonshine one of the guards smuggled in the ingredients for. That's when he told me."

"Told you what?"

The old man's face blanked again. "Who?"

"Cliven Fisker. You were saying that he told you something."

"Told me what?"

"That's what you were about to tell me."

Pickett nodded in understanding, lowering his voice when he resumed. "His secret, you mean."

"Yes, Darl, I do."

"If he told it to me sober, I'd be a dead man. But he was drunk, so I guess he needed to tell somebody, and likely forgot he did afterward."

"What did he tell you?"

"It was about his dad. He thought it was funny. Like he was making a joke. I told you he was drunk."

Cort Wesley just nodded, not wanting to disturb the old man's thinking.

Pickett lowered his voice to a whisper. "You got to kill him, Boone. You're the only man in here with the guts to get it done."

Cort Wesley felt a clog forming in his throat. "Why would I do that? I don't even know him, Darl."

"He's got to die. Because of his secret."

"What's Fisker's secret, Darl? What is it he told you when he was drunk?"

Pickett leaned forward across the table, checking the room to make sure no one else was in earshot. "How'd you like to hear the damnedest thing you ever did hear, Boone?"

"Now that was a waste of time, if ever there was one," said Leroy Epps, once Cort Wesley had driven through the prison gates.

"I take it, based on this secret Darl Pickett claims he's been keeping for forty years, you think he's full of shit, champ."

"That would be giving shit a bad name. Man makes me glad I died when I did, bubba. I'd rather lose my life than my marbles any day of the week and twice on Sunday."

"You can't lose your life; you're already dead."

"Figure of speech. And even though I'm dead, I sure as hell make more sense than that lamebrain."

"Bit harsh, don't you think, champ?"

Leroy's lips puckered. *"Oh, I don't know, Boone, did I tell you I know who really shot Kennedy?"*

"Give it a rest."

"Be glad to, bubba, soon as you stop off and get me a root beer."

Cort Wesley's cell phone rang over the truck's Bluetooth, PAZ lighting up in the caller ID.

"You need to get to the Village School, outlaw," Paz said, when he answered. "There's been some trouble."

71

LA VERNIA, TEXAS

"What do you know about organ donations, Ranger?" Doc Whatley asked Caitlin, seated in a chair he'd set down for her so they could watch the annual Bluebonnet Fest Parade.

"I know there's a black market for them."

"Spoken like a true lawman."

On Whatley's instructions, Caitlin had met him just outside San Antonio in La Vernia where the annual Bluebonnet Fest was underway. She'd never known him to take a day off from work, seemingly always in the office when she called, even on weekends. But here he was on a Saturday, seated in one of two lawn chairs he'd set up in a shaded, grassy knoll where, in a few minutes, the annual Bluebonnet Fest Parade would pass right by them.

Gazing about at the considerable crowd that had gathered, Caitlin figured Whatley must've been here for some time to snag such a cherished, shady spot for himself. The whole thing seemed totally out of character for him, especially given that he was the only person about to take in the festivities who looked to have come on their own.

"Good question, Ranger," he said suddenly.

"I didn't ask one, Doc."

"Your eyes did. I come here every year. My boy always loved this festival, never missed one until he was murdered. I've come back every year since, with my wife at first, until she took sick."

That sickness, Caitlin knew, was alcoholism compounded by serious depression that had never waned after their son had been killed. She felt suddenly uncomfortable in the lawn chair Whatley had placed out for her, having never heard him share anything from his personal life this way. She thought this might be the first time he'd had company for the event, since his wife's decline and ultimate death, instantly glad he'd chosen this place to meet for no other reason than that.

Caitlin had always viewed Whatley as a man bled of emotion, his tragic past having hammered him into submission. Their relationship had been purely professional, to the point that she'd never once had occasion or call to gauge Whatley's emotions. Today, though, his expression was a portrait of sad reflection, looking as if he wanted to smile, but had forgotten how.

Down the street a ways, Caitlin could see the floats, marching bands, civic and veteran's groups lining up for the parade's start behind the town's mayor who, as always, would serve as grandmaster. After parking a good half mile away, Caitlin had passed a kids' carnival and vendor booths packed with handmade arts and crafts. The festival also featured a petting zoo, pony rides, and a Wild West show a few people must've thought she was a part of, based on their stares, not to mention an endless array of food and drink booths. Caitlin noticed a beer garden had been set up this year but, in the true spirit of a family-oriented event, not a lot of attendees were sampling the wares.

"I'm talking about the more medical applications of organ transplantation, Ranger," Whatley resumed, just as the loud pounding of a bass drum signaled the start of the parade a few blocks down.

"I'm a lawman, Doc," Caitlin told him, "not a medical man."

"I want you to think like one. Let's try this a different way: what's the biggest problem with organ donations?"

"That there aren't enough organs around."

"What about those patients lucky enough to get the transplants?"

"Well, I've read about tissue rejection. Guess it's rather common."

"And why would that be?"

"Because it's not part of the recipient's standard equipment. More like an aftermarket replacement part."

Whatley nodded, the way her high school chemistry teacher had when she got a question right. "With a replacement part, the fit is normally pretty smooth. Not always the case, though, with organs because the body sees a transplanted one as a foreign body, like an enemy invader. The immune system swings into action, playing the role of a defending army."

"So doctors prescribe anti-rejection drugs to weaken the immune system enough so it won't recognize the transplanted organ as foreign."

"But there's a problem with that, isn't there?"

"Side effects," Caitlin nodded. "Like with all drugs."

"But these are far more catastrophic, even deadly. And that's only if anti-rejection drugs work, which they don't always do. When they do work, which is most of the time these days, the patient lives the rest of his life with what can be a severely compromised immune system. Often, something else kills him, or her, as a direct consequence of that. You can see where I'm going with this."

Caitlin was starting to. "The two bodies we pulled out of that apartment complex were both organ transplant recipients."

"But neither one of them showed any signs of standard anti-rejection medications in their bloodstreams."

"Maybe that helps explain what killed them, Doc," Caitlin said, recalling Jones's mention of a drug found in the victims' systems the tox screen couldn't identify.

"Quite the opposite, Ranger, quite the opposite."

72

LA VERNIA, TEXAS

Doc Whatley had to raise his voice over the sounds of the approaching parade when he continued. "For decades, patients receiving organ transplants have spent the rest of their lives taking a host of medications aimed at preventing rejection. Generally, that means a combination of drugs that each have their own side effects, which then also need to be treated. Primarily we're talking about the liver and kidneys here, but pancreas transplants are being performed now as well, along with lung, cornea, hearts, and heart valves. The premise of limb transplant has shown great promise as well, and we can assume even more, millions more, patients will face all the complications that come with anti-rejection drugs like Prednisone, Mycophenolate, Tacrolimus, and Cyclosporine before much longer."

"That's quite a mouthful, Doc," Caitlin said, as the mayor and drum majorette leading the Bluebonnet Fest Parade passed by the spot where Whatley had set their lawn chairs. "Can you tell me why it's important to this particular case?"

"Because the bodies of the transplant recipients from that apartment complex contained no trace whatsoever of the drugs I just mentioned. And they weren't alone."

Whatley waited for the parade's lead marching band, playing "Seventy-Six Trombones," to give way to the first in a line of floats, before resuming.

"So far, Ranger, the law enforcement query I put out over the wire has yielded reports of sixteen other transplant recipients dying in conditions identical to the ones as ours."

"Did you say *sixteen?*"

Whatley nodded. "I did, from coast-to-coast, and that number is certain to rise, in large part because natural causes would've been suspected in virtually all such deaths. And, in all cases, that cause was catastrophic organ failure."

"Define catastrophic organ failure, Doc."

"Everything in these victims stopped working at pretty much the same time: lungs, kidneys, liver, pancreas, intestines, hearts in some cases—they all shut down and for good reason."

"What would that be?"

"Based on their degraded conditions, I'd say exposure to a foreign organism. And since those conditions were so pervasive, we can only assume that, whatever this foreign organism is, it attacks healthy organs in a way like nothing I've ever seen before."

"Are we back to a murder investigation?" Caitlin asked. "Maybe something even bigger?"

Whatley frowned, trying to watch the parade passing by and converse with Caitlin at the same time. "My boy wanted to be a doctor."

"I'm sorry I never got the chance to know him, Doc."

"He was doing great in high school science classes." Whatley's gaze had turned distant, as if he was gazing past the parade instead of at the various floats, marching bands, dancers, and civic-minded locals waving up a storm. "Loved coming to work with me on those days we could swing it." His gaze sharpened as he turned back toward Caitlin, interest lost in the festival for the time being. "You remember the two victims from that apartment complex?"

"One had a new liver, the other a new kidney."

"In a perfect world, Ranger, transplant patients wouldn't need to take any anti-rejection drugs at all. The new organs would be treated at the genetic level to make them conform to the body's DNA."

"Treated with what exactly, Doc?"

Whatley smiled slightly at her question, their thoughts jibing. His next words were accompanied by the next marching band to pass them, kind of background music to their conversation now.

"Let's back up a bit first. Your immune system knows you're you thanks to something called major histocompatibility complexes, or MHCs. Something else called human leukocyte antigens, HLAs, encode MHC proteins so a cell can identify itself. So in a perfect world, you'd be able to get these HLAs to encode the donor's MHC proteins, thereby making the body recognize the organ as the recipient's own."

"But this isn't a perfect world, is it, Doc?"

"Far from it."

"And it certainly wasn't a perfect world for the two victims we found inside that apartment complex and the other sixteen you've found so far. You want to venture a guess as to exactly what happened to them?"

"I've already confirmed that they, and the two we found in San Antonio, were part of a clinical trial. I think they agreed to a new treatment methodology that was supposed to somehow trick their human leukocyte antigens into encoding their major histocompatibility complexes so their immune systems would recognize the cells as native to the body's architecture."

"So what went wrong, Doc? What caused such catastrophic organ failure in all these folks?"

"Theoretically?"

"Theoretically." Caitlin nodded.

Whatley went back to watching the next few floats pass, his expression turning sadly whimsical and reflective, before he returned his attention to Caitlin, picking up as if no time had passed at all. "From a biomechanical standpoint, I'd say something went drastically wrong with the cell surface marking. And, whatever it was, it sent the immune system into hyper-drive by making it appear that every single cell in the body was foreign. A massive overreaction that would be impossible to stop once it got going, what immune system specialists might call a cytokine storm. Hardly unprecedented given it's believed that cytokine storms were responsible for the disproportionate number of healthy young adult deaths during the 1918 influenza pandemic that killed nearly a hundred million people worldwide. And this kind of massive overreaction on the part of the immune system is the only thing that can possibly explain what we're facing here. Basically, the participants in this clinical trial had a ticking clock inserted into their bodies, just waiting for the alarm to go off."

"Any idea how long that would take?"

"One of our San Antonio victims received their new organ six weeks ago, and the other eight, neither presenting as anything but positive until right up until the time they took sick. And, near as I can tell, they were dead within a matter of hours, between two and six being a fair estimate. Sit down in your favorite chair, turn on a football game, and by halftime all of your organs have failed so quickly and totally that you never even have the opportunity to call nine-one-one. I didn't mention that, did I?"

"Mention what?"

"That in all the cases I've been able to find so far, not one of the victims managed to call for help." Whatley started to look toward the parade again, but changed his mind. "You can see why I needed to see you about this right away."

"You thinking maybe this clinical trial had something else in mind? You think somebody was testing out a new bioweapon in a way nobody would ever suspect?"

"Not exactly. I don't suspect anything nefarious in the clinical trial itself. I think whoever tried developing the ultimate anti-rejection protocol ended up developing something else entirely."

"A drug capable of killing from the inside."

"Imagine that drug in pill form, Ranger," Whatley advanced. "Imagine it as a liquid, gas, or aerosol. Imagine it baked into cake or sprinkled over neighborhood lawns like fertilizer."

"Is all that even possible?"

"Oh, easily so. Once you've developed the mechanism to alter the body chemistry so drastically, any number of delivery methods could work."

"Then you're saying…"

"I'm saying that whatever pharmaceutical company was testing this drug inadvertently created a weapon that's the biological equivalent of the Manhattan Project. A bioweapon for which there can be no vaccine or treatment. A bioweapon that would come with a one hundred percent kill rate."

Caitlin turned with Whatley toward a vintage Sherman tank being hauled as part of the Bluebonnet Fest Parade on a flatbed truck. Much smaller than the army's more recent incarnations, but its big gun looking scarily formidable from this close up. A Cobra helicopter followed on another flatbed.

"You need to prepare a presentation for Jones, Doc. We need to bring Washington in on this. Let me anticipate Jones's first question for you: how do we find the pharmaceutical company that developed this drug in the first place?"

"I already did," Whatley told her, his features brightening as the last of the parade floats made their way toward them. "Redfern Pharmaceuticals and, get this, they're based in Texas."

"Got an address for me, Doc?"

PART EIGHT

One thing that still distinguishes the modern Texas Rangers from most other law enforcement agents is that they do not wear uniforms. What is probably less well known, however, is that the famed lone-star-in-a-wheel badge worn by today's Rangers was only recently adopted. In fact, Ranger badges weren't commonly worn until the last twenty years of the nineteenth century, and were virtually unknown before the Civil War. There were several reasons for this. One is that a Ranger rarely needed to show a badge to a hostile Comanche or border bandit in order to put the latter on notice that they were on opposite sides of the law. Another is that appropriations for Rangers were so meager that a Ranger felt lucky to get reimbursed for feed for his horse and ammunition for his guns. As Mike Cox points out in a chapter on the subject in *Texas Ranger Tales,* some Rangers also "felt that a shiny star on the chest made too tempting a target."

—"Lone on the Range: Texas Lawmen" by
Jesse Sublett, *Texas Monthly,* December 31, 1969

73

"So you don't make the stuff anymore," Armand Fisker said, once Davey Skoll had finished with his double-talk. "That's what you're saying."

"It's the way clinical trials work," Skoll explained, making sure he was out of striking range.

He had a golf putter in his grasp, but didn't think for a moment it would be much use against Fisker as a weapon. The man must've had a skull full of rocks not to understand the way he'd already explained things to him.

"You're only allowed to manufacture as much of the drug as the trial requires," Skoll tried again.

"Says who?"

"FDA."

"F-D fuck me. Government can eat my shorts."

"Not all of us can operate our business sub rosa."

"What's that mean?"

"Under the radar."

"Business works a lot better that way." Fisker took a step forward, and Skoll matched him with a step back, keeping the distance between them where it was. "You should try it sometime."

"We'll see," Skoll said, and laid a golf ball down a full twenty feet from the pin.

They were standing inside what had been the Redfern Pharmaceuticals break room, when there were enough workers to fill it. Since the facility was down to a mere handful to watch over and guide the work of the machines, Skoll had converted it to a practice putting green, so he'd have something to do when he came to the manufacturing plant. He wasn't much of a golfer; wasn't much of anything when it came to athletics. He'd made himself into a decent enough skier to try diamond-branded slopes because all the fashionable types skied diamonds. If you didn't, you refrained from skiing altogether. In Skoll's mind, the beginner and intermediate slopes were for losers who did their runs around the lowly masses.

"How long will it take for you to get the production line for your magic juice up and running again, Davey?" Fisker asked him, still holding his calm.

"Not long. A few months, maybe."

"Months?"

"It's not as easy as it looks," Skoll said and putted.

The ball curved around the slight rise he'd had built into the practice green, dead on target with the hole, until Fisker stuck his foot out and stopped its roll.

"You put the ingredients in one end, and the pills, or whatever it is you're making, come out the other. What's so hard about that?"

"The measurements, specifications, and ingredients for every drug are different, Arm," Skoll explained, trying to sound as casual as he could manage. "Retrofitting the line requires a substantial commitment and significant capital investment."

"In addition to the rest of my investment in Skoll Inc., you mean."

"Besides," Skoll said, trying to ignore Fisker's sarcasm, "we're almost ready to begin producing those additional lots of Oxy. Your business's lifeblood, Arm."

Skoll watched Fisker scoop up the ball from the stiff, fake grass surface, flinching when it looked like Fisker was going to fling it straight at him. "Don't you be telling me anything about my business."

"Figure of speech, that's all."

Fisker cupped his groin. "This is what I think about your figure of speech, Davey."

How'd I get involved with this Neanderthal? Skoll asked himself.

But the way Fisker was looking at him made Skoll think maybe, somehow, he'd said it out loud, in which case he was about to need far more than just the putter he was still holding to defend himself.

Skoll was spared contemplating the dilemma further, when his phone beeped with a call from the facility's front gate.

"There's a woman here to see you, Mr. Skoll," the guard on duty there told him.

"A woman?" he asked, already trying to figure which of his many bimbos had tracked him here.

"Yes, sir, a Texas Ranger."

74

HOUSTON, TEXAS

Guillermo Paz was waiting when Cort Wesley screeched the rental car to a halt in the Village School parking lot, lunging out with the keys still jammed in the ignition. The colonel had used Homeland Security's chopper, loaned out most of the time to the Texas Rangers, to get here from San Antonio and had then sent it to pick Cort Wesley up from a vacant parking lot a mile from the Walls in Huntsville.

"I want to go see my son, Colonel."

Paz blocked his path when he started toward the dormitory, Cort Wesley slamming into what felt like an invisible force field with a foot to spare between them. "We going to have a problem here, Colonel?"

"Only if you want to answer the Houston police department's questions about your role in this."

Cort Wesley stepped back. "Let's get as close as we can."

Cort Wesley's breath caught in his chest when he saw the three bodies on the grass around the side of the Village School athletic center that was named after some rich alumni. They were still covered by what looked like ordinary bedsheets, soaked through in patches with blood. Then he saw the dark, twisted shapes of motorcycles in the general vicinity and realized the victims could only be more of Armand Fisker's private army comprised of the biker gangs he commanded from coast-to-coast.

Like father, like son.

"The men I had watching your son shot them," Paz explained.

Cort Wesley still had trouble catching his breath. He noticed a crime scene tech taking measurements around a broken window he thought was part of the boys' locker room.

"One of the bikers managed to throw a grenade."

"A frag?" Cort Wesley managed, wondering why no further damage was evident.

"True vintage model, outlaw, so vintage it didn't go off."

Cort Wesley looked at him through the darkness squeezed between two dormitory buildings. "You telling me one of those bikers managed to throw a grenade before your men killed him?"

Paz nodded. "Albert Einstein once said that 'There are only two ways to live your life. One is as though nothing is a miracle. The other is as though everything is a miracle.'"

"I guess I need to opt for the latter," Cort Wesley said, trying not to picture Luke climbing into his clothes when the window shattered and a dark, knobby thing that looked like a piece of stale fruit hit the floor near him.

He got his breath back and fixed his gaze on the massive shape beside him that looked as translucent as Leroy Epps in the darkness.

"I didn't ask you to put men on Luke."

"You didn't have to, outlaw. And I put other men on your oldest before I came up here."

"Why is it I've got this feeling you saw all this coming?"

"I saw, I felt...something, just as I have before. I misjudged it for darkness at first, but now I realize it was emptiness. A void cut out of mankind's heart and soul."

Cort Wesley could only shake his head. "I'd say you were a piece of work, Colonel, but I can't deny the world is looking like a much bigger place than I ever imagined. Reminds me of those video games my boys play that come with rising levels of difficulty. By the time you get up near the top, you're seeing everything differently and seeing things you couldn't see before."

Paz smiled tightly. "Thomas Edison once said, 'There is no supernatural. We are continually learning new things. There are powers within us which have not yet been developed and they will develop. We shall learn things of ourselves, which will be full of wonders, but none of them will be beyond the natural.'"

"I can relate to that, all right," Cort Wesley said, moving in closer to the big man who swallowed him in his shadow. "Now, you want to take me to my son or do I need to find him for myself?"

75

WACO, TEXAS

"You look familiar, Mr. Skoll," Caitlin said to the man who was an inch or so shorter than she, even wearing his shiny new boots. He had a teenager's floppy hair, longer than Luke's and almost as long as Dylan's. It looked more like a wig, right down to the way he raked a hand through it to flip the straying patches off his face, only to have it flop right back. "Have we ever met before?"

Skoll shook his head. "I'm sure I would have remembered, Ranger."

The glint in his eyes, as he studied her in ways she hated, was enough to tell Caitlin everything she needed to know about David Skoll. "This your office, sir?"

"The previous owner's, actually. I haven't had the opportunity to put my stamp on it yet."

"This would be the owner your hedge fund put out of business," Caitlin said, letting her eyes roam the walls while repeating what Doc Whatley had told her about Redfern Pharmaceuticals.

"Many business deals could be classified that way, Ranger. It's called capitalism."

She turned toward him slowly, contriteness forced over her features. "I call it corporate theft."

"I wouldn't."

"What would you call the price gouging you championed as soon as you took over, raising the cost of life-saving drugs by as much as ten thousand percent?"

"Is that what's brought you here, Ranger?"

"No, sir, I'm only here about one drug."

"It might help if you told me the name of this drug," Skoll said, after Caitlin had failed to get the rise out of him she'd been hoping for.

"I don't know if it has a name, Mr. Skoll, because it's still in the clinical trial phase."

"We have any number of drugs working their way toward approval. You're going to have to be more specific."

"Specific? How about the anti-rejection drug that's killed a whole bunch of people it was supposed to save? Eighteen and counting from coast-to-coast." Caitlin checked the code Doc Whatley had provided, which she'd entered onto the Notes app on her smart phone, and read it out loud. "That would be Lot U-two-five-seven-F."

Skoll tried for a harsh glare that made him look like a man practicing his acting in a mirror. "How did you come by this information?"

"So you're denying these allegations are accurate?"

"That's between the FDA and myself. And, even assuming your allegations are true, any number of miraculous, life-saving drugs got off to less than auspicious starts."

"Less than auspicious? Is that how you'd describe the eighteen deaths that we know of, thanks to your clinical study? I'm guessing that's going to turn out to be a very preliminary number, sir."

"I've seen some of the data and I dispute the results. Against the protocol for the study, some of those who died were treated post-surgery. Axiol, what you refer to as Lot U-two-five-seven-F, was never meant to work that way."

"Axiol. Your wonder drug's got a peculiar-sounding name, Mr. Skoll."

"Something I inherited when I bought the company," Skoll groused, adding, "Regrettably."

"If it had worked, would you have charged two arms and two legs for its use, sir, or just one?"

"It does work, Ranger, it just needs to be tweaked. The case trials you're referring to were anomalies and I'm confident the FDA's investigation will determine as such."

The path of Skoll's pacing took him into the reach of perimeter floodlights trying to cut through the darkness beyond the windows. The way the light hit his face made Skoll look even more familiar, but Caitlin couldn't place what it was, or what its significance might be. Whatever it was, she'd stuffed it into a different box she couldn't put her hands on right now.

"So how exactly was Axiol supposed to work?" Caitlin asked him.

"I'm not at liberty say."

"How's that?"

"Unless you want to deal with my lawyers, and sign a boatload of nondisclosure agreements, I can't disclose that information."

"Can't or won't, sir?"

Skoll smirked, his teeth so gleaming white they reminded Caitlin of a freshly painted picket fence before it dried all the way through. "You could also come back with a warrant to try to force me to comply. But I'm afraid I'd have to challenge that warrant in court."

"I wonder if we could even get on the docket before you put Redfern into bankruptcy, the way you did three of the other companies you acquired. I imagine that'll happen sooner rather than later, given the number of wrongful deaths you'll be facing from your wonder drug."

"You mentioned eighteen deaths, Ranger. There are more than five hundred test subjects involved in the clinical trial. And if you knew anything about the survival rate of transplant patients, you'd know that's well within the norm."

"I said eighteen deaths we know about *so far,* sir. The main reason I came out here today was to obtain the master list in order to get a more accurate number, as well as make sure the folks in your study who are still alive are warned appropriately."

Skoll frowned at the prospects of what she was proposing. "That information will require a warrant, too, Ranger."

"I didn't think I'd need one, Mr. Skoll, given that we both want to save lives here. Don't we?"

He looked away from her again and Caitlin realized that every time he did so, he was looking at the same thing.

"Why do you keep glancing toward that door?"

"What door?"

"The one you're trying real hard not to stare at right now."

Skoll yanked his gaze away from that door yet again. "Just the bathroom. I'm having a bit of a stomach issue."

"I'm sorry to hear that."

"You should be, since your baseless allegations are causing a flare-up right now."

"Well, Mr. Skoll," Caitlin said, moving toward the bathroom door, just to see how he'd react, "I'm sure Redfern manufactures a drug that can treat that. Maybe there are a few samples lying around." She stopped, Skoll trying very hard to appear casual, when he looked anything but. "So what form is Axiol manufactured in? Do I need a warrant for you to tell me that?"

"There's a pill form, but we've found intravenous infusion to be the most effective."

Caitlin closed the gap between them, forgetting all about the bathroom Skoll kept glancing toward. "Most effective in killing your test subjects, you mean."

"That's a baseless allegation, Ranger."

"Tell that to the eighteen subjects in your trial we know for sure are dead, sir."

Skoll bristled. "I believe we're done here. You want anything else, get a warrant and talk to my lawyer."

"It's unfortunate you want to play things that way, sir, because I thought we could both do some good here. And I was only getting started."

"And now you're finished, now *we're* finished."

Caitlin shook her head, expressing what looked like genuine regret. "That's a shame, Mr. Skoll, because how else am I going to figure out where I know you from?"

76

WACO, TEXAS

"Maybe you should step away from the window," Skoll said to Armand Fisker, after Fisker emerged from the bathroom where he'd been hiding for the duration of Skoll's conversation with Caitlin Strong.

Fisker continued to gaze through the night at the Texas Ranger's SUV, still parked in the company lot that rimmed the front of the building. "These are blackout windows and she's two hundred yards away."

"Don't discount her superpowers, Arm."

"Wonder Woman she's not, Davey boy."

"No, she's a Texas Ranger, and in these parts that's worse."

Fisker held his ground and turned to look at Skoll. "You handled yourself okay with her."

"I'm still shaking."

"She's got nothing on us, except suspicions."

"She's killed men for less than that."

"You think you need to tell me that after last night?"

Skoll swallowed hard. "I'm sorry. Have you scheduled the funeral?"

"Sons of bitches haven't even returned my son's body yet, and you're not coming anyway. Last thing we need right now are the Texas Rangers, or anybody else, figuring out that we're associated."

"I understand," Skoll said, grateful to be relieved of the obligation.

"And you don't talk to her or anyone else from the Rangers again without a lawyer present. If this goes bad, we need to string it out as long as we can to give you time to get the line up and running again to produce my Axiol. None of this intravenous shit, though. I want it in liquid form, maybe pill, too, not to mention aerosol. Imagine what a mass release of this shit could do to anybody who breathes it in."

"I'd rather not," Skoll said, meaning it. "And I won't be able to hold Caitlin Strong off that long."

Fisker forced a grin, wearing the gesture like an ill-fitting suit. "Then I guess it's a good thing you got me watching your back. You know the size of the army I got backing me up across the world?"

"You mean country."

"No, Davey, I mean the world."

77

AUSTIN, TEXAS

"You want to give me that again?" Jones asked from behind his desk in Austin.

"You heard me," Caitlin said, her mind still swimming with the summary she'd provided of Doc Whatley's revelations on the drug that was killing transplant recipients, combined with her visit to Redfern Pharmaceuticals and David Skoll.

"So let me get this straight," Jones said, shaking his head. "You paid a visit to the man behind this drug, David Skoll, to investigate something you're not authorized to investigate. Have I got that right?"

"We're talking about a potential weapon of mass destruction here, Jones."

"I'll take that as a yes. And in the process of questioning Skoll without authorization, you laid all your cards on the table. Why exactly did I think working for Homeland would change your behavior? You need to read the manual, Ranger."

"Which manual would that be?"

"The one that details how to conduct an investigation involving something as serious as a weapon with the kind of potential you're describing. We could have used David Skoll as an ally, something you've taken off the table." He gave her a long look, so cold and dry that the air seemed to crackle between them. "I'm starting to think the state of your current psyche is turning your judgment to shit."

"You want to say that in English, please?"

Jones tried to look compassionate, not quite succeeding. "Something really bad happened to you eighteen years ago, something you couldn't help but revisit after it happened to another girl who's the same age as you were at the time. I think that impaired your thinking. I think you're chasing boogeymen."

"You've said that to me before, Jones, and it turned out there really were monsters under the bed."

"This isn't Halloween, Ranger. You can take off that costume."

"What costume would that be?"

"The one with a mask of a person who's the only one that can see the light, while the rest of us are stumbling around in the dark." He hesitated, as Caitlin let her stare harden into a glare. "Sit down, please."

"I'll stand, if it's all the same to you."

Jones sat down and waited for her to join him, resuming even though she didn't. "The DNA tests came back on Frank Doyle's blood we lifted off your shirt. It doesn't match the DNA of the man who attacked you or Kelly Ann Beasley."

Caitlin felt her shoulders slump.

"I want you to know I personally showed her the mug shot taken by the Austin police," Jones continued. "Even with all the bruises and cuts you put there, Kelly Ann was sure she'd never seen him before in her life, and that includes the night she was sexually assaulted at Stubb's."

"Did you run David Skoll's file for me?" Caitlin said, doing a bad job of hiding her exasperation.

"Can we deal with one mess at a time? Like the shit show Cort Wesley Masters and his son have officially unleashed."

"What are you talking about?"

"We already had this discussion, but let me highlight the bold points again. You think Armand Fisker isn't on Homeland's radar? You think we don't take someone who's associated with some of the most serious whack jobs the world over seriously? You think this shit show Team Caitlin has unleashed hasn't let the genie out of the bottle? Because, Ranger, here's the kicker: in the past twelve hours or so, a bunch of those associates who are pushing Fisker's dope across their own countries have dropped off the map."

Jones paused to let his point sink in, Caitlin left trying to fit these new pieces into the puzzle she was already assembling.

"Allow me to elaborate," he resumed, when she failed to respond. "The world is truly going to shit. *Mein Kampf* is a number one bestseller in Germany again, because neo-Nazi movements are sprouting up all over the world. That's really nothing new. What is new is the fact that they're thriving, and expanding, because they are swimming in cash."

"All thanks to drug profits from product supplied by Armand Fisker," Caitlin picked up. "That's where you're going with this, right?"

"As rain, Ranger. Armand Fisker's taken his father's work and gone it one better. A national movement of criminal reactionaries who make up biker gangs has become an international movement of the same, organized in a way that makes around a dozen of the most dangerous people in the world beholden to Fisker. It's a true nightmare scenario. And you know the most amazing thing of all? It really does run in the family. Fisker picking up where his father left off, just like you're picking up where your grandfather did in 1944."

"You locate that missing box, Jones?"

He held his gaze out the window for a time, as if there was something to see through the darkness, before fixing his eyes on her again. "Turns out the file wasn't in a real box at all, just a metaphorical one it took some arm-twisting to release on the condition I keep the material under lock and key, strictly classified."

"Which, of course, you're not going to do."

"You remember what I told you about chasing the past, Ranger?"

"The difference being I may be close to finally catching it this time." Caitlin finally took a seat and settled back in her chair, feeling the tension in her muscles gradually let go. "So what happened next, Jones? What happened when my granddad got back to the German POW camp in Hearne?"

78

HEARNE, TEXAS; 1944

"I'm under orders not to talk to you, sir," Captain Lowry told Earl Strong from behind the desk in his office inside the camp headquarters. It had been hastily erected out of unfinished plywood and still smelled of fresh lumber, all of the beams left exposed.

"Well, then, can you tell if those orders came from none other than the director of the Federal Bureau of Investigation? A nod will do just fine, son."

Lowry didn't nod or answer, his gaze flitting from Earl to Henry Druce, the presence of a foreign serviceman clearly unnerving him. But Earl knew something else was unnerving him as well. He'd gotten the same feeling yesterday, during his initial visit to the camp, but had passed it off to three inmates being murdered on his watch. Now Earl understood the source of the man's anxiety, thanks to Witchell Long telling him of Lowry's complicity in whatever was going on here.

"I need to repeat my question for you, Captain?"

"Asking me again won't change the fact that I'm not at liberty to talk to you, Ranger."

Earl glued his eyes to Lowry. "How much they pay you to facilitate Gunther Haut's escape?"

Lowry's lips were quivering now, his teeth beginning to chatter. Earl noted an even deeper sense of anxiety and unease in the way he was clutching the edge of his desk with both hands.

"Now," he resumed, aiming his remarks at Druce this time, "what Captain Lowry may not have a grasp of is that it's one thing to be a traitor to the country, it's quite another to be a traitor to the state of Texas. Rangers have been dealing with that sort of thing for a hundred and twenty years now. Walk fifty feet and you'll probably find yourself over the graves of one or more of the traitors we've run up against."

"You don't understand," Lowry said, his expression desperate and pleading.

"Make me."

Lowry looked stuck between a swallow and a breath. "They've got them."

"Got who?"

"My wife and boys. If I talk, my family will be killed."

Earl moved closer to the desk. "By whom?"

"They didn't introduce themselves. Just showed up in my office with pictures."

"When?"

"Three days ago."

"The day before Gunther Haut escaped. Any notion as to what they found out, what made Haut so important to a whole bunch of people?"

Lowry shook his head.

"And what about these pictures those boys showed you?" Earl resumed. "You recognize anything besides your family?"

Lowry nodded. "My home. Just outside of Abilene."

Earl made a puckering sound, smacking his lips and letting the air from his mouth in what sounded like a low growl. He stole a glance at Druce, then looked back across the desk at Lowry.

"How about you let us help you out of this, Captain?"

Captain Lowry's family lived in a tract home on a parched piece of land in a large plot reserved for families from the nearby military base on the outskirts of a town Earl had never heard of near Abilene. He thought his years as a Ranger had brought him to every square foot of settled Texas, even if he was just passing through. But he never recalled being in these parts, not even once.

It looked as if these identical one-story homes had been dropped one at a time out of a cookie cutter atop parched prairie ground where any landscaping at all would never have taken. As a result, the homes were unshaded, roasting by day in the sun and radiating a collective heat that made the entire neighborhood feel like a sauna. The fact that the housing was temporary, and probably free, likely kept complaints to a minimum. And when they arose, it was doubtful anyone paid attention to them.

Earl edged up to Lowry's address in the mail truck he'd "borrowed" in his capacity as a Texas Ranger, the postman huddled in the truck's rear, stripped down to his skivvies so that Earl could don his uniform. He checked the nearby poles for telephone wires, none in evidence snaking into any of the cheap homes. Not that it mattered, since he couldn't imagine Lowry calling to alert his family's captors that a Texas Ranger was coming. He'd know if he did that, all Earl would find when he got there were bodies and blood.

Earl also figured Lowry knew this might be the only lifeline he got, the only chance to see his family survive their captivity. These weren't the kind of men likely to leave any semblance of a trail back to them, meaning his family's fate was sealed and Lowry damn well knew that. Just as he knew that if he confessed his part in this, to his own superiors or J. Edgar Hoover, his military career would be summarily over.

In Earl's experience, folks trusted the Rangers a lot more when it came to such situations, because of their reputation for getting done what was needed. He figured the unease he'd sensed in Lowry during his first visit to the prison camp in Hearne had been rooted in the captain coming close to telling him the truth then.

He trudged up the walk with single letter in hand, making himself look casual amid the surroundings when viewed from the front window where drawn drapes had been parted so eyes could follow his approach. There was no doorbell, so Earl rapped loudly on the door. Stopped, and then rapped again when no one answered. Louder to make sure whoever was inside grew cognizant of the neighboring homes clustered tight to each other starting to take notice.

Finally, the door creaked open and a sallow figure who smelled of stale sweat peered out.

"I got a special delivery letter here for Myrna Lowry."

"I'll take it," the man offered, his voice spun through gravel.

"I'm afraid it's official government correspondence from the United States military. I'm only authorized to have Mrs. Lowry sign for it."

"She's not home."

"I've delivered my share of letters like this. It likely has something to do with her husband, something she needs to know without further delay."

The man threw the door all the way open and got in Earl's face from the doorjamb. His smell almost made Earl gag, and the only other thing the Ranger noted about him was that his eyes looked yellow.

"Maybe you didn't hear what I said."

"Yes, I did," Earl said, pretending to stuff the letter back in his mailbag. "I sure did."

He came out with his .45 in the letter's place and shot the man in the chest, blowing him backward into the small home's foyer. He heard glass shatter in the next instant, indication that Henry Druce had burst in through the back. Two more shots rang out, followed by a third from a different caliber weapon, after which a thud sounded that could only be a body hitting the floor. Then kids were screaming and a woman was wailing unintelligibly, Earl tracking her voice inside the house to a bedroom doorway where a man with a face that looked tinted by charcoal held a young boy at gunpoint in the room's corner.

"Don't hurt my son, don't hurt my son!" Myrna Lowry pleaded.

Earl leaped over the body Druce had shot in the hallway, making the man holding the boy before him as leverage the last of the three.

"I'll kill him!" the gunman ranted.

"Go ahead," Earl said. "He ain't my boy. And as soon as he's out of the way I'll shoot your guts out and question you while you scream in the worst pain imaginable."

The man ran his eyes between Earl and Druce, trying to disguise the hopelessness he felt. "Kill me and you get nothing."

"You're not German. Your accent says Texas and the way you're holding that gun says you're no stranger to it, but no friend either, the way Captain Druce here and I are. Your part in this ends when you tell me who put you up to it. That's who I'm gonna inflict real pain on, and since you're a Texan, you know well enough to take a Ranger at his word."

The man seemed to collect his thoughts. "I'm leaving and I'm taking the boy with me."

"You're not going anywhere and neither is the boy."

"Please, please!" Myrna continued to wail.

"You don't let the boy go," Earl continued, "and the best you can hope for is to hang for treason. We can run this like you didn't know what you got yourself into, that you didn't grasp the gravity of your actions. That'll be enough to keep you from the end of a rope, providing you talk to me."

The man's eyes skittishly scanned the room, as if trying to see what lay beyond it.

"Nobody's left except you. If dying wasn't part of the assignment, I'd say you can consider the agreement severed. So far no one's been hurt by your hand, and if we keep it that way, you can come out of this alive, if nothing else. Even better than that, lots better maybe, if you draw the right judge."

Earl didn't know whether the charcoal streaks stemmed from the room's lighting, grime, or some skin condition with which the gunman was afflicted. His coarse hair skewed in all directions, as if he'd cut it himself.

"Can you name the man, or men, who put you up to this, the real villains in this picture show?"

"No," the man said, his voice losing a measure of its indignation and his grip on Bo Lowry's son slackening. "But I can give you an address."

Earl Strong and Henry Druce drove north twenty miles to a town comprised of scattered ranches and pig farms, the smell of manure the strongest Earl could ever remember. They'd waited until the police arrived to ensure that Captain Lowry's wife and children were turned over in proper fashion, along with their single surviving prisoner.

The address of the ranch in question wasn't marked, meaning Earl had to find it through a combination of the rough description the man he'd spared had provided and the process of elimination.

"You would have made a splendid soldier, Ranger," Druce complimented, after Earl parked his truck and turned off the lights, now that night had fallen.

"I'll take those words to heart, Captain," he said, letting his eyes adjust to the ribbons of darkness. "They mean a lot to me, especially coming from a man like you. Do a bit to fill the emptiness guilt has left behind."

"I suppose, sir, you were meant to stay here and fight the Nazis on your own ground."

"That does seem to be the size of things, doesn't it?" Earl studied the well-lit house that stood out amid the night, impossible to tell exactly how far away it was. "I'm thinking this place must be a haven for Nazis or, maybe, their sympathizers."

"I'm afraid that particular distinction is lost on me."

"True enough. The bullets from my forty-five sure aren't about to distinguish one from the other, if we go into this shooting. You figure Gunther Haut is inside?"

"If not, whoever's inside will be able to provide a notion as to his whereabouts."

"What do you think of my interrogation skills, by the way?"

"Did you bring your hammer, Ranger?"

They'd advanced a hundred feet onto the property, forgoing the use of flashlights that would have alerted any patrolling guards, when Earl jerked a hand against Druce's chest to stop him in his tracks.

"Something's wrong with the ground," the Ranger said. "I'm seeing bumps, like pimples cut out of the grass and scrub."

Druce followed his gaze, but picked up nothing. "Point one out to me. Lead me to it."

A few moments later, Druce was kneeling over the first raised impression Earl had brought him to. He took a knife from a sheath belted to his calf, and worked it about the slight mound that was no bigger than an anthill, testing what the tip found for him.

"It's a land mine, Ranger," he said softly, rising again. "Crude, crass, and homemade but more than enough to blow your bullocks off with a wrong step."

Earl kept surveying the grounds around them for a flashlight's spray or match's flare, a guard lighting up a cigarette. "Get behind me and let's walk in single file and real slow, Captain."

"If you feel one of them under your boot," Druce started, "don't lift it up again. Some mines are pressure-based. Stepping on it activates the explosives, but it's stepping off that blows them."

"I didn't come this far to get us both killed, sir."

They continued advancing toward the house, avoiding the spill of light raining down from the floods mounted on the roof.

"Something here ain't right," Earl said softly to Druce.

The Brit had his pistol in hand, clearly not trusting the quickness or reliability of his draw the way Earl did. "The lack of guards?"

Earl didn't bother nodding. "Yup, that was my thought. If this is some sort of Nazi hideout, if Gunther Haut is here, there should be at least a couple about."

"None that I can see."

Earl crouched and plucked something off the ground where the light from one of the floods hit it. "Well, this cigarette butt here is still soft enough to suggest there *was* a guard out here, and not all that long ago, either."

They continued toward the house, breaking off to peer through the windows on all sides, and joining up again at the rear of the house.

"It appears to be empty, Ranger," Druce reported.

"Yup, that was my estimation, too. What say we have a look inside anyway?"

The doors were all locked, so Earl resorted again to using a rock to break a window on a door that opened into the house's kitchen. He stuck a hand through, careful to avoid the jagged glass, threw back the bolt, and twisted the knob. Then he eased the door open and entered ahead of Druce.

They walked the first floor together, each with pistols palmed now, finding no one about and nothing amiss. Same thing on the second floor, which featured five bedrooms, all of which looked to have been recently made up. There were a pair of bathrooms upstairs as well, with medicine cabinets fully stocked and towels still slightly damp, either splayed across rods or hanging from hooks. Earl checked the drains, but couldn't tell from them how long it had been since the showers had actually been used.

"They must have left in a hurry," Druce concluded.

"Right, but *who* left in a hurry? If I didn't know better, I'd say this place was a kind of way station for Nazis like Haut to hole up for a time, while more permanent travel arrangements were being made."

"If he was here, though, it couldn't have been for more than a day."

"Let's check the basement," the Ranger suggested.

Earl knew what awaited them in the basement as soon as he eased open the heavy plank door. It had warped, causing it to scratch across the floor and jam to a halt when it was halfway ajar, and it released a coppery stench Earl recognized all too well.

The first body lay at the foot of the stairs, four others lying in clumps on the floor in the same general vicinity. So much blood had spilled from the five victims that it had pooled together in a series of thick puddles on the verge of joining up. From the look of things, absent closer inspection, it appeared to Earl as if someone had taken a Thompson machine gun to them and stitched it up and down their spines. There was nothing like what the blistering fury of those .45 caliber shells could do, a weapon made by the devil to do the work of God.

But not here.

"Oh my Lord," Earl heard Druce mutter, following his gaze to the assortment of Nazi flags and regalia that dominated the walls.

Especially flags, the swastika making its presence known one place after another, as if each of the treasonous residents of this house had one for himself. There were pictures of Hitler and his top cadre, men like Goebbels and Göring, whose faces were well known to Earl from all he'd read and studied about them, in lieu of being able to go and fight them for himself.

Seeing their faces plastered over a basement wall in Texas, in close proximity to the flags of the most murderous, hateful regime in human history, brought the pangs over his being ruled physically unfit for duty back to him. Like an itch he couldn't reach, or a dull throb no amount of aspirin could relieve.

But it wasn't the flags and photos that had moved Captain Henry Druce to invoke the name of the Lord, it was the assortment of weapons stored on a wall bracketed by the two biggest swastikas in the entire basement. Earl recognized German Mauser machine guns and carbines, to go with an assortment of Lugers. There were other pistols and rifles as well, along with gun belts and ammo packs for the heavy machine guns stored on shelving nearby next to long, thick, tubular weapons that looked as if they'd been made to fire the longer German-style grenades.

"Man oh man," was all Earl could think to say, pushing his hand through his hair to scratch at his scalp. "Looks like they were fixing to bring World War II to Texas."

"There are a few weapons missing from where the machine guns are hanging."

"And no Thompson in evidence," Earl added, his boots striking a pair of the gun's expended shells that must've bounced all the way over here. "That tells me whoever killed those boys we stepped over, must've taken it with them, along with a few others, if I'm seeing this wall right."

"Why slaughter their own, Ranger?" Druce asked him.

Earl was looking at the bodies again. "I'm guessing because 'their own' is a relative term. These boys must've been nothing more than grunts, hired help. Easily dispensed with, once they'd outlived their usefulness."

"Because of Gunther Haut."

Earl crouched again and touched a finger to the pooling blood. "This happened in the last hour, Captain. We must've just missed the sons of bitches. I'd like to ask our friend Witchell Long what he knows about this place."

"I'd venture to say he doesn't know it even exists. Haut killed Long's man at the Driskill Hotel in Austin, remember? That means we're facing two different factions here of Nazis, maybe two entirely different groups: one composed of nothing more than sympathizers, probably in it for the profit, the other composed of more soldiering types who genuinely believe in the cause, clearly not reluctant to get into a shooting war."

The Ranger stood back up, his knees cracking. "A shooting war against five men who couldn't shoot back. Drew lines up their spines with .45 caliber bullets when they headed for the stairs. Poor bastards never knew what hit them," Earl said, again picturing the fury of the Thompson, or Thompson*s*, that had done this.

"So the big boys killed their own men and then fled with Gunther Haut."

"That's the way it appears to measure up, doesn't it, Captain?"

"But we've got no idea where they went from here."

Earl nodded. "So what do you say we take a closer look at things upstairs to see if we can find something that can tell us?"

They found a large pantry off the kitchen that had been converted into a kind of command center complete with telephones, typewriters, and an old printing press. Earl was glad for the pungent scent of ink, since it washed the coppery stench of blood from his nostrils.

The Nazis headquartered here hadn't bothered to cover up their presence, and clearly, they had no plans to come back; nobody leaves five bodies in the basement and comes back.

But the weapons, Earl thought, the weapons were another matter. For men like this, weapons were like extra appendages. Men like this never left their weapons behind.

Unless they'd left in a real hurry.

Unless the purpose of their mission called for it.

Gunther Haut...

It all came back to him.

Who the hell was he?

"Did you say something?" Captain Druce asked him.

"Nah," Earl said, checking the contents of a trash can now, "just thinking out loud."

He came to a crumpled piece of carbon paper and flattened it out carefully, so it wouldn't rip, holding it up to the renovated pantry's thin light to see if he could read what it would have stenciled onto a second piece of paper.

"Think I may have something there, Captain."

And that's when the explosions sounded outside, one after another.

The screams followed almost immediately. A group of men, by the sound of things, who'd traipsed across the property without realizing the ground was booby-trapped. Earl Strong and Henry Druce rushed outside with guns ready, realizing almost immediately they wouldn't be needing them.

Even without recognizing them individually, their suits and dress shoes were more than enough to tell Earl the men who'd done the screaming were FBI, Hoover himself likely somewhere amongst them.

"There was a phone inside," Earl said to Druce. "You go get help here on the double, while I see what I can see."

Druce nodded stiffly and retraced his steps back to the house, leaving Earl clinging to the original path he'd taken across the field. He found J. Edgar Hoover standing board-stiff fifty feet away, having figured out his next step might very well be his last.

"Don't move, Mr. Hoover," Earl warned. "You got one on either side of you."

The director of the FBI squinted through the night. "Ranger Strong?"

"Bet you didn't think our paths would be crossing again, not under these circumstances anyway. But, as long as you follow my instructions, you'll come out of this just fine."

Earl could see Hoover swallow hard in the light spilling from the moon that had just risen. "My men..."

"I got somebody calling for help. A bunch are down, some worse than that. Now, sir, I want you to take one step forward, then sidestep a foot in my direction and turn face-on toward me."

Hoover switched on a flashlight he'd been holding and followed Earl's orders, looking like a man who'd woken up in the middle of a tightrope.

"One step to the left now.... That's it, sir. Now, walk straight for me."

Earl met him on a patch of flattened scrub. Hoover was shaking horribly and breathing so fast it seemed he was about to hyperventilate.

"We were both too late, sir," Earl told him. "Gunther Haut has flown the coop. You get a call from the local boys in Abilene about what they found at Captain Lowry's house?"

"You could have called me to deliver the report yourself, Ranger."

"Must've forgotten to get your number, sir."

J. Edgar Hoover groused but didn't challenge him on that subject further.

"You mind if I borrow that flashlight?" Earl asked him, gingerly removing the now folded-up piece of carbon paper from his pocket.

"What is that?"

The Ranger was already aiming the beam at two rows, one on top of the other, of what looked like lines of typed letters and numbers. "Where Gunther Haut and whoever's with him may have gone from here, Director. We better get a move on if we're gonna catch them."

79

AUSTIN, TEXAS

"Four of Hoover's men died that night and three more were seriously injured," Jones finished. "Only Hoover himself and his driver emerged unscathed. He, your grandfather, and Captain Druce must have headed for the train station in Abilene."

"Train station?"

"That's what your grandfather found on the carbon paper: a train schedule, specifically the schedule for trains running from Abilene to Fort Worth that same night."

"What happened when they got there?"

Jones shook his head. "Sorry, Ranger, the file, and the story, ends there."

"There's got to be more."

"I had a hard enough time digging this part up. The rest is buried in a box with whoever really killed JFK. Oh, which reminds me: there was one other thing."

"What's that, Jones?"

"Does the name Bill Kennedy mean anything to you?"

"Big Bill Kennedy?"

"I wouldn't know."

"Well, if it's Big Bill, he was a rookie Texas Ranger right around that time. Nephew of the legendary Ranger Frank Hamer who the governor of Texas herself called out of retirement to track down Bonnie and Clyde."

"Opinions vary on that, Ranger."

"Then they're wrong. Where's Big Bill Kennedy fit into all this?"

"I don't know. His name was on the last page of what I managed to dig up. Whatever else there was is gone for good."

"Well, that sucks."

"All this must've been covered up to spare Hoover the embarrassment of fucking up so bad."

"What about Gunther Haut, Jones?"

He shrugged. "Beats me. After he fled that house and headed for the train station, he dropped off the face of the Earth. There's no record of him any-where, and no record of any continued or follow-up investigation of his escape, or the murders he committed, by the Rangers or any other law enforcement body."

"I think Hoover knew more than he was saying. I think he's the one who orchestrated the whole damn cover-up."

"Par for the course, given his history, especially if he failed to bring Haut to justice. Last thing the country needed at that point was rumors of escaped Nazis running wild."

"They weren't rumors."

"It was only one Nazi, Ranger."

"Clearly a real important one, though."

"I've got something else here to take your mind off all that," Jones said, sliding across the table a manila folder Caitlin didn't recall him setting down in the first place. "Homeland's file on your friend David Skoll. I skimmed it, enough to know he's a real piece of work. SEC has him dead to rights on an insider trading beef, but he's slippery as an eel and will probably skate."

Caitlin lifted the folder from the conference table, but didn't open it. "Gotta love your faith in the system you're a part of."

"My part of the system doesn't employ judges and juries, Ranger, in case you've forgotten."

"No, you employ Guillermo Paz instead."

"That bothering you, all of a sudden?"

"Not even a little bit."

Jones aimed his gaze toward the folder in Caitlin's grasp. "Happy reading, Ranger. As if you needed any more reason to want to shoot this son of a bitch Skoll."

"I'm sure I'll find at least one, Jones," she said, turning for the door.

PART NINE

Still, the Rangers' caseload has continued to grow, along with the rest of Texas. In 1996, a total of 3,680 investigations resulted in 601 felony arrests, 157 misdemeanor arrests, and 598 indictments returned. The Rangers executed 319 search warrants, and secured 2,875 statements of which 473 were confessions to various crimes. The Rangers also recovered $3,129,349.13 in stolen property and at the same time seized contraband which totaled $1,088,659.00. There were 774 convictions for various crimes investigated by the Rangers resulting in 4 death sentences, 48 life sentences, and a total of 6,703 years in penitentiary time being assessed. Additionally, 518 court writs and 568 warrants were served and 107 executive security assignments were handled by the Rangers. The Rangers traveled 2,254,875 miles during 1996 and made 140 separate traffic referrals to appropriate authorities for dangerous drivers or driving conditions.

—"Lone on the Range: Texas Lawmen" by Jesse Sublett,
Texas Monthly, December 31, 1969
(Reprinted from Mike Cox's official history
pamphlet "Silver Stars and Six Guns," published
by the Waco Convention and Visitor Services.)

80

Caitlin stood in the darkest reaches of the front yard, a department store mannequin dressed like her seated in her usual spot on the porch swing, just in case gunmen dispatched by Armand Fisker paid a return visit. She had leaned both her twelve-gauge and AR-15 against the tree she was using for cover, half hoping Fisker showed up himself so she could finish this once and for all.

Cort Wesley would have quite a surprise waiting when he got back from the Village School in Houston, if that came to pass. She hoped he'd be bringing his younger son, Luke, home with him. She imagined the school would probably insist, after Guillermo Paz's men shot three bikers, but not before one managed to toss a hand grenade into the boys' locker room while Luke was changing after soccer practice.

What were the odds of that grenade not going off?

The colonel had told her about the visions he'd inherited from his mother, a woman who residents of the Caracas hillside slum where he'd grown up had labeled a *bruja,* or witch. She listened to Cort Wesley tell her about the lessons imparted to him by his dead cellmate, Leroy Epps. Caitlin herself was sure she'd spotted her late ancestors, including her father and grandfather, from time to time, although she neither conversed with them, nor did they offer her a glimpse of the future. She couldn't say for sure whether their fleeting presence had been conjured up by her imagination, any more than she could attest to the veracity of Paz's visions or Cort Wesley's ghostly conversations.

At least until tonight.

Only two explanations existed for why the hand grenade tossed into the boys' locker room at the Village School hadn't exploded: either it had been a purposeful act engineered by Armand Fisker or...

Go ahead, say it.

...it had been some kind of act of divine or spiritual intervention. Maybe Paz's mother, Cort Wesley's ghost, or some even higher power had disabled the firing mechanism that would've otherwise turned all those kids into pincushions for deadly shrapnel. Sometimes you had to accept the impossible, because nothing else made any sense.

Early into fixating on that thinking, she went inside and upstairs to check on Dylan. He lay atop his rumpled bedcovers in a twin bed that looked two small for him, earbuds connected to his iPhone still in place. Caitlin could hear the muffled riffs of a classic rock song she thought she recognized but quickly lost track of. When sleeping, Dylan looked no different than he had when she'd first met him when he was just thirteen. Maybe sleep really was more than just rest for the body and brain. Maybe it could rewind time and, if you tried hard enough, you could wake up in the midst of another phase of your life. Then she recalled a book she'd read in college by Kurt Vonnegut, *Slaughterhouse-Five,* where a character was forced to relive his life in random order. As Caitlin remembered, it didn't go too well.

She went back outside and resumed her vigil behind the big elm tree, just as happy to be on her feet to avoid the nightmares sleep promised. Every time she drifted off lately, her dreams felt like snippets from an old-fashioned newsreel. Frank Doyle was present in more than his share of the footage. No, he hadn't raped her or Kelly Ann Beasley, but Caitlin had a powerful notion that he knew who did. She couldn't dismiss him being on the scene of two sexual assaults, no matter how spread apart, as coincidence.

Standing behind that tree, Caitlin conjured visions of her grandfather, Earl

Strong, mowing down men in Nazi uniforms from the ramparts of the Alamo, defending the nation from the same spot all those proud Texans had stood up to Santa Anna. The Nazis kept coming and Earl kept shooting, shells flying from the Thompson's chamber, its steel drum packed to infinity with ammo.

She thought of Texas Ranger Big Bill Kennedy, the only person who might know what happened to her grandfather and J. Edgar Hoover next. He'd be in his midnineties, likely riding the range with her grandfather by now, but it couldn't hurt to ask D. W. Tepper to look into it for her.

Caitlin checked her phone to find she'd been out here for more than an hour, when Cort Wesley's truck pulled in to the driveway.

81

SHAVANO PARK, TEXAS

Luke piled out of the truck's passenger seat after him, Caitlin feeling her heart thump at the sight of the boy and the thought of that grenade landing within feet of him just hours before. He lumbered toward her across the lawn, one hand tucked into the jeans that looked molded to his skin, the other holding a backpack until he slung it over one of his sagging shoulders.

When had he grown up so much exactly?

He bounded straight into her arms, wordless and sniffling slightly, his hair damp with sweat. He was taller than Dylan, taller than she, almost as tall as his father.

They separated and Caitlin swiped a tear from his cheek.

"Dylan upstairs?" Luke said, clearing the scratchiness from his voice.

Caitlin aimed her gaze inside. "I didn't know he liked classic rock."

Luke derided her with his gaze, snickering. "Where you been? It's all he listens to."

Then he disappeared inside, Cort Wesley suddenly by her side, the two of them watching Luke close the door behind him before they wrapped their arms around each other's shoulders.

"Who was that again?" Caitlin said, shaking her head.

"I can't even blink anymore. Every time I do, he's a whole other person." He looked up at the department store mannequin dressed like her. "Friend of yours?"

"The idea came to me at the last minute."

"So you've been standing behind that tree?"

"Come on," Caitlin said, taking his hand. "I left my root beer over there."

"Couldn't we do this from inside the house?" Cort Wesley asked her, once they were behind the shaded darkness of the big elm tree. "You know, peer out a window?"

"Not if we don't want the boys to hear us."

"Hear us say what?"

"I can't make sense of what you said happened at Luke's school."

"The grenade didn't go off. I'm still trying to get my head around that." He turned her way with a gaze as black as the contents of the Hires bottle from which she was sipping. "One thing's for sure: this shit isn't going to stop until we take Armand Fisker off the map."

"I think it was meant to be a dud. The real thing would've brought the wrath of God down on Elk Grove."

"They won't find any connection between him and those bikers, Ranger. The whole message was meant just for me." He started to look away, then changed his mind. "I'm sorry, by the way."

"You've got nothing to apologize for."

"I'm talking about your tracking down that guy from all those years ago," Cort Wesley said, leaving things there.

"DNA test results came back negative," Caitlin told him. "He's not the guy."

"I know. Paz told me."

"Who told Paz?"

"You'll have to ask him, Ranger. But he knows where this is headed, too, just like he always seems to know." Cort Wesley stopped, and then started again right away. His eyes held her tighter. "What's the next step for that bouncer you beat the shit out of?"

"I got my share of lumps, too, Cort Wesley, but the man I'm after is still out there. I've waited eighteen years to find him. I can wait a little longer," Caitlin said. "So how'd it feel to return to the Walls prison as a visitor?"

"It didn't feel like anything at all, which is pretty much what I got out of it."

"That old man couldn't remember anything helpful about Cliven Fisker?"

"He thought I was Boone Masters. Darl Pickett's stuck in the 1970s, unfortunately, and what he's got left for brains have turned to mush."

"You got nothing valuable out of him?"

"Valuable? No. Crazy? Oh, yeah, something he claimed Cliven Fisker confided to him over prison moonshine. In other words, I wasted a trip."

"Let's go inside, Cort Wesley," Caitlin said, picking up the AR-15, while he grabbed the shotgun.

Caitlin laid the file Jones had assembled on David Skoll on the coffee table and opened it while Cort Wesley kept an eye peeled out the window.

"What's that?" he asked her.

She started scanning the pages and flipping through some pictures, not really paying attention. "The file on another lowlife we're looking into on something else entirely."

"Are there really this many assholes in Texas, or do we just attract the lion's share of them?"

Caitlin kept flipping. "It's a big state, Cort Wesley."

Caitlin had gotten to the part of Skoll's file that listed all his holdings, both past and present. There were four pages, capsule summaries following each listing. She skimmed them quickly, not expecting to find anything of note until her eyes fastened on one of the last items listed.

"Holy shit," she managed.

82

Frank Doyle glared at Caitlin from the other side of the table in the interrogation room, the chains affixed to the manacles fastened around his wrists rattling. His face was a patchwork assemblage of cuts and bruises, inflicted during the course of their fight, along with a nose swollen to twice its normal size down by the tip where Caitlin's palm-heel strike had done its damage.

"Why don't you ask them to take these off?"

"You're looking good, Frank," Caitlin said, taking a seat across from him and laying the file on David Skoll that Jones had provided down before her. "Looks like none of that damage I did to your face is going to make you any uglier than you already were."

"I'm gonna sue you. My lawyer says I got a case. He says we gotta get in line behind another innocent person you just put in the hospital."

"Except I shot him, so you should consider yourself lucky."

"My lawyer says you identified yourself as a Texas Ranger, even though you're on suspension or something. He says that's the equivalent of impersonating an officer. Your career's finished, from where I'm standing." Doyle gloated.

"Except you're sitting, Frank, and as I recall you came at me before I had a chance to identify myself as anything."

"My lawyer was referring to you talking to the hostess."

"She saw the badge, drew her own conclusions."

"You had no right to be wearing it."

"It belonged to my father and his father before him. It's an heirloom, like a piece of jewelry. And I drove all the way up here today to offer you a jewel of your own: an opportunity to reduce your sentence, maybe walk altogether."

"A suspended Texas Ranger? There a reason why I should believe a damn word you say?"

Caitlin studied Frank Doyle from across the table, paying special attention to the way his eyes kept shifting, as if he couldn't decide what to focus on. "You really don't remember me, do you?"

"I remember you assaulting me."

"I'm talking about eighteen years ago, back when you were pretending to be a college student."

Doyle grinned, showing a black hole in his mouth where Caitlin must have knocked out a tooth. "Best snatch around, lady. You blame me? Guess you weren't much of one to have faded out of my memory."

"Or maybe it was because you weren't the one who raped me, Frank, any more than you raped Kelly Ann Beasley. Her name ring a bell?"

"I'm drawing another blank."

"It took me a while to figure out. Things didn't even dawn on me, when I was sitting in the same room with her. But she looked something like I did eighteen years ago."

"Poor thing."

Caitlin ignored him. "Same color hair, same height or a little taller. Maybe a little shy."

"What does 'shy' look like exactly?" Doyle smirked, rattling his chains dramatically.

Caitlin leaned forward over the manila folder, close enough for Doyle to try grabbing her, even manacled. "Why don't you tell me, Frank? It's why you picked me out eighteen years ago at that party, isn't it? And it's why you picked out Kelly Ann at Stubb's Barbecue at that graduation party a few nights back. Yup, I had you all wrong, making you out to be a rapist, when all you are is a pimp."

"You're not supposed to be talking to me without my lawyer present."

"I'm doing you a favor, remember? I'm the only hope you've got to avoid a long stretch in Huntsville. You think Texas Rangers, suspended or otherwise, ever fail to make a case? You think if we don't have the evidence we need against you, it won't magically appear?"

"The fuck you say?"

Caitlin switched gears on a dime. "It doesn't have to go down like that. I can make this all go away. I just need a little help."

With that, Caitlin flipped open the manila folder and extracted a picture of David Skoll, angling it so Doyle could get a good look. "His name's David Skoll. Recognize him?"

"Nope," he said, after a quick glance.

"You want to try that again?"

"I don't have to. Never saw the man before in my life."

Caitlin nodded and crossed her arms, leaving Skoll's picture on the table between them. "That's funny, because he's your boss, Frank. David Skoll owns Stubb's Barbecue."

"He hired you as a part-time bartender and bouncer," Caitlin continued, before Doyle could respond. "But what you really were was his full-time pimp, same capacity you served in eighteen years ago. Remember that party, us going down into the basement where you handed me that red Solo cup half-filled with punch you got from the bar?"

Doyle tried to cross his arms, forgetting he had the manacles on, rattling the chains again. "I've got nothing to say to you, and I got no clue what you're talking about."

"Of course you do, Frank. Because David Skoll was the bartender."

83

Austin, Texas

Doyle's face had gone white as a sheet. He suddenly looked like a man studying his own breathing patterns.

"When we met for the first time last night, first time while I was conscious anyway, I knew I'd seen him before," Caitlin continued, "but I couldn't remember from where. And I thought I'd hit a dead end when Kelly Ann Beasley said she thought her attacker was a woman. But David Skoll kind of looks like a girl, doesn't he, Frank? With that boyish hair and the face of a cherub, he's kind of pretty. So tell me, was pimping girls for him the only thing the two of you did together?"

Doyle snapped his hands toward her, his elbows jerked back into place by the chains binding him to the steel table.

"I paid a visit to Kelly Ann Beasley on my way here," Caitlin lied. "Turns out she wasn't all the way out when he raped her. After I arrest him, she'll be able to pick him out of a lineup dead solid perfect. When that happens, either you're going down as an accessory, which means you carry the full load, or you testify against Skoll, starting now, in which case you may have nothing to carry on your own. Hell, I'll even drop the assaulting an officer charges."

"I wish I'd killed you the other day," Doyle said, in a hissing growl.

"As opposed to getting your ass kicked by a girl, you mean."

He made a low rumble in his throat, like a dog getting ready to pounce.

"Same girl you served up to David Skoll on a platter eighteen years ago. And there's no statute of limitations on the crime of rape in Texas, in case you didn't know."

"My lawyer's gonna have your badge," Doyle said, not sounding very convincing.

"You mean my daddy and granddaddy's badge? You're lucky it's me sitting here right now instead of one of them, or you'd be wearing a bullet hole in the middle of your forehead. How many times has Skoll pulled you out of the gutter since the two of you fed me GHB in that Solo cup? You've been in and out of jail. Judge let you try rehab instead once, except you ended up getting arrested for stealing cigarettes, and your last known address is a flophouse. I guess it was a good thing Skoll was hiring." Caitlin leaned forward again. "So, tell me, Frank, was this all part of the plan when he bought Stubb's Barbecue? Was pimping and spiking college girls' drinks included in the job description? Skoll's going down, and I'm gonna enjoy being the one to kick his legs out from under him. Decision you need to make is which side of this you wanna come down on. But if I walk out that door without your statement in my hand, your opportunity to make that decision goes away. So we got a short window here. I've got a headache and I hear David Skoll is running a warehouse sale at Redfern Pharmaceuticals in Waco on aspirin. Tick-tock, Frank, time's running out."

Caitlin got up, intending to move for the door, just as she'd threatened. But Frank Doyle's eyes holding fast to her changed her mind. Those eyes were the one thing about him that hadn't changed, hadn't aged with the pathetic adult he'd turned into, beholden to a millionaire's sexual cravings for what meager livelihood he could eke out. She looked in those eyes and it was eighteen years ago again, Frank Doyle coaxing her out of her shell with his looks, his charm, and his smile. Maybe exchanging a quick, knowing glance with David Skoll at the basement bar, as he handed Caitlin the Solo cup that had turned the rest of the night into a black hole and haunted her life ever since.

With that thought, she came around the table and glared down at Doyle.

"David Skoll, Frank. It's you or him. Make your choice."

84

BOERNE, TEXAS

"I knew you'd be coming, outlaw," Guillermo Paz said, looking up from his priest's bedside at Menger Springs Senior Living Community. "I wanted to be here when you came looking for me."

"Why's that, Colonel?"

Paz looked toward his priest. "So we can receive his blessing for what we're about to do."

"No offense, but he doesn't look particularly up to the task."

The side rail was lowered again, so Paz could feed Father Boylston his breakfast, consisting of the watered-down oatmeal he ate for lunch and dinner, too. The spoon looked like something out of a dollhouse kitchen in Paz's massive hand, and Cort Wesley followed the process of him gently easing the next spoonful toward the priest's mouth that gaped gratefully to accept it. Beyond that, the priest he knew had been Guillermo Paz's spiritual adviser since he'd come to San Antonio flashed nothing that even passed for life. Except for an occasional blink, his eyes were blank and unresponsive, not even following the spoon beyond the outskirts of their line of vision.

"Being up to the task is a relative term, outlaw."

Cort Wesley noticed a stack of cards, the size of the playing variety, imprinted with simple words and symbols, fanned across the tray between the bowl of oatmeal and what looked like a kid's sippy cup, equipped with an extra-long straw.

"I've been trying to find a way for my priest to communicate," Paz said, noting his interest, "a means to allow him to better express himself."

"How's that going?"

"Not very well. Once in a while, especially with the YES and NO cards, I think I'm making progress, only to realize it was more likely my priest passing gas."

"Got one of those cards for revenge, Colonel?"

Paz left his eyes on Father Boylston as he responded. "I'm of the same mind on that subject as Nietzsche who said, 'It is impossible to suffer without making someone pay for it.'"

"Now there's someone I can agree with."

"But John Milton said, 'He that studieth revenge keepeth his own wounds open, which otherwise would heal and do well.'"

"That guy," Cort Wesley said, "not so much."

"We'll have satellite reconnaissance and thermal imaging of Elk Grove within a few hours," Paz told him, easing another spoonful of oatmeal toward the priest's open mouth.

"How many men will Jones allow you to bring?"

"As many as we need."

"I get the feeling Armand Fisker's been on his radar a lot longer than he's been saying. I think we're doing his dirty work for him, Colonel. If I didn't know better, I'd say it was Jones who sent those bikers to the Village School last night. That would explain why the grenade was meant to rattle my spine, instead of blow up. I think maybe he set this whole thing up."

Paz didn't look his way or respond, readying another spoonful instead, for when Father Boylston swallowed the last one. "Tell me about the Ranger, outlaw."

"What about her?"

"Last night, in a dream, I saw her cut the head off a serpent."

"She thinks she found the man who raped her eighteen years ago," Cort Wesley said, the candidness of his statement surprising him.

"I hope she's familiar with what Alexander Dumas wrote in *The Count of Monte Cristo*: 'Fool that I am, that I did not tear out my heart the day I resolved to revenge myself.'"

"I'm not sure if she's read the book, but I think she knows that."

Paz finally glanced Cort Wesley's way. "And did you think she'd get in a bar fight with another creature from her past?"

"I like you calling him a 'creature.'"

"Humanity is something that should be earned, not given. The monsters around us come in many shapes and sizes, all of them sharing the desire to see us as no better than they are, to provide a moral justification for their actions."

"If I don't do this, Colonel, Armand Fisker is going to kill both my boys. How's that for moral justification?"

Paz was still turned toward Father Boylston, but Cort Wesley watched him smile slightly in the reflection off the window glass. "How do you feel about the outlaw's words, Padre? Can you bless his intentions, or do you agree with Gandhi that 'An eye for an eye will only make the whole world blind'?"

The priest swiped some stray oatmeal from his lips with his tongue, his mouth working to swallow the tiny portion.

Paz left the spoon in the soupy remains of the bowl this time and selected the YES and NO cards in either hand. "Are you still hungry, Padre? Do you want some more of your breakfast? Look toward the NO or the YES to give me your answer."

The priest just lay there, shoulders supported by the bed's upright position, his mouth making a smacking sound.

"YES or NO?"

The level of compassion Paz was showing the man didn't change the fact that his tone suggested more of a secret police interrogation, his words somehow sounding like they carried the threat of torture behind them to Cort Wesley.

"Come on, you can do this, Padre, I know you can."

The priest's eyes flitted, seeming to regard the remains of his oatmeal for the first time. Then he appeared to regard Paz with the slightest bit of recognition, paying no heed to the YES and NO cards, before the brief flicker of life flashed from his eyes again.

Paz laid the cards down atop the bedcovers. "I'm not giving up," he told his priest, his tone grim and solemn at the same time. "I just want you to know that, Padre. I'll be here tomorrow, and the day after, and the day after that. I wish you didn't need me now, as much as I've needed you all these years. I hate not having your wisdom to guide me about what I've done and what I'm planning, like today when my outlaw friend here wants to know if it's okay for us to remove a man from this world who's tried to kill both his boys. We came here for your blessing."

The bedcovers rustled and shifted, as Cort Wesley looked on.

"Come on, you can do this," Paz implored.

One of the signal cards had slipped to the floor and Cort Wesley plucked it from the cold tile.

"Come on, Padre, you can do this. I know you can."

"Colonel," Cort Wesley said softly, when Father Boylston remained unresponsive, "I think we've got his answer."

Paz turned to see Cort Wesley holding the card he'd scooped up off the floor:

YES

85

As soon as she was back in her car, Caitlin felt sick to her stomach. An unpleasant odor Frank Doyle had dragged into the interrogation room with him seemed to ride her. A smell like milk that had spoiled filled her SUV to the point where she thought a rodent might have found its way in and died beneath one of the seats.

She opened all the windows, but a wave of nausea still overcame her and she opened her door to vomit. Nothing but a few dry heaves and some bile emerged, and Caitlin pulled herself all the way back into the driver's seat. She popped a breath mint shaped like a tire she'd gotten at the car wash into her mouth.

She angled the rearview mirror to get a look at her face and used it make sure she wiped her lips clean. Then she tussled her hair and tried to massage the color back into her cheeks before switching on the radio to get some music on.

Only a few chords had played before her Bluetooth rang with a call from D. W. Tepper.

"Hey, Captain," she managed, pushing the words through her mouth that had gone dry and pasty.

"I don't even want to know where you are," Tepper told her. "I don't need to know, since I'm sure somebody's gonna be calling me before you know it complaining about something you did."

"I found the man who assaulted me, D.W. Frank Doyle's been acting as a pimp for a rapist who's likely left a trail of assaulted women across the entire state."

"So you're in Austin."

"Just about to head back."

"Don't. There's a man in the area expecting you who can clear up some things on another front, an old Ranger named Big Bill Kennedy."

Caitlin instantly recalled the story Jones had told her the previous night about her grandfather's pursuit of the escaped Nazi prisoner Gunther Haut.

"Jones told me you might be interested in his whereabouts."

"Sure, Captain, so I can leave flowers on his grave. The man must be near a hundred."

"Pushing ninety-five as we speak, but still making the rounds to elementary schools to spread the Ranger word. Matter of fact, he's visiting one not far from where you're at right now. I already called ahead to tell him you were coming."

86

WACO, TEXAS

David Skoll knew he had a problem, yet another one. Frank Doyle refused to see the lawyer he'd hired for him, a man with a reputation for running circles around law enforcement. Somebody at Austin police headquarters told the lawyer that Doyle had made other arrangements.

What did that mean exactly?

Skoll had no idea, knew only that it couldn't be good. Only thing the lawyer could tell him was that Doyle had received a visit earlier in the morning from a Texas Ranger. The Austin police, the lawyer explained, had broken protocol by putting Doyle in a room with her.

Her?

Meaning Caitlin Strong. Meaning he was fucked, and how long could it be before Armand Fisker got word that his business associate was going to be arrested on rape charges and take whatever measures necessary to sever all trace of the connection between them? How many of his crazy bikers would Fisker send to Redfern Pharmaceuticals to make sure Skoll never got the chance to do to Fisker what Frank Doyle had done to him? And he didn't expect he'd be able to last very long in jail, not with the Aryan Brotherhood as powerful as ever across the prison system.

"How's the work coming?" he asked Dobie, his windowless office smelling of Doritos and the can of Dr Pepper he'd spilled yesterday that had left the floor all sticky.

Dobie stuck another chip in his mouth. "Almost there. The program's rudimentary, but it should work."

"Rudimentary," Skoll repeated over the hum of the pharmaceutical plant's machines doing what they did twenty-four hours a day. "What's that mean in this case?"

"Basic. I haven't got time to write new code, so I had to improvise. Fortunately, I found a back door into the AM-TECH site and raided their proprietary software for the upgrade we needed."

"AM-TECH?"

"Here, take a look," Dobie said, crunching on his chips as he spun his oversized computer screen around so Skoll could see it.

"Wow," Skoll said, reacting to the man-sized robots packing an arsenal of weapons that AM-TECH was building for the military.

"That was my reaction, too."

"And you can turn our robots into *that?*"

"Close enough, boss, minus the weapons, of course."

Skoll looked back at the screen, passing on Dobie's offer to take a Dorito from the bag he extended in an orange-tinted hand. "Best news I've heard in a while."

87

ROUND ROCK, TEXAS

"You look just like your granddaddy," Big Bill Kennedy said, grinning at Caitlin mischievously.

"I'm going to take that as a compliment, sir."

"Sir? I ain't no sir any more than Earl Strong was. I'm a Texas Ranger." He took off his Stetson and scratched at his scalp through the sparse pockets of hair. "Man oh man, in our day if you'd ever said a lady would be ranging, I don't even wanna repeat the language I would've come at you with."

"Then I appreciate you taking the time to see me even more."

The old Ranger glanced about the playground from the picnic table they occupied, as a big rubber ball bounced past them. "Well, it is recess."

In Caitlin's mind, Big Bill Kennedy didn't look a day over seventy, drawing stares in the playground of Blackland Prairie Elementary School, north of Austin in Round Rock. She had to love any school that featured a Coding Club for fifth graders among its offerings, but still sought to bring living pieces of history into the classroom to remind students of the kind of heroes it took to bring the country that far.

Caitlin had entered a classroom that looked designed and furnished by NASA through a door in the rear of the room and had watched the tail end of Big Bill's presentation from there without attracting any attention. There were a lot of questions about the guns and artifacts he'd brought in for a kind of show-and-tell, the class especially fascinated by the particular histories of the Samuel Walker Colt Peacemaker and the Model 1911 .45 caliber pistols. Her grandfather's Colt had been the first gun Caitlin ever shot, not particularly well, given she was only seven years old at the time.

Big Bill had told Tepper he had a break around eleven, at which point she could ask him her own questions pertaining to history. In particular about what had happened after Earl Strong and Captain Henry Druce of the British SAS, with J. Edgar Hoover in tow, had trailed murderous Nazis from Abilene to Fort Worth.

Caitlin took a sip of chocolate milk from the eight-ounce, squat, boxlike design she hadn't seen since attending a school like this herself, when they'd only served regular milk. "Did Captain Tepper tell you what I came to talk to you about?"

"He didn't have to. And what you're inquiring about, little lady, is something your granddad and I were both sworn to secrecy concerning."

"Like state secrets, national security, that sort of thing?"

Big Bill shrugged his still-formidable-looking but now bony shoulders. "They didn't use those terms exactly back in 1944, but close enough, yeah.

Your granddaddy had been put through the wringer when it came to Gunther Haut, from the time he set foot in that Hearne prisoner-of-war camp. But he didn't learn the truth why until that night I met him for the first time and, like me, I don't think he ever shared it with a single soul afterward."

"I appreciate you doing so on my account, Big Bill."

"Well, little lady, I'm ninety-five years old, and no matter how good I feel and how often I get to dress up like a Ranger again to visit elementary schools, being ninety-five is like holding an express ticket to the O.K. Corral in the sky." His eyes looked a bit faded in color from what must've once been a deep, majestic blue, but they still sparkled with life as they regarded Caitlin. "I can't let this story make that trip with me, and I can't think of anyone I'd rather turn it over to than you."

Caitlin finished her milk. "I appreciate that more than I can say, sir."

"What did I say about calling me sir, little lady?" Big Bill scolded. "And you better reserve judgment on that assessment until after you hear how the story ended."

88

ABILENE, TEXAS; 1944

"My men can handle things from here, Ranger," J. Edgar Hoover said to Earl Strong.

"You mean the ones who didn't get blown up by land mines in their rush to storm a house with nothing but dead people inside?" Earl told him, the night's darkness hiding the grin he couldn't wipe from his face over seeing the head of the FBI damn near piss himself. "My truck's over here."

"You check the IDs on the bodies?"

"Didn't have to know they was dead, back-shot by the real bad boys here. This whole thing's been ugly from the time it started, but it would've been less ugly if you'd told what we were up against from the start in Hearne."

"There is no 'we,' Ranger."

Earl flashed Captain Henry Druce a wink. "There is now, Mr. Hoover."

Earl got as much as his Chevy truck would give him on the forty-five-minute drive to downtown Abilene and the train station where the Texas and Pacific Railroad's line connected the city with Fort Worth. The company had conceived the line way back in the 1870s as part of an ambitious plan to build a southern spur of the transcontinental railroad that would run all the way to California.

"Do we have any chance of catching that train, Ranger?" Hoover asked him, squeezed into the center of the cab with Druce pressed against the door.

"Only if it's late, Director, which does tend to happen from time to time," Earl told him, holding the Chevy at its top speed. "And it's gotta be late by at least an hour for us to have any chance at all. Regardless, whether we even get there or not is up to you, Mr. Hoover."

"How's that?"

Earl braked hard and swung the truck off the road, slinging it down a slight embankment. "See, sir, we're gonna have a little talk, the three of us. Since I'm the one literally in the driver's seat, you boys are gonna tell me what brought you both to these parts here and now, or this taxi ride is over." He looked toward J. Edgar Hoover, hand instinctively straddling the .45 holstered on his belt. "You, Mr. Director, are the reason why Gunther Haut escaped when he did with the help of the camp commander. You're the reason Haut's three bunkmates had to die, so they wouldn't be any the wiser. It all happened because word got to the people behind all this that you were on your way to take Haut into FBI custody for reasons you elected to keep from me." Earl stopped there and moved his gaze across Hoover to Druce. "And you, Captain, must think I'm a fool to believe the British government and the Special Air Service sent you all the way to Texas on some made-up fox hunt, when you knew the fox you were after all along. So unless you boys want Gunther Haut to be in the wind for good, which I'm surmising you don't, you best come clean on what all this is really about and who this murdering son of a bitch really is."

Druce and Hoover stiffened, their breathing starting to fog up the truck's windows, moving Earl to roll down his all the way. There was something uniformly strange about the bent of their gazes, Earl certain it wasn't doubt he was seeing in them, so much as fear.

"Let me tell you boys another thing from my perspective," he told them. "It irks me every day of my life that I never got my chance to fight the Nazis over in Europe. My own grandfather was a Civil War hero fighting for Texas, but my father William Ray missed out on the First World War, just like I missed out in the second. So you might say I'm doing this for both of us. If I can't fight the Nazis in Europe, I can damn well fight them in Texas."

J. Edgar Hoover stopped just short of a smile. Earl realized he had a perfectly round face and a tiny mouth with teeth that looked no bigger than a child's first set.

"You think your sleep is haunted by not going to Europe to fight the Nazis, Ranger?" the director of the FBI asked him. "Well, after you hear what I have to say, you may never sleep again...."

"Is he telling the truth, Captain?" Earl asked Druce, spinning his truck back onto the pavement and pushing the engine harder than he ever had before.

"He is indeed, Ranger, at least according to the best available intelligence."

Earl shook his head, wished he had some tobacco to spit like his own dad, William Ray Strong, but he'd never developed a taste for it. "You boys are a true piece of work. Know the difference between spies, secret agents, and real lawmen? Real lawmen know what it takes to work together."

"Really, Ranger Strong?" snapped Hoover. "I pulled your file in the aftermath of our initial meeting, and that wouldn't appear to describe you at all. You're no more a team player than every other Western gunfighter who thought he could clean up the world on his own, the difference being the world has passed you by."

"Has it now? Well, Director, I'm not really interested in cleaning up the whole world, just my own little part of it you boys traipsed into like you owned it. You think you're the first to show up in Texas thinking we were a bunch of local yokel cowboys who needed schooling on life beyond the great frontier? Bullshit. And the thing all of you have in common is that when you leave, it's always with your tails between your legs, on account of you found something bigger than you were. You're a fool, Mr. Hoover."

Earl could see the man's neck redden beneath the collar of his topcoat, his eyes opening so wide they glistened in the thin light of the truck's interior. "A fool who can make life extremely difficult for you, once this is over, Ranger."

"Yeah? And maybe then I'd get the opportunity to spill my guts that, in spite of everything you knew and who you were up against, you let your men walk straight through a minefield to attack a bunch of corpses. I'm locked and loaded, sir. Sometimes you need a good bar fight, but I don't suppose you'd know much on that count."

"Just get us to that train station, Ranger."

"You a praying man, Mr. Hoover? 'Cause if you are, you better start praying that train is late."

It wasn't. Upon reaching the station, they learned the train had departed for Fort Worth on time forty-five minutes earlier.

"They still got a couple hours before they get there," Earl told J. Edgar Hoover and Captain Henry Druce. "Any chance of rustling up a plane?"

Hoover shook his head, seeming to resist the motion as if hating to show weakness of any kind.

"Well, then, I guess we better get back on the road and burn some rubber. Your FBI's gonna owe me a new set of tires when this is over, Mr. Director, but first I've got a phone call to make."

Fort Worth, Texas; 1944

Ranger Big Bill Kennedy was waiting for them outside the Fort Worth train station when they arrived two hours later. He'd just gotten back to his parents' home from an extended patrol when Earl's labored call from Abilene reached him, repeating his orders twice to make sure the young Ranger had heard him straight.

"You are not to approach them under any circumstances, son. Repeat that for me."

"You already told me twice."

"Then it should be easy for you to repeat it."

"I won't approach them no matter what."

"Don't wear your star or your gun," Earl resumed. "Nothing that might spook them. You got one job and one job only: follow them to wherever they go and report their whereabouts when we arrive at the station."

Having now arrived, Earl could see that Kennedy's nickname was well earned; he wasn't very broad, but was just as tall as any basketball player Earl had ever seen.

Kennedy approached Earl's truck and laid his hands on the open window ledge, breathing hard from nerves more than exertion.

"They checked into the Hotel Texas just down Main Street a ways."

"Must be waiting for another train come morning," Earl surmised, "or maybe something faster. How many are we looking at?"

"Six: five big, one smaller."

Druce and J. Edgar Hoover exchanged a glance.

"Any weapons?" Hoover asked the young Ranger.

Big Bill Kennedy met his gaze for the first time and seemed to recognize him immediately. "No rifles or Tommy Guns I could see on their persons, sir, but I'd bet my britches they were packing pistols from the bulges in their jackets. And they were carrying some pretty hefty valises holding God knows what."

"Heavier firepower will be waiting for them at the hotel, anyway," said Earl. "They had this planned out. By my figuring, they'll make their break at dawn or thereabouts."

"I can have plenty of men here by then," said Hoover, the cracking gone from his voice.

"You can, sir, but you won't, because these boys have been a step ahead of us all along. I'm not saying they've got a pipeline into Washington, but it's a chance we can't afford to take now. That means it's us four and that's it."

Hoover swallowed hard. "Ranger, you may see this as the chance to kill Nazis you were denied in Europe, but this is not the kind of decision a man of your station is equipped to make."

"Oh yeah? This coming from somebody who got several of his men killed in a minefield a few hours back. We're doing this my way, Mr. Hoover, and you will go along or you can ride this out bound and gagged in the back of my truck. Your call, sir."

"This is a tall order, even for three men of your abilities," Hoover said flatly, making no bones about his own effectiveness in a gunfight.

"Oh, didn't I mention the reinforcements I got coming?"

Hoover and Druce looked at each other. "You didn't mention the arrival of more men in the offing," Druce said.

"Who said anything about men, Captain?"

Certain the Nazis inside the Texas Hotel would have posted one of their number in the lobby through the entire night, Earl parked his truck just down the street, but out of sight from the windows. He cut the engine and rapped a hand atop the roof to roust Big Bill Kennedy from the truck's bed.

"You're in charge," he told the young Ranger, who stole a glance inside the truck at J. Edgar Hoover and a decorated British war hero. "Neither one of them makes a move unless you say to make it. That clear?"

Big Bill nodded and Earl turned his gaze inside the truck. "Is that clear to you boys?"

Both Hoover and Druce nodded, too.

"Then we got ourselves a plan," Earl said, climbing out of the truck. "Now, I'm gonna go see about those reinforcements."

"You're alone," Hoover said groggily, straightening his tie and trying to wet his hair into place, when Earl returned over an hour later, maybe closer to two.

"Yes, I am, and you ain't going to a wedding, sir, you're going to a gun-fight."

"But you said you were going to get—"

"Yes, I did," Earl interrupted, leaving it there, until a tight smirk crossed his expression. "Did a whole bunch of deputizing, so much deputizing I could never have rounded up enough badges."

To a man, none of them had any idea what he was talking about and were too tired, and anxious, to ask. Then Big Bill Kennedy climbed out from behind the wheel to cede the driver's seat back to him.

Dawn broke four hours after Earl Strong's return, and almost six from the time he'd parked his truck. The sun struggled to burn through a fog that had lifted off nearby Lake Worth. Big Bill had fetched coffee from a diner and passed the cups out from a wobbly cardboard box, dripping liquid from its underside from some overspill.

The men were barely into their initial sips when the front door of the Texas Hotel opened through the fog and a man wearing a buttoned-up over-coat emerged to check the street, as casually as he could manage. Earl felt sure he was the lookout the Nazis had posted in the lobby through the night, low man on the totem pole, since if anyone was out here lying in wait, he'd be the first one shot.

"Time to go to work, boys."

"Er, Ranger," said J. Edgar Hoover, "you wouldn't happen to have a spare gun, would you?"

"I do indeed, Mr. Director, but you're gonna sit this one out." He continued, before Hoover could protest, "I can't be worried about protecting you on top of everything else, especially given who the real target is here. I'm in charge and that's the way we're doing it," he added firmly, to help the head of the FBI save face.

Everything had fallen into place for Earl Strong, once he'd learned Gun-ther Haut's true identity. What the bunkmates he'd murdered must've learned about him. Why all bets were off on the part of the Nazis committed to preserving as much of the Third Reich as they could, in terms of springing Haut from the POW camp and getting him out of Texas. Why men like Abner

Dunbar and Witchell Long were just bit players in all this, discarded once their minor roles were completed.

True to form, Hoover nodded after Earl laid things out for him. "This is a more important fight than any you would've fought in Europe, Ranger."

"Yes, sir, I believe it is," Earl said, as four other big men emerged from the hotel. They were enclosing a single smaller man he thought he recognized from the camp photo as Gunther Haut, but from this distance through the fog, he couldn't be sure.

And, with that, he pressed down on the truck's horn three times.

The six men had just started moving toward the street in a tight cluster when they heard what sounded like thunder, the ground rumbling beneath their feet. Earl watched them seize up solid in uncertainty, a moment before the flood of cattle rounded Main Street from two blocks up. An endless, churning brown horde cutting through the fog and blowing curtains of steam from their nostrils.

"Let's go!" Earl shouted over the deafening roar.

Big Bill Kennedy and Captain Henry Druce of the British SAS were on either side of him in the next moment, timing their advance from the opposite side of the street and the onrushing cattle. The cattle stole so much of the Nazis' attention, Earl doubted they even noticed the three of them were there, until he opened up with his .45.

The big bullet took one of the Nazis in the forehead, knocking him backward off his feet, blocked from Earl's view by the thundering stampede of cattle down Main Street. He'd paid a visit to the local stockyards, where this very herd had just been brought in for auction the previous day, the owner all too happy to cooperate with the Texas Rangers. He'd insisted that Earl deputize him first, which Earl did, though he stopped short of deputizing all the cattle rolling in the brown, mist-shrouded wave before him.

Big Bill was wielding a twelve-gauge shotgun that looked tiny in his grasp. He pumped out all six shells in the chamber in rapid succession, his first five missing badly, but a sixth taking a leg out from a Nazi who'd begun to push his way through the slowing herd. The man disappeared and Earl thought he heard the man's screams as he was crushed beneath the pounding hooves.

Earl detected the distinctive clack of Henry Druce's Enfield No. 2 Mk1 pistol now as well, the captain nowhere to be seen, having melted into the night in the fashion of the British commando that he was. What the Ranger did see, though, was a third Nazi going down from behind the cover of a mailbox Druce had either shot through or managed a miraculous shot at a shape exposed by no more than a few inches.

Earl, meanwhile, crouched low and waded into the now meandering herd for cover. Three Nazis were down, by his count, leaving two more plus the man who called himself Gunther Haut, when he was really someone else entirely.

No one's ever gonna believe me, Earl thought.

But he didn't care, not since it wouldn't matter if the man was dead, and there was no way Gunther Haut was getting out of this. Earl had lost track of him somehow, glad to see Big Bill pushing the last of the way through the cattle to take up a position closer to the Texas Hotel to stop the remaining Nazis from taking flight back inside the building.

Earl watched Big Bill rise to sight in on one of the remaining gunmen, only to have a Nazi bullet take him in the side and spin him around. He didn't go down, but the kid staggered and dropped lower to shield himself against getting hit again. The first time he'd been shot, in all likelihood, just as this was almost surely his first real gunfight. And Earl could tell by the flow of the herd where he'd last glimpsed Big Bill that the young Ranger was still on the move with the same intention in mind, once he reached the other side of the street.

Earl watched a Nazi pop up out of nowhere amid the herd, spraying fire from his Thompson in all directions. At least one of the shots winged Captain Druce before he could dive behind a car for cover. Earl's ears rang with the Tommy Gun's powerful staccato roar, as its .45 caliber bullets made swiss cheese out of the vehicle behind which Druce had taken refuge.

The herd, meanwhile, reacted to the sudden percussion by picking up its pace anew, the stench of animal hide and manure heavy on the air, mixing with the mist rising off Lake Worth. Earl thought he heard sirens screaming this way, but couldn't be sure, given the high-pitched buzzing that clung to his ears from all the gunfire.

He tried to sight in on the Nazi firing the Thompson, but a fresh spray from its barrel left him diving to the ground, shifting desperately atop the pavement to avoid being trampled. Earl figured the last Nazi in the group would be using the occasion to spirit Gunther Haut away from the maelstrom, now that Big Bill Kennedy had cut off their route back into the hotel lobby.

The Ranger guessed they'd be moving against the grain of the herd and, sure enough, caught a glimpse of the biggest Nazi of all dragging Haut along with him. He was firing a German Mauser machine gun, likely lifted from the wall back at the Nazi stronghold in Abilene, orange flames flaring from its barrel chasing a limping Big Bill behind some trash cans hopefully full enough to keep more bullets from finding him.

Earl got off a couple rounds to at least hold the Nazi at bay, a pause in fire following his shots that likely indicated the big Nazi was jamming a fresh magazine into the Mauser. Earl knew he owned those seconds and lurched upward from his spot at the edge of the stampede, the big Nazi stretching a hand out toward Gunther Haut who'd been swept into the steaming animal horde, his machine gun forgotten for the moment.

Earl got the big Nazi in the chest with one of his last two rounds from the magazine in his .45, then heard an awful, high-pitched scream from the area where Haut had gone down. It lingered for a time, then turned into something more like a gurgle and, finally, shrill cries as the man's final bout with freedom ended with him being trampled to death.

Earl Strong waded into the horde of cattle again, trying to find the man who called himself Gunther Haut to make sure he was dead. But he was unable to push successfully against the grain, and ended up on the other side of the blur of cattle. He found himself standing over the big Nazi who lay on his back, his wheezing sounding as if it were coming from the hole the .45 shell had blown through his chest. He coughed blood into the air, his eyes fastening on Earl hatefully as he died.

The Ranger looked toward Big Bill Kennedy pushing himself out from the cover of the trash cans, dragging the twelve-gauge with him. Captain

Druce, meanwhile, rose from behind the shot-up car, blood leaking past the hand pressed against the wound on his torso.

Moments later, Earl caught sight of J. Edgar Hoover moving down the street tentatively, clinging to the cover of streetlights that offered no cover at all. He spotted Earl and steered clear of the final vestiges of the stampede, the animals finally relinquishing their hold on the day's dawn.

"Did you get him?" Hoover shouted at Earl. "Did you get Haut?"

"See for yourself," Earl said, pointing to the remains of a body revealed by clear pockets in the dwindling herd.

Fort Worth police cars tore onto the scene from the head of street, following the same path the cattle had. There must have been a dozen of them, uniformed police starting to spill out with guns drawn.

"I'll handle this, Ranger," Hoover said, spine straightening and looking once again like the director of the FBI.

"You do that, Mr. Hoover," Earl said, holstering his .45 and eyeing the crushed, barely recognizable form of Gunther Haut lying facedown on the street, his overcoat tattered and torn. "You do that."

89

RED ROCK, TEXAS

"Here's the photo, Ranger," Big Bill Kennedy said, producing a dog-eared, faded prison camp snapshot of Gunther Haut that had been folded in half from his wallet. "Your granddaddy gave it to me as a souvenir."

"That's just like him. I still have the first Colt and Model 1911 forty-five he ever carried. He gave both of them to me on different birthdays."

Big Bill's eyes grew misty. "I don't think there's a man I miss more in the world, Ranger."

"Me, either."

Caitlin hesitated. "The man who got trampled in the stampede, it wasn't Gunther Haut, was it?"

"I suspect it wasn't. There wasn't much to recognize, once all those cattle had their way with him, and your granddaddy got to thinking that maybe he didn't see that big Nazi reaching out to save Haut, but pushing him down into the cattle instead, so we'd figure we got our man. Your granddaddy came to believe that Gunther Haut slipped out the rear of the Texas Hotel, while the Nazis, and that decoy who got crushed to death, came out the front."

"Did he ever find any evidence to support that?"

"Just the fact that a hotel clerk thought he recalled the man who ended up getting crushed to death arriving ahead of the others who came on the train from Abilene. As for me, I never questioned Earl Strong, because I never knew him to be wrong. Hoover had the Fort Worth cops take Druce away and probably put him on a plane back to England after getting him stitched up, before either of us could say our good-byes. Then that sumbitch read us the riot act about keeping our mouths shut on what he'd told us, given that the man who called himself Gunther Haut was believed to be dead and no sense lay in letting out the truth nobody would've believed anyway."

"Believe what, Big Bill?" Caitlin asked him, not sure she wanted to hear the answer. "Who was Gunther Haut?"

The old Ranger didn't hesitate at all. "The son of Adolf Hitler."

PART TEN

We don't have an official uniform. It's Western dress—a hat, boots, a solid-colored shirt, a tie, and a jacket, depending on the occasion. [Department of Public Safety] gives us a clothing allowance of $100 a month, so a $500 hat and a $400 pair of boots cuts into your yearly budget pretty quick. But the way we look is important. I learned early on in my Ranger career that when you approach a crook you're about to interview and you're dressed like a Ranger, he immediately sits up and takes notice and, in most cases, shows you respect.

—Texas Ranger Captain Barry Caver as quoted in
Tracking the Texas Rangers: The Twentieth Century,
edited by Bruce A. Glasrud and Harold J. Weiss Jr.,
University of North Texas Press, 2013

90

ROUND ROCK, TEXAS

"I don't believe it," Cort Wesley said when Caitlin told him over the phone.

"My grandfather sure did, and he took the secret to his grave."

"That's not what I meant. When I paid that visit to Darl Pickett, I thought the old man was crazy 'cause he told me Cliven Fisker had confessed to him in prison over moonshine that Hitler was his grandfather. That makes Gunther Haut his father, and the timeline matches up perfectly when you think about it."

"It also makes Armand Fisker Hitler's great-grandson. So I guess there's a lot to be said for genetics, Cort Wesley."

"You think he knows?"

"I don't know how he could, unless his father, Cliven, told him at some point, which I sincerely doubt."

Caitlin heard Cort Wesley sigh on the other end of the line. "I wonder what Boone Masters would've thought if he knew he'd killed the grandson of Adolf Hitler."

"Maybe he heard the story, too. Maybe Darl Pickett spilled the beans to him. Maybe that's really why your father shanked Cliven Fisker: because he believed it was true."

"The question being, Ranger, do *you* believe it?"

"I know a whole bunch of men died in Texas in 1944 because of Gunther Haut. I know it would have taken more than a rumor or wives' tale to bring J. Edgar Hoover himself out here, along with a decorated captain in the Special Air Service all the way from England."

Caitlin could almost feel Cort Wesley thinking on the other end of the line. "You mean like the stories I've heard over the years about Hitler having a son with a French prostitute or something during World War I when the Germans were fighting over there?"

"That's the rumor that had the most validity, but there are others, including a waitress in Hamburg a few years before that. According to his file, Gunther Haut was an SS officer attached to Rommel's Afrika Korps."

"Hitler's eyes and ears, in other words."

"Not a job he would have trusted to just anyone," said Caitlin. "And sending Haut to North Africa would've kept him away from the front."

"Relatively safe, in other words."

"Haut must've stuck around there after the Allies defeated Rommel at El Alamein in 1942 and then was finally taken prisoner in the wake of the Tunisian Campaign in May of 1943. That's how he ended up in Texas, along with tens of thousands of other German soldiers."

"Except he didn't turn up in Hearne until the spring of 1944, nearly a year later," Cort Wesley noted.

"Because he must not have been captured immediately. After the Tunisian Campaign, Allied sea and air superiority made it difficult to bring supplies in or get someone of Haut's stature out. My guess is he was kept hidden by French officials in Tunis who were either spies or Nazi sympathizers, before he was caught in one of the sweeps that followed over the next year."

"No wonder the Germans worked so hard to get him out of Camp Hearne."

Caitlin nodded. "And they got plenty of bang for their buck. Gunther Haut, son of Adolf Hitler, started a family under the name of 'Rolf Fisker.' Cliven was born in 1947, Armand Fisker twenty-four years later in 1971. The rest, as they say, is history."

She heard Cort Wesley sigh. "We don't know shit about the world, do we, Ranger?"

"No, we don't. Not in the big picture anyway, Cort Wesley."

"That's the only picture is. If I've learned nothing else from you, it's that."

"There's more," Caitlin said, feeling the tension kneading through her muscles.

"I'm still listening."

"I got Frank Doyle to admit David Skoll was the man who raped me. Turns out Skoll's father owned the townhouse where the party took place eighteen years ago. He lived in a neighboring one, was friendly with the students who hosted the party. Doyle said Skoll volunteered to bartend, too, so he could spike the drink of whoever Doyle brought up to him."

"Lucky you."

"I'm on my way back to San Antonio right now to pick up a warrant for Skoll's arrest." She felt herself squeezing the steering wheel tighter. "Why'd he pick me, Cort Wesley?"

"What do you mean?"

"All those coeds at that party, lots of them pretty as hell, why did he single me out?"

"Having not known you at the time, I can't say."

"I can," Caitlin told him. "Because I looked vulnerable and out of place, my status as a social misfit coming back to haunt me."

"So you're blaming yourself?"

"I never should have gone to the party. I was trying to be something I wasn't. And, you're right, now I'm falling into that trap."

"What trap would that be?"

"Believing that my actions precipitated what happened. It's why so many women never report being assaulted; they believe, out of guilt and pain mostly, that they were somehow to blame for what happened, somehow responsible. They feel that's how the world will judge them if they come clean."

"They or you, Ranger?"

"I came forward, Cort Wesley, but that doesn't mean I haven't racked my brain over showing up at the party every day of my life since."

"So showing up made you complicit in the crime, a party to your own assault? Will you listen to yourself, please, Caitlin?"

"I've listened to plenty of other women in the same situation. What I'm saying is that I fit the pattern. I'm not responsible for what happened, but I am responsible for being the person I was at the time. I was responsible for me playing with guns instead of dolls, out shooting when other girls were playing soccer or volleyball. I'm not suggesting I would've changed a goddamn thing, Cort Wesley. I'm saying that showing up at that party I might as well have worn a sign that said VULNERABLE in all caps."

"Which leaves me wondering why you didn't shoot Frank Doyle the other day when you had the chance. You certainly would've been within your rights, yet you didn't even draw your gun."

"I was feeling a different kind or rage at the time, Cort Wesley. I wanted to hurt him, wanted to *feel* myself hurt him. Does that make any sense?"

"Makes plenty, if it's the truth."

"Why wouldn't it be?"

"Because I'm wondering if you wanted your white whale alive. Leave that chapter of your life open just enough to keep the past at arm's length, instead of tucked away for good. Almost like you'd be afraid of losing hold of the rage thinking about that night has allowed you to wield like a jackhammer all these years. I'm wondering if that explains your edge."

"I didn't know I had an edge."

"Sharp enough to cut like a knife, Ranger. But if I ever hear you suggest again that what happened eighteen years ago was your fault, I'll hurt you a lot worse."

"A romantic as always, aren't you?"

"Going up against Armand Fisker will do that to you."

Caitlin wished he was next to her in the SUV. "Yup, here we go again."

91

Cort Wesley stopped at a convenience store before setting off for the staging area to meet up with Paz and his men. He bought a pair of Hires original root beers, twisted the tops off both bottles, and stuck them in the console's cup holders.

"You trying to bribe me, bubba?" Leroy Epps said from the passenger seat, after Cort Wesley had given up waiting for him to appear.

"Be a lot cheaper if you preferred Dr Pepper, like everyone else around here."

"What you want in exchange for that Hires?"

"For you to tell me why my father killed Cliven Fisker in Huntsville."

"Why you figure I'd know?"

"'Cause it's square in your area."

"Like the dead all know each other, you mean? There's a lot more of us around than you living folks; you'd be wise to remember that, bubba. Time may move differently where we at, but that doesn't mean there's opportunity or cause to meet everyone."

"I thought maybe my dad killed Cliven Fisker because he learned he was Hitler's grandson."

"Now, that's a mouthful."

"It isn't true?"

"Didn't say that, only that it's a mighty big world on both ends of the spectrum that finds its own balance. Your dad shanking Cliven Fisker, you about to go to war with his son."

"Drink your root beer, champ."

"I'll get around to it in my time, bubba, because time's all that I've got. And anytime you try changing the subject, it's like sticking a NO TRESPASSING sign in my face."

"Sometimes you get on to things I have trouble following."

"You mean, like fate? 'Cause that's what this smacks of, if anything ever did. Like you and Armand Fisker came out of the womb destined for this day. And I know what you're gonna say next, so spare yourself the bother."

"You mean, how it was his boy who pushed things to the cliff we're hanging off now?"

"Fact that it's true doesn't make this any less fated. That's one of the things I've learned over on this side I'm allowed to talk about. Folks like to think life's about filling in the blank pages, when it's really about turning the pages that have already been filled."

Cort Wesley cocked his gaze briefly toward Leroy, who was leaning forward in the passenger seat, not wearing his seat belt. "You feel like telling me what those pages say about tonight?"

"What, and ruin all the fun that's a-comin'?" Leroy grinned, holding his Hires bottle now. *"No way, bubba, no way at all."*

92

ELK GROVE, TEXAS

Armand Fisker stood in the center of what had once been Elk Grove's meeting chambers, where the town elders, selectmen, councilmen, or whatever they'd called themselves, voted on policy for the town. He gazed toward the short platform on which rested a hardwood, semicircular raised desk. Behind that desk, six chairs waited to be occupied by six men Fisker had never met in person.

The representatives from France, Germany, and Britain had already arrived, having flown into different airports nearby, as arranged. Although helicopters would've made the remaining trek faster, their use would have also attracted the kind of attention Fisker wanted to avoid at all costs, especially with the Texas Rangers breathing down his throat. Leave it to his dumbass dead son not just to pick a fight with an ex–Green Beret, but an ex–Green Beret with a Ranger as a girlfriend.

With those three countries all accounted for, he was awaiting only Spain, Austria, and Italy. Their planes had all landed and they were en route to Elk Grove right now. A few other countries Fisker had invited had been unable to travel on such short notice. And, in the case of several more of the leaders of movements beholden to his drugs for their power, being present on the terrorist watch list precluded them from making the trip overseas.

Fisker had placed placards to match the position of all six chairs, identifying the planned meeting's participants by their countries instead of names none of them would want shared. While he'd never met any of these men, he knew them inside and out from the files he'd practically committed to memory. Not just to get to know them better, but also to learn the weaknesses and vulnerabilities that would allow him to control them and negotiate the most favorable terms possible for all the product he was providing.

Fisker had accumulated so much cash that he had begun offering the pills he supplied at bargain prices, in return for profit-sharing arrangements. Tying up less funds in up-front costs allowed his international partners to expand their networks and hire the kind of operatives who specialized in eliminating all vestiges of competition. Then, to avoid increased scrutiny, on Fisker's instructions, his partners would run those operations as if nothing had changed. That way, governments in the host countries seldom caught on to the concentration of criminal power they were facing. And Fisker's partners were well positioned to bribe inquiring or less cooperative officials with sums easily sufficient to enlist them as willing partners. From there, they were able to build a political power base on which to choose candidates from their own ranks or, even more, become the primary backers of candidates of like minds and values. Fisker, in fact, could see a day where the nationalistic movements he had championed became a unified force running pretty much the whole world.

Business at its best.

Staring up at those six placards now, Fisker wondered if his father ever had an inkling he was building something that would reach such a level. Fisker had never sat down to figure the total gross proceeds his operation generated worldwide, but imagined they were comparable to any number of Fortune 500 companies.

Without the need to pay taxes, of course, or file paperwork, or account for any of their practices.

He should have felt more grief over the killing of his son. Instead, he felt rage. But that rage was tempered with the realization that he'd let his son down. He barely knew his own father. That, coupled with the fact that he, similarly, barely knew Ryan, filled Fisker with an emptiness that made him figure that he hadn't bothered counting all that money he'd amassed because the money meant relatively little to him.

The war hero Masters and Texas Ranger Caitlin Strong represented everything that had dragged down his life. They represented the establishment that had harnessed his father to a jail cell, the very government he had skirted in rebuilding Elk Grove into his own private kingdom where the only rules that mattered were the ones he made up, free from scrutiny and judgment.

But why stop there?

Elk Grove was a microcosm of what people who thought as he did could do with the world if they got ahold of it. From the established order to the chaos that would precede a sea change in the parties holding true power. And now, thanks to Davey Skoll, that chaos had a name: Axiol, or Lot U257F. A disaster in one respect, but a genuine miracle in another, to be distributed across the world as he saw fit to fuel a new level of power rising out of a chaos that was his to dispense. That deadly drug had the potential to unleash chaos across the globe, creating power vacuums with those politicians backed, and controlled, by his associates prepared to step into the void. The life of his son had meant nothing to the likes of the war hero and the Texas Ranger. And so the lives of those like them, from one end of the world to the other, would be given the same weight by Fisker's associates who would now have a weapon of mass destruction at their disposal.

He would be able to measure his success by the number of established governments that fell to a combination of collapse and the rise of populist-style leaders to replace them. Prepared to seize an opportunity that was theirs because Armand Fisker was giving it to them, starting with the six he'd be meeting with tonight.

So while Armand Fisker had never taken much delight in counting all the cash he was making, counting bodies was something else entirely. Starting with Caitlin Strong, Cort Wesley Masters, and Masters' two sons.

Payback was a bitch. That much hadn't changed.

93

David Skoll wasn't at his mansion in Alamo Heights when Caitlin drove straight from the judge's house to serve the warrant for his arrest. So she headed back to the Redfern Pharmaceuticals manufacturing plant in Waco in the hope that he was there. For all she knew, with the walls closing in around him, Skoll was in the wind by now, sliding into some fake identity he'd spent a fortune to make ironclad. Or maybe he'd just fly off to some country that lacked an extradition treaty with the United States.

But something told her that wasn't the case at all; something else told her that this was about more than she was seeing and had been all along. So, with some time to kill and needing a fresh take on what she was missing, she called Young Roger, the honorary Ranger who was a technology expert, over the Bluetooth in her SUV just as the late afternoon sky began to bleed light.

"I owe you a bigger debt than I can ever pay, Rog," she told him. "You helped me catch a ghost from my past who's been haunting me for almost twenty years."

"Thank the computer, Ranger. I just plugged in the data as you gave it to me."

"Don't sell yourself short. And I've got a question for you."

"Hold on, while I fasten my seat belt."

"You driving?"

"No, ma'am. But when you say you need to ask me a question, I know I better anchor myself tight."

"You sound like my captain."

"Is that a good thing?"

"So long as you don't take up smoking," she told him. "There's something else I can't figure out here I want to pick your brain about. By all indications, David Skoll overpaid for Redfern Pharmaceuticals because of a cutting edge anti-rejection drug that went from boom to bust in a heartbeat. What I can't figure is why he did that, even though investment experts I've asked have told me that, even if the drug had worked, his profits would've been marginal at best in comparison to the debt he incurred to purchase the company. So what am I missing?"

Caitlin half-expected Young Roger to plead ignorance on the subject, the other half figuring at least he'd think on the question for a moment. Instead, he responded instantly.

"How much do you know about three-D printers, Ranger?"

"I know they print in three-D. Besides that, not much."

"Okay, what would you say if I told you that a noted surgeon is currently employing a three-D printer to output a fully transplantable kidney using living cells?"

"I'd say that bars must be paying your band's fees in booze."

"Which would amount to one beer, based on how much we get paid. But what I just told you is true, still in the experimental stage and showing incredible promise as a core component in a field that's called regenerative medicine."

Caitlin felt herself shaking her head. "How do you know all this stuff, Young Roger?"

"You ever see me shoot a gun?"

"Was that an answer?"

"No, a point. Anyway, this part of regenerative medicine is called bioprinting, for obvious reasons, and it's already been used for the generation and transplantation of several tissues, including multilayered skin, bone, vascular grafts, tracheal splints, heart tissue, and cartilaginous structures."

Caitlin ran that through her head a bit before responding. "You're not pulling my leg, are you, Rog?"

"Not at all, Ranger. The fact remains that we may not be much more than five to ten years away from organ donations being rendered obsolete, replaced by three-D printers capable of replicating human organs, and even limbs, to precise specifications."

"So what's the catch?"

"The body would still view the transplanted organs as foreign organisms and activate white cells to destroy them. So the real catch is that recipients of the three-D printed organs would still need anti-rejection meds, as much as patients who received traditionally donated organs."

"I believe I get where this is going," Caitlin said, starting to see what David Skoll was up in an entirely different light.

"Every year, only ten percent of patients in need of a transplant find a proper donor and the organ they need. That leaves millions and millions on a waiting list that keeps growing by leaps and bounds. Many of them will die before they ever receive an organ. Others will reject their transplanted organ, in spite of taking traditional anti-rejection drugs, and only a few of these will ever get another chance. So, while the value of a new anti-rejection drug coming to market today would be significant, even substantial, the value of that kind of drug in an era of three-D transplantable organs could reach ten to twelve billion dollars per year."

"Did you say *billion?*"

"Which isn't nearly as farfetched as it sounds, Ranger. Lipitor has made annual profits as high as thirteen billion dollars, Plavix and Nexium both over seven billion. So you want to know why David Skoll would overpay for a pharmaceutical company in the testing phase of a new anti-rejection drug? The answer lies in those nine zeroes."

"And if the drug in question turns out to be shit?"

"Then Skoll would be shit out of luck, but, from a business standpoint, these are the kind of opportunities that investors die for."

"Poor choice of words in this case, Rog," Caitlin told him, starting on again toward Waco. "And, speaking of Skoll, there's one more thing I need you to look into...."

94

Guillermo Paz led the way through the extension of the Natural Bridge Caverns, covering the last stretch to reach Elk Grove with Cort Wesley and a dozen of his best men fifty feet underground. The groundwork for entering this topographical anomaly, located apart from the Texas hill country known for supporting such systems, had been laid by a dig team disguised as a utility crew. That team had dug a vertical trench to access the majestic rock formations that rose from hundreds of feet below, rendering them virtually inaccessible in contrast to comparable caverns located farther to the north.

Fortunately, thermal imaging ground studies, requisitioned by Jones, had revealed the narrow path across an ancient ledge that would connect with a massive underground storage chamber Armand Fisker had erected beneath Elk Grove, providing the access they needed. This unusual landscape feature was one of the reasons why so few oil reserves had been found near the town, accounting in some respects for Elk Grove's demise decades before.

Paz and Cort Wesley crept along that ledge toward a flashing red dot on the GPS devices attached to their wrists that would glow solid when they reached Fisker's underground storage chamber. At that point, some well-placed explosives would chew through the rock and open the door to Elk Grove from fifty feet belowground.

It would take only a few charges to blast through the rock. But ten of Paz's men carried backpacks stuffed with shaped charges designed with a secondary purpose in mind. It was cool down here, only a smattering of natural light emanating from what looked like patches of phosphorus that had collected on some of the jagged walls and towering rock formations a few hundred feet beneath them. Besides that, the dome lights of the hard hats Cort Wesley, Paz, and his men all wore, in addition to the flashlights the heartiest among them dared squander a hand on, provided the sole additional illumination.

"Feels like we've entered hell, doesn't it, Colonel?" Cort Wesley said, as they drew closer to the flashing red signal on their GPS devices.

"Hell is hotter, outlaw."

"How can we really be sure of that?"

Another hundred or so yards passed before the red icon began flashing faster, then went solid.

"Stand back, outlaw," Paz said, fitting four charges into place at the access point to the underground chamber Armand Fisker had dug beneath Elk Grove.

They were fortunate the area's geology had cooperated, given that Cort Wesley knew Armand Fisker would have the one road leading into the town closed off or mightily defended. The valley in which Elk Grove rested, amid a nest of rolling mesas forged out of the dead ground, made an unobstructed approach over land impossible even at nighttime, Fisker certain to have guards and snipers stationed strategically as well. Cort Wesley was beginning to wonder how much its natural defenses played into Fisker's choosing to settle here, wondered if he was even aware of his underground chamber's proximity to the sprawl of caverns not present on any tourist map.

Cort Wesley and the rest of Paz's men backed up along the ledge until they were behind the cover of a curve, the colonel joining them moments later with metallic detonator in hand, thumb ready over its plunger.

"Cover your ears, outlaw," Paz said, and pressed his thumb downward.

95

Elk Grove, Texas

Armand Fisker thought he felt the floor quiver ever so slightly, as he moved his gaze among the six men seated before him, identified in his mind by the placards that listed the countries from which they'd traveled to get here. He chased the distraction from his mind and refocused his thoughts.

"Oh yeah, this is a rare opportunity, all right," he said, the darkness beyond the town hall windows broken only by the well-placed floodlights that cast the town's central square in Day-Glo brightness. "One thing you know about me, I deliver on what I promise. I do what I say I'm gonna do," Fisker continued, running his eyes from England to France to Germany, then to Spain, Austria, and Italy. "I helped you build your networks by undercutting the street prices of your rivals, putting them either out of business or in the ground."

They were, to a man, unremarkable in appearance in every sense but their eyes, which held a steely sense of purpose and assurance. Eyes that dominated their beings, the lighting in the chamber making all of them look black, showing no whites at all. An illusion, Fisker knew, but one he welcomed, as if he were addressing a different species of being here, unburdened by the expectations and conventions almost all men took to their graves.

"I prefer in the ground. You all know about my father's role in all this. Difference between then and now is that he could never have envisioned the kind of thinking that led to the Aryan Brotherhood going mainstream. Because we're not just businessmen anymore, making sure a certain kind of supply meets a certain kind of demand; we're politicians, with the power to affect the way our respective countries go about their business."

Fisker stopped and looked toward England. "Your backing was crucial to Brex-shit, as I call it." France now. "You're backing a political party that thinks a lot like we do about the world, and when they win they'll have your money to thank for it." Austria next. "Your man came this close to winning the last election and will probably win the next, just like in Germany. Nobody labels these movements 'Nazi' anymore. They call them nationalistic, because that's what we are. Our time has arrived, our era has dawned, because the people have finally come around to our way of thinking. You wanna think of yourself as a drug dealer, you're in the wrong room. You wanna think we can run the whole goddamn world, you've come to the right goddamn place."

Fisker waited for any of the men seated up on the platform before their placards to respond, continued when, again, none did.

"Some of you know I lost my son the other day. I'm tired of losing people close to me to guns, rivals, or jail. It's bad for business. You're here today because I got ahold of something that could be really good for business—both as it stands today and will stand tomorrow." Fisker stopped there, prepared to describe for them the virtual weapon of mass destruction Redfern Pharmaceuticals had inadvertently created, without saying too much or too little. "When we started this venture, it was all about eliminating the competition. What I'm prepared to provide is all about eliminating a different kind of competition, defined by whoever gets the fuck in the way of our business, which means in our way period. This is the means for us to create the kind of chaos and panic movements like ours thrive on. This is our golden ticket to the top of the food chain, a weapon of terror as well as action. Bottom line, friends, is that our time has come and I want to make sure we can shape the world in a mold of our own making.

"My daddy started an international movement out of a prison cell," Fisker continued. "But you know what? The real prisoners today are the governments that cower in fear over what we represent and the fact we don't answer to them or anyone else. Look at England, look at goddamn America. Gentlemen, I give you the future, dished out on a silver spoon, where we might not be the kings, but we sure as hell will be the power sitting behind the thrones."

Fisker knew he had them, knew it wouldn't be necessary to go into much more detail, short of providing reports on the actual effects of Redfern Pharmaceuticals' death-dealing drug that David Skoll would be mass producing for him in Waco in whatever form Fisker desired.

Thank you, Ryan, Fisker said in his own mind, realizing he owed all this to his boy getting gunned down, since it had forced a radical change in his thinking. Goddamn kid had finally done something worthwhile.

Then Fisker smelled something, something like kindling burning to start a log fire, familiar in a way he couldn't quite recognize. His first thought was that one of the men before him had lit up one of those fancy European cigarettes. But all of them sat empty-handed, hanging on his next word, because he was speaking in terms they understood all too well. Giving them a means to turn their hate for the status quo into action.

The smell strengthened, coarsening the air, in the last moment before smoke began to drift up through the floorboards.

96

"I thought I made it clear our business was done, Ranger," David Skoll said to Caitlin, when she appeared unannounced on the floor of his automated manufacturing plant. "You're not authorized to be here."

"I brought you something, Mr. Skoll," Caitlin told him, stopping short of plucking the arrest warrant from her pocket. "Something that needed to be delivered in person."

Even up close, Skoll could have passed for ten or even fifteen years younger. He wore jeans more fit for someone Dylan's age and a cheap T-shirt with a logo she hadn't bothered reading. She regarded him in the haze of ambient lighting down here on the plant's floor, picturing a drugged-out Kelly Ann Beasley waking up briefly to a face that did indeed look vaguely feminine.

She looked around her at the machines rolling this way and that. Forklifts toted huge pallets of medications ready to be boxed for shipment. Finished boxes rolled along conveyor belts at this part of the line, while rolling, eight-foot-tall robots that looked like something out of *Star Wars* negotiated the tight confines agilely, scooping up anything that may have strayed from the loaders and conveyors. Elsewhere, farther along the line, all manner of cutting, wrapping, molding, shrink-wrapping, and foiling stations labored without pause in a perpetual process utterly devoid of human hands.

Caitlin wondered how many jobs this plant had once produced, before machines had replaced men. How many families had relied on Redfern Pharmaceuticals to put food on the table, before the likes of David Skoll had taken over? She met his gaze, but kept herself from holding his stare, afraid of what the rage she felt simmering inside her might provoke.

Caitlin didn't need a DNA test to tell her this was the man who assaulted her eighteen years ago. Even though she had no memory of him from that night, his residue clung to her psyche like an itch she couldn't reach. And there was something else, something lurking at the edge of her consciousness.

"That's a nice smell, Mr. Skoll," she complimented. "Be perfect for my boyfriend."

"It's sandalwood, Ranger," Skoll told her, seeming to enjoy the distraction, "courtesy of Taylor of Old Bond Street."

"Sounds English. Been around a while, have they?"

"As long as I can remember."

"Because I remember it from eighteen years ago, the night we first met."

Skoll froze, his face seeming to slide out of his skin. It could have been an effect of the lighting, but the color seemed to wash out of his features, like somebody had taken a scrub brush to it.

"I'm sure you remember that night, sir, or have there been so many others that they just run together? How many other women have you raped, Mr. Skoll, how many between Kelly Ann Beasley and me?"

"I have no idea what you're talking about," Skoll said, finding his tongue.

"Really? I believe I can likely track down dozens of women who'll testify otherwise. See, I had a Ranger tech whiz do a real detailed web search on you, focusing on the nooks and crannies most folks don't even know are there. You ever hear of a company called Efficient Pickup?"

"Can't say that I have, Ranger."

"No? How about the Manosphere?"

This time, Skoll just shook his head.

"Strange, since that tech whiz found a whole bunch of posts you left in the dark about your exploits in their secret chat rooms. Manosphere isn't a place, or even a site, so much as a collection of corners where perverts and rapists gather to swap stories and even exchange strategies for how they facilitate their crimes. They like to call themselves pickup artists. But what they're really adept at is sexual assault and they seem to love sharing their techniques. I'm guessing the user name FUCKMESILLY isn't familiar to you."

Skoll stiffened ever so slightly. "Not at all."

"I find that strange, Mr. Skoll, given that our tech whiz traced his posts on the Manosphere, boasting of his exploits, to an IP address registered to one of your computers."

"That doesn't mean shit, and you know it."

"That remains to be seen, sir, but I'll tell you something that does: I'll bet Kelly Ann Beasley remembers your sandalwood aftershave as clearly as I do. She has a special situation that prevents me from charging you with raping her downstairs at Stubb's Barbecue during that college graduation party." With that, Caitlin finally eased the trifolded document from the pocket of the jacket that dangled just below her waist. "So this warrant is for your arrest on sexual assault charges from eighteen years ago, sir, the night you raped me."

97

Elk Grove, Texas

Paz had triggered the explosives to explode inward, blowing a hole in the rock face of the cavern, creating a charred, jagged entrance to the storage chamber that thermal satellite imaging had revealed. But that imaging had said nothing about its scope or sprawl.

Or its contents.

Cort Wesley felt as if he'd just stepped into a high-end warehouse, with floor-to-ceiling shelving for as far as the eye could see. The first thing that grabbed his attention was a large cache of weapons that included heavy machine guns, rocket launchers, and even a neatly parked array of decommissioned armored military vehicles that had been sold as surplus to arms brokers.

He also noted clear plastic, vacuum-sealed tubs that looked like giant Tupperware containers, holding stores of white, aspirin-like pills. He couldn't even begin to hazard a guess as to how many prescription narcotics the tubs contained, the number too vast to even contemplate. Nor did Cort Wesley bother to fathom how Armand Fisker had managed to obtain pills with a street value that stretched into the tens, if not hundreds of millions. But he heard the voice of Leroy Epps in his head, as loud and clear as in Leroy's regular visits.

David Skoll . . .

Could the pharmaceutical tycoon, who Caitlin was convinced had raped her eighteen years ago, be somehow in league with Armand Fisker?

You bet your britches, bubba. . . .

Still, it was something else stored in pallets on the most shelves of all that made Cort Wesley's eyes bulge the widest and chased Leroy's voice from his head. He actually had to move closer to make sure he wasn't seeing things.

That closer inspection confirmed the presence of an incalculable number of bundles of cash, in denominations of twenty-, fifty-, and hundred-dollar bills, tightly wrapped in plastic sized to fit the pallets on which they'd been stacked and fastened tight. Again, he couldn't even begin to comprehend how much all of this amounted to. But, like the pills, it had to stretch into the millions or tens of millions, at the very least.

No wonder Armand Fisker needed his own town from which to operate the international drug ring founded by his father, Cliven, from the very prison where Boone Masters had killed him in the shower. Guns, drugs, and cash—an unholy trinity that probably made Armand Fisker the most powerful criminal in the country, if not the entire world.

It was clear now to Cort Wesley why Jones had approved and offered intelligence on this operation aimed at bringing down Fisker, once and for all. He was half-surprised Jones hadn't shown up himself in body armor, packing an M4. He also had to figure Jones knew more about Fisker and the extent of his capabilities and intentions than he was saying. Setting all that aside, though, he couldn't care less about the motivations of others, because this was personal for him. Fisker had crossed a line you just don't cross, and neither one of his sons was going to be safe so long as Fisker was alive.

"My men are setting the charges, outlaw," Paz said, suddenly alongside him, following his gaze. "We need to be ready to head to the surface."

Cort Wesley gave the shelves another look before turning to Paz. "There's something else we need to do first, Colonel."

98

As a young man, Armand Fisker had once robbed a bank, the ink bomb planted inside among the bills exploding when he opened the bag, rendering the haul useless. He'd burned all those bills in a rusty trash can in his backyard instead of spending them, struck by the unique smell of burning cash. Sweet and sour at the same time, and noxious enough to make his eyes water. Fisker passed it off as a combination of the special ink and paper used to mint currency, holding memory of that particular scent ever since.

And now he smelled it again, infinitely stronger, carried up into the building on the smoke rising through the floorboards. Up from the storage chamber constructed beneath a hefty chunk of Elk Grove's main artery that was centered under this very building.

My money's burning!

Panic seized Fisker in its grasp. He had no idea what was going on, or who was responsible, but his mind settled on Cort Wesley Masters and the bitch Texas Ranger.

Before him, his six international partners were milling about, their concern flashing over expressions suddenly piqued in suspicion and befuddlement.

"What's happening?" one of them asked.

Fisker ignored the question and moved to the wall-mounted fire alarm. He triggered it, unleashing the rhythmic, alternating squeal that would rally his troops across Elk Grove in a long-prepared, emergency attack response.

They're burning my money!

Thinking that ratcheted up the effects of the chain mail tightening around his insides. Whoever was here, Masters and the Ranger or somebody else, this was no simple frontal assault. It was special ops all the way, with

rock-solid military-level intelligence behind it to boot. Some kind of sanc-
tioned operation undertaken on behalf of an agency his actions had clearly
run afoul of.

Fisker chased consideration of the thought he may have brought all this
on himself from his mind, and grabbed an M16 from a closet instead. He
swung back toward the milling figures atop the platform, babbling to each
other about what might be happening.

"Help yourself," he said to them, leaving the closet door open, before he
surged out of the room for the stairs.

99

ELK GROVE, TEXAS

There was no sign of the invaders on the main drag beyond the former Elk
Grove town hall that was already filling with the members of his organization, summoned by the alarm Fisker had triggered. Many more of them
were spilling out of homes and buildings, armed to the teeth with weapons
of all varieties proudly showcased. A bevy of motorcycles churned about
the hard-packed road, joined almost immediately by fortified pickup trucks
turned into miniature tanks and packing 7.62mm mini-guns bolted to their
trucks' steel beds.

The noxious smoke wafted about the street in thin plumes, the white mist
cutting through the night air like a knife, as more of his cash went up in
flames belowground. If this was meant as a trap, Masters was going to be sadly
disappointed at Fisker's refusal to take the bait. He'd soon have more money,
tons and tons of it, and the opportunity to kill Cort Wesley Masters was
worth every bill that was burning.

"Whoever it is must still be in the storage holds," he told a gathering of
his heavily armed, most trusted cadre who'd rushed to his side, out of breath.
"We move now, we can trap them down there, turn the whole street into a
shooting gallery. So get your men together, and let's..."

Fisker stopped when a series of spits flared beneath him. He felt each like a hollow kick from the inside of his gut. He heard a rumbling, then felt the ground quake around him, portions of it cracking, splitting, and lifting up.

Before him, as Fisker watched with his breath lodged in his throat, the buildings centered around Elk Grove's main drag and central square shook, shifted, and began to sink into the ground.

100

WACO, TEXAS

"You sure about this, Ranger?" David Skoll said to Caitlin, sounding like he was taunting her.

Caitlin whipped out a pair of flex cuffs. "Turn around please, sir."

Skoll didn't turn around. Instead, he smirked, his long hair making him look like a teenager trapped in a man's body.

"You were a lousy piece of ass."

"Say that again?"

"You slept through almost the whole thing. Where's the fun in that?"

Caitlin felt as if someone had touched a match to the surface of her skin. "You really want to make me more pissed off than I already am? Give me an excuse to shoot you and figure things out later?"

Skoll took a step back from her, and then another. "Industrial accidents happen all the time."

"Do they now?"

He continued, as if Caitlin hadn't said anything at all. "You never should have entered this facility unauthorized and unattended."

Caitlin whipped out her SIG. "No more pleasantries, Mr. Skoll. Put your hands in the air."

"Whatever you say, Ranger," he said, smirking again.

Caitlin saw he was holding what looked like a pen in his hand. She didn't give it another thought until light flared from its tip, aimed straight at her.

"Boom," he said, looking past her.

Caitlin wheeled around to follow his line of sight, just as one of the massive robots came barreling straight for her.

101

ELK GROVE, TEXAS

Armand Fisker thought he was dreaming, the sight of the buildings along the main drag that he'd had meticulously restored crumbling into the ground far too incredible to be real. Only when he realized he'd been holding his breath, and started gasping for air already choked with clouds of grit and dirt, did he know for sure that he was awake.

The crackling, blistering, ear-numbing sounds of the buildings collapsing echoed in his mind, clinging to his thoughts. It was like a big branch cracking amplified by a million, a rolling cloud of thunder consuming everything he'd spent years building.

The town hall . . .

His thoughts veered that way in concert with his gaze, trying to see what was left through the thickening clouds. What remained lay in a cluttered heap of wood and debris, no signs of life at all, which meant no signs of his associates from those six countries, save for half of the placard marked GERMANY, blown out of the refuse toward him.

As a man used to power and getting his way, the sense of failure, of defeat, was something utterly foreign to Fisker. Coming so close to his son's death only magnified that unfamiliar feeling of weakness and vulnerability, the shock having bled even the rage and hatred from him to the point that he almost forgot about the scent of his burning money filling the air. That is, until the smells of lumber and dirt replaced it with the rumbling collapse of the buildings around him.

Fisker needed to rally his men, needed to rally them now. And he was moving to do just that, when the armored personnel carriers he'd bought at a virtual heavy arms fire sale sped through the debris-riddled clouds, surging toward him from the far end of the central square.

102

Elk Grove, Texas

Cort Wesley felt the gunner manning the M60 machine gun in his APC open up at the congestion of gunmen, trucks, and motorcycles clustered in what had been the town square when this had still been a town, until just moments ago. Blood sprayed into the air, swallowed almost immediately by the thick clouds that had risen out of the debris of the collapsed buildings. Bikes that had already thrown their riders spun through the air before crashing back down in the path of the APCs to be shoved aside or crushed under the vehicles' huge wheels.

Cort Wesley caught sight of Guillermo Paz driving an APC alongside his, both vehicles' gunners firing in almost eerie synchronicity. The clacking of rounds drowned out the pinging sounds of expended shells clanging off steel, and Cort Wesley's heightened vision recorded one, and then a second mini-gun opening up with its furious, spinning spray of fire.

He felt the big bullets clanging off his vehicle that featured maybe a ton of extra steel for protection. The gunners manning the M60s answered the fire of the mini-guns long enough for more of Paz's men wielding handheld rocket launchers to pop out of the turrets and fire.

The first blast launched one of the pickup trucks airborne. The second sent one rolling, unchecked, down the street where it took out any number of motorcycles, unoccupied as well as manned. The riders who'd abandoned their bikes rushed in all directions, clacking off fire wildly back toward the line of APCs.

Cort Wesley figured they'd be seeking cover behind which to continue the battle. Instead, though, he saw most of the bikers keep right on running, past the debris fields left by the collapsed buildings, varying levels of which still poked over the surface, spouting flames and smoke. Retreating, fleeing, quitting—whatever you wanted to call it—they were gone.

Clearing the street for just him and Armand Fisker.

Guillermo Paz had seen it all before. How men who fancied themselves tough guys, who spent hours and hours pumping iron and shooting up target ranges, wilted in the face of real combat. Big, strong men who knew their way around a bull's-eye that couldn't shoot back. Quite adept at using their weapons to intimidate those already cowering in their path, or waging war when vastly superior numbers and arms made them brave. Put them in a real shooting war like this, though, and the truth of their natures and their competence came through.

By the time Paz lurched out of the APC he was driving, with twin, custom-fitted M4s in hand, the bulk of the enemy had fled into the lowlands toward the hills overlooking Elk Grove. Their initial strategy of claiming the high ground to rain down fire from rooftops and upper-story windows had died when the ground swallowed the buildings they were using. The aim of the gunmen who remained at street level, amid the blowing clouds of flaming debris and ash embers, was typical of those unaccustomed to being fired back upon. Categorized by thoughtless jerks of their triggers that did no more than let the bullets fly in the hope a target might stray into one.

Paz shot the gunmen in the midst of that motion. He was dressed totally in black, including gloves and a long coat draped over the best body armor Homeland Security money could buy, rendering him invisible in the night. He watched the eyes of the men he killed gape, as if trying to discern his shape, their dying thought being they'd been killed by a shape, a shadow more than a man.

He felt a pair of thumps against the body armor covering his side, aimed the M4 in that arm toward a building that had sunk into the ground, with only its peaked roof remaining above the surface. When the gunman spun out a second time, Paz hit him with the M4's fury, in the same moment he sprayed fire with the M4 in his other hand toward a gunman who'd fired at him from behind a rooftop exhaust baffle that now rested on ground level.

By then, only sporadic fire remained, almost all of it coming from his men. The night grew strangely quiet in the intervals between the echoing shots, Paz able to hear the whisk of the breeze blowing the last remnants of Elk Grove past him.

103

WACO, TEXAS

Caitlin realized the light she'd glimpsed must've been a laser, tagging her for the robot, identifying her as a target.

Caitlin thought she heard David Skoll laughing, no longer in view when she drew her SIG and opened fire on the machine wheeling straight toward her, arm appendages stretched forward like daggers. Her bullets clanged off its steel frame, drawing sparks as her ricochets pinged in all directions. With just four bullets left in this magazine, she focused on the thing's head.

A bulb, simulating a robot eyeball, exploded, and coarse black smoke began to rise from the oblong skull itself. The robot wobbled a bit, but surged on toward her, Caitlin backpedaling as she jammed a fresh magazine home. She had just opened fire anew when she heard a fresh whirring sound and swung right to see a second robot coming her way from that direction, too.

They were close enough for Caitlin to smell something like motor oil mixed with burned wires. Still brandishing her pistol, she leaped atop a passing conveyor belt moving in the direction in which Skoll had fled. The whirring sound got louder in the same moment the motor oil scent grew pungent enough to scratch at her throat. Then a shadow of misplaced motion left her diving to the conveyor belt, landing faceup and already steadying her gun on the robot looming over her.

But its pincerlike hand extremity inadvertently smacked her wrist and separated Caitlin from the pistol that clattered to the floor. She tried to push herself back from its grasp, but its heavy steel casing had pinned one of her boots in place. That kept her in the thing's range and allowed it to fasten its pincers on her throat, jerking Caitlin to her feet.

She felt the pincers closing off her air, strong enough to do unspeakable, fatal damage. Caitlin groped wildly, hoping to latch onto some part of the robot with which she might neutralize it. Nothing, though, came within her reach and she flailed wildly at the air, finally managing to get a hand under as close to a chin as the thing had.

Trying to move that was like trying to lift a car by its bumper. No progress at all, Caitlin's lungs thirsting, feeling the first signs of light-headedness take hold. She heard the crackle of glass breaking as bottles jammed on the cluttered conveyor backed up and crashed to the floor, the scent of some alcohol-rich concoction pouring into her nostrils.

Alcohol...

With her consciousness ebbing, Caitlin dipped as low as her knees allowed, reaching for one of those bottles but her grasp coming up just short. She tried lowering farther, felt the pressure increase on her throat, but kept going, the tips of her fingers scraping across the yet-to-be-capped top of one bottle and then another. A twist to the right brought her the extra inches she needed and she snatched one of the bottles up with the world before her turning opaque and foggy.

Caitlin somehow managed to maintain the presence of mind to extend the bottle up and out as far as she could, needing to toss instead of pour the contents into the flashing lights she took for the robot's circuit board. Nothing happened the moment the liquid splashed into place and dripped through. But then Caitlin heard a sizzling sound and smoke began to pour from the area where she'd doused the thing.

The robot jerked her spasmodically and then hurled her through the air, the action more reflexive than planned. Caitlin landed on a pile of boxes tipped from a different section of the assembly line, the thing righting itself enough to roll toward her, its arm extremities jerking about wildly, its head extension twitching and shaking. She got her bearings and groped about the smooth tile for her SIG, remembering it had clattered to the floor somewhere in the area.

Caitlin's grasp locked on it, just as the robot's shadow crossed over her. She opened fire, aiming high for the machine's shoulder area, severing wires that flapped like spaghetti as the thing's pincers locked in place. It continued stretching down toward her, second pincer assembly snapping out at her, when Caitlin lurched to a crouch from which she jammed the barrel of her SIG under the robot's head, fired, and kept firing.

The initial reverberations of the blasts were deafening; Caitlin couldn't even hear the last two shots that finally blew the robot's head from its metallic neck. A dark, viscous liquid burst out instead of blood, showering Caitlin and filling her nostrils with the pungent oil stench. Then the machine seized up, humming like a disc drive when it slowed to a stop.

She leaped back atop the conveyor belt, which came to an end at a series of boxes that had backed up on the line, spilling off in heaps to the side, piling high into a mound. Caitlin pushed herself off the belt in a single, fluid motion, boots hitting the floor just as the mound of boxes blew apart behind the force of a third robot. It slammed into her, nearly crushing Caitlin's foot under its wheels before one of its pincer assemblies closed on her hair and jerked her into the air.

She thought she heard David Skoll laughing again, the mere thought of him more than enough to take her mind off everything except the pistol she stuck into what must be either a socket of some kind or some sort of vent for the heat the things gave off. Whatever it was, the SIG's barrel made for a neat fit, and she fired the last of her bullets from this magazine downward. The robot's works fried so suddenly that it seemed to spasm before locking up, flinging Caitlin through the air.

She crashed into a station on the line dispensing cherry-colored liquid into unmarked bottles of what could only be cough syrup, upending the spigots. The thick, sweet, gooey fluid sprayed in fountain-like fashion in all directions, turning the floor shiny. She went to reload her nearly empty SIG, only to realize she'd lost her last magazine somewhere and scrambled about in search of it, sweeping a hand through the sticky ooze.

Caitlin saw tiny light dancing about her midsection and looked up to see a scowling David Skoll aiming the laser pointer straight her way.

"Kill her!" he cried out, as two more robots surged forward, converging on her from opposite aisles.

Caitlin thought she glimpsed Skoll grinning again, imagining the smell of that familiar aftershave rising off him. Looking younger than Dylan, his soft, almost feminine features making it easy to see how Kelly Ann Beasley mistook her attacker for a woman.

Then Caitlin was in motion, her boots skidding through the collected pools of syrupy liquid, the robots angling her way. She leaped atop the feed sending cough syrup bottles down the line. Caitlin heard glass shattering as she pushed off the bottle dispenser, and projected herself up and over the converging robots.

Charging straight for David Skoll, the path to him free and clear.

104

ELK GROVE, TEXAS

Armand Fisker couldn't believe what he was seeing. Men he'd known for years, decades even, men beholden to him, whose service to his cause defined their very lives and livelihoods, were running away. He screamed after them, cursing at the top of his lungs, even though he knew they'd never hear him through the gunfire still reverberating around him.

Fisker had his own M16 unslung from his shoulder in the ready position, exchanging sporadic fire with the forces inside the APCs while trying to herd those of his men who hadn't fled to him. Some of them were ex-military, but only a sparse few had experienced a true firefight. Fisker himself had been in a few gunfights, but nothing that even approached the fury of this one. The debris clouds still cloaked the bodies of his men who'd fallen, too many to count, the rising stench of their blood adding to the other scents permeating the scene through the night.

The collapse of the buildings had taken the floodlights with them. Now there were only the moon's rays barely penetrating the rolling blanket of smoke concentrated over the street, and the light from the flames blowing out of the ruined structures all around him to break the darkness.

His remaining men fired on the APCs from positions of cover they'd managed to claim for themselves. Not very maneuverable, those APCs spun to screeching halts in the town square he'd claimed for his own until just moments before. Men seemed to flood from them into the night, a stream of specters melting into the darkness.

Fisker refused to accept that his entire world, the empire he'd built, had fallen to so small a force. He didn't care about the bulk of them, just Cort Wesley Masters himself. Fitting comeuppance for him, given that Masters' father had been the one who shanked his. Killing Masters, and orphaning his sons, could still salvage this night, provide solace that seemed unthinkable under the circumstances.

Secondary explosions began to ripple against the debris-riddled landscape, the propane tanks powering the once-revitalized town erupting in blast after blast that left the refuse charred and the air rank with a chemical smell. Fisker moved through the clouds of mist now rich with floating embers and black curtains amid the gray, sweeping his M16 from side to side, ready to fire at the slightest hint of motion.

He had the sense he was walking a tightrope on the edge of a volcano, dodging the pockets of flame that had sprung up everywhere. The latest series of explosions had carved fresh chasms in the hard-paved dirt street, jagged fissures that looked carved by an earthquake measuring ten on the Richter scale, some of them seeming to extend down into the bowels of the Earth itself.

Motion flared amid the shroud before him, vanishing too fast to sight in on. It returned long enough for Fisker to let loose with a spray, then dissolved into the thick, dark air fanning the flames that cast an eerie glow in the pockets open to the night.

Was it Masters? Did I get him?

When no grunt of pain, or thud of a body falling, followed, Fisker rotated the barrel again, fixing on the shape of a man silhouetted against the swirling debris, backlit by the flames churning through the street. The figure was standing stark still, reloading or maybe wounded.

Fisker drew back on his trigger and emptied the rest of his magazine. Certain it was Masters and that if he wasn't dead already, he soon would be.

105

WACO, TEXAS

Another of the robots rolled out into her path when she was almost to Skoll. It lashed its arm out in the semblance of a roundhouse blow, which Caitlin ducked under, knowing she was down to her last few bullets and had to make every one count. The robot tightened its pincer assembly into what looked like a dull tip and jabbed down at her. Caitlin managed to deflect one blow, and another, and finally a third before dropping all the way to the floor and firing her last three bullets into the machine's rolling tread assembly.

The move sent the thing spinning wildly, trying to rebalance itself, only to be betrayed by the tear in the housing and ruined tread on that side. It was still whirling about, a robotic pirouette, when Caitlin surged past it, leaping from one assembly to another, until David Skoll came within range.

She aimed herself at him and projected herself through the air, crashing into Skoll and taking him with her to the floor. Caitlin felt his ribs contract and breath flood from his lungs with a *whoooooshhhhh* on impact. She was vaguely conscious of the remaining reprogrammed robots rolling forward, from the now familiar whirring sound, as she lifted Skoll up and slammed him against the housing of a massive machine that apportioned fully packed plastic bottles of pills into crates for shipping. A repetitive thwacking sound of the boxes being stapled shut hammered her ears, but her eyes suffered no such distraction.

The man who'd haunted her dreams and spun her from sleep with nightmares she could never remember stood teetering before her, hers to control this time. Her faceless attacker looked like a cherub with long hair bunched over his face, covering his eyes but leaving enough so she could see the fear filling them.

"I'll never do a day in prison!" he raged at her, spittle flying from his mouth. "So take your best shot, bitch!"

Caitlin punched Skoll hard in the midsection, feeling the breath rush out of him like air from a blown tire. She was about to hit him again, when he sank to his knees. Skoll's face was scarlet, catching what breath he could in gasping heaves.

"A waste of a condom," he managed between wheezes, still gloating, "that's all you were to me...."

Caitlin heard the robots whirring closer, their wheels scraping over debris from her various brushes with the contents of the line, slowing the machines slightly. She realized Skoll had lost his grasp on the pen-like laser in the fracas, and leaned over to snatch it from the floor.

"Industrial accidents happen all the time, Skoll," Caitlin said, aiming the laser down at him.

She pressed the plunger and hit him with the light, letting it linger long enough to leave whatever digital imprint the robots had been reprogrammed to home in on.

"Hey!" he raged, trying to reclaim his feet only to have the slick floor betray him. *"Hey!"*

Caitlin could feel the heat radiating off the final two robots, the whirring sounds ebbing and then winding down as they slowed. Skoll was still trying to pull himself back up when their shadows swallowed him.

"Jesus!" he cried out, as she eased past him. *"Jesus!"*

Caitlin never even glanced back when his screams began.

106

Armand Fisker let loose with another spray, even though a heavy swath of smoke had swallowed Masters' figure for the moment. He wanted the man to suffer worse than his son had. He wanted Masters to bleed out while he hovered over him, the last words the man would ever hear being Fisker's promise that his sons would be joining him in hell soon.

He moved through the soupy, foul-smelling clouds riddled with the refuse of Elk Grove, narrowly avoiding a yard-wide chasm that had opened in the street belching smoke and flames from what might've been the center of the Earth. The world cleared again before him to reveal a dark tactical jacket, now riddled with bullet holes, hanging on part of a collapsed building's framing.

What the—

Before Fisker could complete the thought, he felt a *swoosh* of air behind him and heard a whistling sound before the night exploded with daylight brilliance an instant before he hit the ground.

Cort Wesley dropped the splintered hunk of two-by-four he'd smashed into Armand Fisker's head and stood over him. The man's face was aglow in the flames sprouting from a propane fire burning up through one of the chasms Paz's explosions had carved in the ground.

"You think killing me ends this?" he rasped, spitting blood, his eyes starting to glaze. "There's a place in hell for you, too. I'm just gonna get there first."

Cort Wesley wanted to gloat and tell him that his great-grandfather was Adolf Hitler, that he owed his nature to his blood and that he was going to die in flames, too. But he said none of this, just moved closer to Fisker and looked down at the blood leaking from his ears and nose courtesy of the blow that had nearly split the two-by-four in half.

"Say hello to your son for me," Cort Wesley told him, through the smoke clouding before his eyes.

Then he kicked Fisker over the edge of the chasm and felt the flames take him with a burst of heat that sprayed upward, lifted by the embers.

"I'm sure he's waiting for you down there."

EPILOGUE

He may not win the laurel
Nor trumpet tongue of fame;
But beauty smiles upon him,
And ranchmen bless his name.
Then here's to the Texas Ranger,
Past, present and to come!
The guardian of our home.

—From *Cowboy Songs and Other Frontier Ballads,* collected by
John A. Lomax, The Macmillan Company, 1922

Caitlin stood next to Cort Wesley, matching ladles in hand at the Catholic Worker House, where they were serving lunch to the endless procession of those grateful for just a warm meal.

"I don't feel bad about it at all," Cort Wesley said to her, watching Dylan and Luke passing out brownies and cookies at the dessert station. "I don't punch Armand Fisker's ticket, he comes after the boys. Plain and simple."

"Nothing's ever plain and simple, Cort Wesley. You know that."

"You mean like you and David Skoll, Ranger?"

"He didn't deserve a day in court. He didn't deserve another day on Earth. He'd had more than he deserved already."

Cort Wesley held the ladle overfilled with mixed vegetables still for a moment. "You sound like you feel about as guilty as I do."

"You want to hear the strangest part? That last moment, when I hit Skoll with that laser, I remembered him . . . raping me," Caitlin told him, making herself say the word. "I had no memory of it for all these years, even in my nightmares, but in that moment I saw it all."

"Maybe it was that aftershave you told me about. I've read that smells can trigger memories."

"I've heard that, too. But it was more than just a smell, like I was being shown something, so I'd know what I was about to do was okay."

"You don't look all that happy about it, though."

"I thought I'd feel better, Cort Wesley, finally be able to put it all behind me. But I don't feel better at all; I don't even feel different."

He nodded, seeming to understand. "What you did can't change the past, never mind erase it. That impression's already bored into who you are, what it helped make you."

"I hope you're not suggesting I still want to hold on to that pain and misery."

"I didn't say that," Cort Wesley told her, holding up on dispensing more mashed potatoes. "You are who you are and you don't want to change that. You may not feel better about this as time goes by, but you'll feel different, like you're being haunted by a ghost instead of a person."

Caitlin spotted a familiar figure join the line at the back and stripped off her apron. "I'm going on break."

Caitlin faced Jones from across a table in the courtyard, the two of them sharing the sunlight.

"You should think about making this gig with Homeland permanent," Jones told her, flashing his customary smirk.

"I think I'll pass on that."

Jones squinted into the sun toward the gleaming badge both her grandfather and father had worn before her. "You could get used to not wearing that, you know."

"Maybe so. But I don't think I could get used to working for someone I can't trust."

"I hope you're talking about the president, and not me."

"The president isn't the one who set me up."

"Come again?"

Caitlin scolded him with her eyes. "You trying to tell me you didn't know about the link between David Skoll and Armand Fisker? You trying to tell me you had no active surveillance on Fisker that put the two of them together?" She shook her head. "You flat-out wound Cort Wesley and me up, and just let us go."

"Freed you to do your thing, in other words, what you're best at," Jones said, not bothering to deny her assertion.

"What's that mean?"

"That the two of you are like something out of Greek mythology, a pair of goddamn Gorgons, since anyone you come up against turns to stone. I just want to make better use of your talents. You should be thanking me."

"You make us sound like a lounge act at Esther's Follies."

Jones looked around him, taking in their surroundings melodramatically. "Keep wearing that badge and that's all you'll ever be. Cross state lines over to my side and you'll be playing Radio City."

"I think I'm doing just fine letting Radio City come to me."

Jones stood up, nodding as if he wasn't convinced. "Suit yourself, Ranger. Somehow I've got a feeling we haven't seen the last of each other."

"Well, Texas *is* the center of the universe."

"I was thinking hell."

"Same thing, Jones, in case you didn't notice."

"What's wrong, Colonel?" Caitlin asked, as they wiped down the tables following the luncheon rush of homeless and others in need through the food line.

Paz kept wiping, pushing so hard on the tabletop it seemed his massive hand was about to go right through. "Something I never told you, Ranger. Just before I left Venezuela for the last time, I was rousting some rebels from the forest. Many of them died fighting for their lives. When I walked through all the carnage, all the blood, I looked down into the dead eyes of a young boy holding a machine gun."

"Killing him changed you?"

"No, the fact that I bothered to *look* showed me I'd already changed. It wasn't long after that I came up here to find myself, I thought. It turned out I didn't like what I found and it's still the same reflection that looks back at me from the mirror. There are moments where I think I've changed, but there are more moments like Elk Grove, where my true nature shows itself again."

Caitlin nodded. "You ever read Edmund Burke, Colonel?"

"Of course."

"'The only thing necessary for the triumph of evil is for good men to do nothing.' Ring any bells for you?" Caitlin asked, stealing a glance at Dylan and Luke throwing wet rags at each other, while Cort Wesley looked on.

Paz's expression brightened, Caitlin resuming quickly.

"We don't get to choose the evil we fight," she told him. "You might even say it chooses us."

He almost smiled. "I wish you had met my priest before his stroke."

"Because I would've benefitted from his wisdom?"

"Because you sound just like him, Ranger."

Caitlin went back to wiping down her table, then stopped just as fast. "Do you believe Armand Fisker was Adolf Hitler's great-grandson?"

"I believe Fisker was evil, and all evil is somehow related. It's what I often brought up with my priest, though not in those words."

"That's not what I asked you, Colonel."

"Yes, it is. We put names and labels on evil because that makes its existence easier to bear for us. But the fact is it's all the same, no matter the face it wears. And that's why no matter how much of it we vanquish, there will always be more."

Caitlin smiled and this time Paz joined her. "Good to know our place in the world is secure, Colonel." She looked back toward Cort Wesley, who'd joined his sons in a pitched battle of rag tossing, the boys ganging up on him by the look of things. "But once in a while, it's nice to do some good in a place like this, too, where we don't have to use our guns to make a difference."

"Accidents happen, Ranger," Paz told her.

"Yes, they do," Caitlin said, her grin broadening. "All the time."

Author's Note

Those familiar with this page, where I provide some insight into how I came to write the book you've just finished, are used to me pointing to something like a newspaper article or *60 Minutes* segment as the genesis for the story. It was different in this case, because *Strong to the Bone* started with me wanting to challenge Caitlin as I'd never challenged her before. Provide a deep look into a part of her psyche I'd never previously explored.

Sexual assault is a scourge, leaving its mark on hundreds of thousands of women in the United States every year. Giving Caitlin such a cross to bear after eight books seemed like a great challenge for her character, as well as a way for me to weave something emotionally vital and visceral into the context of the story. Challenging yourself as a writer means challenging your characters. Not letting you, nor them, get lackadaisical, especially after eight books when many series like this have long since tired.

Of course, I needed a plot, too, and if you've been with me for the last few Caitlin Strong books, you know I've cast the Chinese (*Strong Darkness*), the Russians (*Strong Light of Day*), and ISIS (*Strong Cold Dead*) as villains in consecutive tales, making Nazis the next obvious choice in that succession. So I googled "Nazis in Texas" and came up with a ton of hits about the German prisoner-of-war camps that dotted the Lone Star State in the latter days of World War II, exactly as I laid out in these pages, including the camp in Hearne.

Sometimes truth really is stranger than fiction.

So much of the book grew out of that notion (including the twist about the identity of one of those prisoners), but I also needed a "MacGuffin," as Alfred Hitchcock might call it, which came to me in the course of a discussion with a good friend of mine named Stan Israel who'd received two liver transplants in the course of a week after his body rejected the first. We got to talking about the future of anti-rejection medication, and Axiol, the clinical trial drug developed in these pages, was born in that discussion. Lots more research needed to be done, of course, and, if you're wondering, yes, the notion of transplantable, replacement organs being produced by 3-D printers is very real (Thank you, Natalia Aponte!).

Truth being stranger than fiction again.

My editor, Bob Gleason, served up the idea of a lawless biker town when he told me such places really do exist—I think he mentioned California, maybe around Barstow or way farther up north, as a setting for a few of them.

The Aryan Brotherhood really was founded in prison and I probably don't have to tell you that the rise of nationalist movements across the globe is very real, too. What's different about *Strong to the Bone*, though, is that the villain's world-altering plot doesn't exist from the get-go. Instead, it develops organically over the course of the action. So I guess this time out I really relied on my characters to do the heavy lifting for me.

Hopefully that produced a whole bunch of fun hours of reading for you, enough so that I'll see you again next year when Caitlin and company return in *Strong as Steel*!